TRIQUETRA

THE WINTER WARS

By

Jo Cox

Copyright © Jo Cox 2018
This book is sold subject to the condition that it shall not, by way of trade or otherwise, be lent, resold, hired out, or otherwise circulated without the publisher's prior consent in any form of binding or cover other than that in which it is published and without a similar condition including this condition being imposed on the subsequent publisher.
The moral right of Jo Cox has been asserted.
ISBN-13: 9781731203007

DEDICATION

To John, without whom…

And Tabetha for her encouragement.

This is a work of fiction. Names, characters, businesses, organizations, places, events and incidents either are the product of the author's imagination or are used fictitiously. Any resemblance to actual persons, living or dead, events, or locales is entirely coincidental.

CONTENTS

Chapter 1 .... *1*
Chapter 2 .... *6*
Chapter 3 .... *11*
Chapter 4 .... *15*
Chapter 5 .... *20*
Chapter 6 .... *26*
Chapter 7 .... *32*
Chapter 8 .... *39*
Chapter 9 .... *44*
Chapter 10 .... *48*
Chapter 11 .... *53*
Chapter 12 .... *61*
Chapter 13 .... *67*
Chapter 14 .... *73*
Chapter 15 .... *80*
Chapter 16 .... *85*
Chapter 17 .... *90*
Chapter 18 .... *95*
Chapter 19 .... *99*
Chapter 20 .... *103*
Chapter 21 .... *107*
Chapter 22 .... *113*
Chapter 23 .... *117*
Chapter 24 .... *121*
Chapter 25 .... *126*
Chapter 26 .... *131*
Chapter 27 .... *136*
Chapter 28 .... *142*
Chapter 29 .... *149*
Chapter 30 .... *160*
Chapter 31 .... *167*
Chapter 32 .... *174*
Chapter 33 .... *180*
Chapter 34 .... *184*
Chapter 35 .... *191*

Chapter 36 197
Chapter 37 203
Chapter 38 211
Chapter 39 218
Chapter 40 223
Chapter 41 229
Chapter 42 235
Chapter 43 240
Chapter 44 246
Chapter 45 250
Chapter 46 257
Chapter 47 273
Chapter 48 281
Chapter 49 287
Chapter 50 303
Chapter 51 309
Chapter 52 316
Chapter 53 322
Chapter 54 330
Chapter 55 337
Chapter 56 346
Chapter 57 357
Chapter 58 364
Chapter 59 372
Chapter 60 380
Chapter 61 388
Chapter 62 396
Chapter 63 403
Chapter 64 408
Chapter 65 417
ABOUT THE AUTHOR 426

Chapter 1

The noonday bell, ringing in the courtyard reached the ears of the young man perched on a window ledge, scuffing his boots against the golden stone walls. He glanced sideways, grey eyes focused on a large, ornately carved door further down the corridor as it creaked open. After a moment's quick assessment of the young woman who came out, he released the breath he had unconsciously been holding and rose to meet her.

Callie was not as tall as he was and the thoughtful expression she turned to him came from bright blue eyes. With copper-coloured hair and fine bone structure most people would identify them as siblings but not necessarily twins.

"So," Raff raised an eyebrow, "what did he want you for – what's going on? Don't tell me they are sending you to Nilsport?" She shook her head. "Well, thank the Lady for that!" There was genuine relief in Raff's voice. "I mean… I know you're good at what you do, Callie, but you won't even graduate until the end of summer and a battlefield is really no place for a weather witch!"

His voice faltered as she slowed her step and turned to face him. "I'm sorry to hear you say that, brother, because a battlefield is exactly where I'll soon he heading."

"But you said…"

"Not Nilsport. The Council has received intelligence that the Kerrians have sent a force through Arco's Gap."

"What? The bastards!" He was genuinely shocked.

"They overran the outpost, but one of the rangers escaped and raised the alarm. They obviously know most of the army is committed in the west."

"But," Raff spluttered again, "we have a treaty."

"Had, a treaty. It seems there's some sort of internal war going on. Right this minute it's impossible to say whose forces these are. Come on, we're missing lunch."

The pair jogged across one of the courtyards and made their way to the dining hall. The student tables were fairly full although High Table, where the Masters sat, was almost empty. Collecting their meals, they squeezed in at the end of a bench occupied for the most part by their year-mates; a complete mix of warriors, healer and magecraft trainees.

"At last," two or three of the other students chorused, trying to catch Callie's attention, which was firmly fixed on her food.

"Callie! What did he want? What have you done now?"

Raff grinned. His sister seemed to visit the Dean's office more often than most students, and normally on disciplinary matters, but he didn't speak. Callie shared most things with him, but this might concern the safety of the realm and so was not a matter for gossip. He could just imagine the look on their father's face if they treated a matter of intelligence so lightly: but then, their father was the King's Defence Minister and General of the Armies.

Callie deflected the questions with skill and her denial that she was to be sent to Nilsport obviously rang true. For all that, she made a brief meal before excusing herself, arranging to meet Raff later.

Back in the cubicle room that she occupied during the college terms, Callie took a moment to think about what she would take with her. Usually graduating Mages were accompanied on their first tour of duty by experienced or veteran magic-users. Unfortunately for her, nearly all of the Mages except the Academy teaching staff and those tasked with protecting the Royal Family itself, had gone west to Nilsport where it looked like the Frystlanders were making yet another attempt to get themselves an ice-free port on the Musta Meri Sea. Incidents with the Frystlanders never ceased entirely, but when they had managed to make an alliance with the Ice-landers, a few months previously, matters had escalated into a far larger conflict, which showed no signs of ending.

Callie packed sensibly and swiftly. High-born, the D'Arcourt family had been in Service to the Crown for generations; active service. In many ways Callie's education had been a mirror of her brother's and she was more than capable of using the weapons that decorated the walls of her room. Only the late emergence of her Mage gift had prevented her from continuing the military training she and Raff had started on the same day. Even now, on days of tedious magic theory she resented having to give up her arms training. Only Raff's agreement to continue teaching her himself had kept her from storming out of the college entirely.

Finished packing, she made her way to the college library, taking a side turning into the map rooms. Geography was a compulsory subject for all Academy students. Unlike many of the other nations of the Feldermark, by far the majority of senior military officers in Lithia achieved their rank through talent earned promotion. For that to work, all recruits received as much education as they could handle, with adapted teaching for those who showed particular skills.

Callie unrolled the maps showing the eastern borderlands where the massive Skyfall range ran southward to the southern sea and separated Lithia from Kerria. The mountain peaks were high and virtually impassable by anything larger than the nimble mountain goats, except at Arco's Gap where the Snow River ran out.

In winter when the river froze over, the local mining villages had to defend themselves from both the silver mountain wolves and Kerrian raiders. Callie made a few notes and tucked them into her pack then headed for the stables where she found Raff. She had intended to check her mount carefully before the long winter trip but realised Raff had done it for her. He was nearly as good with animals as Megan, their older sister who was an animal healer. Jessa would have behaved perfectly for him and not just because of the apple she was still crunching happily.

"She's fine," he smiled. "I take it you'll be heading out pretty soon?"

"Dawn tomorrow, if everything can be sorted by then."

"Why shouldn't it be?" He raised an eyebrow.

"The Dean wouldn't tell me who else is going apart from the reserves, until we all meet up after dinner tonight. He said it was for security reasons – and you know what that usually means. Some titled brat has probably got in on the act."

"Any idea who?"

"Not really. The princes are already away. Mikheli is at Nilsport and Jerran on that trade embassy to Cirdar. As well as the regular reserves I know there will be some rangers and scouts and we are to meet up with other forces at Barnard's Castle. Lord Barnard obviously has quite a few men in uniform but won't want them to move far from the mines. You can't really blame him. I mean if the Kerrians are making a serious sortie it will be the mines they are after; mines we really can't afford to lose right now."

"That's exactly what Mother said. Oh damn, I forgot to tell you. Mother's back and wants to see you before dinner."

"What?" Callie groaned and levered herself off the hay bale she had settled on. "Is she here?"

"No. She's at home but she'll have to attend dinner at court later so you'd better hurry."

*

Esme D'Arcourt smoothed her formal court gown and dismissed her maid as her daughter inched open the door of her dressing room. Callie eyed her warily, but the smile lighting her mother's face was a warm one and crinkled the tiny lines by her eyes. She was a tall, elegant woman; her auburn hair only now showing the first signs of grey.

"Thank Havens I got back today, sweetheart." She gave Callie a quick hug. "I hear you are heading east in the morning." Callie nodded; not surprised that Esma already knew about her mission. Esma born near and raised at court had always had her own sources of intelligence. "Callie dear. Tell me honestly, how do you feel about it? Are you nervous?" Callie hesitated. Nothing but the truth would serve with her mother; nothing ever did.

"I am nervous," she admitted slowly, "but possibly not for the reasons you might think." Her mother waited quietly.

"I think I'm afraid that I will be… ineffective. I think they are only sending me because I'm the least useless of the Mage-gifted still left at college. Not because I'll be any help. I'm only a weather witch. If things turn out badly," she saw her mother's tiny flinch, "I know I can defend myself, but how can I help the others if all I can do is tell them the weather is set fair so tomorrow will be a good day to die? They need a Battle Mage. I think they will regard me as a liability; extra unwanted baggage." She sighed, well aware she was exaggerating.

Her mother smiled. "Knowing you can defend yourself means I can put my worries aside. As for you, Callandra, you are intelligent, imaginative and determined as I have often found to my cost." Callie grinned. "Now is the time to use your gift for the unexpected. That creative streak that has landed you in detention; how many times?" She paused, apparently doing mental sums while Callie blushed. "Well it might be a strength where you are going." She eyed her daughter thoughtfully. "You know that in normal circumstances you would be with an experienced Mage on your first posting. That Mage would guide you and direct you. You won't have that. You won't have someone else's experience to lean on – but neither will you be limited by what they think is possible."

"The situation as far as I have heard is flexible and changing very fast – just like you do! I have every confidence that you will use your talents well, although…" She hesitated, and then spoke slowly, choosing her words with care. "Callie, it really is important that you remember you are part of a team. It would be unprofessional to let personal feelings, irritations and antagonism, however justified, affect your contribution to this campaign."

"But—"

Her mother stopped her with a quietly raised hand.

"You can act with maturity and good sense. Your father and I both know you will be a credit to us. Just remember – stop and think. Don't just react; even when things seem unfair."

A sudden knock at the door heralded the return of Esma's maid with a cloak and notice that the carriage was at the door.

"Take care, my sweet." Another brief hug and Lady D'Arcourt was gone in a flurry of velvet and the memory of a fragrance.

Chapter 2

Callie made her way to her own chamber and stood in the doorway. It was a pretty room but had an air of disuse about it. She pulled open the wardrobe door. It still held day dresses, ball dresses, a velvet cloak barely worn and a tray full of satin ribbons that made her smile. All things a proper young lady might have enjoyed. She wondered briefly if she was a disappointment to her mother in that way but had to admit that both her parents had respected her choices and had never tried to make her into something she was not.

Callie dropped onto the stool in front of the dressing table and turned her mind to her immediate future. She would be going into a battle zone: a real battle zone, not a training exercise. She had been honest with her mother. Her fighting skills were impressive but as she had learnt from her father, battle was unpredictable. If things went badly there was a chance she might not make it back. She wished Raff was going with her. A stray thought struck her. If she couldn't take her brother, she could still take something family.

Retrieving her jewel case, she sifted through the contents. Near the bottom she found what she was looking for: an ornately decorated box. It contained a curiously shaped pendant on a long silver chain and in a twist of silk several fairly plain silver rings.

The pendant too was made of silver, with an intricate design she could never quite pin down. It was a pointed oval in shape and towards one end there was a blank circle as if a gem once attached, had vanished; but it was still attractive. It had been a gift to Callie from her grandmother. Two years previously, when Lady Vesta, her mother's mother, had fallen ill with no hope of recovery, she had stoically put her affairs in order. Callie remembered her fondly as a calm and kindly woman. She had been very pleased, almost relieved when Callie's Magery had emerged, and had immediately given her the jewellery. Callie had tried to refuse the gift. It was obviously very old; a very valuable heirloom, but Vesta had explained in a few words, that without Magery, the pendant would be an attractive piece of jewellery but nothing more, so of no use to Esme, while Megan's Mage gift was not 'the right sort.'

Callie had hounded her grandmother for more information, trying to discover how the pendant would be useful to her, but Vesta had simply smiled at her frustration and declared she really did not have the answers Callie was seeking. She let the long silver chain slide through her calloused fingers then slipped it over her head to lie concealed beneath her clothes. With a last glance around, she made her way out of the house and set off back to the palace.

The streets were very busy. Caught up in the press of people heading for the winter market Callie began to fear she would be late. She was jogging as she approached the small assembly hall and paused at the end of the corridor to get her breath back.

For a moment she was pleased to hear other footsteps approaching from the opposite direction; but only for a moment. As well as the footsteps she heard a well-bred instantly recognisable voice, raised, as it invariably was, in complaint. *Damn and blast*, Callie groaned inwardly. Prince Mikheli was back. The Crown Prince was a man with an exaggerated idea of his own abilities and a massive sense of self-worth and entitlement. Surely he wasn't to be part of the Wildwater foray?

Although trained in all the arts of warfare Mikheli lacked all tact, and tended to regard advice, even from experienced army officers as personal criticism. King Theon had at first denied Mikheli's loud-voiced demands to go to the western war. His reluctance no doubt due to the fact that he himself had ascended the throne when his elder brother had been killed in a skirmish.

Finally, the Crown Prince had been allowed to go and if only half the stories Callie had heard were true, his meddling and interference had caused no end of trouble. It seemed a pity that Jerran, his younger brother, who by all accounts was a useful warrior, was employed almost solely on trade and diplomatic missions.

Callie had nearly reached the meeting room, close enough to make out the Prince's words when he spoke again in that voice that always seemed tinged with contempt.

"So let me get this right. The only Mage you'll have is an untried girl; a weather-witch and not even finished training?" Callie froze in mid-step. Mikheli was complaining about her! "What are they thinking? You're not a babysitter. Still, don't be surprised if she runs straight back to her classroom."

Callie seethed as she darted forward into the assembly room, unable to hear the quietly voiced reply. How unjust! They hadn't even met her yet and she was being written off as a liability.

She grabbed a seat with some of the scouts she knew, and looked about her. As she had expected the meeting was made up of squad leaders and their senior officers. She studied the crests on their uniforms and identified archers, swordsmen, engineers and the one or two blank tabs that could mean anything from diplomat to assassin. In one thing Mikheli was correct. She really was the only Mage present.

When Prince Mikheli entered the room the gathering quietened swiftly. He was accompanied by several men including, surprisingly, his brother Jerran. Callie knew one or two of the others by sight. Colonel Ferran, an experienced and respected army careerist, who must be approaching retirement, was listening to a younger man, of an age with the Princes who looked slightly familiar, although she couldn't put a name to him. Two she did know had Prince Jerran sandwiched between them; Lords Nevis and Hadley. Close cronies of Prince Mikheli, they were rich and privileged, arrogant and irresponsible and heirs to position of power. Callie's path had crossed theirs once or twice and she was completely certain that only her father's position at court and possibly her already notable fighting skills had saved her from the problems some of her friends of lesser status had had to endure at their hands. Barrack-room gossip said they had far too much influence with the Princes and she hoped strenuously that this was untrue.

It was not a long meeting. It soon became clear that Prince Mikheli would not himself be part of the expedition; news which sent a ripple of barely concealed relief across the room. His attendance was to support his brother, who actually would be going, by offering his 'expert' strategic advice. As Callie had heard stories of how hard the regular officers had had to work to prevent the Prince getting himself and far too many troops killed, she struggled not to laugh at that and certainly thought she saw Colonel Ferran's lips twitch though he said not a word.

The plans Mikheli proposed seemed to Callie to be very full of 'ifs and buts', but she consoled herself with her father's oft repeated maxim, that no battle plans lasted beyond the first contact with the enemy and they would soon be far from the Crown Princes' influence. She wondered if Prince Jerran was cut from the same cloth as his brother and hoped, for the success of their mission, that he was not.

When the meeting concluded and the royal party left with strict instructions for a dawn start, there was hesitancy amongst the group to disperse. Callie turned to her neighbour, Gilligan, a scout and talented swordsman she had often sparred with in core training.

"Gilly, who was the man talking to the Colonel? He wasn't introduced so I suppose we are all meant to know him."

Gilly smiled: "That's Lord Dexter and actually you probably wouldn't know him. He's rarely here at court."

"He's royal?" she questioned.

"Distantly I suppose." Gilly nodded thoughtfully. "A cousin, I think. The family estate is on the borders so he is usually there."

"Great!" She almost spat her disapproval. "Two of them."

"Callie! Hey! Calm down." His steady voice pierced her simmering anger. "You should at least give them a chance."

"Why? They aren't giving me one." He raised an eyebrow.

"I overheard them complaining about taking me – a mere weather-witch – not even finished training. I believe the word babysitting was mentioned."

"Ah! Well I'm not sure yet about Prince Jerran, but Lord Dexter must have been fighting for ten years or more and he is well liked by his men. That should tell you something. You don't know them and they don't know you – so this is your chance to show them what you can do." He slapped her on the back as he rose.

"Now I thought it wouldn't harm to get a little more edge on this." He patted his sword. "Shall I take yours?" His eyes twinkled as she handed over her weapon. Go and get some sleep. You'll need to be on top form for the next few weeks." She glared. "Yes, I know it's not fair but being what you are you're just going to have to be better than the rest of us."

"Hardly a challenge." She ducked the cuff he aimed at her and they parted.

Chapter 3

Although Lord Barnard's keep occupied a commanding position, with the White Water River visible from the highest towers, it was not actually in the Iron Valley. When the original keep had been built to defend and hold the border, centuries earlier, the first Earl's lady had objected to the proposed location close to the great mines. She had had her way and instead the castle was built at the head of an attractive wooded valley, just to the west.

The journey there had involved hard riding, dawn to dusk for six days, with simple camps set up more often than not by moonlight. The first two nights the royal party had peeled off to retire to one of the inns that dotted the road nearer to Derryn but from the third night out, hostelries were few and far between.

By the end of the first day it became clear that there would have been tension between the royal contingent and the regular forces if Colonel Ferran had allowed it. The Lordling's loud-voiced demands for even greater speed had been firmly blocked by the Colonel who was not prepared to see his horses foundered on the wintery roads just for the saving of half a day. Callie was all admiration for the man and his refusal to be provoked. Although it wasn't usually the Prince's voice raised in irritation he was always surrounded by his entourage, or in his large tent placed noticeably distant from that of the Colonel.

The nobles, it seemed, were unaware that canvas walls are not sound-proof. More than once Callie wished Prince Jerran would have the sense to silence the constant complaints and criticism of his friends who were only now discovering that winter warfare was deeply uncomfortable; but he made no move to do so. It occurred to Callie that the choice of Ferran as commanding officer had been an excellent one. With a different leader the nobles' behaviour might have affected morale or undermined the Colonel's authority but no such thing was happening. Colonel Ferran's reputation was unassailable. His successes in the field were legion and many of the troops had served with him in other campaigns. As Gilly said, sitting by their campfire, it just made the young lords look out of touch and ignorant. Will, who had trained Callie and her year group in woodcraft and was acting senior scout agreed although his choice of words was somewhat stronger.

Darkness had rapidly fallen on a short winter's day when they first sighted the lights on the ramparts of Barnard's Castle. Strongly built in a traditional northern style, the entrance was via a narrow tunnel allowing at most two horses to walk abreast, but the inner courtyard was large and roomy. By the time Callie swung down from her horse she was chilled to the bone. She followed Gilly's troop towards the stables to find a stall and fodder for Jessa. It had been drummed into her in training that a warrior must tend to his mount before seeing to his or her own comfort, and it had been a hard, cold road for the horses too.

Beyond the stable door her attention was drawn to the other side of the courtyard where the massive doors of the inner keep stood open. Prince Jerran was talking to an older man, grizzled and solid but finely dressed. She presumed this must be Lord Barnard himself: royalty would certainly expect such a personal greeting.

She unsaddled Jessa with practiced speed and gave her a brief rub down, then grabbed her pack intending to find the mess and the barracks. It would be good to be warm, dry and clean. The barracks at Barnard's Castle were well built and maintained and even boasted the luxury of a bath house.

After a solid meal relaxing at a mess table, it was a while before Callie's instincts began to bother her. None of the squad leaders were present. Captains sometimes messed with their men but not always, so their absence was not unusual and she assumed the nobles would be dining privately with the Earl but where was Will? "Where are the squad leaders?" she asked the table at large.

Sinto, one of the archers, raised an eyebrow at her. "They are all at the big strategy meeting. I'm surprised you aren't there too."

"Strategy meeting? I wasn't told about it." A small pulse of anger stirred in her stomach.

Sinto smiled sympathetically. "Can't say I'm surprised, Cal. Those nobles think women are good for just one thing, and it isn't battle tactics. Daft though. It will be harder for you to help if you have no idea what's been planned."

"Where is the meeting?" Callie frowned.

"The Justice Hall – it's in the old part of the keep." He pointed vaguely as Callie rose to her feet, then grinned. "Oho, I know that look. Take it gently, Callie. Remember, the enemy are the ones outside the castle!"

Callie smiled briefly at him then flew across the hall and headed back across the courtyard checking the sky as she did so. There were guards outside the double doors of the Justice Hall. Guards unwilling to listen to her or let her in. They were civil enough, but confident that anyone meant to be at the meeting had arrived long since. Offering a silent apology to her mother, Callie squared her shoulders and turned her focus inwards. Her power rose, filling her, until her body tingled then she directed her will towards the guardsmen. With exquisite care she froze their feet to the floor, immobilising them before pushing the doors open and entering the room.

The Prince was sitting at the centre of a huge paper-strewn table with his advisers on one side and Lord Barnard and Colonel Ferran on the other. The squad leaders and captains sat on rows of chairs facing the table. Most of them looked up as she moved forward, heading towards an empty seat.

"By our Lady, now what! I said no interruptions." It was a moment before Callie realised the words were aimed at her by the Prince's aide who glowered petulantly. "I said to bring refreshments later – or did you bring water?"

"Did I bring…?" She took a deep breath. "Your Highness," she ignored the Prince's adviser, "if you want refreshments I'm sure that can be arranged but I am not part of the kitchen staff. I am your Mage. I am sorry I'm late but somehow notice of this meeting didn't reach me." The Prince she noticed looked surprised and uncomfortable.

"As for you." She turned her gaze back to the aide. "You want water? Happy to oblige." She channelled a wisp of power and the Prince's retainer found himself under a minute rain cloud that released a heavy shower of water all over him. He leapt to his feet shouting, swearing and trying to dodge the downpour to no avail as it followed him, to the door. There was a stunned silence as it banged shut behind him then Lord Barnard cleared his throat.

"Milady. Grateful as we are for this impressive demonstration of your skills could you perhaps?" He made a gentle gesture with his hands. Callie turned the water off with a business-like smile and took an empty seat. She knew she shouldn't have done it but was simply too angry to care; and the quickly stifled laughter from those around her was balm to her soul.

Chapter 4

It might have been an hour or so later by her reckoning that Prince Jerran and his entourage withdrew. A long hour to go over Prince Mikheli's proposed strategy of charging straight through Arco's Gap and engaging the enemy head on. Suggestions that perhaps the Kerrians might not be sitting still waiting to be slaughtered were dismissed out of hand. The nobles seemed to regard the Kerrians as disorganised bandits and the Frystlanders as barely more than savages. It worried Callie that Colonel Ferran, who must know better, had not opposed the plans more strongly. She had seen an exchange of looks between him and the Earl once or twice, but nothing had been said. Then again, as the meeting closed she had noticed the two men had not followed the royal party back to the reception rooms or guest wing, but had quietly slipped through a side door almost concealed by heavy drapery. A couple of other men had followed them but she hadn't been close enough to see who.

Callie lingered as the hall emptied. Maps were still spread across the front table and she quickly settled herself on one of the chairs to take a closer look. They were clear, detailed and impressive. The outpost, now held by the invaders, was at the northernmost point of the river valley just before the Ice Falls. In deep winter the Wild Water River froze over and the cascade with it, creating a stunning wall of ice that marked Lithia's border.

If the Kerrians had taken the outpost they must have crossed the frozen river north of the falls. Arco's Gap was basically the valley on either side of the river. In spring with the snowmelt it was virtually a lake with the floodwater lapping at the feet of Arco's Bluff, a hill rising to the west. If the Kerrians held both the outpost and the heights the situation might be much more serious than they had expected.

According to the Earl no news had come from the mines in several days, so communications were already compromised. That would make it harder to co-ordinate a defence. She wondered how the Kerrians had used the nine days' grace they had had before the King's forces had arrived. The terrain was difficult; more suited to guerrilla tactics than the face-to-face battle Jerran's party was advocating.

Callie ran her finger along a line skimming between the Iron Valley and the Skyfall Mountains. It was marked as a logging track and she wasn't sure whether it might be a weakness or an opportunity. The only other access was by the main road into the valley, stone-paved to take the weight of the ore carts, which ran between thick pine forests, with endless opportunities for ambush by a hostile force already in place.

A flicker of apprehension made her frown. In her studies she had excelled at strategy and tactics and her natural ability had been recognised and nurtured by her father. She found herself running through his approach – analyse the situation. Identify strengths and weaknesses, your enemy's and your own. Is there a best strategy? If not, what is the least worst option?

She was so deep in thought that she did not realise she was no longer alone until a hand reached past her to tug the map she was leaning on. A pair of dark brown eyes looked her over with interest and their owner smiled apologetically.

"I'm so sorry but I'm afraid I do need to take these now."

"Of course." She stood up to move away but the man caught her arm. "Please let me introduce myself. I'm Lord Dexter, and if you are our Mage you must be the Lady Callandra D'Arcourt." He smiled at the involuntary grimace she gave when she heard her full name, but added, "I owe you an apology. I'm sorry you weren't informed of the meeting."

"Why are you sorry?" She raised a questioning eyebrow. "Surely it wasn't your job to round people up, Lord Dexter?"

"No," he acknowledged, "but I did put together the list of people to attend, and it seems your name was left off, by mistake."

"By mistake?" Her tone showed exactly how much she believed that.

Dexter grinned, flashing even white teeth at her. "I didn't say it was my mistake." Callie felt herself relaxing the smallest amount. "You looked very interested in the maps." His voice became deliberately neutral. "Have you any thoughts on the proposed tactics?" She studied him for a moment or two while he rolled up the parchments. He had asked the question seriously and was waiting for her answer.

"The strategy is foolhardy and dangerous, unless you have way more information than you shared at the meeting. The season and the terrain are against us. The Kerrians aren't fools and this time they seem very determined. The outpost has never been taken before, has it?" He shook his head. "And this time they have involved the Frystlanders and that could bring new elements into play."

"Trolls?" His voice wasn't quite sceptical.

"Possibly. They aren't at Nilsport – and aren't needed to defend the Holmes at this time of year so they could have come south."

"True." He considered the idea thoughtfully.

"And what have they been doing for the last nine days? If they haven't captured the mines they have established a blockade so tight we have lost contact."

Callie handed him the last map – the expression on his face was a compound of surprise and no little admiration. He seemed to come to a decision. "Please – come with me." He turned and walked, arms full, across the hall to the side door she had noticed previously. It didn't seem to occur to him that she wouldn't follow, so she did.

He led her along a plainish corridor and pushed open one of the doors. The room was occupied, and Callie found herself meeting the curious gazes of Lord Barnard and Colonel Ferran. A third man she did not recognise leant against the wall by a window looking out at the falling night.

"Dexter?" There was a question in the Colonel's voice as he looked her over. Dexter smiled. Although a generation younger than his counterparts he was utterly confident in his actions. Callie recognised that certainty: she had seen it before. It was the confidence of a man who has fought for his life and won; not uncommon in soldiers but rare in someone as young as he seemed.

He drew her forward "This is Callan…"

"Callie," she interrupted.

"Callie D'Arcourt, our Mage. She was studying the maps, and as we have just been discussing our resources I thought it would be a shame if we overlooked one."

Colonel Ferran held out his hand and shook hers. She felt the callouses resulting from a lifetime of horses and swordsmanship.

"Callie." He spoke her name as if it was known to him and his next words confirmed it. "The last time I saw you; you had just fallen off your father's warhorse and broken a tooth. Do you remember?"

"Um, I remember the horse." The men laughed and the Earl gave her a brief bow, which she returned in kind. "I did hear that they might have found us a Mage, but the rumour mills have been working overtime, and when you weren't at the strategy table I thought I must be mistaken." She opened her mouth to explain but paused at an infinitesimal shake of the head from Lord Dexter who had begun spreading the maps on the huge desk.

"Callie was saying exactly what we were. We need more information; there are too many unknowns. We will be sending out our best scouts tomorrow and then we should have a better picture so…"

"How are your woodcraft skills?" A new voice broke in. "Please answer honestly." Callie turned. The shadow by the window was studying her intently as he moved towards them, the candles flickering on hair so fair it was almost silver.

"My woodcraft skills are excellent." She met his grey eyes boldly because she was telling the simple truth. Evading a twin who could almost anticipate her every move had trained her exceptionally well.

"You are a weather witch." He paused. "I am scouting tomorrow. You should come with me. When you see the lie of the land, the river and the forests you will know how best you can help." He finally blinked. "I am Liss. Will you meet me at the postern gate an hour before dawn?" Callie looked at the others. Obviously they were waiting for her decision, which was easy to make. She would really value a chance to see the terrain.

"I'll be there."

"Good. Dress warmly." He nodded at the others and silently left the room.

"Well, that was interesting." Dexter exchanged a glance with his companions before turning back to her.

"Callie, as I understand it, the Prince has decided not to call on your services at the moment."

"It seems that way." She nodded.

"I am very much in the same boat. I have my own troops here, as does Lord Barnard, but His Highness has decided that they are not needed for his planned action, so we are requested to 'patrol the area' and possibly help mop up any of the defeated Kerrians after his battle.

"I'm sure it has absolutely nothing to do with the fact that our men are not part of the Royal Army and so remain under our own control." He gave a wry smile and Callie was aware of Colonel Ferran and the Earl nodding slightly.

"Although that is frustrating in one way it does allow us some liberty. As you said in the hall, we need much more information before we proceed. The Prince wishes to rest and prepare tomorrow and launch an attack the following day, so we have twenty-four hours to get a clear picture of what we are facing. I don't really know what you might be able to do, but there will be a place for you in my troop if you want to be involved?"

Once again Callie had the sense that Lord Dexter was really looking at her: really thinking about her. She didn't hesitate. "I'm here to help any way I can. Count me in."

He smiled, obviously pleased, and Lord Barnard drew her closer to the maps.

Chapter 5

It was barely false dawn when Callie approached the postern gate. The castle was still sleeping although the guards were alert and watchful. She saw Liss in the shadows staring at the sky. She knew it would be a fine day when the ribbons of night fog dispersed; crisp and bright.

Although she was warmly dressed he handed her a fur-lined surcoat mottled in shades of blue and grey matching the one he wore himself. They would be well camouflaged against the winter world.

Callie had wondered if they would ride but was not surprised when they set off on foot. They would soon have had to leave their mounts anyway. She followed Liss down the road from the castle. He moved fluidly and silently, hardly leaving footprints in the light dusting of fresh snow that had fallen overnight. When they were well clear he beckoned her closer for a few quiet questions. Did she know the scout hand signals? Yes. Was she good with her bow? Yes. Was her short sword just decorative? No. All her answers seemed to please him, except the last one. Had she ever taken a life? Not knowingly.

Near the castle, the trees had all been cut down a bow shot or more from the road, but soon the dark pines crept closer. At the first opportunity Liss led the way off the road heading through the forest north-west to Arco's Bluff. Nothing disturbed the pre-dawn quiet.

They slipped through the trees as the land rose. Callie had almost begun to relax when she saw Liss freeze and motion her down. The dawn quiet had become a silence and she almost thought she caught a scent of wood smoke.

They crept cautiously upwards. Arco's Bluff reached a tree-crowned summit before falling away much more gradually back to the valley floor beyond. She wondered how much further they could go towards the Kerrians before being spotted. Liss crouched, listening, and Callie schooled herself to patience. They waited until she thought she was getting cramp and frostbite… but there. A discord – a noise that should not have been. She tracked Liss's gaze until she could make out two lookouts, very well concealed and unmoving.

Liss signalled that they needed to move higher so would have to pass the men: not easy when the slope they were climbing was getting steeper and narrowing.

"We need to distract them." He looked at her. "Can you break a branch over there?" He pointed.

"What?" She looked at him blankly.

"You can control the wind – do so." She gulped at the matter-of-fact confidence in his voice. She supposed in theory it should be possible. The air was always moving on the heights so her tool was to hand.

She focused inwardly then reached out with her will to feel for the breeze gusting above the tree-tops. The half-dead tree Liss had pointed out had a lightning-blasted limb standing fairly clear of the trunk. She grasped the wind and visualised what she wanted to happen, then aimed at the broken branch. It sheared off instantly, taking several others with it, and fell heavily through the undergrowth.

Callie was so surprised at her success that she almost forgot to follow Liss as he sped up the hillside behind the backs of the lookouts. A few hundred feet higher tucked into a patch of evergreen shrubs she steadied herself and caught Liss's eyes on her. He smiled. "Well done – perhaps a little less power next time." She nodded, grinning, then gasped as her eyes processed what she was looking down at.

She and Liss were positioned a bare few feet from the edge of a steep basin that dived away to the north and east. It was absolutely full of tents. No, not tents, she corrected herself, yurts. She felt her stomach turn over. The Kerrians didn't use yurts. These were the portable dwellings of the northernmost Frystland tribes, sneeringly referred to as Trolls for their formidable size, and they were here in force. She was dimly aware of Liss counting and notching a tally stick with his knife as she watched.

The silence was odd. How could so many warriors make so little noise? A silence that was suddenly broken by the sound of crying: a child crying. Callie was wondering if there was something wrong with her hearing, when she saw movement down below. Several Frystland warriors pushed into one of the yurts and the squealing abruptly ended. When they re-appeared they were dragging a sobbing woman with them, who clutched an infant to her breast.

As they neared the largest yurt, the felted door was drawn aside and several men appeared. The Frystlanders were all huge, dressed in fur and leathers. It was their boast that they felt neither cold nor pain and if not actually the trolls of legend, they apparently had much in common with that lost race.

The last man out of the tent was older than the others, slighter of build and more colourfully dressed. Over his furs he wore a woven cloak that glowed in the first rays of the rising sum. Liss crouched lower and she heard his low voice. "A Shaman. They've brought a Shaman."

The old man approached the woman who clutched her infant more tightly as it whimpered once more. Callie bit her lip. She did not want to watch what she feared might be about to happen, but could not drag her eyes away. The Shaman did nothing for long minutes, standing quite still, his eyes closed, then he placed one hand on the head of the woman and one on the child. Almost immediately the crying stopped. At the old man's nod the warriors released the woman who made no move to escape but just stood there gazing up at the old man. He gently turned her shoulders and propelled her back in the direction of her tent. Callie thought she saw the woman smile and her infant wriggle. She definitely saw more women emerging from other yurts as the camp began to stir. Several of them also carried babies or tended to the eldest and frailest tribal members, moving aside as the older children wove their way silently through the camp herding domestic animals. She looked at Liss, whose face held the same expression of shock as her own.

*

The sun was noon high when Liss next called for a rest and Callie was more than grateful. Her legs aching from the days of riding were protesting the mountaineering. Leaving Arco's Bluff, they had scouted the Ice Falls, a sight Callie found both stunningly beautiful and awe inspiring, and observed the outpost for some time. The Kerrians were obviously using it as their headquarters, and while they watched, dog sleds and messengers on shaggy mountain ponies had arrived and departed. Worryingly, some of them seemed to be coming from the Iron Valley itself, and as they headed in that direction they had to move deeper into the forest several times to avoid discovery.

They slipped quietly along animal trails through the trees on the lower slopes of the Skyfall Mountain until finally they were close enough to see the oldest, Blackstone Mine. The compound gates stood wide open and the place was crawling with Kerrian soldiers: far more than Callie had expected. There was no sign of the miners and the ramshackle village that had obviously surrounded the stone buildings had been burnt to the ground. The Kerrians were fully armed and seemed to be dividing their attention half inwards, half outwards. She wondered if the miners had retreated into the underground workings, creating a stand-off, but could not imagine a good outcome. They were hopelessly outnumbered and surely not prepared for a siege.

At the Deep Delve Mine the picture was the same. There were many more Kerrians on high alert, and although several of the buildings remained intact, there was no sign of Lord Barnard's people, so it was with some dread that they followed the banks of the Silver Stream towards the last mine. It was only mid-afternoon but already the daylight was beginning to fade and Callie was beginning to think she would never be warm again. She was about to ask Liss how much longer they would be out when a gust of wind moving the still air of the valley brought the noise of fighting straight to them.

They moved forward towards the Silver Stream Mine as quickly as they dared. The Kerrians had yet to storm this last compound. The gates were still closed, but from their vantage point it was obvious the defenders, for all their courage could not win. They were about to be overwhelmed by sheer numbers and the walkways of the palisade walls were covered with bodies. Callie felt sick and helpless. People were dying as she watched. "We've got to do something." She looked at Liss.

"Yes Callie. You're right, we have to do something. We have to get back to the castle and tell them what is happening so that a proper force can come and fight the Kerrians and re-take the mine."

"Re-take the mine? It isn't lost yet."

"But it soon will be." Although his voice was calm and reasonable she could see the tension in his face. "Two more warriors cannot make a difference here. We must report back."

"Wait." Callie's mind was racing. What had her mother said? Be creative. Be inventive. She looked up at the towering mountains, closer to Silver Stream than at either of the other mines. She closed her eyes and tasted the wind, felt for the snow thick and dense on the higher slopes.

When she opened her eyes Liss was studying her face with an indecipherable expression. "You have an idea. What can you do… and how?" There was a strange ring of hope and confidence in his voice. Hope and confidence in her.

"I can start an avalanche." He blinked.

"Can you control it, once it runs?"

"A good question, I think so."

Remarkably he didn't challenge her, just studied the terrain with sharp grey eyes.

"Callie, think ahead. If you can swamp the Kerrian forces, could you take the snow further forward?" He pointed. "To the narrows?" She nodded, seeing his plan.

"We need to prevent reinforcements, but first we need to warn our people."

"How?" He smiled and reached for a strange long arrow, its top wrapped in a dark gauze. "As soon as they see this sign our people will run for shelter. Here in the mountains there are many avalanches, mostly at the hands of Mother Nature so there is an alarm system, but timing will be crucial. How long do you need?"

She frowned. "Release it when you see the snow break past that col." She pointed.

Liss squinted then looked back to the fighting. "Do it." He reached for his tinder and she reached for the snow.

The taste of frozen water was in her nostrils as her magic reached out towards the towering peaks. "There!" A subtle instability of new snow fallen on a base that had previously melted. She gathered her will and the wind chiselled beneath the snowy blanket. It quivered and she dug deeper. She felt the edges of a great snow slab begin to tremble, start to slide and finally break free.

Thousands of tons of snow began a wild merciless descent towards the valley. She tapped Liss's arm and saw the arrow fly a bright red flame against the darkening sky. She braced herself as the immense rumbling grew louder and nearer, mesmerised by what she had started.

Strong fingers shook her fiercely. "Control it." Liss held her steady. Gods, could she? She took a deep breath and flung her strength towards the cataclysm she had created.

The sounds from the valley floor changed. Panicked screams rose from the soldiers who saw what was approaching. Horses ripped their tethers and raced away into the darkness out of the path of thundering destruction. Callie felt herself wavering then Liss's hands were on her shoulders, steading her. "Nearly there, nearly there." The snow was almost at the narrows. "Now hold it back."

She tried, then tried again. It slowed but it did not stop. Her chest felt tight, constrained and her frustration morphed into a strange wild anger. She pushed harder and as heat suddenly raged through her body her power exploded. The great wall of snow slowed then stopped moving. It reached right across the valley, sealing it. Where an army of invaders had stood there was a field of pristine snow, just reaching to the top of the stockade. It was strangely beautiful, Callie thought as the setting sun painted stripes of pink, grey and gold over the blank white canvas. Then the colours faded and she saw only blackness.

Chapter 6

It was good to be dry, comfortable and warm; especially warm. Her body noticed these things as she slowly surfaced from the darkest of dreams. Eyes finally open, she saw that she lay in a comfortable chamber, probably a guest room and definitely not her cot in the barracks. A lamp burned softly on a nightstand and she sat up in bed reaching for the water left beside it. She ran fingers through her tangled hair. She felt bone weary, as if she were recovering from an illness, but knew as her mind re-ran events that she had taken no injury. She sipped her water thoughtfully.

With the briefest of light taps her door opened. Dexter looked surprised, but pleased to see her awake, and after a few words to a page stationed at the door he stepped into the room and planted himself at the end of her bed.

"My timing is impeccable." He smiled. "How are you feeling?"

"Honestly? Like I've just completed the twelve labours of Sesstice." She groaned and tugged the coverlet higher, finally realising that she wore very little under the covers. He nodded.

"Liss said that would be the case. He also said you would be hungry." He grinned as her stomach rumbled in agreement. "I've sent for food."

"I take it Liss brought me back?" Dexter nodded.

"He borrowed a dog team and took it along the Eagle Cliff track. He told us what you did. He was very impressed and believe me, that doesn't happen often." He paused as a clattering beyond the doors announced company and returned with a laden tray, which he placed carefully on the bedside table. Callie pounced on the food and almost inhaled two savoury rolls before reaching more carefully for a huge bowl of thick soup. Dexter watched her with a slight smile. Hi-bred ladies were usually very dainty in their eating; something that obviously bothered Callie not at all.

"Liss reported fully on all you saw as well as what you did. The Prince's scouts confirmed some of it although they got nowhere nearly as close to the Troll camp as the two of you."

"The Prince sent out scouts too?" There was a definite edge to her voice.

"Of course he did. We all knew we needed more information." She snorted, to be brought up firmly by a raised finger and a stern look.

"Callie, don't make the mistake of thinking Jerran a fool. He isn't. In many ways he is quite astute. He is still young and learning, which can't be easy in a court full of sycophants. He can think for himself and it's a shame he defers so often to the older idiots he is surrounded by." Dexter's voice and expression were both earnest.

"I'm sorry – you say he's young. He looks the same age as you."

"Fair point, but we have had very different upbringings and I haven't had to play second string to an older brother. Anyway, the battle royal is on hold for the moment. There will be a war council after an early breakfast and you are expected to attend; in the Prince's quarters." He looked at her assessingly then made for the door. "It's nearly midnight now. A few more hours' sleep should see you fine." Then he was gone, closing the door quietly behind him.

Callie finished her soup slowly, gave herself the briefest wash and fell back into bed. It took her a little while to drop off and she mulled over what Dexter had said. Talking to him felt a lot like talking to Raff only older and more experienced. She realised she was already trusting his judgement although their acquaintance was brief and tried to work out why. Colonel Ferran and Lord Barnard respected him, as did Liss. His men, as far as she had seen were disciplined in a way that spoke of good leadership and fairness. She was beginning to feel he would be someone she could rely on and if he wasn't writing off the Prince then, very well, she would reserve judgement. On that thought sleep reclaimed her.

*

Breakfast in the mess hall was busy and fairly rowdy. Her friends were full of questions and she was grateful that Will and Gilly were able to field many of them, as they too had been out scouting the previous day.

At the quarter bell, she followed them through the inner keep to the Prince's apartments. Colonel Ferran, Lord Dexter and Prince Jerran were already leaning over the maps in heated discussion and when Lord Barnard and Liss appeared the doors were closed; today's group a much smaller gathering. Will and Gilly settled by the doors in case they were needed and Colonel Ferran called the meeting to order and began the briefing. Now that, Callie thought privately, was interesting. Colonel Ferran, not the Prince. He outlined the situation in a few words. The mines needed to be relieved as soon as possible, if any of the Earl's workers were to be saved, but to access the Iron Valley, the Prince's forces would either have to skirt perilously close to Arco's Bluff or take a more easterly road, which ran uncomfortably close to the Kerrian-held outpost.

Callie listened with interest and no small degree of anxiety. It was clear the size of the Kerrian force, even excluding the Frystlanders was far larger than anyone had bargained for. When her previous day's exploits were warmly applauded she felt strangely little satisfaction; there was so much more to do. They needed to relieve the mines urgently, their forces were outnumbered and the main route into the Iron Valley was effectively under Kerrian control.

With their problems set out before them there were several long minutes of silence as each of them reviewed their options. It was the Prince who spoke first, directing his attention to Callie. "Lady Callandra may I formally introduce myself?" He offered her a smile, made up, she decided of equal parts chagrin, charm and hope. "I'm Prince Jerran, the man who so resoundingly and foolishly underestimated you." He reached for her hand and shook it firmly with what seemed like genuine friendliness. "Please forgive me. Your actions yesterday were little short of miraculous. Gilly tells me the avalanche wall across the narrows froze overnight and nothing and no-one will be going through that way until the spring." He paused. "Is there any chance you could do something similar at Deep Delve or Blackstone?"

She reluctantly shook her head. "I don't think so, I'm sorry. The mountains are lower and further out from the valley floor. Also I don't think they held the same depth of snow."

"Liss?"

"That would be my feeling too. We might improve our chances if we send one force down the old logging trail at the same time that we approach from the west."

Colonel Ferran and Lord Barnard exchanged glances and the Colonel frowned heavily. "Any force going down the main route to Arco's Gap will be at the mercy of the Kerrians and the troll forces on the bluff. We could lose a lot of men and we don't have a lot of men to lose. Is the logging trail clear of the avalanche?"

"Yes, just above it and useable," Liss confirmed.

"The numbers are worrying me." The Earl leaned back in his chair. "Although I hate to think of my people at the mercy of the Kerrians, perhaps we should hold off and request reinforcements."

Dexter shook his head. "That would be four days' hard riding each way and time needed to call up reserves. I don't think we have another two weeks to play with."

Callie scratched her head. "Four days each way? Didn't we take six?" Dexter nodded.

"We did but we set up relays on the way here. Messengers will be able to change horses and keep moving." She flushed, wondering what else she had missed.

"As I see it, we need to try and neutralise some of the Kerrian forces." Liss was looking at Callie consideringly. "Callie, would you be able to make fog?" She grinned.

"Certainly, but wouldn't that cause problems for our men too?"

"Not necessarily." Liss sketched a few lines on the map. "If you could create a fog bank here," he drew a semi-circle from the bottom of Arco's bluff to a point just east of the outpost, "I think we might be able to get into the Iron Valley."

"Is it possible to be that precise?" The Prince glanced up at her and looked impressed when she nodded.

"They would surely know we were up to something," Colonel Ferran looked at the map thoughtfully, "but there is no way they could risk their mounts and it would take out their bowmen." Eyes met around the table in agreement. "Then that's what we'll do."

The Prince looked pleased. "We'll leave at dusk."

"No." Callie's objection was out of her mouth before she had time to think.

"No?" The Prince looked distinctly startled.

"I'm sorry, Highness, but what you are asking me to do, well, it will not be easy. If you need the fog to last for some time I'll have to meter my strength... pace myself." She almost chuckled, mentally hearing her least favourite teacher's voice – *Save your strength, Callie, pace yourself.* Who knew he would be so right?

"So what would work best for you?" The Colonel's gaze met hers unblinking.

"Sunrise, please. It will be fine tomorrow and I can build on the overnight valley fog, and then use the sun." To her relief he nodded and they turned back to attend to details, the Prince's hazel eyes the last to leave her.

With most of a day free Callie attended to a few domestic chores then made her way out to the stables with apples from the breakfast hall in her pockets. Jessa was looking bright and bored and pointedly turned her back as Callie approached. It required quite a lot of petting and bribery before she blew into Callie's hair and stretched her neck to be scratched.

"That's the first time I've heard anyone actually apologise to a horse." Dexter emerged from a stall a little further down the stables.

Callie grinned. "My father says you should always treat those who work for you with respect and gratitude and Jessa works very hard for me." The mare snorted in apparent agreement and they both laughed.

"If you need anything for her or any help with her, just ask Walter." He pointed out an elderly man giving instructions to one of the stable boys.

"You are obviously very familiar with Lord Barnard's castle."

"Yes. I spent a lot of time here when I was younger. Is there something you need to know?"

"Can you direct me to the armoury? I had my sword sharpened in Derryn but I'm not happy with my knives."

He looked at her weapons, and she braced herself for the sarcastic comments that so often came the way of women warriors but he merely led her to the stable door and pointed. "I'm sorry I can't go with you, Callie, but I'm expected elsewhere." He made to leave, then turned back looking slightly embarrassed. "Talking of saying sorry, I owe you an apology for last night." She raised a puzzled eyebrow. "For barging unchaperoned into a lady's bedchamber in the middle of the night. I don't know what I was thinking."

"Forget it, Lord Dexter. You were treating me like any other member of your team and I hope you will continue to do so. On that basis you are always welcome to barge into my room in the middle of the night." He wiggled his eyebrows at that and she burst out laughing.

"Don't you have somewhere to be?" He nodded and set off back to the inner keep still chuckling, while she made her way to the armoury. There was a short queue and she leant against the wall in the wintery sunshine. She liked Dexter's attitude. Women did fight, both in the army and the guards. Although far fewer in number than the men, and despite there being quite a few notable female warriors many of the rank and file male troopers still believed they were superior. As for herself, she was yet again unique. Men and women fought; Mages didn't.

The queue edged forward slowly and a pang of homesickness struck her. Dexter reminded her of her kind, clever, irritating twin. In her mind's eye she could picture him so clearly. As it was late morning he would be outside the lunch hall trying to accidentally cross the path of Mia, a healer student he seemed very interested in. Mind you, there were many young men interested in Mia. She was lovely; a dark-haired, pale-skinned beauty with a figure to die for. In fact, she was someone Callie would have loved to hate, but to make matters worse she was genuinely kind and pleasant. Sickening really. Callie was nudged back to the present as she reached the front of the queue and her knives were taken from her.

Chapter 7

It was bitterly cold in the fortress courtyard in the hour before dawn. Most of the troops were assembled beyond the gates, their horses snorting cloudy breath into the frosty air. Callie murmured gentle nonsense to her mount as she watched Gideon, Lord Barnard's eldest son, talking to Colonel Ferran. She couldn't see the Prince and wondered whether his noble companions had decided to stay in bed and perhaps join them all for a little light war making after a leisurely breakfast.

She didn't look for Dexter, knowing he had headed out with his men along the Silver Stream back trail even earlier. A hand on her arm startled her. Liss with his silver hair and grey eyes looked like a frost wraith in the half light. Even his stallion was grey. She hadn't heard either of them arrive but was glad to have him beside her. He had been a steady presence the previous day. It had helped.

Jerran was actually standing in the stable doorway, reluctant to face the pre-dawn chill until the last possible moment. He shivered and wondered if the Colonel and Gideon were as impervious to the cold as they appeared. Gideon at least was used to the northern winter and Jerran noticed fur edging his gilet and cloak. Callandra talking to Liss was wearing so many layers she appeared round; a waste of a delightful shape if first impressions counted. The young Mage seemed calm although so much would depend on her. He studied her thoughtfully, his interest roused. She had pulled off an incredible feat the day before. When he had fully understood what she had done he had been more than startled. Dexter, it occurred to him had seemed less surprised. Dexter who seemed somewhat to have adopted her.

He turned that thought over in his mind. Perhaps it was not so surprising. Callie was small, feisty and obviously intelligent, the last being a quality that few women of his own acquaintance seemed to possess. But more than that he wondered if he was the only one who had noticed how very much she resembled Dexter's sister Miri, with her chestnut hair escaping from her hood and curling in the damp air as she talked to the Isseni.

And that too was interesting. For Dexter to show an interest in Callie was one thing. For Liss to do the same was another story altogether. Liss was Isseni, and acted as ambassador for that country when necessary, but he was so much more. His skills as a warrior, strategist and linguist had earned him a remarkable reputation. He was not part of the royal forces, although he was often attached to the army. He had, to Jerran's certain knowledge carried out sensitive missions for King Theon. He was very clever and perceptive, so if something about the young Mage had caught his attention, then she was someone worth watching.

The Prince mounted up at the Colonel's signal and made his way across to the war leaders, waving a greeting in Callie's general direction. He was glad Liss was staying by her. Despite her show of power the previous day, the fact remained that their best hope of recovering the mines was dependent on her blocking the enemy cavalry and archers with her Magery. If she failed, if she could not buy them enough time to relieve the mines before they turned to face the rest of the Kerrian forces they would have the enemy on both fronts and many men would die. That would be a heavy burden for an experienced, battle-tried Mage to bear and she was neither of those things.

The war party rode for nearly an hour before they halted and Callie was beckoned forward. They were not far from the sentry post where Lord Barnard's men kept watch on the enemy. First true light would be with them soon, but here the long shadows of the Skyfall Mountains made night linger. When the sun finally rose above the peaks the valley fog would quickly disperse.

Liss led Callie forward slowly, their horses silent on the soft snow until they slipped into the very edge of the treeline. Without the fog the whole of Arco's Gap would have been visible from this point. They stood at the bottom of hills that ran up to Arco's Bluff, knowing that high above them the Troll lookouts would be waiting, watching and more importantly at the moment, listening.

Callie dismounted, ignoring Gilly's quickly stifled objection and handed Jessa's reins to Will, who tied them to his own horse, leaving his hands free for his bow. Objectively Callie knew she could do what she had to do from horseback, and if things went badly, she would be slower to escape if she had to mount her horse, but she also knew with a visceral certainty that went beyond teaching that she had far more control and maybe even far more power when she was literally grounded. A fact she had been able to demonstrate to her teachers. A fact they had been unable to deny or explain.

Liss watched her very closely. It was time. She reached out, feeling her way through the air currents. The air was cold but moist. High above a winter sun offered light and just enough warmth. She drew the strands of her weather working together and the mist began to thicken, until a dense blanket blotted out the approaching day, plunging the valley back into semi-darkness.

She moved her focus and pushed shape into the fog, extending it forwards towards the Ice Falls outpost and clearing the eastern side of the valley where the war party must ride. She buried the lower slopes of Arco's Bluff in dense white clouds, then she breathed a sigh of relief, echoed, she was amused to hear by Will and Gilly. It was done. Now, she had to hold the weather working; anchor it in place. She bowed her head in concentration, moving into the almost trance-like state that lessened the strain on her power.

A blanket was draped around her shoulder, but she moved not a muscle. The Colonel leading the troops forward gave her a nod and the Prince waved in salute but she did not notice. Nor did she see the faces of the men moving silently past. Their expressions as they looked at her, nervous or grateful. Few of them had had direct experience of Magecraft except at the hands of healers; Battle Mages being so rare, and to see a slip of a girl rearranging nature was strangely shocking. Before long only churned snow showed the passage of the solders and Arco's Gap appeared empty once more. The army had managed to slip past into the Iron Valley.

Jerran rode beside Colonel Ferran and Gideon. Once clear of Arco's Gap they began to move faster, the need for silent running now less important than the need for speed. For all her strength Callie would eventually tire and they did not want to find the enemy both ahead and behind them.

When the Blackstone Mine palisade loomed, they did not slow down, but raised their shields and skirted round it out of bow-shot range. Then they raced forward up the valley towards the cliffs that towered over Deep Delve. Here the compound was three-quarters of a circle abutting the rock walls. The gates, obviously repaired and strengthened were tight shut and Kerrian archers manned the walls. They had even hung a Kerrian flag from the sentry tower. Jerran heard Gideon swear under his breath and spit at the sight of it.

"I fear we have come too late, if that is anything to go by." Jerran's heart sank. Surely if the invaders were that entrenched there could be no miners left alive. He had addressed his remark to Gideon and was more than pleased to see him shake his head.

"Our miners will be tucked up in the workings. We have had many raids over the last few years. There are well-laid plans and drills for our men. This," he pointed towards the flag, "this is just to add insult. Right now this little force will be shitting themselves." His gaze panned over their own forces quickly moving into position.

"Will we start the attack on the Colonel's mark, or yours, sire?" There was hesitancy and a distinct question in Gideon's voice. The Earl's son was obviously still not entirely certain who was in charge here: Colonel Ferran or the Prince.

Jerran winced inwardly, realising his aloof behaviour had added to this uncertainty when in truth it was no more than nervousness on his part and an awareness of how little actual experience he had. He schooled his expression to one of cordial neutrality, a skill trained into all royals from birth. "On the Colonel's mark." He almost tasted the easing of tension around him.

"When we have fully engaged the Kerrians, after the archers draw back, you will hear a horn sound: Arco's horn. That will be a sign to our miners to come out fighting."

"Arco's horn." The Prince's eyes widened.

"Well they all believe it's Arco's horn."

"And it's not?" Jerran wasn't sure what to make of that. Gideon grinned.

"Well, it could be. My father said it was found when a very old part of the castle was being cleared for repair work. The point is, it matters to the men." He hesitated. "Obviously we don't know how many men will be fighting fit but even a few attacking from the rear could tip the balance so timing is crucial."

"The men are in position, sir." One of Ferran's captains trotted up to them. "Ready the archers." The order was relayed as Jerran checked his weapons one last time and then the first fire arrow was lit and fed to the next and the next. The bows were raised and aimed and as the Colonel's arm fell, flames screamed through the still air to fall on the timbered walls of the Deep Delve Mine.

The palisade walls were constructed from northern pine; so were the walkways, some barns and even a simple barracks. Green pine, resinous and flammable despite the weeks of winter snow. It seemed long minutes before the first flames took hold, then snapping and spitting one building after another caught alight, sending the Kerrians diving off the walls for cover. Jerran quieted his horse as he watched the mayhem spread.

"Here they come." The gates were opening, and the Prince took a deep breath as he looked at the opposing forces. They were steady and disciplined, not the disorganised rabble he had been led to believe. He cursed himself for a fool and drew his sword, unconsciously moving forward until a firm hand snagged his horse's reins. He looked up furiously and met the steady gaze of the Earl's son. "Gideon, get your bloody hands off my horse." Gideon released the reins immediately, not looking the least bit chastened. "I intend to fight." Jerran's words spilled out half statement, half challenge, but Gideon merely nodded.

"Indeed, and I would fight at your side, Highness, but we must not be in the first rank. Trust me, sire; there will be plenty of Kerrians for all of us and moving too far ahead of the main force will earn you no great honour, just an early death."

He smiled at the Prince and looked back to the field. The

exchange had taken mere seconds and the Kerrians were only now advancing. "Engage the enemy." Colonel Ferran signalled his captains and ahead of them battle was finally joined. In moments horses and men jostled and fought, the destriers kicking and biting as their riders pressed forward.

Jerran looked behind him where the men of his personal guard were grouped beside a squad of Gideon's men. He noticed with a start that Nevis and Hadley were also there slightly to one side. They had been so unusually quiet he had actually forgotten them. It occurred to him that they both looked very nervous and the air of experience that their extra years had conferred on them seemed to have disappeared.

He turned his attention forward again. "There." The Colonel was pointing to the edge of the melee. "Don't let them flank us." And they were off, racing towards a group of Kerrians hell bent on evading the fighting. The Prince was aware of Gideon on his left and the enemy ahead, then a sword was thrust towards his throat and he parried with the skill that hours of training had won him.

It wasn't like the practice bouts or the tourneys or the salle. He cut and slashed, thrust and stabbed until his arms were trembling and his coat was dappled with blood and sweat, all the while storing image after image of this thing called Battle. A boy so young his helmet was falling in his eyes, looking stupidly at where his hand was missing. A toothless veteran holding his spilling guts in his hands. The stench of vomit and loosened bowels and the bitter copper tang of blood in his mouth.

He heard the horn sounding in the distance and the noise within the compound rose to a ferocious pitch, for the shortest time before it died away altogether. Finally, finally, there was no-one left beyond Jerran's blade. Gideon, still beside him slapped his shoulder and offered him a water bottle as they picked their way forward towards the compound past the charred remains of the walls.

Maybe eighty or so miners were clustered around Colonel Ferran, who had been one of the first through the shattered gates, but they turned as one, when Gideon rode forward. He knew these men, Jerran realised, watching him offer a nod here, a hand there and once a very firm push on the shoulders of a giant, a man determined to say his piece although his face was sheeted in blood from a head wound.

Gideon shoved him towards one of the stone buildings where a makeshift hospital was already setting up.

No-one paid Jerran any attention. He was not recognised at this northern outpost of Lithia. It was an unfamiliar feeling. He was plainly dressed and his simple armour now bore the marks of battle. The previous night Nevis had ordered the servants to take Jerran's armour to be checked over. It was an exquisite suit emblazoned with the royal arms and given to him by the King when he came of age. It had been brought back a while later just as he and his friends had been leaving his rooms to go to the strategy meeting. He had instructed the servants to place it on the armoury stand.

As chance would have it, just outside his door he had bumped into one of the prettier laundry maids brining up fresh linen. A comely woman with a pleasing shape and knowing smile, he had waved Nevis and Hadley on ahead and dallied for a few minutes hoping a well-placed compliment or two might earn him a night-time companion. Then loud laughter had erupted inside his rooms and caught his ear. He had opened the door quietly and seen the servant holding up his ornate breastplate and regaling a page with the armourer's opinion of nobles who didn't know the difference between a parade and a bloody battle. The armourer had also apparently foretold that many of the families who spent all their time at court would be dying out soon either because of in-breeding or wearing armour that made them such bloody obvious targets.

Jerran had been furious and mortified and was further annoyed to see his laundry maid had slipped away. Lord Nevis, calling him had forced him to walk away from the mockery. Then the strategy meeting had taken a while and required all of his attention so he had been much calmer by the time he returned to his chamber and unfortunately, solitary bed.

Yet somehow, while he slept his saner self had decided the armourer had a point and despite the loud objections of his friends the next morning, that his dress must reflect his rank the work of art had been left on the stand. It was his plain but well-made training armour that he had reached for at dawn.

Chapter 8

His musing was cut short by his horse tugging at his reins. The others were dismounting and taking a few moments to re-order themselves. He joined the Colonel and was amused to be offered a huge meat-filled roll and a leather tankard of hot spiced wine.

"How long have we got?" he asked Ferran through a mouthful of beef. The Colonel stretched himself and cast a weather eye at the sky. Late morning by the look of things.

"No time at all, Highness. We are more or less finished here and we need to tackle Blackstone before our Mage has to withdraw. Blackstone won't be so easy. They know we are on our way Dexter will have blocked the Iron Valley entrance by now so they cannot seek reinforcements but they are fresh, we are not and an enemy with his back to the wall will always fight twice as hard. What was your butcher's bill?"

Jerran flushed with chagrin. "I didn't…" He had not thought to check his men for wounded and realised that must have been where he had seen Gideon heading. The Colonel took pity on him.

"Didn't know where to find the healers? That way, lad." He pointed to the building Jerran had spotted earlier and turned away to talk to one of his captains.

The barn-like building was well organised. Men and women were attending to the walking wounded with speed and efficiency. "Highness." He looked further, seeing areas set up with simple cots. Lord Hadley was lying down on one with a heavily bandaged shoulder.

"What happened?" Jerran knelt down beside him.

"I took an arrow." He gestured to his armpit. "They've dug it out; it happened early on. Surgeon reckons I've lost a lot of blood." Although he winced he looked strangely smug. "I'm sorry I won't be able to go on with you. Such bad luck!"

Jerran nodded and smiled. "I hope I'll catch up with you later. We are moving out almost immediately." Hadley nodded.

"Be safe, sire." His head was nodding as the Prince rose to go. Jerran found only two others of his men amongst the seriously wounded. The dead had been taken elsewhere. For all the fighting had been so fierce they had got off lightly.

Back in the courtyard he retrieved his horse from one of his guards who had watered the stallion and thrown a blanket over its back then mounted up. He found himself once again next to Gideon. It seemed to him that they had lost some men but gained others. Quite a large squad of men, their faces still black from the mine, were lined up beside the regular troops.

"Those men." Jerran couldn't quite believe what he was seeing. "Surely they aren't coming with us?"

"Of course they are." Gideon looked perplexed.

"They have been besieged in a mine held by the enemy for the last week. Are they fit to fight? Don't they need time to rest and recover?"

"They will rest and recover when this is over." Gideon looked across at them. "I couldn't stop them coming if I wanted to, which I don't. Many of them will have family or friends at Blackstone. Fighting alongside trained forces they get a chance of payback." Jerran tried to digest that idea.

"If they are on foot won't they slow us down or arrive after the event?"

"The men will double up. We don't have far to go," the Colonel explained, turning his horse beside them and watched attentively as the miners began to mount behind Lord Barnard's own troops. He rode forward, motioning for Jerran and Gideon to follow him before he turned to address the force.

"Men, you have fought well. For that I thank you but there is more to do. You all know what you are fighting for." He bowed his head to them as they cheered, then turned his bay to lead the way across the churned snow back towards the Blackstone Mine.

*

The hours passing so swiftly in the fighting passed very slowly in the icy fog below Arco's Bluff. Liss watched the forward sentries take turns walking a perimeter to check for every movement and to keep from freezing.

He watched the sentries and he watched the scouts but most of all he watched Callie. She still stood firmly and the wall of fog had thinned not at all. Where the land widened into the water meadow below Arco's Bluff, was perhaps a mile from the Blackstone Mine and probably the same again to Deep Delve. The thick drifts of snow blanketed the land and gave a slightly eerie silence to the scene, but sound travels oddly in the mountains, small noises echoing and large noises muffled.

Once or twice a distant clamour disturbed the peace, come and gone so fleetingly the men looked at each other for confirmation but when the faraway clarion call of the horn shivered the mountain air they knew what it meant. Could read from it a report on the progress of the battle. Fighting might be hot work but waiting on guard in the snow was not. Liss did not object when the scouts lit the tiniest fire with charcoal bricks, and Gilly mulled wine in a small pot. When he wrapped Callie's gloved fingers around a hot cup he earned a brief grateful smile but no words.

Will had chopped bracken and spread it beneath the trees for the horses to stand on and they had dozed beneath their blankets quiet and uncomplaining for some time when Liss noticed their ears prick up and their heads lift.

He signalled the scouts. "The horses sense something." He nodded towards Callie. "I'll guard. You go." They had nodded and slipped into the edge of the fog bank. The sentries, aware of the scouts' departure readied themselves along their positions checking their weapons. For a long time, they heard nothing then a sound of scuffling followed by a heavy thud brought Liss, bow drawn, to stand in front of Callandra.

At first he could see neither of the scouts then further away a figure stepped briefly clear of the fog into the bright sunlight. He was a small man, darkly clothed under a bright cloak that swirled from his shoulders. He looked at the sunlit road leading towards the Iron Valley then his eyes swept back to the sentries before he melted back into the fog. "Hell," Liss cursed under his breath. He doubted Callie had been visible, small as she was behind him, but the man had seen what they were up to before he had vanished.

He cursed again a short while later as Gilly appeared between the trees dragging a body. Will was unconscious and there was blood on his face. "What happened?" Liss ran his hands expertly over the woodsman, finding no other signs of injury.

"We ran into two of their scouts. I got one but the other took Will down and escaped. Sorry."

Liss dismissed the apology. "It's a miracle they didn't come sooner. Was your scout wearing a long cloak?"

"No," Gilly shook his head, "short tunic, fur-lined gilet. Why?"

"We saw another. We'd better get ready for company and prepare to withdraw. They still won't be able to use their horses or archers while Callie holds her weather-working and even if they lead their mounts clear it will all take time."

Gilly looked slightly reassured then darted past Liss to grab the young Mage who looked suddenly unsteady.

"Callie?" Liss kept his voice low.

"Liss," she sounded strained, "someone is trying to interfere with my magic. I can feel it."

"Can you hold it?" He could see she was beginning to shake.

"Not for long."

Liss turned back to Gilly. "Ride as fast as you can to Blackstone and warn Lord Dexter and the Colonel that the Kerrians will be coming sometime soon." He watched as the scout leapt on his horse and raced away towards the Iron Valley. The sounds of fighting seemed nearer and clearer now. The battle for Blackstone was likely to be fierce and if reinforcements were able to attack from the outpost or Arco's Bluff things might go badly for their men.

Callie had held her weather-working with little effort once it was in place. The existing dampness, sun and snow had all reduced the power she had needed to create and hold the fog but now she felt a counter-force pushing against her. Her head began to throb and she looked on with dismay as the thick blanket she had created began to thin and fade.

Noises, once muffled reached them ever more clearly. Noises of horse and harness and armour. Shapes became visible. In the distance the Kerrians and their allies were moving into battle formation. Callie estimated a scant quarter of a mile between the outpost, now just appearing and the entrance to the Iron Valley where Dexter's men waited: slightly further for the Frystians, who showed no eagerness to engage.

Liss put a hand on her shoulder. "Drop the fog, Callie; save your strength, they can already see enough." His voice was grim as he swiftly reached the horses. "We may have to retreat."

"But we can't just abandon them." Her eyes were huge in a pale face.

"We may have to, Callie, unless you have any more tricks up your sleeve. We retreat and live to fight another day."

She looked at the strange man whose presence had been a steady comfort the whole long morning. What he said made sense but… this wasn't just 'an army' anymore. It was people she knew, faces she recognised, warriors she had bunked with, sparred with, laughed with. She felt slightly sick inside and looked around her frantically for inspiration.

Unsteady on her feet, she slumped down on a carpet of grey-brown pine needles by the fire, her head on her knees. She felt the faintest tremor run through the ground and realised the Kerrian forces were moving forward. They were too far away for her to see any details and the winter sun high overhead was dazzling on the snow and ice but there was no doubt. They were on their way to the Iron Valley. The forces of the Earl and the Prince would be trapped. It looked like they had lost their gamble.

Chapter 9

"Gods above." Dexter schooled his face to a professional calm he was far from feeling. The fighting was not going well at Blackstone and the soldier before him brought Colonel Ferran's request that he bring his troops back to support the royal forces.

The Colonel's messenger had arrived only minutes after the scout Liss had sent with news that the Kerrian forces were clear of the fog and heading in his direction. He visualised the map they had spent hours poring over. No, he could not take his men back to Blackstone. If the worst came to the worst the Colonel would have to break off the action at the mine and leave a besieging force until more troops were available. If the Kerrian forces advancing from Arco's Bluff were allowed free rein, this border incursion, already larger than any he could remember would escalate into full-scale war; and Lithia was already fighting in the west.

He could not take the risk. He drafted a brief note to the Colonel, relieved in a corner of his mind that it was to the Colonel, a military man who would understand his decision even if he would not be happy with it. He wasn't at all sure how the Prince would have reacted. He called his men to order and moved them forward to their holding position, where the land rose slightly before once again falling away as it became the Iron Valley, then he drew his sword, and waited.

"We must go." Liss reached a hand down to Callie. She shrugged the blanket from her shoulder, rolling it up as she looked over the valley. It was beautiful in a winter white way. A heavy night frost had set diamonds on the snow fields, sparkling in the sun and at the top of the valley the great Ice Falls shimmered, so massive although so far away. All that water frozen until the spring thaws came. It would all look very different then, if only…

She caught her breath then trotted clear of the trees, still staring. It was such a long way but it might be possible if she was strong enough. "Callie?" She turned and stilled Liss's question with a raised finger.

"Liss." Her blue eyes locked with his grey ones. "Are you a Mage?"

He slowly shook his head. "Not in the sense that you mean." She almost smiled at the ambiguous answer.

"But you have quite some knowledge of Magery." He simply nodded. "I have an idea. There might be something I can do if only I have enough power. Can you…?"

"No," he interrupted, obviously knowing what she would ask. "I cannot give you extra power, I cannot link." Her shoulders sagged. "What were you thinking?"

She offered a wry smile. "I was wondering if I had enough power to melt the Ice Falls. Delusions of grandeur or what?" She gave a mirthless laugh. Although Liss's eyebrows shot up she was grateful that he didn't laugh out loud. She turned back to her contemplation.

"Well, have you?" Liss's voice quite steady, quite serious.

"I… I really don't know. I doubt it. How much power would it take?" Liss chuckled.

"As I don't think anyone has ever thought to do what you have just suggested, the only way to find out is if you give it a try." Callie's jaw dropped.

"Do you think I should? It's insane."

"Well maybe it is but Callie, we have nothing to lose. If you succeed you will save many lives."

"And if I fail?" She bit her lip.

"If you fail, let me see, I expect you'll have a blinding headache, but no-one will fault you."

She took a deep breath, looking again at the distant sparkling ice-wall. He had the right of it. There was really nothing to lose.

"I'm going to try."

"Nice day for it." She grinned at his dry humour. His piercing gaze dropped from her suddenly as if he had made a decision and he moved swiftly to Will's horse and started rummaging through the scout's supplies. "Prepare yourself." He returned to her carrying of all things a small shovel. Callie, absorbed in planning out her Magery only vaguely noticed as he began to clear debris from the forest floor and turn over the thin soil, creating a clear circle about three feet across. "Come," he beckoned, "sit." She snagged her blanket, unrolling it but he snatched it from her hands. "On the bare earth, Callie; even in the earth. Trust me." She eyed him curiously as she settled where he pointed and was struck again by how grounded the earth contact made her feel. "Are you ready?"

"Not quite. I need to create a really strong shield: one the Shaman can't break." She reached inwards and found the heart of fire that was her Mage gift. She cocooned it, wrapped it, encased it in intricate wardings. "Now." Liss nodded. This time she reached for her power and outwards to the Falls then upwards to the winter sun. She focused her will and sent her awareness deep into the frozen river, trailing sunlight, sun warmth, sun fire behind her. She visualised the river in the spring, wild and tumultuous with great slabs of ice breaking free and plunging hundreds of feet to shatter on the rocks below.

The river was frozen, lost in its winter sleep; yet deep down a tiny stream still trickled. She tried to push it faster, tried to warm its cold eddies, sprinkle its crystal depths with sunlight and seed it with warmth. Nearly. So nearly. By the Gods it was so hard and she was already tired. She tried again, hardening her will yet knowing her strength was failing. She could feel herself weaken. Then Liss's hands were on her skin. He removed her boots and tugged off her gloves. "What the…?" He pushed her bare feet and frozen hands deep into thin black soil.

Her head reeled in a moment of stomach-plunging disorientation then she felt a new power well up through her body. It had texture and grain and colour as if she could taste the earth and rocks. It rose steadily, filling her, and she slowly reached for this new and old part of herself and gave it direction, sending it out towards the Ice Falls.

There was an almighty cracking, an explosion of sound as a huge sheet of ice fell from the front of the falls. Water spurted out behind it with immense and terrifying force. There was another rumble. Then groaning and shrieking in slow motion, virtually the entire front of the great cascade fell away, tumbling down to the rocks.

The ice she had melted poured out, a surging torrent, carrying ice floes, tree limbs, even rocks with it. Dimly, distantly, she heard screaming and Liss muttering, "Good Gods," but she could not see. She was the river, she was water, sun and earth and her mind was stone.

Thunder rolled across the valley and Dexter's men rose to their feet all along their battle line watching in disbelief as an apocalyptic flood was released from the frozen Ice Falls. A wall of water hurtled across Arco's Gap deepening second by second, moment by moment. They stood silently, fearfully, looking on as their enemies drowned. A few, very few of the Kerrians, better positioned or swifter to react fled to higher ground, forcing their ponies up near vertical slopes between the close-set trees but still the water rose.

"Sir? What?" One of Dexter's captains looked at him, white faced and questioning.

"I don't know, Griff." He shook his head. "We will no doubt find out more later." He gazed a moment longer. It was a mesmerising sight. The whole valley that was Arco's Gap was now a virtual lake where white-water currents swirled and tumbled the bodies of the fallen. He pulled himself together, looking around. "It seems there's no more work for us here and we're needed at Blackstone. Get the men mounted up and let's be on our way."

Chapter 10

On his third attempt Jerran finally managed to sheathe his sword, noticing in a detached way that his hands were shaking. He dismounted slowly, wondering whether his legs would actually hold him up. They did, but only just. He looked at the men close by him, his personal guard. Every one of them was grey with exhaustion. The fighting had been intense, the Kerrian force much larger than they had expected.

Truth be told things had been balanced on a knife's edge when Lord Dexter had arrived with his own troops; men who were all fresh and rested.

"You're needed, sire." Fife his sergeant pointed across the courtyard where a figure waved and beckoned. "We'll see to your horse." He waved someone forward to take Warrior's reins. Jerran nodded, trying to make his brain work.

"And Sergeant, will you check on the wounded?" Fife nodded with a salute. Neither of them mentioned the many, many dead.

The stone-flagged forecourt of Blackstone Mine was only lightly covered with snow. Snow now grotesquely stained red and pink with blood. So this, he thought, was warfare in winter. The daylight was already fading but the sunset spilled more scarlet along the valley floor illuminating the charnel house he picked his way through. It reminded him of the paintings of hell to be found on the walls of low churches.

Gideon, he thought it was Gideon, was waving him towards the large stone refectory that squatted relatively unscathed to one side of the mine workings. It seemed a long way away and he was soon shivering but once through the heavy doors a wall of heat hit him so that he stumbled and almost fell onto the bench where the officers had gathered. Colonel Ferran eyed him sharply but said nothing, merely handing him a sturdy silver flask. He didn't know what it was, didn't care what it was. He took a deep gulp and felt fire burn through his body. "What the…?"

"It's a local brew." That was Gideon. "A sort of methaglyn only quite a lot stronger. Have some more. you look like you need it."

Jerran didn't argue, just sat and sipped and tried to make sense of what he was hearing.

"So you are certain we cannot return across Arco's Gap?" The Colonel, startled, was obviously repeating a question.

"Colonel, it's a lake, and if you ask me, it will be for some time to come. The ground is frozen so there's nowhere for the water to go." Dexter, who looked annoyingly alert, was shaking his head.

"Then we'll have to travel back along the logging road."

The Colonel thought for a moment. "We have far too many injured who can't be moved. We'll leave them here and get the Earl's healers out to them. Dexter, send Lord Barnard notice of what passes here and when we'll be back. Gideon, we'll patch up those we can and move out in half a mark; leave at least two squads. I think we got all the Kerrians but let's not take any chances.

"The Blackstone miners have paid dearly today and there are very few of them left who are fighting fit."

He looked round the table. "You fought well, gentlemen, but there are still duties to attend to." He nodded in dismissal and Gideon and Dexter moved away rapidly.

Jerran took a deep breath and another sip. "Do you have any orders for me, Colonel?"

Ferran looked the Prince over once more then smiled briefly.

"Get your wounds seen to if you want to ride back with us tonight." Then he turned away after gently removing his flask from Jerran's reluctant hands.

Wounds? The Prince sat a moment longer then realised Fife had returned to his side. "I'll show you where to go, milord. That leg might need stitching up, but if you can bear it I'd wait until you're back at the castle. Lord Barnard's healer is one of the best, they say."

Jerran heaved himself upwards staring blankly at his left leg where his chain mail hung in tatters, and his breeches, slashed wide open were caked with blood.

"I didn't notice it."

The old sergeant simply nodded. "It is often so in the heat of battle, but once it's all over every bruise and blow comes back to haunt you. It will be a slow road home with so many injured and taking the logging trail at that."

"The logging trail? Why?"

They had reached the rear of the stone building, which once again had undergone a rapid transformation into a field hospital. Fife made a movement towards the front of the line of men and women waiting for attention but the Prince hauled him back and settled on another of the benches. "We'll take our turn, Fife. I can see for myself there are many here worse set than me." The grizzled veteran eyed the Prince then grunted in agreement. "The logging road?" Jerran prompted.

"Yes, milord. What I heard from Lord Dexter's men was quite the story. It seems the Frystians have their own magician, a 'Shaman' they were calling him." Jerran nodded.

"Well this here Shaman finally breaks our lady's weather-working and all the forces are lining up across Arco's Gap and spilling out of the outpost about to come in our direction. Then Lady Callandra snaps her fingers and takes down the ice falls and melts half the river too."

"What?" Jerran shook his head in disbelief.

"Really, sire. They all saw it. There's this almighty crack, then a flood like the end of days and Arco's Gap is now a lake. That's why we are taking the long road home."

The men were silent for a moment, each trying to imagine the forces brought into play by the young woman they had left at the roadside hours previously.

A rather shrill voice drew the Prince from his thoughts. "You there! Fetch me a surgeon." Nevis. For a moment Jerran felt a flicker of relief that his old friend had survived the fighting, but only for a moment. Nevis was standing a short way behind him with no injuries visible to a quick glance, unlike the trooper he had just despatched on his errand.

Jerran was trying to summon the energy to intervene when the trooper returned trailing behind a very tall, rather stout woman with iron-grey air and a no-nonsense expression. She stepped in front of Lord Nevis looking him over carefully, hands on hips. "You're not the surgeon." Nevis was well known for stating the obvious.

"That's the truth," the woman agreed. "I'm Maggie, the blacksmith's wife."

"I need to see the surgeon urgently. Kindly go and fetch him." The young lord drew himself up to his full height only to find he was still eye to eye with the matron.

"Lad," the woman gave him a cheerful smile, "there's many here that need to see the surgeon urgently but if you have enough energy to make a song and dance about a little wait, well then you are obviously not one of them. If you need a dressing or a bandage one of us will be with you soon."

She turned to go. Nevis, Jerran noticed, was turning an interesting shade of red. "How dare you?" His voice, it seemed, could get even higher. "It appears someone needs to teach you your place." He took an angry step forward. Jerran sighed in exasperation and stood up. Nevis always demanded every courtesy due to his rank, no matter how inappropriate the time or place.

"Will." His voice wasn't loud but immediately caught the young lord's attention.

"Sire, what are you doing here?" Jerran fixed him with a steady gaze.

"I'm waiting, waiting to see a surgeon." Lord Nevis blushed looking confused.

"But sire, you could…" His voice trailed off while he pointed to the front of the line.

"Yes Will, I could, but there are many men here with worse injuries than mine." He staggered slightly and found himself steadied by the formidable dame who had just faced down his friend.

"Now you, lad, you look like you've lost rather a lot of blood. If you are hoping to ride out tonight 'twould be best if we get you wrapped up right away."

"Lad?" Lord Nevis's voice seemed now to have moved back to his childhood treble. "Woman, do you know whom you are addressing?"

Jerran held up his hand, silencing the irate young man and moved over to the cot his nurse was indicating. He found himself stifling a surge of hysterical laughter that only dissipated when Maggie, murmuring, "This may sting a bit," poured what he felt sure must be concentrated acid into his open wound. He fought to stay conscious and was still reeling when Maggie, dressing his wound with swift efficiency told him he could go.

Jerran settled back down at the refectory table to recover while Fife went to retrieve Warrior. Looking through the small window onto the courtyard he could see daylight had entirely fled. Men were working steadily by torchlight, mainly moving bodies out of the courtyard to somewhere beyond his view.

The sergeant reappeared at the door. "Time to go, milord, the troops are mounting up." Jerran took his time, each step a huge effort. In the courtyard Fife looked him over, wordlessly cupping his hands to help the Prince reach Warrior's back. Then he snagged Jerran's winter cloak, unrolled it and tossed it to him, inclining his head at the quietly murmured thanks.

Fife had been the head of the Prince's bodyguard for perhaps eight years. An experienced man, sensible and responsible but somehow slightly detached and distant. Jerran caught at the thought that something had changed and he felt it again when he turned his horse to join his men. Of the twenty he had ridden out with at dawn, twelve sat their mounts beside him. Four were too badly injured to make the ride home and the others, men he had known for years, had made their last journey. He gritted his teeth as the order was given to move out and cantered into the night.

Chapter 11

When the Ice Falls finally shattered, flooding the entire valley, it took Callie a moment or two to register that she had completed her task, she could let go. She tried to draw her strength back into herself and failed. Her power and will seemed as intangible as the diamond dust sparkling and vanishing in the winter air. Liss's anxious face appeared before her unfocused gaze and she tried to smile before finding even that was too much effort. She crumpled against his cradling arm and he lowered her to the ground. He slipped his hand to her neck to feel her pulse and cursed as it brushed across her strange pendant. It was red hot and seared a long burn across his fingers.

Hesitantly he drew her scarf aside and pulled open the neck of the thick tunic she was wearing. The tear-shaped pendant almost glowed against her pale skin. He moved to wrap her clothing higher for their journey home and the jewel slid slightly to one side along its chain. The Isseni's eyes widened. Where the pendant had lain there was an outline almost etched on Callie's skin. He touched it lightly. It looked like a burn but felt quite cool and it did not match the shape of the pendant. The central section was the same, like an elongated raindrop but the scar, for want of a better word had three distinct petals. He gasped and swallowed hard. Surely it couldn't be; here, now, at last? For a moment his grey eyes shone strangely with light or tears.

Hearing Will moving slowly Liss pulled himself back to the present, wrapping Callie warmly and restoring her boots and gloves. The lieutenant from the watch post had offered some of his men to see Liss and Callie safely back to Barnard's Castle. With Will now conscious but obviously concussed and Gilly away to Lord Dexter, Liss had accepted gratefully. He mounted his horse and Callie was lifted up in front of him, with Jessa tethered to one of the troopers.

They rode slowly. News of the events at Arco's Gap had been sent earlier. Lord Barnard rarely took the field himself these days but was always there standing firmly behind his sons and his men offering support, relief and sanctuary as needed. Liss knew the Earl would have spent much of the day on the ramparts; the faster to intercept messengers and runners as they arrived from all quarters, so he was not at all surprised to see Lord Barnard standing on the steps of the keep as he finally drew Shadow to a halt.

"Again?" The Earl raised an eyebrow at Liss's burden even as his servants rushed forward to lift Callie down. "Is she injured?" He gave a sigh of relief when Liss shook his head. "Well thank the Gods for that. Try and remember her father is the King's general, a man of action rather than words when he is displeased and permanent damage to his daughter would tend to have that effect.

"So, what's the story? A little weather-working surely shouldn't have reduced her to this state. Is the lass weak?" His eyes followed as Callie was carried away.

"Quite the contrary, milord." Liss dismounted and let the stable master lead Shadow away. "Did you get the report?" Lord Barnard nodded guardedly as they walked back into the building.

"I got 'a' report. Frankly I wasn't sure what to make of it."

"Well…" The Earl stopped him with a gesture.

"Come to my study before dinner when you have had time to catch your breath. I'd like to hear it again coherently, from an eye witness, and if our warriors will have to take the back road, we won't be seeing them for hours yet. I'll send Tallis to see Lady Callandra." Liss smiled. He doubted Callie actually needed the services of the Earl's healer but it would do no harm to check.

"Thank you, milord." He offered the Earl a swift bow and made his way to his own chambers, glad to be alone at last. He needed time to think.

It had been just past midnight when most of the armed forces had finally reached Barnard's Castle. There were many injured and the Lord's household had swiftly swung into action. This was not the first time and likely would not be the last that injured warriors and horses would arrive at the fortress needing aid. The healer and his team salved, stitched, cut and cauterised by the light of torches and oil lamps until the skies began to lighten once more.

*

Tallis had sent journeymen straight off to Blackstone with other helpers and supplies from the Earl's dispensary. They would do what they could there before checking in on Deep Delve and finally Silver Stream. It was unlikely they would be back for a week or two, and the healer devoutly hoped there would be no more freshly wounded for a while. In the years since he had come north into the Earl's service, winter raiding had been a more or less annual hazard, but this time the action was on an altogether different and very much larger scale. Apparently it could have been even worse.

He listened as he stitched and patched men back together and heard the tale of the ice-wall and the young Mage. The young woman who had saved them from a large part of the Kerrian forces, by shattering the Ice Falls, melting half the frozen Wild Water River and turning Arco's Gap into a lake. He had visited her hours earlier when she had arrived back with Liss, the Isseni. As far as he could determine there was nothing physically wrong with her, she just wouldn't wake up.

Tallis, as a healer had some Magery of his own, but healing was a gentle power. If he overextended himself, worked too long without rest, he knew he would suffer with headaches and dizziness and he suspected and hoped that this was Callie's problem but on a grander scale. He was fairly confident that she would wake whole and sound once her body had recovered, but if she didn't… He sought out his bed wishing, as he had so many times before, that there was some rapid way of contacting colleagues in the capital who had greater knowledge of the arcane than he possessed.

It was still full night when Callie stirred briefly. She didn't bother to open her eyes – that was still too much effort – but she knew immediately that she was safe, in her room in her bed. She identified the noise that had disturbed her, distant and muffled as it was, as men and horses. The army must have returned. She wondered idly if she should be helping but couldn't think how and her common sense told her she was still drained, still exhausted. On that thought she shut her eyes once more and only opened them again when the mid-morning sun found entry through an uncurtained window.

She took her time rising and dressing and although breakfast was over, as a guest in the castle she had no difficulty coaxing a tray from the cooks. She was still sitting alone at a refectory table when one of the pages tracked her down with a summons to the debriefing meeting. She knew she had to attend. She also realised as she made her way to the Earl's study how little she wished to report on her actions.

The men were calling the fighting 'The Battle for Arco's Gap' and it had been far more battle than winter raid as evidenced by the men lost and injured. Reports had to be written and relief supplies directed back to the mines, so another day passed before Dexter found himself free of urgent duties. Standing at the side of the great courtyard, he had just waved off a small company who were heading back to the capital, Derryn, with news for the King. Gideon was leading the party, Lord Barnard being firmly of the mind that the King would listen more closely to news from someone who had actually been involved in the thick of the fighting.

Dexter had expected Jerran too would be among those going but Healer Tallis had declared the Prince in no way fit to make the journey; his wounds both more numerous and more serious than at first thought. Lords Nevis and Hadley both superficially injured rode beside Gideon. The Prince had been quite determined that they had done their part and should go and no more could be expected of them.

It had been an interesting scene to watch as Jerran had thanked them profusely for their advice and noble service, while still insisting they must return to their anxious families. Their objections had been half-hearted at best. They seemed to have lost much of their enthusiasm for war now that they had actually experienced it, but had been immensely gratified by the Prince's fulsome praise. Dexter, for a brief instant had detected something altogether unexpected in the Prince's earnest demeanour. It had seemed to him that the young royal was struggling very hard to keep a straight face then the moment was gone and he wondered if he had imagined it.

A movement at the stable door caught his eyes; Callie, someone else he wondered about. She looked to have been checking on her horse in the rear stalls before setting out back across the courtyard to the keep. The whole area was busy, men and women coming and going constantly. While Dexter hesitated a group of men appeared, obviously off duty, laughing and chatting as they headed towards the barracks. He saw the exact moment they recognised Callie and as one they all fell silent. In fairness they all nodded respectfully in her direction, but with body language that showed wariness, almost fear. There was no chance she hadn't noticed; of that he was certain.

On impulse instead of calling out to her Dexter slowly followed behind the young Mage. He realised he had hardly seen her since the fighting, days before. She had been at the debriefing meeting, but now he came to think of it, it had been Liss who had made the report from their position, not Callie. He hoped she was alright. In many ways it was he himself who had drawn her into the middle of the fighting, and she had done so well that he had forgotten that she had never been in battle before; so well that he hadn't kept in mind just how young and inexperienced she was.

He cursed himself. He should have checked. In better times she would have had a mentor with her to support her first field endeavours and make sure she was not overwhelmed. He walked a little faster after her up the stairs of the keep. He presumed she was heading back to her room but she carried on past it, turning up yet more stairs until she reached a corridor with exits leading on to the battlement walkways.

Dexter waited a few moments then climbed the last steps. Callie was standing, arms wrapped tightly around herself looking out across the valley. From this side of the castle, at this height it was altogether possible to see sun glinting off the distant water that yet covered Arco's Gap.

Dexter hesitated a moment more wondering if he should leave her in peace when he heard a stifled sob. He stepped clear of the doorway. "Callie?" He spoke softly but she swung round, startled. Tears were silently tracking down her cheeks. Dexter tried frantically to think of something to say; anything to say. She was biting her lip, trying so valiantly to recover. For a second she looked so like Miri his younger sister that he simply forgot about words, stepped forward and opened his arms wide, closing them around her a moment later, holding her firmly and steadily until she stopped shaking.

Callie found herself clinging to a man she barely knew. He held her comfortingly closely and didn't seem to mind that her tears were soaking his chest. For long minutes he stroked her hair, gentling her as one would a startled animal before his head dropped absolutely on top of hers. He was that much taller than she was. It was such a natural gesture it almost made her smile. She supposed she should feel embarrassed but oddly did not. It felt like hugging Raff only a bit different.

When she stirred in his arms Dexter released her immediately. "I'm sorry." They both said it at the same moment. He gave her a thoughtful look.

"I can't think of a single thing you need to be sorry for, Callie. I, on the other hand can only apologise. After dragging you into the thick of battle on your first field trip I have given you precious little support. Actually strike that; for precious little, read none. I am so sorry."

Dexter looked so entirely disgusted with himself that Callie felt herself genuinely smile for the first time in days. "I'm fine." He raised an eyebrow. "No, really!" The eyebrow still hovered. "Okay, I may not be great right now, but I will be fine. You see," she hesitated, "I thought I knew what it would be like."

"You couldn't have known. No-one does until they've lived through it." He shook his head.

"I know that's true, but Dexter I had a very unusual upbringing." She was shivering. He squatted down, pulling her into the lee of the parapet and wrapping an arm around her.

"How so?"

She stared in front of her. "When I decided to become a warrior my father wasn't pleased but he didn't try to dissuade me. What he did do, was make me, and my brother, sit in the corner of his study when couriers came, or scouts, and make us listen to first-hand accounts from the battlefields. He took us with him to a field hospital. He made us go and talk to veterans who had one eye or no legs. He wanted us to see the reality of war; not to have any delusions of conquest and glory." She turned her sapphire eyes to meet his; her face was so young and so serious.

Dexter took a deep breath, trying to absorb what she said. "Well that would certainly make you readier than most. Your father sounds like a man of vision."

She smiled fondly. "He is, but…" She paused.

"But?" he prompted.

"Here it has all been different. When I fight with my sword, I am face to face with the enemy. I kill him or he kills me. But when I add Magery to the mix it all changes." She sighed "With the avalanche and the flood," she stared down at her hands, "they didn't stand a chance. And I didn't kill one or two, three or four. Liss said there were about 200 men at Arco's Gap. I feel like a butcher." Her voice shook again and he tightened his arm about her shoulders.

"Callie."

"Don't tell me it's—" He laid fingers gently to stop her mouth.

"Callie. Yes, you killed many men. That's what warriors do. Your Magery is another weapon. In some ways it is still like your sword. You choose when to use it and you don't use it lightly." He sighed. "I have been fighting here in the borders for more than ten years now and it never gets any easier. Some of the Kerrians are vile, Callie. What they do when they capture a settlement beggars belief." He grimaced. "I actually still have nightmares about some of the sights I've seen."

She saw his mouth flatten and his eyes looked distant. "What you did with your Magery really saved countless lives and prevented immense suffering." He grinned. "I think some of the men want to raise a shrine to you."

She shook her head. "I think many of them are afraid of me, afraid of my power and that's another thing." She hesitated, but it seemed ridiculously missish not to share her secret fear with a man whose lap she was all but sitting on. "My power."

"What about it?" He was interested and curious.

"It's hard to explain. I think it's changing." He looked a question.

"I've always been strong. That's why they thought even as a weather witch I might be of some small use here. So, strong but not this strong. Not nearly this strong. I don't understand what is happening. If we were back in Derryn there are people I could speak to but here…" Her voice tailed off.

Dexter considered all that she had said and mentally re-ran the immensity of what she had accomplished in the last few days. He couldn't remember even hearing of anything similar before. The power she had used was as she said, quite extraordinary.

"Right then. It seems we need some answers and although we are miles from Derryn I can think of two good places to try right here. Lord Barnard's grandfather created one of the best libraries outside the capital here at the castle, something about being snowed in for weeks at a time, and it has always been maintained. Scholars still travel here from Derryn to study. That's one place we may find some answer." He slowly withdrew his arm and stood up.

"And the other?" She paused thoughtfully then their eyes met as they spoke together.

"Liss."

Chapter 12

As it turned out, both the resources they sought were together. Liss, when they found him, was in the library, a part of the castle Callie had yet to visit. He almost seemed to be expecting them, drawing them away from the study tables to a side room with deep leather armchairs. "Liss," Dexter began but the Isseni stopped him.

"Callie, are you well?" She nodded. "Your head; no double vision or dizziness?"

"I'm absolutely fine, Liss, just rather confused and full of questions."

"I'm not surprised," he half smiled. "and my friend Dexter thought I might have some of the answers."

Dexter grinned. "Something like that." Liss fixed his piercing gaze on her.

"Well, in some ways he's right. I imagine," he started slowly, "that the thing worrying you the most right now is your Mage power?" She didn't question how he knew.

"Absolutely. These last few days. Where does it, I mean, how can I, I've never…" Her voice tailed off in total bewilderment. Liss stopped her with a raised hand.

"Dexter, there was no-one in the library when I came in, please check that it is still so and lock the doors." Callie and Dexter exchanged baffled glances, but nothing more was said until Dexter resumed his seat on the leather couch. Liss smiled gently. "I know that was all very melodramatic but it really would be best that this conversation remains private at least for the time being.

"Callie." He turned back to her, steepling his long fingers. "Where to begin? Do you remember asking me if I was a Mage?" Callie nodded.

"Yes. If you were, I might have been able to harness some of your power and make a stronger working, but you said you weren't."

"Actually," he corrected, "I said not in the way you meant. I do not have power that you could access, but my people have some innate talents not known in the northern lands and Lithia. One of them is that we can recognise and identify Magery in others. We can tell how weak or strong a Mage is, and what is the nature of their Mage gift.

"When I saw you at the palace I could hardly believe my eyes. To my inner sight most Mages glow. You don't. You absolutely shine." He paused briefly. "When I enquired and was told you were a weather witch, the sort of magic user employed to keep enough rain over the farms' fields, it didn't make sense. Also the 'taste' of your magic was unusual to me; nothing I recognised." He grimaced. "Appearances can be deceptive. I may not look particularly old but I am not a young man." He waved his hand at the library.

"I helped Mayen stock this library when first it was built."

"Mayen." Dexter looked shocked. "Wasn't he Lord Barnard's grandfather?"

"Great-grandfather actually: well remembered, Dexter. My point is there really shouldn't be any Magery around today that is unknown to me, but now there is, and Callie it's yours. It made me think. On our scouting trip I was watching you closely. One or two things you do; things that you are probably not even aware that you do, raised my suspicions or perhaps suggested an answer that was more or less confirmed at Arco's Gap." He paused, lost in thought for a moment.

"Liss, please," Callie pleaded. "You are really worrying me."

"Sorry." He smiled apologetically. "Now do you remember when you tried to melt the Ice Falls?"

"Of course."

"Can you tell us how it felt as it actually happened?"

She looked at Dexter who nodded encouragingly. "Well…" She thought back. "When you said to go ahead and try it, I centred myself and built my wards then reached for the weather." She saw him shake his head briefly but he motioned for her to continue. "Then I aimed my focus and will at the Ice Falls. I remember thinking how very far away they were and how arrogant I must be to remotely imagine that I could affect something so huge. Then I did feel my way behind the Ice Wall down to the tiny unfrozen stream.

I remember trying to force the sunlight and the wind into the cracks and the crevices but then I just wasn't quite strong enough." She was silent for a moment and Dexter watched fascinated as the emotions played over her face.

"Then what, Callie?" Liss prompted.

"Then you half buried me in the earth; my hands and feet. Gods, that was cold." She threw him a fierce glance before returning to her memories.

"Then?" he nudged again.

"Then I seemed to get a second wind, my power recharged. It was a huge, heavy power boost. It just filled me up. It was a slow and steady flow, not fireworks, and I realised I could do it. I splintered the ice and melted part of the river, pushing the water out as hard as I could. It was incredible, but I don't really remember much after that."

"No, you more or less passed out at that point."

"So what does it mean?"

"I think it means you are no weather witch, Callie. If I'm right, and actually I'm rarely wrong," he ignored Dexter's unimpressed snort, "you are an altogether different creature. I think you might be an Elemental Mage."

A stunned silence followed this pronouncement. "What? Good God, Liss." Dexter's face was a picture. "Are you serious?"

"Never more so."

"But I can't be. Elemental Mages don't exist anymore. There haven't been any for, I don't know, hundreds of years."

"Actually, over a thousand years." Liss pointed to one of the books lying back on his table. "I just looked it up."

Callie ran her fingers through her hair. "Liss, I don't think you can be right. I know I'm good with air and water, but I can't use the others."

"Callie, you do use the others. At least you certainly harness the power of earth. That's what gave you enough strength to take down the Ice Falls. Think about it. When you want to use your Magery you prefer to be on the ground, don't you?" Callie stopped to think. He was right. She always dismounted unless it was unavoidable and had always performed better outside.

"What about fire?" Dexter queried.

"Yes, what about fire?" Callie wasn't sure why she was so sceptical but needed to be convinced.

"Callie, you came into your Magery exceptionally late, if I've heard correctly." She nodded. "That is often a sign of the unusual. Now, what I have suggested is a theory, an idea. You know you can work with air and water. I know you use the earth. Fire, we need to verify."

"Surely her teachers would have realised if her gift is what you think it is? Everyone who attends the Academy is tested," Dexter chipped in.

"They are, but no-one would have been looking for this outcome. As you said, there has not been an Elemental Mage for 1,246 years. Also, my reading tells me that although previous Elemental Mages worked with all the elements, they invariably had a stronger affinity for one or two and their connections to the elements did not necessarily develop evenly or all at the same time. It might be that when you were tested at the Academy you had yet to develop your links to earth and fire."

"If they exist." Callie nodded her agreement with Dexter's continuing doubts. "So really we need to test this out?"

"Exactly." Liss nodded. "If Callie agrees."

She looked at the two men, her mind whirling. What Liss had suggested seemed unbelievable. Elemental Mages were the stuff of legends, and yet it would explain so much. She hesitated. "Wouldn't it be better to wait until I'm back in Derryn? I could speak to the Masters at the Academy."

"You certainly could do that," Liss agreed. "Although none of them will have had any experience with this type of magic if I'm right, and there may be another factor for you to contend with." The Isseni rose to his feet and began nervously pacing the room, his face very troubled. Dexter watched, amazed. He had known Liss for years and never ever seen the man so entirely rattled.

"Liss?" What is it?" The Isseni stopped his pacing and turned to face Callie.

"When you collapsed I was checking your pulse and I saw your pendant."

She reached for it automatically, puzzled. "My pendant?"

"Your pendant and your mark."

"What mark?" She looked confused.

"On your throat. You really haven't seen it?"

She shook her head. "I'm not one for mirrors, you can probably tell that by the hair."

Liss smiled, his gaze swept the room then he scooped up a polished oil lamp and held it out to her. She stared at her reflection and pushed the pendant to one side revealing the strange shape beneath it; reddish brown against her creamy skin. Dexter at her shoulder touched it lightly with a finger concern in his eyes. "What is it? Did you burn yourself?"

"No. Not that I remember. It doesn't hurt."

"Callie, how did you come by that pendant?"

"I inherited it from my grandmother. It's been in our family forever. It's odd really. I've never worn it before but for no very good reason I went looking for it just before we left Derryn. Has it really burnt me?"

"No, it burnt me but it only marked you."

Callie dropped back into her chair. It was all too much. Dexter saw the near panic in her face.

"Liss, perhaps we should just deal with one thing at a time."

The Isseni lost some of his air of distraction and drew a deep breath. "You are right, Dexter. Callie, your Mage gift… do you wish to explore it?"

She considered carefully. Liss might be mistaken, in which case nothing, but if he was right the sooner she knew the full extent of her powers the less chance there was of disaster. "I think I must but how do we do this?"

"We'll set up a series of experiments." Liss thought a moment. "It would be best to do this away from watching eyes. Are you both free now? It's still early in the day."

Callie nodded. "I'm free."

"And I can be if you give me a mark." Dexter mentally reviewed his duties.

"Very well, we'll meet at the stables a mark from now. Dress warmly and please don't mention this to anyone just yet." Callie and Dexter made their way to the doors, unlocking them while Liss tidied away the books he had been working on.

Chapter 13

On the other side of the castle Jerran awoke for the second time about mid-morning. It had been a lot earlier when Della, one of the saucier housemaids, had left him. Although he never minded losing sleep for a good cause, and she had been a very good cause, he was still recovering from his battlefield injuries.

He knew he was still tired but he was also restless and decided as he dressed that a short ride might help, especially as Warrior became a handful if he was under-exercised. With that thought in mind he strolled slowly down through the keep. Glancing out of a window on the stairs his gaze was caught by the sight of Liss, Lord Dexter and the Mage also preparing to ride out. He wondered where they were going. If it wasn't too far he might be able to catch them up.

Ladon was supervising one of the stable boys when Jerran finally reached his stallion's stall and confirmed that the others were only riding to the Earl's nearest hunting lodge, a scant couple of miles off the Southern High Road. Why, he couldn't say; although he seemed to have plenty more to say when he realised the Prince intended to ride out alone.

Jerran firmly declined all offers of an escort. With Lords Nevis and Hadley heading back to Derryn he found himself actually alone: a situation so rare he planned to enjoy it while he could. Besides, he would eventually catch up with the others; not that he was in a hurry to do so. He trotted through the winter landscape, the snow muffling the sound of his horse's hooves. It was very lovely with the snow-clad trees sparkling in the winter sun and here and there rocky outcrops laying shadows of grey and purple across his trail.

Jerran estimated that by the time he had ridden out of the castle courtyard, he would have been about half an hour behind the others and was just beginning to wonder where they were and if he had gone astray when he heard what sounded like an explosion. It was a short-lived but violent percussion and his hands tightened involuntarily on Warrior's reins, startling his mount. Looking all around him he saw nothing untoward. He was about to set off again when there was another one.

This time he got a sense of direction and nudged Warrior hesitantly forward, loosening his sword in its scabbard, his mind raising and discarding possibilities. If Dexter's party had encountered Kerrians or Frystlanders who had managed to survive Arco's Gap they might be in trouble.

Through the trees where a track left the main trail he saw a distant rooftop that could only be the hunting lodge. The building was set below a ridge that would offer needed shelter from the bitter north winds. Dismounting, he also noticed recent hoof prints on the snowy path ahead of him. The others had definitely come this way.

Instead of approaching the building directly Jerran circled left, staying in the cover of the trees and trying to calm his horse, as yet another explosion sounded. A break in the trees let him look down onto a small field, a meadow that fell away to one side of the hunting lodge. It was fenced as if it would normally be used for livestock or horses, but housed neither at present. Liss, Callie and Dexter were below him, perhaps a couple of hundred yards away and obviously not in any difficulties.

Jerran was about to call out to them when there was a blinding flash of light and a further explosion. He tried to make sense of what he was seeing. Was Liss setting up targets and Callie trying to destroy them? He stood watching thoughtfully. She was not so much trying to blow them up as, "Good Gods," set fire to them. He swore as a column of flame leapt up fifteen or twenty feet high from the nearest target. At first the fire was white hot, then, apparently following instructions from Liss, that he was too far away to hear, Callie shrank the inferno.

It continued to burn, and following shouted suggestions from both men, Callie began to shape the flames into a spear, a flight of arrows, a whip. The Prince watched in amazement. So much power, so much control and he had thought her a mere weather-witch. He crouched down as the used target was replaced by another, obviously of a different material. He was so absorbed in what he was watching that he barely registered Warrior's restless stamping; so absorbed that he did not realise he was no longer alone until his head exploded with pain and he fell face first into the snow bank over which he was peering.

Down in the meadow Liss and Dexter gathered up the burnt remains of Callie's fire-raising experiments. Callie slumped against the fence. She simply didn't know what to think. Liss had arrived with a sack of random items – wood, stone, material, even metals. He had set them up as targets and asked her to try and set fire to them.

Callie knew she could cast fire. All Mages, of any discipline could, but only to light a candle or fashion a Mage light. Only true Fire Mages could do anything more, so why could she? She had set fire to twigs, paper, fabric and green branches and was still able to do so even when Liss and Dexter had increased the distance to the targets. When Liss had asked her to make her fire hotter, she had created an inferno that had exploded a nearby snow-covered log. She could not explain how she had done it. She had just known on an intuitive level what was needed.

The trio made their way back up to the Lodge where an elderly couple of the Earl's retainers fussed over them with cold meats, hot drinks and a glowing hearth. Liss seeming entirely unsurprised by the events of the morning sat silently watching Callie who gazed into the fire. Dexter wondered what she was thinking. He wondered if she realised how radically the power she was coming into would alter her life.

Finally, she sighed. "So I'm an Elemental Mage." It was more statement than question and marked a level of acceptance. Liss nodded.

"Callie, I realise that this is already a lot for you to deal with…" He tailed off and she threw him a sharp look.

"I can hear the 'but' you aren't saying. If there is more, tell me. Now is the time." Her voice was shaky but determined if those two qualities could co-exist.

"Callie, may I see your pendant?" Dexter looked as puzzled as she was, but she eased the slender chain over her head and passed it to him. He ran a long finger over the intricate design whistling softly.

"Unbelievable."

"Liss, cut it out, we've all had enough of the magical mystic for one day. What's the story?" Dexter's exasperated tone made Callie giggle.

"If I'm right…"

"'And I usually am'," Dexter and Callie chorused together.

Liss coughed in mild annoyance. "This may be even more important than the advent of the first Elemental Mage in a thousand years. I think this may be part of a very powerful talisman. You said you got it from your grandmother?"

"Yes. She gave it to me when my Mage gift appeared. I know it's a family heirloom but I don't really know much more than that. I thought it should have gone to my mother or Megan, my older sister, but Donna Vesta said without magic it would just be a piece of jewellery, so useless to my mother and Megan's magic somehow wasn't the right sort. She was absolutely certain it had to come to me."

"Yes, she would have been." Liss handed it to Dexter who examined it with interest before returning it to Callie. "Without powerful magic it would be purely decorative, but with Mage gift so much more."

Liss rose. "Come, we need to return to the keep. The winter days are short."

"Oh no, no. No you don't." Callie stepped in front of the Isseni and physically pushed him back into his chair. "So much more? So much more? What exactly do you mean by that?"

Dexter stifled a grin at Liss's startled expression. People didn't prod Liss in the chest or push him into chairs. They just didn't. He found it entirely delightful that either Callie didn't know this, or really didn't care.

Liss raised an eyebrow and gave the young Mage a stern glare. It had exactly no effect on her. In fact, she folded her arms and started tapping her foot. Trying not to laugh Dexter put a hand on his friend's shoulder. "I know that look, Liss, you don't want to speak until you are certain of your facts, but just for now, what are you thinking?"

"I'm thinking you young people are very impatient." He sighed. "Very well. My thoughts. In your histories there are heroes and villains, Gods, Kings and magic." They nodded. "In the Time of Light, when magic was stronger than it seems to be nowadays, many magical artefacts were created."

"Like Markes's spear?" Callie interrupted.

"And the Swords of Destiny?" Dexter added.

"Exactly. Those you mentioned were particularly famous and are closely linked with Lithia, but there were many others with equally remarkable stories but less well-known.

"The engraving on your pendant Callie, is not a pattern, it is actually a runescript. I recognise it but cannot decipher it without some research. Going on the shape I think your pendant may be a part, indeed the key part of a Triquetra."

"A what?" Neither Dexter nor Callie knew the word.

"A Triquetra. It's a strange shape like a three-petalled flower."

"Like Callie's mark?"

"Yes. Your part, Callie, would be the key because it should include a stone."

"So there are another two parts to it?"

Liss nodded. "They would fit together to make the whole piece."

"So, were there many of them?" Dexter inquired.

"No, and almost all of them were sacrificed at the time of the sundering."

"The sundering, that was real? I thought it was a myth."

Liss's face held a strange expression. "Oh, it was real. The Kigali with their demon hordes had scourged and destroyed all the eastern lands. The magical and mundane battles of the great war slaughtered millions. Whole nations were destroyed. Finally, in the Time of Dark, the elder races that survived came together and shared their skills and their powers, and defeated the enemy. They saved the western lands but the cost was appallingly high. The elves, my kindred, gave all their magic and withdrew to Isseni. All we were left with were our two talents." He stopped speaking, his eyes seeming to look back in time.

"The Triquetra?" Callie asked quietly.

"They were almost all destroyed during the wars. One or two were thought to have survived. The greatest Triquetra, the talisman that finally defeated the Kigali, was so powerful that after the war it was broken into three pieces. Each piece was entrusted to one of the human Mage families for safekeeping."

"Why human Mage families?" Dexter looked confused.

"They were the only ones left who still had enough magic."

"Gods above, and you think Callie's pendant may be part of one?"

"I'm certain it is. The only question is which one?"

"No! The question is, what does it do?" Callie persisted. Liss shrugged.

"The commonest story is that they acted as a magnifier of magic power."

"Like Callie needs that." Dexter snorted.

"And…" Liss quelled him with a look. "And they were used for communications."

"How?" Callie stared blankly at her pendant before slipping it back over her head.

"I really don't know." Liss was apologetic.

"More experiments for you, Callie." Dexter smiled wryly. "Now, are you going to let Liss up? It's definitely time we headed back."

Chapter 14

Callie was feeling tired as they arrived back at Barnard's Castle. Temperatures hovering around zero and using her Mage gift had left her with a strong desire for a rest before dinner but a message had been left at the stables asking all three of them to meet up with Colonel Ferran and the Earl as soon as they returned. Both men were looking at one of the great maps spread across the Earl's desk when they finally reached the study.

"Ah, good, you're back." The Colonel's smile was somewhat forced. "We may have a problem." He looked behind them. "Where's the Prince?"

"Jerran didn't come with us." Dexter exchanged a glance with Liss. "In fact I haven't seen him at all today. I thought he was resting?"

"He was but Ladon said he decided to take Warrior out. He said he had seen you leave earlier and would catch you up." The Earl looked puzzled.

"Perhaps he changed his mind and rode another way?" Dexter shrugged. "So what's come up?"

"We've just had a slightly alarming report from our scouts." The Colonel gestured to Will and Gilly standing to one side.

"As you know we have been patrolling all along the Iron Valley.

We have also had men patrolling the Westway and there has been no activity there so we seemed to be left with an encampment of Frystians on Arco's Bluff. This has been under observation but only from a distance. I asked these two," he waved a hand, "to get as close to the camp as they could, to see if they were showing any signs of withdrawing; no point in fighting if we don't need to."

"From a distance the camp appeared as normal, but up close there's nothing there. The tents are just branches and so on."

"A glamour," Callie blurted out, startled.

"That seems to be the case."

"To cut to the chase," the Earl was a man of fewer words than the Colonel, "they have gone. As they are not heading back north, into their own lands, they must have turned west."

Dexter moved swiftly to the map. "If they are not on Westways, are you saying they are on the Spring River?" The Colonel nodded, looking ever grimmer.

"I must go." Dexter's voice sounded harsh and urgent. The Earl nodded.

"Yes. I think you must. I ordered your men to be ready to ride, as this may be another part of their incursion."

"And I want you to take half of the royal forces too," Colonel Ferran added. "I would have confirmed that with the Prince, were he here, but in his absence I have that authority. They are ready to move out." Dexter nodded his thanks and was gone.

Callie walked to the map. "Where have the Frystians gone?" Liss ran a slender finger west in a line from Arco's Gap.

"That is the Westway; the high road that runs east to west until it eventually joins up with the Traders Road to Nilsport."

She nodded. "The hills west of Arco's Gap are thickly forested and almost impassable, but at this time of year, the Spring River freezes over and acts as another road."

"And Dexter?"

"Dexter's lands run below the Winter Hills. Winter's Keep, his home, was built where the river turns and flows south."

The Colonel pointed to a symbol on the map. "It commands an important strategic position but that does mean it sees quite a lot of action." The two men exchanged glances and Callie wondered what they knew that she did not.

The troops, already on standby, had departed the castle before Callie had even got back to her room. It left the whole castle with an oddly quiet and empty feeling. Still tired she flung herself onto her bed and considered all that had happened that morning. She was an Elemental Mage. The life she had been anticipating, had been taken from her for the second time. In the old stories, Elemental Mages had been famous or notorious, but always notable public figures. Their immense powers had been employed and exploited by Kings and Councils, something Callie realised she would hate. She took off her pendant and looked at it again. Liss's face came back to mind. His expression had been one of disbelief and hope and even a flicker of fear. What was there about her jewellery that he found so alarming?

Callie wished she had someone she knew and trusted to talk to. She missed her twin. Although they constantly argued, their minds were so well attuned that Raff could always help her. He was a thinker and saw ramifications that flew right over her head. Half asleep she tried to think where he would be at that precise moment. It was Thursday so weapons training would be finished and he had probably headed into the city to their favourite inn, The Broken Arrow, with their friends.

She could picture him so clearly. He always sat with his back to the wall; usually on one side of the mantle. [Oh, Raff,] she groaned out loud.

[Callie?] She could almost hear his voice.

[Don't you 'Callie' me, Raff. Where's my twin when I need him?]

[CALLIE!] She shot bolt upright on her bed.

[Raff?] Her eyes scoured the room. Empty, as she had known it was. She ran to the door and flung it open. A long corridor disappeared into the gloom of approaching evening. There was no-one in sight. Callie slipped back into the room, her heart racing and leant against her closed door.

Alright. Had she been dreaming? No. She had been dozing but

she was certain she had heard her brother's voice. So what, exactly, had she been doing? She lay back on the bed and tried to remember her thoughts. Thorsday. Raff, the Broken Arrow. Her hand brushed across her pendant. [Callie.] His voice was so loud she jumped dropping the pendant again. Nothing. She stared at the jewel in her hand.

[Raff?]

[Callie? Callie, when did you get back? I can't see you through the crowd. Come over to our table and I'll get you a drink. Where…?]

[Raff. Shut up.]

[What?]

[Raff. I'm not in Derryn.]

[But?]

[Raff. I'm not in Derryn. I'm at Barnard's Castle, in my room either talking to you or going mad.] Her voice trailed off and there was a long silence.

[Callie, are you still there?]

She nodded then cursed herself for an idiot. He couldn't actually see her; at least she didn't think so. [I'm still here.] Another long pause.

[How in the seven hells are you doing this?] The pendant felt warm in her fingers.

[I think…] Then she hesitated, remembering Liss's advice. [I really can't explain, but can we try something? Can you try and contact me tomorrow?]

[When… and how?]

[Just try and picture me as clearly as you can, say, standing with Jessa in the stables.]

[Like when we're doing one of Longstone's meditation exercises?]

[Yes, exactly.] There was a brisk knocking on her door. [Raff, I've got to go. Hopefully, possibly speak soon?] Callie slipped her pendant back over her head and approached the door anxiously: not at all sure she could cope with any more surprises in just one day.

Outside one of Lord Barnard's pages was hopping anxiously from one foot to the other. "Milady, your presence is requested with all speed in Lord Barnard's study and if it please you to come warmly dressed and fit for riding."

"What? Why?" The young lad who had looked pleased the moment before having successfully delivered his message now just shook his head. Callie gave him a smile and a thank you and managed not to swear until the door was closed. She swiftly put on her thickest tunic and grabbed cloak, scarf and gloves before making her way down to the Earl's study. The door stood ajar revealing a motley group of people. Lord Barnard stood with Will and Gilligan and one of his own scouts, a man she now knew as Tore. Ladon, the stable master was also there along with a leather-clad stranger who was talking to Liss.

"Here she is." Liss spotted her immediately and broke off what he was saying.

"What's going on?" Callie was immediately aware of the tense atmosphere.

"The Prince is missing." He looked both concerned and exasperated. "When he rode out this morning he told Ladon he meant to join up with you but he never did. Reece here has found his horse tethered at the rear of the Hunting Lodge, but there was no sign of the Prince himself. We need to find him now."

"Now?" Callie looked blankly towards the windows. "But it's dark and it's beginning to snow."

"Exactly. If he's injured in a ditch somewhere, he's not going to last a night in these temperatures, and if the snow sets in we'll lose any chance of tracking him. Swiftly now." The Earl made shooing motions with his hands and they all hurried off towards the great courtyard and stables.

As Callie had noticed, a few flakes of snow were drifting down from the night sky; she reached out lightly with her Mage gift. The snow clouds were a solid blanket extending for several miles; not something she would be able to move without help. Liss made his way to her side. "Sorry to drag you out again Callie, but this doesn't add up and if we are walking into another situation I think it's a good idea to have our best Mage with us." He grinned.

"You mean your only Mage." She shivered, too cold to smile as they mounted up and moved out, beginning to retrace the route they had followed earlier in the day.

On the main road the snow was too broken and churned up for the scouts to identify individual tracks, but when they reached the side trail up to the Lodge it was a different matter. Leaving their horses with the small detachment of soldiers the Earl had insisted upon, they followed Reece up and round the ridge behind the lodge building. It was clear a horse had been left standing there for some time.

Callie waited by the path while Liss and the scouts went over the ground minutely, their expressions grimmer by the minute. "Do we search the area?" Callie hadn't been able to hear the quiet discussion. "It would be best to double-check." That was Tore, who promptly directed the detachment of soldiers to spread out and move in a line up the hillside, to search for the missing royal. They moved slowly. Callie's feet were soaked and frozen and she was just wondering how much colder she could get when one of the guardsmen at the farthest point started shouting and waving his torch.

When she caught up with Liss and Tore they were pointing at a tiny trail that wiggled through the back of the trees. It bore the imprint of paw prints and sled marks. "Damn, that is not what we wanted to see." Liss scowled. "We'll have to follow and follow now, before the snow wipes out the tracks. Reece, pick someone to return to the keep and tell Lord Barnard that it looks likely that the Prince has been taken by the Frystians and we are going after him."

Callie drew in a breath of wintry air. So that was the story they had read in the snow.

It was perhaps half an hour later when Liss called a halt. Even through the steadily falling snow Callie was able to recognise the huge looming outcrop that was Arco's Bluff. They waited under the trees while Reece dropped to the ground casting around on the western road then back to the north, moving with the silent skill of a woodsman. In minutes he was out of sight.

She reached again towards the snow clouds and flinched; things were about to get a whole lot worse. She nudged her horse alongside Shadow just as Reece returned. "The sled is running along the treeline beside the lake, heading north towards the Ice Falls. They definitely haven't turned along the Westway."

Liss swore again. "We will have to follow them and find out if they are heading due north, or if they are hoping to follow the others down the Spring River. We…"

"Liss," Callie interrupted. "I don't think that would be wise. The weather is moving. I can feel it."

"Blizzard?" He looked a question. She nodded.

"Or even Asksno."

He stared at her. "How long do we have?"

"Maybe half a mark. It's going to be bad." Liss grimaced.

"We need to find the Prince but I will not wilfully risk other men. Reece, are you willing to continue?" The Earl's man nodded.

"I'll track them. I know these lands. If need be I can find shelter for one but not for all of us. Do you take them on the Westway to the next Waystation?" Liss nodded.

"I'll do that. Send word or meet us at Winters Keep. Swiftly now." He turned his horse's head and signalled to the others to follow, setting a brisk pace as they tried to outrun the coming storm.

Chapter 15

When Jerran came slowly to his senses it took him several attempts to open his eyes, then he rather wished he hadn't. The world was flashing past him at speed in shades of grey and white. He realised his wrists were tightly bound and with a gag in his mouth he was unable to clear the coppery taste of blood. He had a monumental headache, not helped by his head banging against The rear of the sled in which he lay as it hit patches of uneven ground.

He could not turn far enough to see who was behind him, but murmured voices indicated the sled driver had a companion. The guttural exchange sounded like Frystian. It was all very odd. Frystians didn't take prisoners, so why had they taken him? His head swam and he closed his eyes, drifting back into a semi-conscious stupor that seemed to last for hours. He realised he must finally have slept because the next time he opened his eyes, it was full night and he was being carried bodily into some sort of tent.

He was put down, not too roughly on a pile of furs. The men who had carried him were quite simply giants clad in fur and leather, their long hair held back by leather thongs. One looked Jerran up and down as if he was prime livestock then they loosened his wrist bonds slightly, removing the gag and pointing to a waterskin on the floor nearby.

Jerran opened his mouth to ask any one of the hundred questions on the tip of his tongue only to see his captors disappear back through the doorway. With some fiddling the Prince managed to get himself a drink of water, which was surprisingly cold and fresh, then crawled to the entrance flap of his tent and peered out. Immediately in front of him stood a guard fondling a very long, sharp spear. It was snowing heavily but the man appeared oblivious to the atrocious weather conditions.

Jerran could see very little. When the gusting wind swept the snow aside for a brief moment, he got an impression of more tents and animals, before the white curtain fell again. He crawled back to the furs. Even if he had the means to free himself from his bonds, to try and escape into the blizzard would bring him a quicker death than any he now faced.

He considered his situation. He was alive and relatively uninjured. He would be missed and people would come looking for him as soon as the storm was past. His captors had given him water and shelter. He was still trying to figure out why when he drifted off once more.

It took very vigorous shaking of his arm to draw him out of a deep sleep, probably occasioned more by concussion than exhaustion. A Frystian woman was crouched beside him, placing a steaming bowl of soup and a hunk of bread next to his furs under the watchful eyes of his guard. He nodded his thanks realising he was really hungry; not a surprise as he had left Barnard's keep at mid-morning the previous day. The soup smelled appetising but he noticed he was not offered any eating irons. He mimed the difficulty of eating with bound hands but the woman gave a disinterested shrug and indicated that if he wanted it, he must drink it, before she left.

He thought it was perhaps mid-morning when the tent flap was next drawn back and four men entered. Three were obviously warriors, tall, muscular men, warmly dressed and well-armed. The fourth man was slighter and older and Jerran noticing the line of tattoos that ran from his silvery hair down the side of his face, guessed he must be the Shaman Callie and Dexter had mentioned.

They settled themselves in a semi-circle, observing him closely and muttering to one another. Jerran schooled his face to look expressionless. Unless he gave himself away, it would never occur to them that he might understand their tongue. Few did, and that might be his only advantage in his current situation. "Why am I here?" He aimed his question in Lithian somewhere between the oldest warrior and the tattooed man. "What do you want with me?"

The second warrior spoke quietly to the others obviously translating. "We mean you no harm. We mean you no harm but we wish to speak with you."

The translation was accurate. Jerran raised an eyebrow indicating his head where congealed blood still stained his face, and his bound hands.

"Unfortunate, but necessary." The oldest warrior spoke. "I am Einar. I am leader of this clan. We believe you are also a man of rank among your people?"

Jerran's mind reacted. They could not know and he did not wish them to know that he was royal but he would admit to rank. His clothing, his weapons and his horse would already have confirmed this. "I am." He nodded, wondering if he was to be held for ransom, not something he had ever heard that the Frystians did.

"Very well. If you give your word not to try and escape, we will unbind you. Later we will set you free."

Really? So he had nothing to lose. "Then I give you my word." The third warrior sliced through his bonds with a lethally sharp dagger and Jerran rubbed feeling back into his wrists.

The oldest man "Einar" continued. "We wish to speak to your leaders. We wish you to take a message to them. You have the weapons of a warrior and you have rank. Will they listen to you?"

Jerran spread his hands. "They might, it rather depends on the message."

The Frystians exchanged glances and after a long pause the Shaman spoke. "The clan of the Snow Fox does not want war. We come in peace."

Jerran raised an eyebrow. "And yet less than a week ago you stood with the Kerrians as they invaded our land."

The old man nodded then beckoned Jerran to the door of the tent and pulled it aside. "What do you see?"

The Prince looked out. The snow had stopped. There were many tents, campfires, sled-dogs, women and children. He looked at the Shaman. "What I see I don't understand. Since when have the

Frystians brought their women and children to war?"

"Since to leave them behind would mean a quicker death." There was suppressed anger in the Chieftain's voice but the Shaman quelled him with a look and returned to sit. He looked at Jerran sadly. "As you see I am old. I have lived many winters and hoped my bones would rest in the snows of our clan valley but it seems I must walk a different trail.

"In the far north life is hard. So it has ever been, but we, too, are hard and we have survived generation after generation in the wildness of the taiga following our herds and the seasons. But now that is no longer possible. Last summer the ice did not melt and our children are starving. Our animals can find no forage and the herds dwindle.

"In the autumn when all the tribes gathered, it was decided that some must seek other lands to live in. The clan of the Snow Fox was one of those chosen. We travelled south. Raven and Bear clans travelled west."

"To Zeeland?" Jerran interjected curiously.

"Certainly that way." Einar nodded, obviously trying to gauge his reaction to what had been said.

"We need land. Here in the north of Lithia there is much land, empty land and few people."

"It still belongs to the Lithian kingdom." Jerran kept his voice neutral and even.

"Yes it does." The Shaman agreed. "And yet what harm would it do if our people lived here? The land is virtually wild. We need new land so our people can survive. Land we would treat with respect. We do not believe land belongs to men. We believe men belong to the land. This is the message we wish you to take to your leaders."

Jerran was silent for a moment, considering. "They will say that the land is empty to prevent your people gaining a foothold beyond the Winter Hills; a foothold that might be the first step in an invasion." A heated exchange followed the translation of his words and the Prince observed just how tense the Frystlanders were. The Shaman put a firm hand on the Chief's shoulder.

"We do not wish to fight unless we have to."

"Then why did you stand with the Kerrians?" Jerran made no effort to hide his scepticism.

"Our agreement with the Kerrians was simply to defend their backs at Argabron." Arco's Bluff? "And this we did. You did not see any Frystians fighting."

Jerran stopped to think. That might just be true. "If you lived within the Lithian borders where would your loyalty lie? Do you think the king would accept an independent enclave within his borders? Would you?" The Shaman smiled.

"Your King already allows this to happen; West Lithia."

Jerran was startled. How did these nomadic tribesmen know of the tiny Principality on the borders of Westerland and the Southern Sea. "West Lithia is independent, but it does not belong to a larger nation as you do. You are the Snow Fox Clan but you are also Frystians."

The men turned away talking rapidly and he tried to listen to their conversation, while looking disinterested. He distinctly heard the Shaman arguing that he should be told all, while Einar and his deputy were objecting on the grounds that they must not show weakness. It was Einar who ended the discussion. "There are other reasons why we would not be a threat to Lithia, but these are serious and secret matters only fit for discussion with your leaders. You have learnt enough for now. When we release you, you will take our words to your Lords. We will take no actions against your people until we hear from you, although we always hold the right to defend ourselves." He touched his hand to his sword and heart as if making a binding vow.

Jerran took a deep breath trying to analyse what had been said, and even more, what had not. His every instinct told him that he was only seeing half a picture. "Very well, and when will you release me?" The men relaxed almost imperceptibly.

"We are travelling along the Spring River. In three days if the weather holds fair, we will reach Forest Gate where the river turns south past the great castle. We will stay there and you will go on." Jerran nodded, mentally running the route in his head. They weren't west enough for the great castle to be White Wold so it must be Winters Keep. Dexter's land. That promised to be an interesting meeting.

Chapter 16

The Lithians rode fast through stinging snow and darkness for what seemed like half the night and when the Westways station finally appeared Callie was so cold she could barely release her horse's reins. She would have tumbled to the ground if Liss had not steadied her. The waystations all had barns and stabling attached where horses and other animals could shelter, and being out of the scything wind was a blessed relief in itself.

The horses were swiftly settled, roughly brushed, fed and watered before their riders braved the outdoors again. The main building, beyond the porch area held a bunk room, an open area with tables and a stove and one further smaller room. Logs stacked ceiling high ran along one wall, both inside and out. It was pitch dark and Callie smiled as the solders tripped over each other and swore. The stove was laid ready and she lit it with a thought and kept it roaring while pails of snow were melted on the top.

They shed their outer clothing to drip and dry and draped their blankets near the fire until they were warm enough to find their beds. Callie's last thought, before she dropped off, was one of gratitude for the roof over her head on such a night and pity for Reece out in the blizzard seeking the missing Prince.

*

Liss did not hurry them the next morning. The snow had stopped, although the day was grey and raw. They had lost the trail of the missing royal with no chance of finding it after the blizzard, so Callie was still toasting her feet and drinking a steaming cup of tea by the stove when the Isseni approached her. "Callie, how are we fixed with the weather?"

"No more snow today, and I think clear skies to come in the next day or two but it's going to be cold." He nodded. "Are we going on, or back?" Her comment acknowledged, they were out of the picture when it came to the Prince's survival.

"We'll go on. If we keep on the Westway we can notify all the patrols as we meet them and when we get to Winters Keep, we can see how things lie with Dexter. If he's not already up to his neck fighting we may be able to head up Spring River, or his scouts may already have news."

"Winters Keep is one of the Marcher Castles, isn't it?" Callie found the name familiar but couldn't immediately recall why. Liss nodded. "So Dexter's father is the marcher Lord?"

"No." Liss looked grim. "Dexter is himself the Earl."

"Really?" Callie was surprised. "But he's so young!"

Liss said nothing for a moment then, "He is in fact the oldest surviving member of his family."

Surviving member? "Oh Gods! Winters Keep. The massacre." She gasped as her memory finally caught up.

Ten years ago a horde of northlanders had managed to storm the castle. They had put all the inmates to the sword: every man, woman, child and babe. As Winters Keep held such an important strategic position it could not be left in the hands of the enemy so the royal army had fought to recover it. When they had eventually recaptured it they had found evidence of atrocities that had left experienced warriors and even her own father white-faced and shaking. If she remembered correctly the Earl's sons were both absent at the time. One of those, the eldest must be Dexter.

"Dexter wasn't there when it happened, was he?" Liss shook his head.

"No, he and Blaine his younger brother were at Barnard's Keep.

Against all advice he got himself to Winters Keep as the King's forces finally broke through, so he was one of the first into the castle. It was very bad by all accounts. Anyway, come on, time to go."

It didn't take long to clear up. The men brought in more logs and reset the fire and stove leaving the waystation ready for the next benighted travellers and headed to the stables. Callie was standing by Jessa feeding the mare apples from the bin when Raff's voice made her jump and nearly drop them. [Callie, Callie are you there?] The soldier next to her gave a puzzled look as he moved away. [Are you okay?] She beckoned Liss into an empty stall at the end of the stables.

[Raff] She spoke out loud so that Liss could hear. [I'm here.]

[Goddess] His voice in her head again. [So this really does work.]

[It certainly seems to.]

[So can you talk to other people or is it just us?]

[I...]

[Talk to Gregor, he's right here.] Greg was Raff's closest friend, so someone she knew well.

[Good morning, Greg.] There was no answer. She tried again. [Greg? It's Callie here, what are you doing?]

[He's talking to you but you can't hear him, can you?] Raff's voice again.

[Afraid not.]

[Well that's really interesting.]

[Interesting! It's bloody amazing. Where are you now? Just wait until I tell—]

[No.] She almost shouted. [Please promise you won't tell anyone about this, at least not yet and make Greg promise too. Raff, it's important. I need to figure some things out first. We are at a waystation on the Westway heading towards Winters Keep. There are quite a few "situations" brewing. Please.]

[Okay, little sister, you've got it. Greg says you're to take care, Callie. He doesn't like to think of you in the Badlands.] Callie winced. Unfortunately, Greg had a huge crush on her. He was a really nice person. So nice that on more than once occasion, she had wished she could feel more for him than sisterly affection but for her, the spark simply wasn't there.

[Listen, Raff. I've got to go. I'll try and keep in touch if my adviser thinks that's a good idea.]

[You have an adviser?]

[Bye, Raff]. She slid her pendant back beneath her shirt. Liss looked on, fascinated and once again disturbed.

"You spoke aloud so I could hear you although I couldn't hear your brother. I presume you could have had the entire conversation silently?" She nodded. "So the stories are essentially correct. It can be a communication device. Who else have you contacted? What are its limitations? Do you think distance will affect it?" They led their horses outside, while Callie explained how recent this discovery was.

"It may only be Raff that I can contact, being my twin and so on."

Liss shrugged as he mounted Shadow. "Possibly, but it has to be worth at least trying other people… and there may be other things it can do." He tailed off, looking annoyed with himself.

Callie didn't know what was on his mind so she just nodded her agreement as they moved out slowly through the fresh snow that covered the great Westway road. They had many miles to go.

*

Jerran was also travelling west. The tribe had packed up and moved out not long after his discussion with the Chief and the Shaman. It moved slowly; all but the eldest or weakest on foot. All the tribe's possessions were loaded on sleds and the herd fanned out all around them. He had been given a fur-lined cloak that was heavy but immensely warm, and the warriors had shown him how to bind his boots with strips of sealskin that gave purchase on the icy ground. Although they moved slowly they kept on moving hour after hour with only a short rest in the middle of the day.

As the light began to fade a halt was finally called and the camp swiftly erected. Vidor, the Frystian who spoke Common and had kept him company for part of the day, indicated he should help raise a tent if he wanted one to sleep in, so he duly obliged.

The tribesmen watched him warily and he watched them with

lively curiosity, so little was actually known about their culture. Almost all contact between the Frystians and the Lithian Kingdom had involved bloodshed. To Jerran they seemed organised and hard-working, going about their allotted tasks quietly and efficiently. There was some play where the very youngest children were concerned, but from about seven or eight years old it seemed everyone had jobs to do.

He was just finishing a large tasty bowl of stew when Vidor and the Shaman appeared in front of him with another warrior in tow. They squatted down so their conversations could be quieter.

"This is Arne, one of our scouts. He has been checking the back trail and says we are being followed."

Jerran waited, making no comment. "It is only one man." The scout added a few words. "A woodsman." He kept his voice even.

"That is not surprising. You know I am a man of rank and so I would certainly be missed."

They nodded. "It would be easy to kill the man." Vidor made it sound unimportant. "Or we could take you there so you can speak with him; tell him what we have agreed."

"And show him that I am alive." Jerran nodded in understanding. Nothing more could happen. The odds of escape were too slim and he had given his word. It had already been a long day and now it looked to be a long night too.

Chapter 17

Callie had ceased to be enchanted by the snowy landscape long before they finally approached Winters Keep. They had passed a second waystation in the early afternoon and stopped at the adjacent inn for a creditable lunch. While there, Liss had called in at the Guards' Office and with the Earl's authority asked that all patrols look out for a "missing noble; the Earl Setryn" lost near Arco's Gap, the outermost point of the patrol's circuit. Callie admired the duplicity. Prince Jerran actually was the Earl Setryn but she seriously doubted anyone in the road guards would be aware of this.

Callie had not realised they were nearing their destination until Liss sent Will and Gilly on ahead to see how the land lay around the Winters Keep fortress. The rest of the party approached more slowly to avoid getting caught up in fighting if the Frystians were ahead of them. By this point Callie had decided she would actually prefer to fight a dozen trolls singlehanded than sit her horse for very much longer, so she was relieved when the scouts returned announcing the road to the castle was clear.

Winters Keep was not at all what Callie was expecting from a border castle. Unlike Barnard's Castle, which was stocky and dark, Winters Keep had several tall towers and the silvery grey stonework gave an impression of height and light. It was built where the Spring

River made a wide loop and it towered over the river valley with the Winter Hills rising behind it. Winters Keep the town, ran along one side of the valley below it. Set behind a massive curtain wall, it was connected to the Westway by a well-paved road.

The castle gates were tightly shut, the portcullis lowered and watchful guards armed with crossbows followed their every move as they approached. This was a citadel on high alert and yet, once acknowledged, they were brought into the courtyard with swift efficiency and their horses led away for some well-deserved attention.

"Liss," a voice hallooed from the ramparts and Callie looked up to see a man waving down at them. For a moment she thought it was Dexter and her spirits rose but Liss raised a hand and waved back.

"Blaine."

"Blaine?"

"Dexter's brother. Come and meet him."

The Isseni led the way into the castle, making it nearly to the great hall before Blaine reached them. The men exchanged a brief embrace before Callie found herself introduced to the heir of Winters Keep. He looked very like his brother, perhaps a shade fairer and a little more solid but the family resemblance was strong. He took her hand in the way that often led to long-winded and fanciful compliments, then frowned briefly, muttered, "Goddess, you're frozen," and to her delight dragged her through various groups of people to the Great Hall's enormous fire and pushed her down into a very soft chair.

Liss strolled behind them; a look of amusement on his face. "I'm frozen too, Blaine." The young man grinned.

"Rubbish, Liss, we all know you have ice in your veins, but what were you thinking dragging a lady like this through the winterlands?"

A servant appeared behind him with mugs of hot spiced wine which they clutched gratefully. "Lady Callandra, in my brother's absence, welcome to Winters Keep." She smiled her thanks. "Before you ask, Liss, no the Frystians haven't got this far yet and we have patrols out in all directions. Dexter will be back soon. He thinks if they are moving down Spring River, they will be here in the next day or two, but so far no sign." His face became serious for a moment, an expression that didn't seem to suit it.

"Your men have gone to the barracks and your horses are safe and sound, so when you have unfrozen we can get you settled too. Is there any news that can't wait until dinner and Dex?" He looked relieved when Liss, after a moment's hesitation shook his head and a few minutes later they were following him to adjoining guest rooms in the west wing.

*

Callie had barely dropped her bags on the floor before a quiet knock at her door announced a servant with extra wood for the fire already burning in the small hearth and the offer of water for a bath before dinner if she should want it. An offer she gratefully accepted so she was soon neck deep in steaming soapy water.

She finally felt completely warm as her aches and pains faded and also relieved that for a moment she was not hurrying, or even moving.

After her bath, with time to spare before dinner, she curled up on the gigantic bed and turned her attention once more to her pendant. She steadied her breathing and allowed herself to drift into the semi-trance state she normally sought when she was practising her Magery. Liss's idea that she might be able to contact people other than Raff, with whom she had a strong connection, intrigued her. This time instead of her twin she tried to focus on her father. She let the sense of him crystallise in her mind. His hair thick and grey springing back from a broad forehead, tanned by many years spent on active service. His hands long fingered and strong. The scent of him, spicy and warm. She pictured him at his desk in his study.

[Father.] The man in her mind would have raised his head from whatever document he was reading and his eyebrows would flicker as they did when he was startled.

[Callie?] He could hear her!

[Yes Father, it's me.] She could hear the smile in his voice.

[As I am not in my dotage (despite what you and your brother think), am I to assume we are speaking through some esoteric use of your magic?]

She laughed, admiring again his speed of comprehension. [Almost exactly right, sir. There have been some interesting developments in my magic and I am exploring possibilities at the moment.]

[I see. Are you still at Barnard's Castle?]

[No. Not anymore. I've just reached Winters Keep.]

[Winters Keep? What on earth are you doing there?]

[Looking for Prince Jerran and trying to avoid a war with the Frystians.]

[Good Goddess, Callandra, make sense please. The Frystians I understand although I thought they were at Barnard's Castle, but what's this about the Prince?]

Callie paused as she thought through what she could say.

[Father, do you know Liss?]

[Certainly. I have known Liss for many years, both as the Isseni Ambassador and as an adviser to the King. Why do you ask?]

[I am travelling with him and he wants the information I am about to tell you kept quiet, at least for the moment. Is that all right with you?]

[Yes,] he answered without hesitation.

[Well it looks like Prince Jerran has been abducted by Frystians. We were tracking them but lost the trail in a blizzard yesterday.] There was a long silence. Finally, Callie broke it.

[Father, I know it is a lot to ask. I mean I do realise that I'm asking you to conceal the fact that one of the royal Princes may have been taken hostage and you are a royal adviser, but Liss…]

[No, Callie, that's not what is giving me pause. If this is recent?]

[Only yesterday.]

[Well then, no such news could reach us for at least a week or more by known means, so I won't be in any trouble but, Callie, are you absolutely sure of what you are saying?]

[Well it's all circumstantial at the moment but Will and Gilly identified the sled tracks.]

Another pause.

[Well now I am worried. Frystians don't do this. They are fairly simple people. Hostage-taking and abduction; there would have to be a very particular reason behind that. They have been, with only one exception, very predictable.]

[And what was the exception?]

[The assault and massacre at Winters Keep where you are right now, my dear. It was…]

[I know about it. Liss told me. But why do you feel it was so strange?]

[Think, Callie. Frystians are nomads. Towns and castles mean nothing to them and yet they actually overran the citadel at the cost of hundreds of lives, only to virtually abandon it a few weeks later.]

[They abandoned it? I thought the royal army won it back?]

[And so it did. But apart from slaughtering all the inmates, including children, which is another thing Frystians don't do, the royal forces found many clansmen apparently dead by their own hands. There were few defenders to fight.] Callie digested this startling information.

[I've never heard that before.]

[No, you wouldn't have.] Her father sounded grim. [At the time the crown needed a morale boost, so much was made of recapturing the castle and the strangeness of the whole event was buried. Anyway, if Liss thinks the matter of your missing Prince should be kept quiet, I won't say a word until I have to. Liss always has his reasons, few of which he'll share, but I do trust the man. Just keep me informed, my sweet… and be wary.]

[I will, Father. Don't worry.]

She broke the contact thoughtfully and dressed slowly for dinner hoping her casual clothes would not cause offence, although she couldn't imagine Dexter caring about something so unimportant. Her stomach growled and she found herself hoping their host would not be delayed on his patrol and that dinner would be on time. What a pity she didn't have a close link to him. She would have suggested he get a move on as she was hungry.

Chapter 18

Although dinner was served for most of the castle inmates in the great hall, Callie was guided by one of the pages to a private dining chamber where Liss and Blaine were already waiting. She had just accepted a drink when Dexter arrived looking frozen to the bone. He eyed them thoughtfully and coming to his own conclusions ordered the servants to put the food on the table and not to return until called.

When the door was closed he gestured to Liss and Callie. "I'm delighted to see you but this isn't the season for social visits, so what's happened?"

"We've lost Prince Jerran." Callie heard Blaine's sharp intake of breath.

"Dead lost, or mislaid lost and how?"

"Not dead we hope." The brothers listened intently while Liss explained.

"So you are thinking of going up Spring River from this direction?"

"Yes."

Dexter nodded. "We can certainly do that, but we went quite a long way up today. They were not anywhere in sight but one of my best scouts, Finn, did not come back with us. He is going on further tomorrow. If we ride out, we should be able to meet up with him about mid-day." He released a breath. "I realise it's the Prince we are talking about. I would be genuinely sorry if anything bad happened to Jerran. He proved himself a valiant warrior, but there's no way I want my men fighting up there in the Winter Hills. We are going to have to wait for them to come to us."

Liss frowned. "On the bright side, if the Frystians have taken Jerran, rather than killing him immediately, it speaks of some purpose, so they are likely to keep him safe." He shook his head. "It's odd. Not something they would normally do."

"That's what my father said," Callie blurted out without thinking.

"You discussed the Frystlanders with your father before you came away?" She nodded, grateful for the misunderstanding.

"Anyway there's nothing more for us to do right now except enjoy our dinner and I know you are starving, Callie, and I didn't actually make dinner late, so eat up."

Callie nearly dropped her knife. What did he just say? No, surely not. It must just be coincidence. She concentrated on her meal, aware of Liss's piercing gaze fixed upon her.

Having obtained Dexter's cheerful consent and even invitation to go along with the morning party, Callie opted for an early night. A comfortable bed in a warm room was always a treat when out in the field. She fell asleep almost immediately only to waken a few hours later thinking she had failed to extinguish her lamp. She groped for it still half-asleep then felt it cold under her fingers.

She sat bolt upright drawing her dagger from under her pillow (weapons-master Krill would have been proud of her), peering into the darkness while her brain finally caught up with what her eyes were seeing. Her pendant was glowing gently. She groaned. Why couldn't strange and arcane events take place in broad daylight, say just after breakfast? She was still tired and with no more thought she flung the jewel irritably across the room aiming for the chair by her door, then leaned on her elbow, her jaw dropping. The light from the pendant had grown stronger. Goddess. She stamped across her room and picked it up meaning to slip it under her pillow only to stop as the light dimmed. Thinking rapidly, she walked around her chamber. It was brightest as she headed towards her chamber door.

Impulsively she flung it open, walking barefoot out into the stone corridor.

Dexter was yawning as he made his way to his bed. The demesne of Winters Keep required a lot of management and decisions that only he as the border Lord could make. With the threat of the approaching Frystians and his absence supporting Lord Barnard, things had got behind and after dinner he had worked for some time in his office.

The Keep was now quiet about him although he heard the distant shouts of the men on watch on the ramparts, so it took a minute or two for a nearer noise to attract his attention. It sounded like swearing. Definitely swearing. Instead of turning into his rooms he strode past and edged round a corner to look along the corridor leading to the guest wing.

A woman clad in a night robe of the sheerest material was marching away from him. After pausing for just a moment to enjoy the view, or establish who it was (his conscience couldn't decide) he followed behind as quietly as he could.

Callie was cursing quite audibly and moving with a strong sense of direction and purpose. As he followed she went down a flight of stairs and along a short internal gallery that took her to the entrance of the Garden Tower then stood there muttering crossly. The door, as Dexter knew full well, was locked. He scuffed his feet noisily so she would know someone was coming and walked into view.

Callie swung round. "Dexter." A sudden realisation of how odd and inappropriate her behaviour must seem brought a flush to her cheeks. The Lord's face was carefully blank. "Is there something you need, Lady Callandra? I'm sure the servants could bring you…" His voice broke off. He was staring at the light source she held in her hand. "What is that?" Callie gulped.

"It's something I think I may need to explain to you. It wants me to enter the tower but the tower is locked."

Dexter took a calming breath. "Perhaps explanations might be better back in your room. He looked down. "You look cold." Callie blushed again as she realised where his glance had strayed.

Back in her room she grabbed her cloak and moved over to the hearth where Dexter was adding logs. When he was finally sitting in her armchair she held her pendant out to him and told her story with only a few omissions. Dexter didn't know what to think. This young woman, curled up on the rug by the fire intrigued him. Her power was immense. Her humility and common sense rare and her breasts… He schooled his thoughts.

"So you think your pendant was leading you to something in the Garden Tower?"

Callie nodded. "What is in the Garden Tower? If you don't mind me asking?" Her voice was hesitant. His face had not been as expressionless as he might have hoped.

"It was my sister's clinic and still room. Miri was a skilled healer. She used to work in the tower. It has an outside door as well and people knew to find her there. When, when we lost her, I locked it. The castle's present healer has quarters near the barracks. I don't know what any of this means but I will take you there and we'll see what happens as soon as we have time." He rose. "Try and get some more sleep and Callie, if you do go wandering again perhaps you might, er, wrap up warmer. He winked and shut the door behind him.

Chapter 19

The next day dawned cold but bright and Liss led them off shortly after breakfast heading up the frozen Spring River. They were able to ride further than Callie had thought as Dexter's foresters had laid a cinder path a fair way along the river's edge to a lookout point, but soon enough they were on foot.

Dexter took the lead with Liss and Callie immediately behind him. Two experienced arms men brought up the rear with a third remaining behind to tend to the horses. They moved slowly and Callie reached out to check the weather. She was pleased that nothing bad was approaching. In some ways she found rain and snow the easiest weather forms to both identify and control. They were more tangible than wind and sunlight. The day, although bright was still overcast and her thoughts slid from the absent sun to the element of fire.

Apart from the experiments at the Hunting Lodge she had not had any time to explore this further. Although she was warmly clad in a fur-lined coat the cold, dry air seared her lungs and she found herself toying with the idea of casting a spell for warmth. She wondered if the others were as cold as she was and without thinking sent her Mage gift towards them.

From one moment to the next her view of the world changed and she stopped dead, nearly tripping up the rear guards. Superimposed on the reality she knew were vividly coloured images. The ground was blue-grey. The snow-crusted trees were also grey with the thinnest core of gold and her companions shone bright gold and red. For a long moment she was lost in the wonder of it until Liss shook her gently. "Callie?"

"Liss, I think I can see heat, or sense it. Not in the way of weather working and sunlight," she anticipated his next question, "it's quite different."

She turned to one of the arms men. "Is your left foot colder than your right one?" The man nodded.

"It is that, my lady. I have a hole in my boot that I haven't taken the time to get fixed; more fool me."

"Well, well. That could be very useful indeed, Callie. How far can you feel or see?"

Callie pushed her senses outwards. "I don't really have a way of measuring distance. Uh oh. There are people coming."

"How many?" Dexter tensed and the guardsmen drew their weapons.

"Only four and they are on foot."

"Right Miles, brush our back trail. Liss and Callie take cover there." He pointed to a thicket. "Finn, here with me." In seconds they were invisible; deeper shadows in the gloom beneath the trees.

They did not have long to wait, and Liss and Callie exchanged glances when they heard the approaching men, apparently having a convivial chat. Liss, looking out through the concealing undergrowth made a startled noise, quickly stifled, and a few moments later Callie could see what had amazed him.

Prince Jerran was walking down the river way chatting idly to his captors, two tall barbarians clad in fur and leather. The third man wore clothing typical of a Lithian woodsman. At Dexter's signal Liss and Callie allowed the men to walk past them then slipped behind, while Dexter stepped in front.

The Frystians immediately placed themselves around the Prince, axes in hands. There was a moment of tension then the Prince shouted in recognition. "Liss, Dexter, Callie." He muttered something to the Frystians who lowered their weapons the least amount. "Well met."

"Milord are you alright?" Liss walked forward slowly.

"I am. I take it you were looking for me?"

"For you and for them." Callie was startled by the tone of Dexter's voice. His weapon still very ready for use. Jerran stepped away from his companions, towards the young Lord, putting his arm around his shoulders and so to all intents and purposes disarming him. "We need to return to Winters Keep, Dexter. I have much to tell you and these men need to tell their Chief that I have been safely delivered. Finn here can confirm that."

For a moment it looked like Dexter was going to argue but he sheathed his sword under Jerran's watchful eye and turned away, engaging in a low-voiced conversation with the third man; obviously his scout. Callie was not close enough to hear a brief exchange between the Prince and his erstwhile captors, but watched with interest as they chatted briefly and departed.

Liss quickly joined the Prince and Dexter slipped back beside Callie. "Can you check that they really are withdrawing?" He didn't meet her gaze and his expression was troubled.

"I am checking, Dex, they really are going." He said not another word all the way back to Winters Keep.

Once the Prince had had a chance to clean up, they all reconvened in the private dining room for a late lunch and listened with interest to Jerran's account of his abduction. Callie was puzzled by the strange atmosphere in the room. It should have been relief. The royal Prince was back with them unharmed, but there was palpable tension.

Liss finally interrupted the Prince. "Jerran. You have told us you were taken because the Frystians want a spokesman to our government but what is it that they actually want?"

The Prince hesitated for some time and it seemed to Callie that he was deliberately avoiding looking at Lord Dexter. Finally, he made his mind up. "They want land. They want to live in The Barrens and offer allegiance to the Crown." He hurried on. "I think this idea has some merit and I will take it to my father."

There was a general intake of breath and a murmur of disbelief. Dexter shot to his feet. "I can't believe you are even considering this.

The Frystians are animals. Have you gone mad?" He leaned over the table towards the Prince, firsts clenched. Callie saw Jerran's face stiffen into what she thought of as his 'royal expression'. He also rose to his feet and fixed Dexter with a stern glare.

"I think you forget who you are talking to." There was a brief pause.

"And so do you." Dexter stormed out of the room.

The Prince closed his eyes and Callie thought he bit his lip before he sat down slowly. No-one spoke until Liss stirred. "You will need to return to Derryn swiftly then, milord. I also need to go there, and Callie?" He turned to her questioningly.

"Yes. I need to go back too. My assignment was to Barnard's Keep and that is finished, and there are other reasons, as you know." She tailed off, trying to remember what Jerran knew about her magic.

The Prince nodded. "If it can be arranged I would choose to leave at first light. We can take a small escort from the royal guards. It would be wise to leave most of the men here. The Frystians of the Snow Fox Clan gave me their word that they will not attack or even move closer until they hear back from the King and I think I trust that, but there's no reason to tempt fate."

Chapter 20

Callie was just finishing checking over Jessa when she saw Blaine ride into the courtyard, returning from patrol. He waved to her then dismounted, leading his horse into the other stables. It occurred to Callie that he wouldn't know what had been happening so she headed in his direction. "Blaine." His cheerful expression raised her spirits a little. "Do you have five minutes?"

"For you, Callie I have five minutes, five hours, five days, five…" She laughed, it was impossible not to. "I'll take over here, lad." The stable master began to unsaddle Blaine's horse. He nodded his thanks and followed Callie back into the keep. "Is there news?"

"There is indeed. We have our Prince back." He looked pleased.

"Thank the Goddess; in one piece I take it?"

"Yes. At the moment."

"At the moment? Is he in danger?"

"You tell me. Is Dexter likely to kill him?"

"Dex? Why, what happened?" They settled on a window seat while Callie explained.

The humour fell from Blaine's face completely and he whistled. "No. That idea wouldn't have gone down well with my brother." He studied his hands. "I take it you know about the massacre?" She nodded. "Dex was at Barnard's Keep doing his service and Gideon was doing his here. You know how it's done. Thankfully Gideon had returned home for a family wedding, or he would be dead too. I had gone with him. I was meant to be a page boy. Dex was one of the first back into Winters Keep when our troops broke in. He won't talk about it, but I've heard enough to understand why he had nightmares for nearly a year. Now to hear the Prince thinks we should welcome the Frystians into our land. Well, that would be hard to stomach. I'd better go and find him. Thanks for telling me, Callie." He rose slowly. "If you are all leaving tomorrow, dinner will be in the great hall so I'll see you later."

Callie had wondered if Dexter would actually appear at dinner, but realised she had underestimated him. He was a polite and courteous host, although he made no effort to initiate conversation, leaving that burden to Blaine. As soon as possible after the meal Jerran withdrew, excusing himself with the honest reason of an early start the next day. No-one else lingered.

Callie took less than no time to pack her bags then had a relaxing bath and sat by the fire drying her hair. She had been able to contact her father with minimal effort, becoming accustomed to the strangeness of her amulet. He was fascinated to hear the Frystians' proposal, and like the Prince found some merit in the idea, which annoyed Callie for reasons she couldn't pin down. Even so, he acknowledged Dexter's attitude was entirely understandable.

Breaking contact, Callie found herself worrying about her host. His bitterness and rage at the Prince's announcement had been very disturbing. The expression on his face was at the forefront of her mind. As her hand brushed across her pendant she gasped aloud and froze. She could see Dexter in his study: actually see him. He was alone sitting in a low chair staring into the fire, holding a very large goblet. As she watched, he attempted to reach for the bottle beside him but missed and slid off the chair spilling a puddle of what looked like brandy onto the floor by the hearth. Callie watched in horror as the sputtering fire ignited the liquor sending small blue flames flickering upwards across the floor to where Dexter slumped.

The next moment she was out of the door, flinging her cloak around her as she raced down corridors. When she threw open the study door it was all exactly as she had 'seen' it. Dexter was half lying on the floor staring at the puddle of flames and his smouldering breeches with a bewildered expression. Callie ran past him, grabbing the water jug from his desk and emptying it over the growing fire then beat out the last few flames with a heavy tapestry cushion. Acrid smoke sent her across the room to open the window before she righted the bottle and picked up the goblet. Dexter watched her with the detached interest of someone truly drunk.

"Callie," his voice was slightly slurred, "did you want a drink? Be my guest. Oh." He smiled. "That's right, you are my guest. Let me have a drink with you. We can share the bottle."

"Perhaps another time, Dex." Callie shook her head. "I think it's probably your bed-time."

"Really? Is it late?"

"Yes, really. Come on." He got to his feet by crawling up the furniture, and stumbled across the room crashing into the door frame. Callie threw a backward glance to check the fire really was out then slipped his arms around her shoulders as they staggered slowly back along the corridors.

Eventually Dexter stopped. "This is my room. I can manage from here. Thank you." Callie smiled a goodnight and walked away. She was hardly round the corner when an unmistakable thud sounded behind her. She retraced her steps. Dexter was sitting on the floor in front of his door. He looked up at her quite crossly. "The door doesn't work."

"The door?" She stepped past him and flicked the latch. Dexter, who had regained his feet look at her with an expression of amazement. "Was that magic?"

She couldn't help it but just burst out laughing. "Yes, Dexter, of course it was magic." She draped him over her shoulder again and they traced an erratic path through a private living room into his bedroom. Dexter's eyes lit up when he saw his bed and he took a long step forward promptly tangling himself in Callie's cloak. He landed on the bed with Callie on top of him. "That feels nice," he murmured putting his arm round her, then smiled and closed his eyes.

"Am I intruding?" Blaine's bemused voice sounded from the doorway.

"No you're bloody not." Callie managed to wriggle free from Dexter's arms but unfortunately left her cloak behind. "He's your brother, not mine. You can see to him and could I please have my cloak back?"

Blaine grinned, eyeing her appreciatively. "If you insist." He tugged it free of his brother and returned it with a bow.

"Goodnight gentlemen." She headed for the door hearing Blaine cursing behind her as he tried to remove his uncooperative brother's boots, and Dexter's voice half asleep mumbling.

"I'm not her brother. I don't want to be her brother. Why is my leg wet?"

"I have no idea. Why do you smell toasted?" A snore greeted that question.

Although he was not looking his usual alert self, Callie had to give Dexter credit for seeing his guests off at an unspeakably early hour the next morning. He had offered her a short but obviously sincere apology for his behaviour the night before, which she had laughed off. He had also apologised that they had not had time to investigate the Garden Tower and invited her to return for that purpose if ever she chose to.

Every instinct in Callie's body told her she would have to do exactly that, so she accepted his invitation with gratitude. That, more than anything, seemed to convince the marcher Lord that he hadn't irredeemably offended her.

Chapter 21

The road from Winters Keep to Derryn was well maintained but mostly unpaved. Liss estimated their homeward journey would still take the same time as their outward journey although they were further west and nearer to Derryn. They had pressed hard on their way to relieve Lord Barnard's forces and their return carried no such pressure.

The first two nights were spent at waystations and Jerran, without servants or other nobles found it strange and liberating. The guards included men-at-arms he had fought alongside and this gave him a measure of acceptance he had never previously known. After a long day in the saddle, the tiny part of him used to service would have liked to have his horse taken care of and his bed made up, but looking around him he could see every man had already turned his hand to a task. Every man and, of course, one woman, Callie. She was already brushing down her mare and he had heard her offer to help with the cooking when she was done.

He watched her with fascination. These men were comfortable around her for the most part. They treated her as if she was a senior officer, offering a mix of respect and camaraderie. Callandra D'Arcourt, with a pedigree nearly as good as his own and immense Mage power; she was entirely unpretentious. She settled her horse and the next moment began chopping onions with one of the scouts.

Jerran started untacking his horse.

The third night was a cold camp under canvas, which was unfortunate as Callie had predicted a gale blowing in. There was no chance of reaching the next village or town; the distances were simply too great. They stopped fairly early and pitched camp in the shelter of some traveller pines, pinning their shelter down with rocks as well as pegs. They ate cold trail food and had just managed a hot drink when the storm broke and they all dived into their tents.

Liss and Jerran felt that guards would not be necessary in such weather, so everyone settled in to sleep out the storm. The guardsmen were two to a tent with Liss and Jerran sharing. Callie curled up alone in her fur cloak and was only grateful that she could use her Magecraft for warmth that allowed her to sleep.

When the storm departed and the wind dropped, it was the absence of noise that actually woke her. She felt for the weather, glad that it now seemed set fair, then used her heat sensing to check on the men. They were all hunkered down as she was expecting and she was about to try for more sleep when she realised there was one man-sized heat source outside just beyond the trees. If it was one of their men who had slipped out to relieve himself well and good. If it wasn't… She waited but the person didn't move. After a little while she slipped her boots on and picked up her sword and dagger, edging silently into the darkness.

The man was sitting on a fallen log gazing out over the hills that fell away to the south-west. As soon as she recognised the Prince she turned to retreat, but he spun round startled, then relaxed as her face became visible. "Callie! What are you doing out here?!"

"I woke after the storm, realised there was someone out here and came to check it was one of our party. Is anything wrong?" He shook his head and sighed.

"No. Nothing at all. I'm just making the most of this." He waved his arm at the snow-covered landscape now illuminated by the moon and a million stars. "I love it; the space, the freedom."

"The cold?" She noticed him shiver. He smiled.

"Well maybe not the cold but it is beautiful."

"Yes, it is," she agreed.

"I like being out here where things are so much simpler."

She sat down beside him. "What things?"

He looked at her warily and she thought be wasn't going to answer. "Out here you find shelter or you freeze to death. You defend yourself or you die. You work or you don't survive. It's simpler, it's honest. No game playing, no jockeying for position."

She chuckled. "Except round the fire."

He smiled then looked away, lost in thought. "I take it you were thinking about the Court?" He glanced back at her and nodded then shivered again. Without thinking she extended her warmth to envelop him and saw him relax a little.

"The Court. Now I think of it, I don't recall seeing you there, Callie. Admittedly I am away a fair bit but I think I would have remembered."

She grinned. "No. You wouldn't have seen me. As I've yet to finish my training I am not obliged to attend. I don't suppose you have that option."

"No, I really don't and I guess you won't either in future." It took a moment for his matter-of-fact statement to sink in.

"I beg your pardon?"

"Your Mage gift, Callie. Powerful Mages are usually attached to the Court. Didn't Liss say you might be the first Elemental Mage for a thousand years?"

"So?"

"Well obviously there will be many people wanting to…" He hesitated.

"Use me?" He shrugged apologetically. She felt her anger stirring. "No chance. There's no way that's going to happen. I've already had my life turned upside down once when my damned Mage gift first appeared. I wanted to be a warrior. I wanted to join the Land Knights but no. I had to sit in a classroom studying weather patterns to help our farmers, instead of improving my combat skills."

"But that's—"

"Yes! Yes, I know it's important." She only realised her voice had risen when he put a finger to his lips, glancing round at the sleeping camp. "Jerran, I do know it's important, truly. But that's not what I wanted to do." She hated the whine in her voice; apparently so did he.

"Well you're not the only one who hasn't been given a choice." He sounded bitter.

"Meaning?" His hazel eyes darkened and his gaze locked onto hers.

"Do you think I wanted to be a trade ambassador? I spend my time away arguing tariffs with money-grabbing merchants and ministers, who are too busy feathering their own nests to care about the people. Then when I do come home I am paraded in front of possible political partners like a prime steak in a butcher's shop." He looked away, rubbing a hand over his face.

Callie sat silently for a minute, thinking. Finally taking a deep breath she turned to face the Prince, putting her hand briefly on his arm. "Jerran, I apologise. I have been taught to think things through before I speak but I guess I'm still a work in progress. I've just been making all the superficial assumptions that everyone does, haven't I? You know; Prince, Power, Privilege." She hesitated. "If it was your choice what would you do?" He shook his head.

"It doesn't matter."

"I'd really like to know." He half smiled.

"I'd make your choice, Callie. I would be a warrior aiming for the Land Knights but it won't happen. Mikheli has that privilege." He gave a mirthless laugh. "I was only allowed to join this trip for two reasons. Firstly, because the King's advisers like to keep an eye on our border Lords. They have a lot of men in arms and they need them but it does make the crown nervous."

"And the other reason?"

"I'm sure they thought the fighting would be over long before I got there. I doubt very much that anyone imagined I would actually do battle."

"But you did."

"Yes. I really did. For the first time in my entire life I felt I was where I was meant to be, where I belonged... and I don't imagine it will be allowed to happen ever again." Silence fell between them. Callie became aware of a heat source approaching over the field. She signalled to Jerran and they watched silently as a snow fox trotted out from the hedge, its black-tipped tail waving behind it, stopping to sniff the air before going about its business.

It broke the strange intimacy of their night-time conversation. Callie stood up. "I'm going to try for some more sleep. See you in the morning." The Prince nodded and continued gazing into the distance.

*

Callie had wondered whether the Prince might avoid her the next morning. If he might regret having shared his dreams with her, but found the opposite to be true. When the road allowed for conversation, he beckoned her to join him with Liss and their conversation ranged far and wide over kingdom matters.

Callie found it fascinating. Jerran was thoughtful and very well informed. She was fast coming to the conclusion that her first impression of the Prince had been unjust. He was turning out to be an easy travelling companion, as they rode south.

They had to endure no more cold camps, as larger villages began to appear on their route and on the last night before they would make Derryn, their inn was able to offer them a private parlour as well as the usual facilities. Jerran had asked Liss and Callie to remain after their meal as he wanted their thoughts before he completed the report he would make to the King the following day.

They had both listened with interest to all the Prince had to say about the Frystians and why it would make sense for the Barrens, the empty lands south of the Winter Hills, to be occupied. He made a good case but Callie, who felt she was beginning to read the Prince a little better had a strong sense that she wasn't being shown the whole picture.

"Jerran, what aren't you telling us?" She refused to be quelled by his blank look and Liss's bemused expression. "I just know there's something bothering you." He hesitated a moment or two then shrugged.

"It's nothing I can put my finger on. I honestly believe the Clan want to live in peace and work with us and yet there is something they are not telling us. There are things that don't add up. In their camp, although they did not know that I understand Frystian, their speech was very guarded around me. But I did overhear bits and pieces. Yes, the herds are dying and their people are starving but there's more to it than that. There's something else badly wrong in the north. One of the tribes they will no longer even mention, and when they released me and brought me down towards Winters Keep, Einar the Chief had to compel my guides. They said they did not want to set eyes on their nation's shame."

"Did they mean the massacre?" Liss asked.

"I think so but they would not speak of it. Anyway, if the King agrees to their request someone will have to return and let them know and designate a land area, arrange a treaty and so on, or if he refuses they must be driven off. If it's me, and it may not be, I would like to go north and see for myself and for the safety of the Kingdom, just what is going on." He hesitated. "I was wondering if that happened, if you two might fancy coming along for the trip."

Liss nodded immediately. "I think that's a very good idea, Jerran. Things are moving that may affect us all and we need reliable information. What about you, Callie?"

She bit her lip and frowned slightly. "I do need to return to Winters Keep when I am free to do so, but I'm honestly not sure what's going to happen to me when I get back to the Academy. I can't hide my Mage gift if I'm to have any chance of learning about it and although I don't want to be 'used', my least worst choice might be to volunteer to go to Nilsport." Jerran nodded his understanding.

"You're right – that way you won't be conscripted and you might be able to lay down some conditions of your own."

"Such as?"

"Well, how long you'll be committed for. Who you will work with, report to, that sort of thing."

"Oh. Yes, I see." Callie looked very thoughtful for a moment, and then a sudden flashing smile lit up her face. "Yes indeed."

"Callie." Liss and Jerran's voices chorused in alarm.

She rose. "Sleep calls." She waved them an airy goodnight and departed for her room.

Chapter 22

When Derryn finally lay spread out beyond them, they halted briefly to re-order the party. The Prince would ride in front with his personal guard, followed by Liss and Callie; the remaining arms men bringing up the rear. Eyeing the Prince speculatively, Callie nudged Jessa alongside Jerran's mount. "Jerran. Would you do something for me?"

"If I can." He looked curious.

"When we start riding again would you try and sort of blank your mind – try and empty it."

"Why?"

"For no bad reason, I promise you. I'm still sort of experimenting with my Mage gift. Liss knows." The Prince switched his gaze across to the Isseni, who raised an eyebrow but nodded. "What's going to happen?"

"Maybe nothing. Probably nothing."

"Okay. I'll try, but you understand I have no Mage gift." Callie nodded and pulled Jessa back into position as Fife gave the order to move.

"What are you up to Callie?" Liss sounded more curious than worried.

"You'll see. I have an idea but it may not work." She patted Jessa's neck and slowed her pace allowing a distance to grow between her and the Prince. When she judged it far enough she felt for the spark of her magic, and with one hand on her reins and one on her pendant she focused on Jerran. The minutes passed and she concentrated harder. Ahead the Prince suddenly pulled up his mount. He turned in his saddle, obviously expecting Callie to be a few feet behind him, then waited as she and Liss caught up. His expression was indecipherable.

"The snow fox had a black tip to his tail?" He spoke as if the words were being dragged from him.

"Yes." Callie's smile lit up her face.

They stared at one another until Liss's voice broke the moment. "Well, well. Very interesting but I think you are worrying your men, milord." Jerran nodded with a very thoughtful glance at Callie; he slowly trotted forward once more.

Callie was delighted with her experiment. The Prince had heard her. It had required far more effort to contact him than to contact her father or brother but it was possible. Liss, she found utterly impenetrable while Dexter was fairly simple to reach, although she had yet to figure out why. Thinking of her twin she found his 'signature' with no difficulty and asked him to meet her at the family house as soon as he was able.

At the Palace Gates, Jerran and his escort detached themselves, while Liss turned away towards the Academy leaving Callie to ride on alone. She was pleased to be home. Leaving Jessa to the stable boys for a good rub down and some pampering, she reached her own room feeling dirty and weary and for once made no objection when the housekeeper organised a bath and clean clothing for her.

Afterwards, somewhat revived and finally unpacked she was just contemplating lunch when Raff strolled in and enveloped her in a brotherly bear hug. It felt very good. "The hero returns," he cheered, eyes crinkling.

"Hardly," she laughed, relaxed at last.

"I don't know. If you did only half of what I've heard it's damned impressive so, spill the beans. Tell me everything." They settled at the lunch table.

Raff was a good listener, hardly interrupting until she ended, pulling the pendant out from under her tunic. "Good Lord." He fingered it gingerly. "So, it's not this pendant that's turned you into an Elemental Mage?"

"No, Liss says all such Magery is innate, but he does think that it magnified what I was able to do, unskilled as I am."

"Hmm. I must say, Cal, when I heard your voice that first night in the Broken Arrow, it was so clear I thought you were in the porch, hanging up your cloak. And you spoke to Father?"

She nodded hesitantly. "I almost felt I could see him. Do you think that was just my imagination?"

He shook his head. "I doubt it but anyway that's easy enough to check; where he was and what he was doing. Did you see me?"

"Were you just beside the fireplace between Gregg and Hal?"

"I certainly was."

"So I really did see you. That's amazing." Her face fell.

"What's up? You look worried."

"I am worried. Jerran said…"

"Oh, so we are on first-name terms with the Prince now, are we?"

"Shut up. It's not like that. Actually, he's not like that." Raff raised his eyebrows but let it pass. "Jerran said that most really powerful Mages are attached to the Court and in royal service. I would hate that. I don't want to be used." She glared. Her brother gave her a straight, not particularly sympathetic look.

"Callie, you're not making much sense."

"What? I thought you'd be on my side."

"Cal, I'm always on your side, but just think it through. The Court, yes, I totally agree – a total snake pit but I doubt that's where you would be needed." As she took a deep breath he held up his hand, forestalling her.

"Don't even begin to say that you'll feel 'used' if they ask you to go to Nilsport. If you had completed your warrior training you would have been posted wherever your superiors needed you. As I will be – no picking and choosing in that. If I understand all you've done, you could act as a Battle Mage – only more so." She digested that for a few minutes. "You keep saying, if they 'ask' me."

"I do," he nodded, "because you still haven't graduated, you aren't in the King's forces and you are a noble. All they can do is 'ask' you, Callie. Mind you," he met her gaze, frowning, "the fighting isn't going well at Nilsport. There have been some heavy losses since the Ice-landers got involved. You know Anders?" She nodded; he was one of their year-mates. "His brother Stefan was killed in the last assault."

"Goddess." She put a hand to her mouth. "So you think I should go?"

He winced but met her eyes unflinchingly. "If you feel confident in your new Mage power it might save lives."

Callie toyed with her glass of wine, letting her thoughts settle. Raff sat quietly opposite her; a familiar and always comforting presence. She sipped her wine then raised her head. "Right. First things first. I am not confident in my new Mage gifts. I need help or at least advice."

"Then go and talk to your teachers. Try Wiston or Lauder."

Callie nodded. "I'll try and speak to Master Lauder. I've never found anything magical that man doesn't know, and at least he has a sense of humour."

Raff butted in. "I expect he finds the idea that you have become possibly the most powerful Mage on the planet hugely entertaining, whereas it's probably giving the Dean apoplexy." They both laughed. "Come on. I've got to get back to barracks and as there's no time like the present, I'll walk you up to the College." He rose to his feet.

"Give me five minutes." Callie shot out of her chair and ran up to her room. Her jewel case was where she had left it before leaving for Barnard's Castle. The carved box, which had contained her pendant, still lay on the top and she opened it quickly, tugging out the twist of while silk and putting it in her pocket before grabbing her cloak and following Raff out of the building.

Chapter 23

The Academy when they reached it was bustling. Still term time, students were spilling out onto the grounds leaving or going to classes. The distant sounds of warrior training made a backdrop to the nearer chatter and for a brief moment, Callie wished for the silence of the winter nights in the hinterlands. There could not have been a greater contrast.

Leaving Raff, she made her way to the Faculty building, inwardly amused that this must be the first time she had gone there voluntarily. Most of the Masters would be busy teaching, but she hoped the one she sought might be free. Master Lauder was probably the oldest member of the existing staff and taught a reduced number of classes, mainly occupying his time with research.

Confirming at reception that he was in his study, she wandered along the well-trodden corridor to his room at the far end and knocked on the door. "Come in, Callie." His voice was deep and calm. She didn't even bother guessing how he knew it was her. He waved her to one of the old armchairs facing his cluttered desk and smiled. "Welcome back, Callandra. How are you feeling?"

She felt all the tension that had been holding her together, leave. "I really don't know, sir."

"Well, that's not at all surprising. If I tell you that Liss has already dropped by and updated me on what's been happening to you, would that help?" Callie grinned.

"I should have known."

"So." He looked her over carefully. "How can I help you?"

Callie shrugged. "I have absolutely no idea. How can you help me?"

The old Master laughed. "As there are no Elemental Mages, and haven't been for centuries, as you well know, there is no-one here with that experience to tutor you, but we do have quite a lot of information and historical records. You are going to have a lot of reading to do." He waved at the pile of books perched neatly on one corner of his desk. "I looked these out after talking to Liss."

"What are they?" Callie eyed the hefty pile dubiously.

"They are historical accounts of some of the most famous Elemental Mages and what they achieved. Some of them are journals; there is even one diary. They will show you some of the possibilities of your gift. The 'what'. As to 'the how', I think you'll find all the techniques you used with your weather magic will transfer.

"Liss tells me that you have already experimented with earth and fire. As to your amulet, I believe you have managed some long-distance communication?"

"Yes." She nodded and pulled the pendant over her head for him to study. His eyes widened as he looked at the rune marking and he appeared very thoughtful as he ran a finger across the incised curve. "Do you know what it is?"

"Possibly." He pursed his lips. "The runes are Moreni, which makes it very, very old."

"Can you read it?" she asked hesitantly. Master Lauder brushed his unruly hair out of his eyes, and looked at her.

"Not immediately."

"Oh Goddess, why does everything have to be so mystical?" she muttered crossly, provoking a chuckle from the elderly Mage.

"Liss told you that many magical items were crafted in ancient times using wizardry long since lost to us. Nowadays these items are few but not unknown. This one as you have established is…"

"Good for communications," Callie butted in. He shook his head.

"Not exactly that, Callie, and not just that either. You are good at communications, your will linked with your air magic ensures that. The pendant is magnifying the latent ability that already exists in you."

"So?"

"So, it will help you connect very easily to people with whom you have a natural link, people you are very close to or know well. You might be able to link with some others now. It will be harder but not impossible. Usually talismans like this had what we call satellites."

"What are satellites?"

"A good question and not an easy answer. They can be various different things; jewels, heraldic tokens…"

Callie tugged the twist of silk from her pocket and untied it revealing a dozen plain silver rings. "Rings?" Master Lauder raised an eyebrow. "I only just remembered them. They were with my pendant."

The Master prodded them with interest then nodded. "Well, well. See they have similar runes engraved within. I suspect that if you gave one of these to a perfect stranger you would then be able to establish a link."

He ran the rings through his fingers then stopped abruptly before picking them up one at a time, studying the runes and separating them into two piles. Callie watched, fascinated. "Yes, I see." He looked up at her. "These ones have a rune for listening. These others are marked for both listening and speaking. How very convenient."

There was silence while they both considered the implications of their latest discovery. Callie shook her head, trying to clear it. "I really don't know what to do next." It was an admission few of her teachers would ever have expected her to make, but she had never been made to feel uncomfortable by Master Lauder and his expression was as kindly and uncritical as ever.

"Liss tells me you are thinking of going to Nilsport?" He phrased it as a question. Callie nodded slowly. "As you haven't graduated yet, you would need (and the King would need) our consent to release you." She nodded again.

"I've no idea what, if anything I might be able to do, but Raff says the war is not going well and if I can save lives I should." She wondered if he might argue but he did not.

"Raff is right but you are young, you are inexperienced and you are one of my students. If you are to go, either as a volunteer or at the request of the Palace, and I'm sure there will be a request from the Palace, I would insist upon certain conditions. Firstly, you need at least a week here, to read all those books. They will show you the way Elemental Mages have worked before.

"Secondly, you will need to set up communication links. Raff would be the logical choice; and finally you will probably find yourself right on the battlefields. Even when warded you will be vulnerable as you exercise your Magecraft so you will need a warrior escort of the highest calibre to defend you."

Callie nodded that all made sense then she grinned wickedly. "Actually Master Lauder I have some ideas about that."

Chapter 24

Back in his stall Warrior looked well satisfied as the stable hands untacked him and started brushing the journey dust from his black coat. Jerran lingered offering an apple, his feet reluctant to tread the well-worn path back into the Palace; back into his life at Court.

His mood darkened as he made his way to his own quarters in the royal wing. Everyone he passed bowed and smiled or tried to engage him in light conversation. His jaw began to ache, as well as his head, as he forced himself to be at least polite. He found he was walking faster and realised, wryly that if his rooms had been much further he would have ended up running.

He sent a note to inform his father of his return and headed for a bath, trying to figure out why he was so tense. Cleaner and a little more relaxed after a long soak, he was still unwilling to tackle the pile of correspondence awaiting his attention in his living room. Most of it would be invitations, and most of those from nobles with eligible daughters. He was in no mood to deal with them, instead sorting through his weapons. His sword needed attention so he left it to one side and had just hunted out a whetstone and some oil to sharpen his dagger, when there was a knock at his door.

As he opened it the person outside lunged at him and he whipped the dagger upwards, to find himself staring into a pair of huge terrified brown eyes. "Salli." He drew back, startled. "I'm so sorry."

The young woman at his door slowly let out her breath. "Jerran," she squeaked. "They told me you were back and it's been absolutely ages, so I slipped away." She stepped through the doorway. "Have you missed me?" She smiled and dimples appeared beside her generous mouth.

"How could I not?" The words slipped out smoothly even as Jerran realised that he meant not one of them. He moved past her, dropping the dagger onto the table. She slipped her arms around his waist, her pert breasts crushed to his chest, peering up at him through long lashes.

"And are you going to show me how much?" She licked her lips.

Jerran stared down at her. A pretty and willing young woman was pressing herself against him and it was having exactly no effect on him. He cleared his throat in confusion with no idea what exactly he was going to say or do, when another brisk knock on the door spared him the decision. "Oh damn." One of the King's messengers stood outside with a note, which he scanned quickly. He conjured up a disappointed expression. "I'm so sorry Salli but I have to go to the King, and give him my report."

She pouted. "Do you really have to go?"

He raised an eyebrow. "Then, shall I come back later?" Her smile faltered as he shook his head.

"Salli, I really don't know how long I'll be, and just back I have a lot to attend to."

He re-opened the door. "I'll be along shortly." He dismissed the messenger and went to retrieve his report then gently ushered his visitor out. "You'd better go, Salli. I'd hate you to get into trouble because of me." Her face cleared a little at that and she bobbed a curtsey as he strode past her along the corridor, patting her bottom as he did so and eliciting a small giggle.

The King's "office" as he called it was on the ground floor of the palace; a large room with windows opening onto a small courtyard garden. A corridor led circuitously back to the audience hall and another led to the many offices of his ministers. It was a light, airy chamber with a round table, as well as the King's desk and some more casual seating.

When Jerran knocked and entered, he was not unduly surprised to see his father already in discussion with several advisers, including Liss and General D'Arcourt, his Minister of Defence whom the Prince now listed mentally as Callandra's father.

The King rose at Jerran's arrival and came swiftly round the table to envelop him in a bear hug. "Welcome back, my boy. I've been hearing of your adventures. I'm glad they've left you more or less on one piece." He looked Jerran over carefully then waved him to an empty chair. "I've got the meat of the events from Liss here," he nodded in the direction of the Isseni, "but now I want to hear your version."

He settled back at the table, giving Jerran his complete attention, and the Prince began his report.

It took some time, with questions from all sides. King Theon was an intelligent man and had made it his business to ensure that his sons, both bright themselves, had had the best of educations, so he treated their input and opinions with respect. When Jerran had finally finished, the King was silent for some time in deep thought. "Ivor?" He looked to General D'Arcourt.

"An interesting idea, sire, very much a double-edged sword. On the one hand if the Frystians hold true, we would get some settlement in the Barrens, possible trade and a buffer against other Frystian clans. But if they have treachery in mind we will have given them a foothold on our side of the Winter Hills." The King nodded.

"Liss?"

"The General has the right of it, although as Snow Fox Clan is so very small, to be blunt, they would not be hard to deal with, if they played us false." He paused. "What worries me more is what we are not being told. Like Prince Jerran, I suspect there is more going on in the north than we know. Your agents in Kerria and the north have gone silent, and although there have never been many traders from those parts, there are now none at all. I think we need more information."

King Theon nodded. "I agree. I also ought to let the Council have a chance to discuss this. Some of the marcher Lords certainly won't be happy if we consent." Jerran thought of Dexter and couldn't argue. The King signalled to his secretary. "Erich, we have another meeting tomorrow to discuss Nilsport. Please add this to the agenda." The man scribbled a note with brisk efficiency.

"How are things going at Nilsport?" Jerran queried. His father looked grim.

"Not well. It's virtually a stalemate."

"If it was just the Frystians, the action would be over by now but the Ice-landers have changed the balance," General D'Arcourt chipped in. "Our forces have sustained substantial losses and report that the fighting is the fiercest they have ever known, which also makes me think there may be some substance to what Prince Jerran is suggesting. If the Frystians feel their homeland is under threat they may be fighting for survival."

"That being the case," the King spoke slowly, "I find your account of the fighting at Arco's Gap very interesting. You seem to confirm what we have already heard from Gideon and Liss, that the Lady Callandra's intervention made all the difference there."

"Absolutely. She is very powerful and," Jerran smiled, "very inventive." He detected the General's lips twitch.

"Perhaps we should send her to Nilsport." King Theon rubbed his eyes, thinking out loud, and was interested to see the humour vanish from his son's face.

"You could certainly ask her if she wishes to go." Jerran's voice was almost aggressively neutral. "Callie; Lady Callandra is still a private student at the Academy and has not, as far as I am aware, signed up to any service."

"I take your point," the King spoke mildly, "but if she was interested we might be able to come to some arrangement with the Academy." Jerran nodded after a moment, briefly, reluctantly.

"Now we have other matters to discuss, which involve budgets and taxes. You are welcome to stay, Jerran, but if you want to…"

Jerran laughed, shot to his feet and headed towards the door at speed. "I'll see you later, Father."

"At dinner please, Jerran. We will need to meet again to discuss the embassy to Westerland."

Jerran closed the door quietly, the smile wiped from his face. A few months previously the King had made a first overture to Westerland raising the possibility of a marriage between the Westerland Princess and Prince Mikheli. This had met with a favourable response, as Westerland and Lithia shared borders and trade. Now, further, more specific negotiations needed to take place. Jerran shuddered. The Westlanders were a very correct people and much given to formal dinners with endless speeches. After the last trip he had prayed never to have to return. A prayer that evidently hadn't been answered.

Back in his room the pile of correspondence on his desk hadn't got any smaller. He settled to it, realising it could hardly make his mood worse, and he would then be free after dinner to get very drunk.

Chapter 25

Callie left her meeting with Master Lauder, weighed down with books and advice. Dumping the hefty volumes on the desk in her academy room, she finally unpacked and dealt with the domestic chores of laundry and cleaning. After writing up the notes on her field trip to be handed in to her mentor, she curled up with *The Elemental Mage in History*.

As the Senior Master of the Derryn Academy, Master Lauder usually only dealt with graduates or very advanced students. The late emergence of Callie's Mage gift and her objection to it, had led her into conflict with other faculty staff and finally Master Lauder had agreed to tutor her himself because he felt it was slightly less painful than listening to the constant complaints of his colleagues. He was a man of endless patience and vast learning. He also had a very lively sense of humour and Callie had appreciated very quickly how lucky she was to have him, so if he said she needed to read these books then no question, she would.

She was soon so absorbed in the stories of the great Mages that it wasn't until the light had faded so much she could hardly see that she realised how late it was. Pulling her head out of her book she became aware of noise all around her and realised her year-mates were arriving back from their various classes and duties.

Popping her head out of her door she was met with cheers,

teasing and hugs. It was definitely good to be back. Stories of her exploits, mostly wildly exaggerated, were repeated and challenged all though dinner and when she finally headed for bed she felt talked out. Raff had eaten with her group and they arranged to spar the next morning. After all, Callie could only read for so many hours at a time and she knew she needed to maintain her weapon skills if, as seemed likely, she was to be sent back into action.

On her way to the dining hall she had found a note in her pigeon hole from the Dean telling her briefly that the possibility of her service to the Crown at Nilsport had been proposed. He had therefore required that she drop into his office the next day to let him know what she wished to do and how she felt about the idea. Lying in her bed at last, Callandra had tried to decide what she really did feel about it. Arco's Gap had changed things for her; changed her, and she had fallen asleep wondering how much.

Raff was sitting on a bench in the large practice hall when Callie found him next morning. He watched her approach, weaving her way smoothly between fighters paired off for sword work, and reflected, not for the first time, that somehow he never thought of his sister as a small woman. It was only when she stood next to some well-muscled warrior that it became apparent. He knew what she had told the Dean simply from the expression she wore.

"So, you're going."

"Yes." She waited to see if she needed to defend her decision, but Raff just nodded.

"I'm not going to try and talk you out of it, Cal. Things really aren't going well there. I've been talking to some of the wounded and men back for leave. Anything you can do to end it… well…" He didn't finish his sentence. Callie slumped on the bench beside him.

"That's what I think too, Raff, but honestly, I have no idea what I can do. I mean they already have Battle Mages there. Really experienced, powerful, Mages, who know what they are doing."

"Really experienced, powerful Mages who so far have only prevented Nilsport from being overrun. I don't expect you had the faintest idea what you were going to do at Arco's Gap until you got there, did you?"

"Well, I…"

"Did you?"

"Oh shut up. I hate know-it-alls. I'm going to carve you into tiny pieces for that."

"In your dreams. When do you go?" He rose to his feet and unsheathed his sword, checking his practice armour. Callie did the same.

"I still have a few days. Master Lauder has laid down some very precise conditions for me to go." She fell into a fighting stance.

"What conditions?" Raff queried suspiciously, noting the air of innocence she had assumed.

"You'll just have to wait and see." She raised her weapon and the bout began.

*

It was on the third day after his return from the north that Prince Jerran was again summoned to see his father. He had spent the intervening days with friends who were more than happy with his plan to forget his woes by drinking himself into oblivion. Unfortunately, it hadn't quite worked out. His friends had soon achieved the drunken stupor he had been aiming for while he had become more and more sober. He had also found the exaggerated tales told by Hadley and Nevis of their battlefield prowess at Arco's Gap increasingly difficult to stomach. In fact, he had withdrawn early on both nights and, not in the mood for softer company, the only thing he had taken to his bed had been the notes from his previous embassy to Westerland.

King Theon had a distinctly bemused expression on his face as he looked his son over. So much so, that Jerran racked his brains trying, unsuccessfully, to recall any recent indiscretions he might have been guilty of. "Is something wrong, sir?" Best to get it over with. The King sighed.

"Not wrong exactly, Jerran, but I don't like being manipulated and in this case there's damn all I can do about it."

"About what? Has something happened in Westerland?" The King was watching him closely but his bewilderment was obviously convincing as Theon sat back and shook his head. "

You won't be going to Westerland."

"I won't?" He tried not to let his delight colour his voice. "Am I to go north then to sort out the Frystians?"

"Not immediately. It seems," his father took a deep breath, "that you are needed at Nilsport."

"Nilsport?" The announcement was so unexpected he just opened his hands in confusion.

"Jerran, Nilsport is becoming a war of attrition. We are bleeding troops and war is costly. We now have a new weapon available to us: our Elemental Mage."

Jerran started. "She has agreed to go?"

"She has," Theon nodded, "but the Academy is determined to safeguard her in every way, and I have had to meet their terms."

"Which are?" Jerran pressed.

"Right now she is being intensively tutored and advised by Master Lauder himself on everything we hold on record about the Elemental Mages of the past. When she goes to Nilsport, as she will actually be on the battlefield, she will need her own guard; a small elite detachment. Communications will also be of paramount importance. I am given to understand that Lady Callandra can speak mind to mind with one or two people; her brother, her father," he paused, "and you. Is that so?"

The black-tailed fox! Jerran grinned. "Yes sir. Actually it is."

"And what precisely is your interest in Lady Callandra?" The King raised an eyebrow and the Prince briefly regretted his reputation with the ladies. At least this time he had nothing to hide.

"Actually sir, I regard her as a friend."

"A friend? She's a very attractive young woman and you regard her as a friend?" The King sounded entirely unconvinced.

"Sir, I really do. The thing is, she doesn't act like the women at court. She doesn't flirt. Doesn't give a damn what she looks like. Speaks her mind. I think we deal well together."

Theon studied him a moment longer. "In that case prepare yourself. You will ride out on Moonsday. Consult with Fife about who you should take. Lady Callandra's brother must be included in the group. I will give you a royal order to give to Mikheli. I can't have both my sons on the battlefield so he'll have to come home, at least for a while."

Jerran whistled. "He's not going to like that!"

"No. That's why it will be a royal order," the King agreed.

"What about the Snow Fox Clan?"

"The Council voted in favour of allowing a settlement; on fairly strict terms, mind you. Liss has agreed to return to Winters Keep and get that set up, although if Nilsport can be concluded in short order you still might find yourself heading north again before too long. Now, off with you. You have a lot to do." The King offered a tired smile and Jerran accepted his dismissal.

He stood for a moment outside the King's chambers trying to process what had just happened. He wasn't going to Westerland to fence with words; he was going to Nilsport to fence with swords. His spirits soared as he set off for the barracks to find Sergeant Fife. After that, he thought a little chat with the Lady Callandra might be in order.

Chapter 26

What had been intended as a bit of exercise to relieve her stiffness after sitting reading for hours, turned into something else entirely for Callie. Veris the weapons master, having been informed by both the Academy and the King's office that she would be going to Nilsport had 'offered' to help her brush up her skills. An 'offer' from Veris being a command by any other name. She had been put through all her forms and even a session of unarmed combat. She had lost count of how many times she had ended flat on her back, and sitting on the bench feeling her bruises, her only consolation was that Raff was doing no better.

He had bounced through the door of the Salle an hour earlier, full of the news that he would be going to Nilsport with her and had enjoyed a laugh at her expense at the trouncing she was receiving at the hands of the weapons master and two of his senior students. His laughter stopped abruptly when Master Veris announced that in consideration of this news he would be next. If anything he had been harder on her brother on the entirely reasonable grounds that he would essentially be part of Callie's bodyguard.

Sore and dripping with sweat they headed for hot baths, agreeing that having earned a trip to The Broken Arrow, they would gather their friends and meet later for supper. Callie had had little free time since returning from the north and with Nilsport just days away she felt the need to be doing something ordinary. She wanted to gossip with her friends and know the decisions she made were not matters of life and death but matters of ale or cider.

They headed out fairly early and sitting at the long bench table that had become the students' through constant use, Callie was happy to let the conversations wash gently over her. Raff was just organising a second round of drinks when the noise level in the tavern dropped suddenly then surged in a hiss of excited whispers.

A young man had just walked in and was looking about him with interest, ignoring, although obviously aware of the stir his arrival had caused. Raff gulped and nudged Callie, whose attention was entirely on Chloe, one of her best friends. She caught the direction of her brother's gaze, her eyes widening in disbelief. "Callie, isn't that?"

"No!" Chloe squeaked as Callie elbowed her in the ribs before standing up and waving at the stranger. "Rhys. Over here." Prince Jerran grinned and made his way between the tables dropping into Raff's seat.

"Callie, finally, I've been looking for you."

"And you've found me. What are you drinking? Raff's just getting them in."

The Prince gave a genial nod in Raff's direction. "A half of ale if that's okay?" Callie's brother nodded and continued on his way to the bar.

"Rhys?" Jerran's attention was drawn back to the table by the pretty girl sitting next to Callandra. She had a puzzled expression on her face. "I expect you've been told before, but you look just like Prince Jerran."

"Yes, I'm afraid it has been mentioned before." He lowered his voice into a conspiratorial tone that still reached everyone on the table. "Same family actually – just the wrong side of the bed-clothes." He ignored the sound of Callie choking on her drink.

Chloe gasped. "No: you mean our King…"

"Fathered me? Yes, I'm afraid so. Do you mind if we don't talk about it?" He looked down at his hands, his long lashes dropping over his hazel eyes, presenting a picture of discomfort. Callie thought it a masterful performance.

Chloe patted his shoulder. "Oh Rhys, of course not. I do apologise. That's so awful for you but it really doesn't matter here. Are you at the Academy?"

"Not now." Jerran shook his head. "I'm a warrior."

"At Nilsport?" one of Raff's friends chipped in.

"Rhys was fighting with Lord Dexter's forces at Arco's Gap – that's where we met." Callie intervened.

"Oh right." The explanation seemed to satisfy everyone and after a few introductions attention was further diverted as Raff arrived back with a tray of drinks. It was a friendly gathering but Jerran quickly realised there would be no chance for private conversation with Callie, so he just sat back and sipped his ale. When a fairly noisy argument broke out he turned to Callie with a raised eyebrow.

"Rhys?"

She shrugged. "I like the name."

Raff leaned forward, his eyes sparkling. "Trust me it could have been worse. Rhys was very important to her."

"Oh – an old friend?"

"Yes."

"No." The twins glared at each other.

"Alright, he was my favourite dog." She bit her lip, looking at Jerran with some trepidation. Jerran burst out laughing.

It was far from late when Callie and Raff made their excuses to the assembled company and drew Jerran with them up the hill towards the barracks. On the way the Prince told Callie about the other arms men he had chosen to create an elite bodyguard squad for her. She was oddly disappointed that Liss would not be going with them, although in view of his status perhaps she shouldn't have been surprised but she was pleased to hear that Gilly had volunteered, knowing him to be an excellent swordsman as well as a talented scout. Jerran thought she might well recognise the other men too. They certainly knew who she was having all fought at Arco's Gap.

By the time the residences were in sight most arrangements had been discussed and Raff, yawning, mightily wished them goodnight and departed. Jerran was about to do the same when Callie stopped him. "Jerran, have you time to come to my room? There's something I want to give you." She took a couple of steps and turned when she realised he wasn't following her. The expression on the Prince's face, a mixture of surprise and uncertainty made her groan. "Good Goddess, Jerran, your virtue is safe with me. Now come on." She was pleased to see he looked slightly embarrassed as he caught up with her.

"Not the most luxurious accommodation," he commented, looking about him at the simple bed, desk and wardrobe that comprised the entire furniture in her room.

Callie shrugged. "It's fine. We don't usually spend much time here." She moved books off her desk and rummaged around inside, producing a small bundle that she untied and emptied on her bed.

Jerran saw a pile of silver rings. "What are they for?" He watched as Callie separated them into two piles.

"Master Lauder thinks they are 'satellites' to the pendant I wear. You remember when I contacted you mind-to-mind on the road home?"

"I'm not likely to forget it," he grimaced. "I was so startled I nearly fell off my horse!" She laughed.

"Well, I was trying to see if you have the sort of mind I can link with. You do." He nodded. "But it was hard work, much harder than contacting my brother, or my father; people I have a really deep link with, people I am close to."

He nodded. "That makes sense."

"Master Lauder thinks the rings might make things easier. Try one of these. Some of them only allow a wearer to hear me. These ones," she pointed, "should also allow the wearer to speak to me, to make the contact." Jerran slipped one on his finger.

"Ready?" He nodded and Callie reached out very softly. The Prince flinched then smiled.

"Yes I do think Chloe is pretty. Although she's not as pretty as…" His voice trailed off withered by an icy glare. "Don't even think of completing that sentence." He closed his mouth.

"Now, was that clearer?"

"Yes. Much clearer and louder."

"Brilliant." Callie was delighted. "Now your turn. Think something at me." Jerran paused for a moment then Callie blushed uncomfortably. "There's no need to thank me, Jerran. It was pure self-interest. If I'm going into battle I want to be protected by the best and I heard the men talking about you at Black Stone."

He shook his head but said nothing more. "I'd better go before I do get you into trouble. I'll see you after breakfast on Moonday. Goodnight, Callie."

"Goodnight, Rhys." He chuckled as he walked away.

Chapter 27

They took the traders' road out of Derryn heading north-west and quickly settled into a ground-eating pace. Rain over the past few days had washed away the light covering of snow, although Callie warned them that there was more to come. Still, inns were plentiful along the route so they had no fear of cold camps for some days to come, if at all.

Raff found himself watching the group with interest, feeling at first almost an outsider. The others had all fought together at Arco's Gap and that shared experience had forged a subtle bond. The Prince fascinated him. The D'Arcourt family were nobility, so he and Callie had been presented at court aged sixteen but were not expected to be part of that world until they reached their formal majorities at eighteen, in the summer. In practical terms this meant that he had met Prince Jerran once, and only once, before their night at The Broken Arrow.

He had certainly heard many stories about both Jerran and his brother; most of which were unflattering. But Raff, although the less voluble, more thoughtful one of the twins, had a well-founded respect for Callie as a judge of character. She obviously both liked and respected the Prince so he determined to keep an open mind regarding at least this one of the royals.

As for Callie herself, the changes Raff saw in her, ran deep. He was glad to be there to watch her back. He was also glad, on a much more prosaic level when they crawled damply into The Travellers Rest at Minark, a large village, perhaps an hour's steady riding from Nilsport itself. They had chosen to leave the traders' road at Bailey Bridge and followed the lesser road that had brought them to the coast, making their way beside the Black Sea that was living up to its name under lowering skies.

Warm and dry for the first time in hours, they enjoyed a substantial and tasty meal, even if it was a bit too heavy on the fish for Raff's taste, while they discussed what needed to happen the next day. Gilly had been sent on to the command centre at Nilsport with news of their impending arrival. They planned to link up with him the next morning.

Jerran, well aware of how little his older brother was going to like being summoned home, had decided to get that unfortunate duty over with as soon as possible. He intended to seek out Mikheli first thing. Then they needed briefing with the most up-to-date information on the fighting. The Commander of the King's forces at Nilsport was, at least in theory, Colonel Jago, a vastly experienced officer who had come to prominence twenty years previously in the Ostland Wars. Unfortunately, his war record and strategic brilliance did not, for Prince Mikheli, counterbalance the problem of his ignoble birth. Ignoring the meritocratic structure of the army and refusing to believe any 'commoner' could be talented, the crown prince's constant interference and pursuit of his own vainglorious ideas, had all but brought the campaign to a standstill.

Jerran, although he had a true fondness for his older brother was not blind to his faults, and en route, had even considered privately whether just removing Mikheli might be enough to turn the tides of the war; regardless of any contribution Callie might make.

Glancing across the table at her, it occurred to him that she had been far too quiet for far too long and her face had an unnaturally closed expression.

"What's the matter, Callie?" He interrupted Raff's wittering with no apology.

She met his gaze startled. "Nothing."

He raised an eyebrow then just waited and Callie saw she now had

Raff's attention too. The pause lengthened. Jerran had a look she was coming to know. He wasn't going to let it go. She groaned. "I, just, the thing is I've only been on a battlefield once. Everyone is expecting me to make a difference. What if I can't?" Raff looked chagrined. He should have been the one to realise how anxious and worried his sister was; not a man she had known so briefly.

The Prince nodded his head. "I suppose strictly speaking that's true, but bear in mind, for all their experience, the Battle Mages here, haven't been able to win us the war. You will do your best, I know. I've never seen you be half-hearted about anything. If things go well, great. If not, we will be no worse off than we are now. Will we?" He waited.

"No," she finally huffed. "I suppose not."

"Right then. Stop being so hard on yourself. You're obviously tired so go to bed." Callie gave a wry smile and rose to her feet. "As Your Highness commands." She headed for the stairs and they both watched her until she had quite disappeared.

"Dammit. I should have noticed." Raff looked annoyed with himself. The Prince shrugged.

"You'll notice next time… and there will be a next time, Raff. Callie has it right about the weight of expectation on her. It will be up to us to make her job as easy as possible."

"Do you really believe she can make a difference?" Raff asked hesitantly.

"I don't doubt it for a minute. I think she is only just getting used to the vast power she now commands." In his turn he paused. "If you had seen it, Raff. It was stunning but also terrifying." He chuckled. "I just thank the Goddess she's on our side. Now we need some sleep too."

Raff, Callandra and the remaining arms men presented themselves at the military headquarters in Nilsport, just before mid-morning. Gilly had been on the steps waiting when Jerran had arrived some time earlier, and having established that the Crown Prince had taken over a large summer residence belonging to one of the city notables he had taken Jerran off to meet with his brother.

Although Nilsport was the ultimate goal of the Frystians and their

Ice-lander allies, the port was not as yet actually on the front line. The town, set behind sturdy walls, had a permanent garrison, so there were soldiers everywhere, off duty or on rotation. The battle-lines of the front were nearly two miles further north-west.

Gilly had had to ride on to the entrenched positions there to pass his messages to the commander and then returned to Nilsport with the news that Colonel Jago would be returning to headquarters before mid-day. They settled down to wait in his adjutant's office and were re-joined by Prince Jerran shortly before the Colonel and his staff rode into the Courtyard.

It seemed to Raff as he found a seat at the table of the hastily convened conference that their welcome had been cordial rather than enthusiastic. The Colonel had read out his copy of the King's Order requiring Prince Mikheli's immediate return to Derryn to all his senior officers and there was no disguising the ripple of relief that ran through the room.

He, however, still seemed wary, looking them over, while obviously conducting some internal debate. Finally, he squared his shoulders. "Prince Jerran."

"Sir?" That response produced a lightning-fast flicker of one eyebrow.

"I do like things to be clear. I understand that Prince Mikheli is required at the capital but now you are here. Do you mean to take his place, assume his duties?" Raff thought several of the officers and even the two men he had identified as Mages held their breath.

"Sir," Jerran's voice was calm and steady, "I am replacing my brother only in the broadest sense (you know… the royals are fighting beside us sort of thing, in case that has any effect on morale). I regret that I cannot undertake his 'duties' as such as I have duties of my own. I am to all intents and purposes leading the bodyguard of our Mage the Lady Callandra."

There was a loud exhalation of breath round the table. Colonel Jago looked both relieved and startled. "Thank you for clarifying that, Prince Jerran. Now Lady Callandra." He eyed her curiously and Callie resisted the temptation to try and look fierce or impressive. "When we got news of your arrival from Gilligan last night, I thought it best to bring back two of our Battle Mages to try and work out how you might be able to help and co-ordinate with them. Let me introduce you, unless your paths have already crossed?" She shook her head. "Mage Terran," he indicated the older of the two men, who smiled and bowed slightly. "Terran, Battle Mage and part-time healer. Yes. Really." He smiled at her reaction to his strange combination of talents, making his grizzled hair fall into his eyes. "And this is Mage Lewin." He dropped a heavy hand onto the shoulder of the younger man who had short blond hair and a determinedly bland expression.

"So, Lady Callandra. How much battlefield experience have you actually had?" Terran's voice was not unfriendly but Callie had a moment of panic and was horrified to hear herself announce, in a wavering voice that she had only been on a battlefield once. The Mages exchanged dismayed glances.

"And you were a weather witch?" Mage Lewin guessed. She simply nodded. An uncomfortable silence spread round the room lengthening painfully until it was finally broken by the Prince who burst out laughing.

"Stop teasing them, Callie." He cuffed her gently as if they shared some private joke. "Gentlemen, the Lady Callandra has only been at war once so far, so I suppose she was, literally, telling the truth. But that once did include saving Lord Barnard's Iron Valley and defeating the combined Frystian and Kerrian forces out of Arco's Gap singlehandedly." There were gasps around the table. "And it's true that Lady Callandra is a weather witch… but that's not all she is." He looked across at Raff who picked up his cue.

"As well as a weather witch Callie is an Elemental Mage."

"What? Good Goddess." The Mages looked far more shocked than the military officers who simply did not appreciate the enormity of the announcement.

"But there hasn't been an Elemental Mage for…"

"1,042 years." Callie spoke up. "Well, that's according to Master Lauder."

"Master Lauder confirms you?" Mage Lewin looked stunned.

"Certainly." Callie's voice had regained its firmness. "He has been mentoring me as much as possible since I returned from the north. I still lack experience," she met the gazes of the Colonel and the

Mages, "but what I do not lack is power." They took a moment to digest this.

"Perhaps she could help take out the siege engines?" Lewin's whisper to Terran reached the Prince's ears.

"Gentlemen," he smiled at them challengingly, "you need to start thinking on a very much grander scale and we need to look at the maps."

Chapter 28

By the time lunch was announced Callie felt she understood the military situation. There had been several attacks by the Frystians, which had been repulsed. In previous years, as losses mounted the northerners had always retreated but now they had dug themselves into entrenched positions and were busy building siege engines that boded ill for Nilsport if the lines should be overrun.

By mid-afternoon they were standing on the eastern end of the deployment, where the Winter Hills gentled before running down to the river valley.

The enemy force spread before them was much larger than either the Prince or Callie had expected and Raff looked quite shocked. "That's quite an army," Jerran remarked quietly.

"Yes, it is." Colonel Jago's voice was grim. "And we suspect we are not seeing all their forces. So far our scouts haven't been able to get close enough to the forest." Callie and Jerran's eyes met.

"Well I imagine we should be able to help with that." He drew her forward and she nodded in understanding.

"Just give me a moment." She grasped her pedant and turned her focus inward.

"What we think—" Mage Lewin began.

"Quiet." Callie glared at him and started again.

"I was just…" Mage Lewin began again and Raff stifled a laugh as the young Mage found himself in a headlock with the Prince's arm across his throat.

"Be quiet." The man nodded as Jerran slowly released him and he started rubbing his neck. He looked to his colleagues his expression, shocked and offended but Terran's eyes were on Callie.

She let her mind range out across the land until she reached the distant woods. The heat signature was intense. There were many hidden troops in small groups. Callie became aware of subtleties, different textures in her mind, like different flavours on her tongue. Another strangeness baffled her for a moment then she smiled as she identified horses.

She turned herself slowly, ranging back and forth. Raff, fascinated by the sight of his sister using her gift, was abruptly brought back to his own duties by Jerran nudging him, none too gently with his drawn sword. "Raff! You are part of Callie's bodyguard. You shouldn't be watching her; you should be looking for threats to her."

Raff flushed and drew his own weapon. "Uh oh." Callie came back to them suddenly. The Colonel and Major Durrant exchanged dubious glances but it was Terran who spoke.

"What did you see? Feel?" He had obviously realised what she was doing.

"You're right. They have a lot more men both in and behind the woods."

"Damn. I don't suppose you could estimate how many?"

"About 1,000 on foot and there is another force behind them – maybe 300 or so and they have horses."

"The Frystians don't have horses," the Major chipped in.

"No, but the Ice-landers do. I doubt the horses have been there long. It's winter. Fodder will be problematic so the chances are they have only recently arrived."

The Colonel pondered the information. "I wonder if that's what they have been waiting for. They have just been sitting there the last couple of days, refusing to engage, and I don't want to order an advance as we are really in our most defensible position where we are. Hmm. Callie. Can you scan eastwards, deeper into the Winter Hills?"

She nodded and the men encircled her again. She turned slowly then suddenly stopped, moving her head back and forth. She came to herself looking anxious. "There are troops moving into position just behind the hills."

"On horse or foot?" The Colonel's voice was clipped.

"On foot. They already extend beyond the end of our lines, but they are moving slowly."

"They are trying to flank us." He turned to the Major. "Logically, they will try and synchronise the attacks. Warn the captains that we can expect action on two fronts. They won't use the horses at night so we may well face a red dawn." He looked at Callie. "Thank you, Lady Callandra. I think I now understand why you warrant a Prince as a bodyguard." Callie just shook her head as the Colonel led them back towards the camp.

Jago's huge tent encompassed both his private quarters and a command room with a map-strewn table in the centre and chairs haphazardly around the side.

"Miles," he signalled to a lieutenant almost hidden behind a huge pile of paperwork, "will show you where you are billeted. I suggest you get some rest. I think a dawn attack most likely although we can't be sure." He turned away as they followed the junior officer out.

The young man cleared his throat nervously. "There are two tents free together near the other Mages, Highness, Lady Callandra. I know it's not what you must be used to but…"

"It will be fine." Callie gave him a sunny smile. "I was in warrior training before I became a Mage. Can you remember what those tents were like?"

He chuckled, relieved. "I certainly can. Over there." He pointed to a sturdy tent with two substantial rooms. "And the other one." He hesitated. "The thing is, Prince Mikheli never actually stayed here overnight so…"

"Why am I not surprised?" Jerran shook his head. "But I don't think six of us will fit in that tent. I think I'd prefer to share with

Lady Callandra." He paused and winked at Callie who glanced at her brother's outraged face before she burst out laughing. "And of course you, Raff." the Prince finished genially.

They ate round a campfire in the company of several other Mages who had extended a cautious but on the whole, positive welcome.

The commissary had produced a tasty stew and the bread was fresh. For a while Callie just listened as the Mages discussed what they had been doing. Most of them could deliver an explosion or what was, in effect, a lightning bolt, but not over any great distance and with only limited impact.

The realisation of how much greater her own Mage gift was, reduced Callie to introspective silence. She did not realise Terran had moved to sit next to her until he patted her arm. "Lady Callandra?" She started.

"Oh, Callie, please." He smiled.

"You are looking very anxious. Are you worried you might not be able to reach the enemy forces or the siege engines? Perhaps I can help?"

"No. It's not that at all." Callie studied the older Mage. His face was reddened by the cold but the deep lines beside his mount spoke of good humour. For someone with such a violent gift, he radiated steadiness and calm.

"I can reach the forces. I can destroy the siege engines – probably all of them." His eyebrows shot up at her matter-of-fact tone but he didn't speak. Callie stared into the fire. "You know what Jerran said. I really did destroy an entire army. It was destruction on a grand scale; so many lives lost. The thought of doing it again fills me with horror. It makes me feel sick." She glanced at Terran, who looked thoughtful. "I know we are at war – a war we didn't start, but I really wish there was another way." He rose to his feet.

"Let me sleep on that and Callie, you should too." He shoved her in the direction of her tent and she went not at all reluctantly. She picked her way past the cots set out for Raff and Jerran in the outer room – to her brother's evident disapproval – and prepared for sleep. It occurred to her as she shed her outer clothing that if first impressions counted she was going to get on well with Mage Terran. She seemed to have found herself a mentor after all. It eased, if only slightly, the worrying weight of her Mage gift.

It was not quite light when Raff woke her. "We are wanted in the command tent right away." She threw on her clothes, armed herself lightly and stepped outside where Jerran was stamping his feet to keep warm. Lamps and a small brazier made the Colonel's tent a puddle of light and warmth as the chilly camp stirred into life around them.

Mugs of hot spiced cider or tea were pressed into their hands as the Colonel beckoned them to the map table. There was an unmistakable air of urgency. He eyed Callie in a business-like manner. "Lady Callandra. Mage Terran suggests that you concentrate on the siege machines. At the moment they are beyond the range of our Battle Mages, but you just might reach them. He also has an idea for dealing with the flanking force, which he will explain later. Now communications can be a problem so I'll assign you messengers."

Callie held her hand up to stop him. "No need, Colonel. Raff will take care of that." Raff nodded, and the Colonel after a moment of bafflement simply nodded.

"I'll trust you know what you are doing. May the Goddess bless the day. Let's do it."

In the semi-darkness they dismounted at the slightly elevated position the Mages had chosen as their viewpoint. Raff, looking out onto mist and the last rags of the night could see nothing of the enemy lines. It was only when one of the Mages sent a flame shooting into the sky that he was finally able to make out the engines that were edging forward from the shadows of the sheltering forest. Callie stared into the darkness. Jerran had offered her the eyeglass he now used himself but she had no need of it.

"What do you think?" Terran appeared beside them. "That flare was put up by Crae, who has probably the farthest range of any of us. So we won't be able to do anything for a while yet; probably not until those monsters are close enough to wreak havoc on our troops."

Callie hesitated.

"If you need to wait?" Terran's voice was calm; unjudgmental.

"Oh. No." Callie smiled. "I was just thinking that when I burn them, I could send the fire on into the forest. That would sabotage an orderly approach by the Frystians. If that would help?" The men all stared at her.

"You think you can burn the soaking wet forest?"

"Well only if you want me to." She thought she heard Jerran chuckle quietly.

"Be my guest." The Colonel stepped to one side as Jerran signalled defence for Callie. He saw she was biting her lip. Minutes slipped by. Terran and the Colonel began to look disappointed but Jerran knew Callie had yet to begin. She was bracing herself for what was to come.

[Callie!] She started, eyes opening wide as he spoke in her mind. [Now would be a good time, Callie. I've got an assignation to keep with one of my brother's chambermaids, so if you could do the honours and get it over with, I'd hate to disappoint her.] The brief message was loaded with not so subtle innuendo. Callie grinned and squared her shoulders as she narrowed her focus and looked about her for a fire source to lessen the demands on her power.

She scooped flame and ember from half the campfires and moulded them with her mind then sent fire arcing across the soon-to-be battlefield. She pressed heat and flame against the two enormous trebuchets. They were draped in heavy wet cloths and hides that caused her not a moment's delay. When they were alight beyond saving, she moved to one side then the other, reaching for the Ballistae that could spear three or four men with every shot. These were more numerous than she had expected, but by the time she was sure she had them all, a line of fire a hundred yards wide, lit up the sky.

She took a breath and reached for the chilly breeze, ever present so close to the coast and drew it to her. Her hair swirled around her like flames as she channelled it, shaped and refined it and sent it forward to meet her fire. Then she pushed and a wall of flame surged into the trees. Clouds of steam rose into the sky then fire flickered along the forest boundary, first yellow then red then white hot as she unleashed her will. The forest was ablaze. The men beside her looked on in mute amazement as the ordered ranks of the Frystians descended into chaos. Men burst out of the woodland trampling over their comrades in their haste to avoid the inferno.

Colonel Jago studied the scene before him and turned to his staff officers. "Gentlemen, signal all ranks to advance immediately." He moved away followed by Raff.

Terran looked between the distant fires and the slender girl beside him and gently shook her arm. "Callie, Callie you can stop now." There was no sign that she had even heard him. He looked at Jerran anxiously. "We need to call her back before she loses herself to the elements. I have heard of this." Jerran stepped closer and prised her fingers away from the pendant she clutched so tightly. He held on to her hand and called into her mind. For a moment he was aware of wildness, wind and flame and a river of power, and then he found her, like the eye in the centre of the storm. With heavy sarcasm he suggested that she had impressed everyone quite enough and they were now getting shit scared so could she kindly stop it.

Callie came to, with a suddenness that amazed Terran. She met the Prince's gaze, her face alight with laughter, and chuckled wryly. "Well there's no need to be so rude about it." Then she swayed and both men reached to steady her. Terran pushed her down onto the nearest rock and unscrewed a flask. "What is it?" She eyed the offering doubtfully.

"Medre; a most reviving draught." She sipped and tasted honey on her tongue, and then felt fire in her stomach. She licked her lips.

"Well I guess that's breakfast taken care of. So what's next?"

"We need to—" She held up her hand for quiet.

[Callie!] Raff's voice was clear in her head. [The scouts report the flanking force has been sighted. It's moving in fast and it's larger than we thought.]

She relayed his message word for word. Terran gaped, thinking ruefully that around Callie he was losing the capacity to be surprised.

[Tell them we are on our way.]

Chapter 29

They cantered along the camp supply road until they reached the eastern end of the deployment. The sound of fighting, constant beside them. Jerran swore under his breath. The Frystians held the high ground here, and advancing rapidly they had already cleared the woodlands. The royal forces were being decimated. They leapt off their horses and ran to the nearest rocky outcrop that offered cover and visibility, and Callie's heart sank. The Frystians far outnumbered the Lithians. She racked her brains trying to think what to do. Jerran swore again, his face tight-lipped and bleak. "Unless we can stop them, we'll have the enemy behind us, and they will have an open road to Nilsport."

"Callie." Terran caught her shoulder. "I had an idea last night after we talked. Can you cast 'stun'?"

"Sorry, no." She looked chagrined.

"Right then. I can but you will have to lend me some of your power. Are you all right with that?" Callie hesitated, studying the Mage intently, then nodded.

"Just tell me what I have to do." Terran reached for her hand.

"Hold on to me and don't let go until I tell you, whatever happens. You'll need to drop your shields."

On a battlefield? Callie winced.

"Jerran." He turned to the Prince "Both our lives will be in your hands while we do this working." The Prince nodded and signalled his men to encircle the Mages, weapons drawn. "Ready?" Callie nodded and released her shields. First, she was aware of Terran's hand around hers; strong, calloused, warm, and then the brush of his mind on hers. It felt odd but not actually hostile. She tried to relax as he forged a link, reaching cautiously towards her core power. They joined and she vaguely heard him gasp before he steadied himself and turned his focus outwards. Entranced, she braced herself against the outward flow of her power and the temptation to slip into Terran's mind and waited.

Jerran's hazel eyes flickered back and forth as the two Mages settled to their work. The fighting had not slackened and at any moment they would be in the range of the Frystian archers. He'd no sooner had that thought then Alleyn, the youngest of his men spun round beside him clutching an arrow that now decorated his left arm. He slumped to the ground, pointing to a group of men who were running in their direction with clear purpose. As they ran they split again, half heading to where two Battle Mages were trying to clear a passage for the wounded.

"They are trying to take the Mages. Get ready." Jerran drew his dagger in his left hand and set himself in front of Callie as a giant of a man sprang round the rocks, raising an immense battle-axe above his head. The Prince dived to one side under the blow, rolling swiftly back to his feet and stabbing the Frystian in the side, before pivoting to gut the warrior who followed behind.

The Frystians were big men and Jerran realised that speed would be their only advantage. "Don't let them close with you!" he shouted, only to see Narry almost swallowed up in the embrace of a monster that seemed to be trying to rip him apart with his bare hands. He dared not turn away from the man in front of him who was edging ever closer to the Mages. Then Narry's opponent staggered and fell to one knee, hamstrung from behind by Alleyn who had lunged from where he lay. The man was down but still wielding a blade. Jerran leapt sideways, fielding blows from both Frystians so neither could turn on Alleyn, the sweat running into his eyes. His blade flashed back and forth seeking an opening until finally with a twist he slid the sword into one man's armpit and watched him measure his length on the rocky ground.

Looking about him he saw that for the moment they were clear of the fighting. Gilly tugged his sword free of the last Frystian and made his way to Alleyn's side, as the Prince once more stood guard.

Suddenly silence descended across the field, a startling contrast to the previous wild noise of battle. The fighting had stopped. The Frystians were falling like skittles, in ones, twos, groups and dozens, lying motionless where they fell. One or two of the King's men tumbled alongside them, losing their balance as resisting weapons fell from nerveless hands. "What the hell?" Gilly looked to the Prince who in turn eyed the Mages speculatively. Terran drew in a deep breath and released Callie's hand, looking about him with immense satisfaction. Callie took a stumbling step or two before she steadied herself and blinked at what she was seeing. Then her face lit up.

"Are they dead?" Jerran asked, quietly looking at the many, many fallen men.

"Not at all," Terran grinned, "they are just sleeping."

"Sleeping?" Jerran's jaw dropped.

"Terran that was brilliant." Callie hugged the older Mage who winked.

"Well I wasn't sure it would work – and I'm certain it has never been done on such a grand scale before; we have your power to thank for that."

"How long will it last?"

"Several hours at least, that's why it was a better choice than 'stun'. There will certainly be time enough to capture and restrain them, or… Actually what shall we do with them?" The Mage looked bemused.

"Jerran," Callie interrupted, finally realising that there were dead Frystian bodies all around them. "What happened here?"

"Oh, we had a bit of company, while you were busy. We'd better check on the other Mages as well. You were all distinctly targeted."

"I'll do that now." Terran moved away. Jerran nodded and turned to Callie.

"You'd better let the Colonel know the situation. I think I know how we can deal with these Frystians, but there are a few things I'll need to find and I won't leave you, so are you okay to come with me? Gilly needs to see to Alleyn and Narry." He pointed towards the battlefield. Callie, relating information back to Raff simply nodded and followed as the Prince picked his way between the bodies littering the hillside.

It was deeply unpleasant. The heavy weapons of the Frystians caused massive damage to frail human bodies and on more than one occasion Callie thanked the Heavens that she had not had time for a real breakfast or she would certainly have lost it. They finally found what Jerran was seeking at the very back of the enemy deployment. Three elaborately carved wooden poles, decorated and inlaid with semi-precious stones had been driven into the earth to overlook the fighting. One was a snow bear, the fur and claws still attached. Another was a wolf, its yellow eyes picked out in amber, and the third looked like a leopard seal.

Callie looked at them, fascinated. "So these are Clan Totems?" Jerran nodded.

"I learnt about them when I was with Snow Fox Clan."

"What do you plan to do with them?"

"I plan to end the fighting." He handed the Totems to his men and they made their way back to their mounts, through the strange landscape of the sleeping and the dead.

It was perhaps mid-afternoon when they wearily gathered again in the Colonel's tent, Callie having refused to attend any further meetings until she had been fed. She had expected to see Raff and was disappointed, but not surprised to hear he had gone to check on Alleyn and Narry in the surgeon's tent and had not yet returned.

Colonel Jago was looking very chipper and eyed them with a mixture of satisfaction and trepidation. Fighting on the main front had been fierce but disorganised on the part of the invaders who had lost cohesion with the forest fire and the destruction of the siege engines. When it became clear that the flanking force had also failed, the Frystians had broken off the engagement and retreated back beyond the burnt forest.

Having brought them up to date Colonel Jago turned his attention to Jerran. "Highness, I now have a battlefield full of sleeping enemies. I confess I have no idea what I'm to do with such a number of prisoners, but Mage Terran tells me you have a plan?"

The Prince nodded. "I think we need to let them go."

"What?" Major Durrant's voice seemed to have risen an octave. "Are you…? I mean…"

"Major." Callie lowered her head so no-one could see her smile. She knew 'that' voice. The 'royal' voice. "As the Colonel says, such a number of prisoners would create immense logistical problems. We are certainly not going to slaughter them, so we need a way to make sure they leave and do not return. Is that not so?"

"Indeed, Highness, but exactly how do you propose to do that?" The man was really struggling to keep sarcasm or scepticism out of his voice.

"I shall give them a choice between imprisonment or swearing oath on their clan totems that they will stop fighting. If they so swear, then they will be free to leave and they will have to leave." There was a long silence.

"You think swearing an oath on their clan totem would truly bind them?"

"I don't 'think it' I know it. Any warrior who broke such an oath would find himself 'sekur aettin', which means clanless; an outlaw. He would not survive long. It's a death sentence by another name."

"Then make it so," The Colonel looked thoughtful, "and it might be best if you yourself…"

"Yes, I agree." The Prince was ahead of him. "Seek out the Chiefs and senior warriors. You can identify them by their facial tattoos. Secure them and bring them forward so Terran can undo his spell casting. I'll go and clean up."

It did not take long to organise matters. The Colonel and his senior officers and several Battle Mages stood in a semi-circle facing the Frystian forces. Terran and Callie stood to one side and Raff, reappearing, took a place behind his sister. The Clan Chiefs, awake but securely bound stood silently watching as Terran twisted his spell casting. The clansmen across the battlefield woke. They were aware but unable to move. All eyes watched as the Prince appeared, and a gasp could be heard as the Frystians realised he held their clan totems.

Jerran cradled the poles in his arms as he approached the Clan Chiefs. He placed them carefully on the ground and laid his own sword across them, before addressing the men in their own language. The choice before the clan leaders was no choice at all, and they knew it. After very few words the leader of the Wolf Clan nodded and Jerran signalled for his bonds to be cut. He knelt, placing one hand on his clan totem and one hand on Jerran's sword and gave his oath. The Snow Bear Chief swiftly followed, and finally the Chief of the Leopard Seal Clan. Their words spoken, they picked up their totems and walked away.

Jerran, his armour partially concealed beneath a splendid velvet cloak, a thin gold filet on his head, stood silently. He radiated an authority and certainty that the Frystians obviously recognised. He had dealt with the enemy with courtesy and respect, although wounds had had received in the recent fighting had barely stopped bleeding.

It was sometimes easy, Raff reflected, to forget that this man was second in line to the throne. His competence was very impressive and thinking over what he had accomplished in that single day made Raff wonder what kind of a King he would have made, had he been Theon's first-born son.

Finally the Prince walked back to the ranks of the Senior Officers, who were watching as the northmen, released from Terran's control picked up their weapons and walked away without a backward glance. As Jerran approached, something in the way the Colonel's staff were all looking at him, made his face close up. To Callie it seemed that a space had grown up around the Prince, once again isolating and distancing him.

This Prince was a man she had grown to like and depend on. A man who had saved her life yet again. No. She wouldn't stand for it. She stepped forward, tugging at the cloak and catching his eye. "Well, are you going to take that poncy thing off now so we can go for a beer?"

Jerran's face cleared and he burst out laughing. "As you wish, Lady Callandra." He swirled the velvet. "Don't you like it? I found it at Mikheli's house. Only thing is, I'm not entirely sure whether it was his own or belonged to one of his lady friends." Callie chuckled as they walked back to the camp, with Raff and the Colonel's staff close behind.

Callie was halfway through her second beer when she nearly fell asleep in her bowl of stew. She could no longer keep her eyes open and Terran ordered her straight to bed. She didn't argue, which worried Jerran more than her obvious exhaustion. Terran saw his eyes following the young woman as she left the steamy mess tent. "Don't worry, Highness. I drew an incredible amount of power from Callie when I cast that sleep spell. Her energy levels are really low right now but she'll be fine by morning." The Prince relaxed slightly.

"You're sure?"

"Absolutely." Terran nodded. "So the only question is, which one of us should finish her beer? I really do hate waste."

As Jerran approached their tent some time later, it belatedly occurred to him that perhaps he should have found somewhere else to sleep. Raff had returned to Nilsport town with Colonel Jago, whose delight at the twins' instant communication was likely to keep that young man busy. He hesitated at the entrance, then decided that the rules of reputation could not really apply to a war zone and slipped inside.

He shed his armour as quietly as he could and collapsed with relief on his cot and drifted into sleep to the gentle awareness of someone breathing nearby. He slept peacefully for some time but he slept lightly. When the noises reached him, he had a hand on his dagger before he had even sat up, but a quick scan of the moonlit tent showed no intruders.

He padded across the floor and pulled aside the divider. Callie was tossing and turning, clutching her blanket with white-knuckled fingers. He stepped beside her cot and put a hand on her arm, shaking her gently. "Callie, Callie." She did not wake. In the dim light he saw horror and terror race across her face. She whimpered and even in her sleep he saw her bite her lip. Bite it so hard that blood beaded and ran down her chin.

He shook her harder, his voice louder. Nothing. He knelt and reached closer, putting his hands on either side of her face then sought the link to her mind. Darkness engulfed him and the sense of a vast malevolence. He recoiled and almost retched. Then he took a deep breath and pressed forward again until he felt the bright coppery spark that he identified as essentially Callie, and called to it.

It felt like trying to pluck a leaf from a raging torrent. He called again and again, with all his will. After minutes that felt like hours Callie shuddered and Jerran wrapped his arms around her shaking shoulders. She turned into the warmth of his chest, her breath still coming in gasps. He said nothing just held her until she calmed. "Gods above, Raff, what was that?" Her voice barely more than a whisper, trembled.

She was still shivering when she raised her head. Her eyes widened in confusion and she blinked, trying to understand how her brother had turned into Jerran. "Raff had to go back to Nilsport with Colonel Jago." The Prince kept his voice quiet and very, very neutral. "I apologise for intruding but you seemed to be having the mother of all nightmares." Callie stilled, so caught up in her memory that the inappropriate intimacy of their situation never crossed her mind. "What was it?"

"The heart of darkness." She muttered the words then repeated them louder. "The Heart of Darkness. Jerran I don't know what it means, but I know it's important." She took a deep breath, finally becoming aware of the warm shoulder she leant against and the flimsiness of the shift she wore. Jerran saw if in her eyes and gently moved back.

"Will you be alright now?"

"I think so." She managed an almost smile. "I'm sorry for disturbing you and thank you."

He nodded and caught himself on a yawn. "I'm next door if you need me." He slipped away back to his own bed and Callie settled down again. She was still tired but possibly too afraid to sleep.

Even after such a restless night it was still early when Callie reached the mess tent, so she was surprised and delighted to find her brother already there and tucking into a huge breakfast. Colonel Jago was worried about the behaviour of the Frystians and had come out early to meet with his field officers. Given the extent of their losses, followed by the withdrawal of three clans the previous day, he had anticipated that the Frystians would begin to retreat. That they were not, gave him further cause for concern. After his meeting he intended to wait until the scouts returned before heading back to Nilsport and he wanted Raff along.

They chatted quietly for some time, pleased to be without other company for once. Of course she told him about her nightmare and then couldn't decide if she was glad or sorry when he took it so seriously. She finally agreed to his suggestion that she consult Master Lauder about it when they returned to Derryn, unless Mage Terran could help. Mention of Terran reminded Callie that she had promised to go to the field hospital and check on Alleyn and Narry for Prince Jerran, and Raff was happy to show her the way.

The Aid Station was one of the few facilities within stone walls. What must once have been a farmhouse had been adapted to accommodate the injured until they could be taken back to Nilsport. It didn't take long to find Callie's escort. Alleyn was sitting beside a camp bed, pale and with a heavily bandaged arm, but obviously doing well. The same could not be said for Narry who lay unmoving on the cot.

Alleyn was in conversation with a tall grizzled man that Callie assumed to be one of the surgeons, until he turned slightly at her approach and she recognised with surprise that it was Mage Terran himself. "Callie. Hello," he greeted her in his usual genial manner, "and Raff." He extended his smile to include her brother. "I take it you are checking up on your men?" Callie nodded.

"How are things?" She looked between the two soldiers. Alleyn grimaced.

"I'm doing fine, milady. 'Tis nought but a flesh wound. Narry's not so good." He looked worriedly at his friend.

"Do they know what is wrong?"

"Beyond the cuts and bruises he has a chest wound and broken ribs. More than that we can't tell."

"He has internal bleeding. His lung has collapsed." It took her a moment to realise the voice was her brother's. He took in their startled expressions and flushed slightly. "I've seen it before. Remember Saffi?"

"Saffi?"

"One of our dogs. She impaled herself. Raff looked after her."

"Do you have the Healer Gift?" Terran asked softly.

"Me? No, of course not." Raff shook his head energetically. The old Mage studied the young man before him and raised an eyebrow, gesturing to Narry. Raff shrugged uneasily. "I just seem to know what's wrong."

"And yet you say you have no healing gift?" Callie, watching wide-eyed could tell her brother was, for some reason on the verge of panicking.

"I don't; I'm not… it's only with animals. I've never touched people."

Terran laughed softly. "Many healers first find their gift when dealing with animals, pets, livestock. Did you not know that?"

"Really? For my sister it was the other way round."

"So healing Magery is already in your family?"

"Well, yes. I suppose so." Raff sounded startled. Terran laid a firm hand on his shoulder.

"Raff, trust me. Healing gift is rare. If you have even the smallest amount of it, you may be able to help Narry. The lad is already beyond anything I can do. You can do him no harm. Why not just try? If it doesn't work none will fault you." He pushed Raff gently forward. Callie saw both fear and eagerness on her brother's face as he reached for Narry's hand lying limp and white on the blanket.

Alleyn, who had watched the whole scene play out in silence slipped out of the chair and Raff settled himself beside the cot. He glanced once more at the Mage and his sister then he set his mind and slowly extended his awareness into the warrior's body. Gliding from the peripheries that were relatively undamaged, he moved to the disaster area that was Narry's chest, exploring hesitantly and cautiously. As he had suspected, Narry's ribs were broken in several places and one had punctured a lung, which had collapsed and was nearly full of blood. He almost panicked then remembered the drills Callie had told him about, had complained to him constantly about when first she began to develop her Mage gift. Step by step. Step by step.

He imagined Narry's ribs sliding back into place, aligning themselves carefully, then willed them to be whole and strong. He visualised sealing the blood vessels that still pumped Narry's life away: largest to smallest. It was all happening in his mind and yet it felt like exhausting work. Work he was not used to or prepared for.

He felt his focus, his concentration fray and his will begin to falter even knowing that if he stopped now, he would not be strong enough to start again and it would all have been for nothing.

Then someone took his other hand. Callie! He would always know her touch. She offered him her power, a source so deep and rich and full that he marvelled. "I need a tube and a blade quickly." He ran his fingers over the young man's chest, until the tools were slipped into his hand. He plunged the lancet deep through layers of skin and muscle, sliding the tube through a second later. He envisaged the pooled blood moving slowly up the tube. Up and out, clearing the lung.

He was dimly aware of voices and swearing behind him but dare not let his attention lapse. It took time. Time he now owed entirely to Callie, but finally the lung was clear. He pulled the tube out, sealing layer upon layer of flesh behind it until it finally popped free. He drew back into himself, dizzy and weak until a shock of energy from his sister brought him back to his surroundings.

Callie crouched beside him, her face blank. Terran gave him a long look and gestured. He was absolutely covered in blood. "Raff, that was truly impressive. Next time a little warning perhaps?" Then he laughed.

"I'm so sorry." Raff stuttered an apology.

"Lad, I don't think you ever need to say sorry for saving someone's life." He pointed at Narry who, even as they watched, took a deep breath and wriggled into a more comfortable position.

"I'd better go and clean up." He walked away. Callie got to her feet and gave Raff a hand up.

Alleyn cleared his throat. "Sir? Thank you, sir. Narry and me. Well, we've been friends forever. We're from the same village. I'm so grateful. I didn't realise you were a Mage too." He turned back to his sleeping friend.

"Neither did I." Raff's voice was a whisper.

Chapter 30

When they stepped out of the Aid Station the winter sun was higher in the sky and a chill wind whipped at them, bringing a flush of colour to their cheeks. Callie pushed her brother down on to the bench beside the door and looked down at him thoughtfully. "How long have you known?"

"I didn't know. Not exactly. Not until just now." He gazed at his feet.

"Raff." There was a distinct warning tone in her voice.

"All right. Sometimes I wondered. You know, all the animals." Callie stopped to think. Raff was known to be really good with any creature he came across, and there had rarely been a time, as they grew up, when he hadn't been tending some poor injured beastie.

"But why didn't you say anything?" Callie persisted.

"I nearly did. Then your Mage gift emerged and you had to give up Battle School. I didn't want to disappoint Father and I honestly did enjoy Warcraft."

"Did? Past tense?" She sat down beside him but he still refused to meet her gaze.

"You know I was so pleased to be sent here with you on this trip." She nodded. "I was even more pleased when the Colonel insisted that I stay with him at Nilsport." He finally looked at her. "The battlefield made me feel so sick."

"It was pretty bad," she agreed. "I thought I was prepared, but some of the things I saw…"

"No." He interrupted "That's not it. I could feel so much pain from the injured, I thought I would pass out. I'm not at all sure I could go out there again." He looked ashamed, and Callie sat quietly for a moment rethinking the past hours.

"Raff, when you healed Narry you did it in the way I was taught. Focus and will and extending your consciousness, didn't you?"

"Yes." He nodded. "But I'm not used to it and my own power didn't last long. I wouldn't have managed if you hadn't helped me." She brushed that aside.

"When I melded my power with yours, Raff, I found it easy to do. I wasn't surprised because of our link as twins, but it was more than that I think. You don't have any shields do you?" He looked blank.

"Gods above, Raff, no wonder you nearly passed out. It's the first lesson we learn. Here, let me." She linked to her brother and used a thread of power to cocoon his fragile core. He gave a huge sigh of relief.

"Thank you. Whatever you just did, thank you." He arched his neck as if to throw off a headache. "So what do I do now? Father will be so upset."

"No, I really don't think he will. Remember he went against Grandfather's wishes when he chose to follow The Way of the Sword. You can't change what you are, Raff. You need to accept it."

"What, like you did?" She was almost pleased to hear the heavy sarcasm back in his voice. "Fair comment. I deserved that, but listen. Over the last few weeks I think I have finally found my own way. I may no longer be a simple warrior, but I am using my own unique skill set to carry on fighting and you will too." She measured the sun with a calculating eye. "Come on, big brother, we are due back at the Command Tent."

Jerran was pleased to hear the good news about Alleyn and Narry when they met up with him a short while later, but his was the only cheerful face. The scouts reporting back had confirmed that despite their depleted forces the Frystians showed no signs of withdrawing. On the contrary, there had been an air of expectancy about their camp that was slightly alarming. At the Colonel's request, Callie scanned the nearby area, looking for any signs of reinforcements but found nothing new. It was agreed that Raff would once again return to Nilsport with the Colonel while Callie remained at the forward camp with Jerran and the rest of her bodyguard in case hostilities resumed.

After a simple lunch Callie retreated to her tent, and after checking her weapons, curled up to try and catch up on her missing sleep. It seemed like minutes but was actually several hours later that she opened her eyes to find Jerran shaking her again. "What now?" Even as she spoke she became aware of Raff shouting her name [Raff.]

[At last! Callie, Nilsport is under attack.]

[What? How?]

[A huge fleet of ships has been sighted. Almost all the Mages are at the front line. The only forces here are the city militia.] Callie locked eyes with Jerran.

"Ships, heading for Nilsport. Where did they get ships?"

Jerran snapped his fingers. "The Ice-landers have a fleet on the North Sea. They must have sailed it right found the coast. If they make landfall Nilsport will be lost. How far away are they?"

[Raff?] She relayed the question.

[A quarter of a mile; maybe a half. They were hidden by mist. There is an on-shore breeze so they are coming in fast.] Callie cursed herself.

"I should have noticed. You don't get mist with an on-shore breeze. Someone has managed a minor weather working." Jerran paced the tent looking grim.

"There's no way we can get troops back to Nilsport in time and even if we could that would be an indication for the Frystlanders to attack." Callie thought hard.

"I need to get to the sea – now!" She was strapping on her armour as she spoke then they raced across to the Command Post. It didn't take long to pass the dire news on to Major Grinter the duty officer. A veteran he began re-ordering the troops before they could even leave the tent.

They wove a rapid path between the troop positions that guarded the sea-end of the battle line. Callie gave a sigh of relief when her boots finally skidded onto the mix of sand and pebble that edged the shores west of Nilsport. She scanned the horizon, her heart in her mouth, but was still too far away to see the enemy.

They loped along the foreshore beside the encroaching waves until rounding a promontory they stopped in shock. The sea was dotted with white sails: many, many of them, and they were speeding towards the land. "I think we just found what the Frystians have been waiting for." Callie quivered as fear ran through her veins then felt Jerran's hand on her back.

"Steady. Stop thinking 'fear', think 'mayhem'!" He winked. Callie squared her shoulders and settled to her task.

She liked working with water. It was already moving, flowing, and full of usable tensions and currents. She dropped her shields and let her mind drift into the brine, tasting it; learning it. The tide was coming in and she doubted that even her power could reverse such an essential, natural rhythm. She would have to try something else. She crouched where the water puddled and pooled beside the rocks and reached a hand forward circling it until the water swirled into a tiny whirlpool. Then she brought her will to bear on her creation, which grew and spread like ripples on a pond. She reached up into the stormy skies and felt for the sea breeze, twisting it with her will and directing it down to her whirlpool. She held the two constructs in her mind's eye then brought them together.

The sea began to boil and hiss as a huge maelstrom formed, spinning faster and faster even as it widened. Callie took a deep breath, reaching for her pendant, then pushed. The vortex sprang forward and raced down upon the hapless fleet. Ship after ship was caught up and sent hurtling on a mad and deadly helter-skelter ride, into the gaping maw at the heart of the whirlpool. Others were soon dead in the water as sails and rigging failed under the ferocious forces she had unleased.

The nearby arms men watched the annihilation of their enemies with shock and fascination. Jerran watched Callie. Then, at last he put his hand on her shoulder. [Enough.] He spoke into her mind and pulled her hand from the pendant into his. The wind died almost immediately and with a ghastly sucking sound, loud enough to reach the shore, the maelstrom filled and vanished, spitting a few last spars onto the boiling surf.

Callie's legs failed her, and she clung weakly to the Prince who scooped her up, dropping onto the nearest rocks and wrapping his cloak about them both. He pressed a flask into her shaking hands; more of Terran's medre, and she gulped gratefully, as he gently rubbed some warmth back into her arms. The sea still raged and churned, but only five of the huge ships were still afloat, and through his eyeglass Jerran could see that they were all badly damaged.

The jingle of harness behind them made Callie turn to peer over Jerran's shoulder. Gilly and Razz were just above the beach on horseback, leading Jessa and Warrior.

"If you are able we should probably still head for Nilsport."

Jerran set her on her feet and led the way to the waiting men. "Those last few ships will eventually come to land. I don't think they will be anything the militia can't handle but it's best to be sure."

Callie groaned but mounted up, following Gilly as they set off at a steady pace for the nearby town. [Raff.] She reached for her twin. [I've taken out…]

[We saw. That was unbelievable. The Colonel says to say thank you – you have saved the town. Where are you now?]

[On the Nilsport coast road. Jerran thought we should still come; in case they have anything else up their sleeves?]

[Then I'll see you soon. We are heading out right now with the militia. Take care.] He broke the connection and Callie turned her attention to Jessa. The route they had taken was not the main road to Nilsport, but a rougher track that ran right beside the beach, following the contours of the rocky coastline. They hacked gently until rounding a final cove they could see Nilsport ahead in the distance.

As the path dropped briefly below the sandstone cliffs, there was a sudden clatter of tumbling pebbles and shale. For a moment Callie thought they must be caught up in a landslide, then a heavy body slammed into her from above, knocking her from her horse to land breathless on the gorse and heather covered bank beside the trail.

She lay stunned then struggled frantically. She was pinned beneath a gigantic Frystian warrior who grabbed her hair with one hand, then slammed her head back into the ground, twisting his grip to bare her throat for a killing stroke from the huge axe he held above her. She blinked away stars and struggled again, desperately, hopelessly. The warrior moved not an inch and her efforts only seemed to amuse and even excite him. The axe glittered in the winter sun and Callie took what she thought might be her last breath only to see the Frystian's eyes roll backwards. He dropped her head again and his own fell down onto her, dribbling blood from his mouth and from the exit wound of Jerran's sword that now pierced his heart and nestled against her own armour.

The Prince looked Callie over, his sparkling hazel eyes battle bright and concerned, then seeing no obvious injuries he tugged his blade free to whirl back into the fray that continued behind them. By the time Callie had heaved her assailant to one side, the ambush was over and eight north-men lay dead beside the path; giants every one. She rose unsteadily to her feet, feeling a lump on the back of her head that stained her fingers red. She watched Gilly and Cormac calmly dragging bodies off the trail while Razz coaxed Jessa back towards them. Jerran stood nearby, eyes darting back and forth before he finally wiped his sword on a tussock of grass and walked over to her.

"Looks like they had an advance party in place. There may be others." He patted his horse and Callie took Jessa's reins from Razz with a murmur of thanks, leaning against the mare until her legs stopped shaking.

"Do you think they were after us?"

The Prince considered for a moment then shook his head. "I doubt it. It was random chance that we came this way right now. I expect they were meant to join up with the forces on the ships, or protect them as they landed." He eyed her thoughtfully for a moment. "It might be worth finding you some sort of uniform though."

"Uniform? Why?"

"Travelling with a military escort but wearing civilian clothes marks you out as someone important."

"Says the Prince of the Realm." She flicked an eyebrow as he grinned. "Do I look really important to you right now?" He looked her over. She had blood on her face and in her hair that tumbled down about her shoulders. Blood also patterned her armour across her torso. Her loose trousers were slightly torn and encrusted with mud and salt water. Oddly enough, he thought, she looked superb; gory certainly but superb. Callie flushed at his long assessing stare and mounted up looking uncomfortable. Jerran cursed himself for a fool as she turned away and nudged her horse forward; her expression guarded. After a moment there was a whisper in her head. [Okay, maybe it's not about you looking important – but. I admit it. I just love women in uniform.]

In spite of herself Callie's lips twitched before she uttered a deep groan. The man was such an idiot. She edged Jessa close to Warrior and thumped him.

Chapter 31

Reaching Nilsport was rather an anti-climax. The militia, supplemented by the off-duty troops in the town had been more than enough to deal with the terrified, injured and demoralised Ice-landers who had finally made it ashore. The Mayor had been concerned at the number of prisoners he had had to accommodate but the horror of Callie's maelstrom had impressed on many of them, that they were lucky to be alive, and they gave very little trouble.

Colonel Jago had left them a message expressing his gratitude and making clear that nothing more was required of them. He also invited them to dine with him later in the mess. Callie was delighted to discover that rooms had been arranged for them at The Mermaid, an inn practically next door to the barracks, which actually had a bathhouse at the back.

They left their horses in the military stables and Callie took some time brushing and grooming Jessa, grateful for the mare's steadiness over the last difficult week. Jerran's horse had been left to the stable hands as the Colonel's staff officer had messages for him from Derryn and the King. Callie assumed the Prince would be staying at the mansion Mikheli had requisitioned, but expected he would turn up for the Colonel's dinner. That thought made her realise how quickly she had got used to having him around; not something she would have put money on just a few weeks earlier.

Her own room when she finally found it, was warm and spacious with a large soft bed, and a little later, clean and dry with the prospect of a decent meal and a good night's sleep ahead, she finally began to relax.

Nilsport had been a garrison town for years, with a large contingent of permanent troops, and the facilities reflected that situation. The main mess hall used by ordinary militia and troops on attachment was almost full. Callie waved to Gilly and Razz as she made her way through, to the anteroom at one side where the senior officers ate.

There were about a dozen people within, most of whom, to her relief she recognised. Shouted congratulations and compliments filled the air at her arrival, making her blush, and keep her eyes firmly down on the glass of crisp white wine a servant had put in her hand.

As other conversations resumed, she finally looked about her. She was not, as she had at first thought, the only woman present; there were three others. Two, she recognised as Mages, were talking to Terran, whose booming laugh made her grin and the Colonel himself introduced her to the third. "Lady Callandra please be known to Major Lessep, the head of the Nilsport militia. She has been very keen to meet you."

Callie shook the firm hand that was offered. Major Lessep was a tallish wiry woman with short greying hair but bright eyes. She thanked Callie sincerely for saving Nilsport from the Ice-lander fleet but when Callie, embarrassed, tried to brush it off, she was stopped with a raised finger. "Lady Callandra, don't undervalue what you did. We may have been able to hold off the Ice-landers long enough for troops to return from the front. I say 'may' advisedly but even if we had, it would have been with great loss of life. You need to let people thank you."

Callie flushed; it almost felt like being told off by her mother. "The thing is," she blurted out, "it's just random chance that it's me – that I have all this power."

Major Lessep smiled at her sympathetically. "I understand what you are saying, Callandra, and in one way, yes that is true, but it isn't random chance that you are here right now. Here on a battlefield, before, as I understand it, you have even finished at the Academy – is it?"

There was a long pause. "Well…" Callie acknowledged at last. "If you put it like that."

"I do." The major nodded. "Now the Colonel is signalling for dinner to begin."

Callie's seat at the long table was a couple of places to the left of the Colonel, facing Raff who in turn sat beside Terran. The place to his right was empty and the charming staff officer beside her explained that Prince Jerran was expected but had been held up. In fact, the first course had been cleared and their glasses refilled before the Prince finally appeared. He offered brief apologies to the company and took his seat beside the Colonel looking more than a little preoccupied.

Raff raised an eyebrow at his sister questioningly but she gave the faintest shake of her head. She had no idea what, if anything, was wrong and was wondering if it was even her place to ask when the door opened again to admit one of the Colonel's aides who passed the commander a folded message. Jago read it swiftly and smiled, giving a brief direction to the messenger, and then he tapped a fork against this glass, waving the piece of paper. "Ladies and gentlemen, I have good news. The Frystians and the Ice-landers are withdrawing entirely. The war is over."

Cheers rang round the table, echoed a minute late by a roar from the main mess hall. The Colonel rose to his feet. "I toast you all and thank you for the valour you have shown and the blood you have shed in defence of Lithia."

They all drank, and as the Colonel resumed his seat Jerran remained standing. "On behalf of my father King Theon I too must thank you all. May I also offer the toast to the fallen." He turned to one side, spilling a drop of wine that fell like a bloodstain on the floor.

"The fallen."

The moment of respect was genuine but brief as the heavy weight of war slipped away and relief and good cheer filled the room.

It was a convivial evening. Plans were loosely put in place for the following days, if events unfolded as expected. The Colonel's scouts were tracking the retreating enemy but there seemed little doubt that the withdrawal was real. For the first time in days Callie turned her thoughts homeward. It would be good to see her friends and sit at the back table in the Broken Arrow with nothing more expected of her than a homework assignment.

She found she wanted to talk to her father. So much of what he had taught her and shown her had become real on the battlefields. Raff needed to talk to him too, and she had agreed to go with her brother to the Academy. Raff would need very specific training in healing magic in view of his age and the level of power he had already demonstrated despite his lack of crucial basic skills.

She had been a little shocked and surprised to discover how wary he was of Magery in general, thinking he should have become used to it living with her and indeed their older sister. Although her own efforts to reassure him seemed to have made little headway, from what she could overhear, his conversation with Terran sounded much more optimistic. She was really pleased that the veteran battlemage would be returning to Derryn with them. He felt like someone she had always known and hoped he was someone she always would know.

As Raff had also taken one of the reserved rooms at The Mermaid Inn, at the end of the evening they walked the hundred yards or so together, strolling despite the cold; warmed by good food and quite a lot of wine. Raff finally turned to his sister. "So what's up with Jerran?" Callie looked blank.

"Damn, I forgot to ask, then when I remembered he had already gone."

Her brother gave her a look. "What?"

"He looked worried." Callie thought back. Yes, that was true, although he had maintained a perfectly civil table conversation about nothing of importance. Actually, that wasn't a good sign either.

Raff prodded again. "Someone should talk to him."

"So… why don't you?" She didn't know quite why she was being so contrary.

"Because Callie, you seem to be the closest thing that man has to a real friend."

"Honestly?" She took a moment to digest the truth in that idea and gave up trying to argue. Her brother would not let it go. "Fine. I'll talk to him the next time I see him."

Raff opened the door to the inn and Callie stepped through. It was late and only two tables still held drinkers. Two tables and one low settle beside the hearth. Jerran was sprawled in front of the fire, his shirt neck open and his hands cupping a very large brandy goblet. "I guess there's no time like the present." Raff eyed the Prince with concern. "I'll see you in the morning."

Callie sighed then walked across and dropped on to the settle beside Jerran, who glanced sideways at her, but didn't speak.

"Jerran."

"Callie."

"You left before I had a chance to ask what's wrong."

"Nothing's wrong."

"Nothing?"

"Nothing." He sipped his brandy in silence.

"Do you know, Jerran," Callie continued in a light conversational tone, "I have been exploring these mind-to-mind Mage links." He didn't speak but she knew he was listening. "I think I now understand how the ancient Mages could take information from another person's thoughts whether they were willing or not." She let a silence grow. "So I ask you again. What's wrong?"

"You wouldn't." His eyes met hers in surprise and shock.

"No. Of course I wouldn't, because we are friends and so you will tell me anyway."

A reluctant smile curved his mouth and he took a deep breath. "My father is sending me to Westerland."

"Oh. Why?" Callie stopped to think. Lithia had always had good relations with their south-westerly neighbour. "As an honour escort to Princess Serenna. She will be visiting Lithia for her formal betrothal to Mikheli."

"I see." She didn't although she spoke the words. Did Jerran have an interest there? "Are you not in favour of the betrothal?" She phrased the question as diplomatically as she could.

"No. Absolutely not."

"Because…?" Callie wasn't sure what if any answers she would get.

"Because Serenna really dislikes my brother." Not what she had been expecting. "You know Serenna?"

"Yes, quite well. She's kind, sweet, quite intelligent. She likes books and gardens." Callie tried to picture such a woman with the irascible and often arrogant crown prince. It was not a good fit. "She has to marry him? There's nothing to be done?"

He shook his head. "Both countries want a marriage alliance. I even offered to marry her myself when it was first proposed. She would have much preferred that, but I'm not the crown prince and her father wouldn't agree."

"You have feelings for her then?"

The Prince gave a wry smile, but shook his head. "Only as a friend. I know this has got to happen, but it's a disaster in the making. Mikheli can be – difficult. He has his good points but he and Serenna…" He brooded, glaring into the fire. "I shouldn't let it get me down; certainly not today when we really do have cause for celebration but this is going to make two people I care about unhappy and I hate it that there is nothing I can do." He swallowed more of his brandy. After a moment Callie put her hand on his arm.

"Jerran there is a lot you can do and will do. Serenna will weather it all much better just knowing she has you there as a friend; a friend with influence. If you can make Mikheli understand that you, in the most platonic way, care about Serenna, that must help too."

Jerran rubbed his hand across his forehead and sighed. "Do you really think so?" His glance sought reassurance and she nodded firmly. "I do hope you're right, Callie."

"I'm always right."

"Oh yes, I forgot briefly. Thank you for reminding me." She laughed.

"So you won't be heading back with us to Derryn?"

"No. I'm to go straight on from here. The embassy departed some time ago and is already on the way back. I'll meet up with them at Satine. I wasn't sure you would be going back to Derryn yourself."

Callie looked askance. "I thought you might split off at Vale and head back to Winters Keep." She shook her head.

"I certainly must go to Winters Keep but right now I really need to return to the Academy with Raff. We need to find him help and I think perhaps, I may need some too."

"So you might be there for a while?"

She nodded. "And strictly speaking I'm still a student at the Academy until midsummer."

Jerran looked startled. "I keep forgetting how young you are, Callie!"

"So quoth the Greybeard." She rolled her eyes at him.

"What do you plan to do after that?" She frowned, staring at the dying fire.

"I'm really not sure." Jerran hesitated, eyeing her speculatively.

"You know Liss thinks there's something badly wrong in the northlands, I mentioned it before. My father may send me there – or at least as far as the Barrens to endorse and finalise our agreement with the Snow Fox Clan. If he does, I hope to go further and find out for myself what's happening. So if you happen to be free at that time?" He let the offer hang in the air.

"Maybe." Callie grinned and got up. "I need some sleep and so do you."

Jerran rose to his feet beside her. "Callie, do I need to give this back to you now?" He held out his hand and the firelight flickered across a silver ring. She shook her head, noting that he actually made no move to hand it over.

"No, keep it. You don't know when you might urgently need an Elemental Mage and I like having a Prince at my beck and call." He laughed as she smiled up at him.

"Thanks for everything." They uttered the same words at the same moment.

The Prince put his arms round her and gave her a quick hug. "Goodnight." She headed up the stairs. Jerran watched her go then threw the last of his brandy on the dying fire.

Chapter 32

Callie and Raff didn't rush on the journey home. News of the Frystian defeat had already been sent to Derryn, thanks to the royal courier service, and they were weary. When they did finally reach the capital the twins went first to the barracks, where they found that they were requested and required to each write a report on their parts in the actions at Nilsport. Reports that would be presented at a further debriefing meeting. While Callie went through her personal mail, Raff went across to the Academy to explain his situation to the Dean who listened sympathetically and took it upon himself to make necessary further arrangements for Raff's retraining. Both matters underway they retrieved their horses once more and headed back into the city to the family house where they found both of their parents waiting for them.

They were enveloped in warm hugs that spoke of relief at their safe return as much as deep affection. Esma, aware that her son held her a little longer than usual, tipped his face up and met his grey eyes. "Are you alright, my sweet?" Raff gave a lopsided smile.

"I think so. I'm just really glad to see you; to see you both. You know I am really tired of being an adult. It's not what it's cracked up to be."

"The beginning of wisdom, my boy." The General winked. "Now go and do what you need so we can sit down to dinner at a good hour."

They did. The evening meal was a simple one and private, General D'Arcourt dismissing the servants so Callie and Raff could talk freely. Although dinner started quite early it was very late before they headed for bed. Walking up the stairs yawning, Callie found herself thinking, not for the first time, how lucky she was in her parents. Her father's astute questioning made her remember and consider details and observations she hadn't even been aware of making in the turmoil of the battlefield.

Raff had nervously told his own tale. It was soon obvious, even to him, that his father was fascinated rather than disappointed at the new direction his son was about to take. During the telling, Callie caught a pointed exchange of looks between her mother and father and demanded to know what lay behind it. It was her mother who explained.

Apparently when Callie's late, but strong Mage gift had emerged the General had suggested they get Raff retested by the Academy, finding it hard to believe that only one of a pair of twins would be gifted. Esma had dismissed the idea. In her defence she had felt sure that Raff would speak out if he noticed any developments. She was utterly mortified that she had been so wrong and offered to go with him back to the Academy to explore study possibilities; a suggestion that Callie and her father found hysterically funny, but Esma took some convincing that her son, even though he had just returned from a war, might manage to talk to the Academy staff without his mother holding his hand. It was a good evening and Callie was still counting her blessings as she fell asleep.

They stayed at home the next day. After writing their reports, Callie needed to go shopping having discovered just how hard winter warfare could be on her wardrobe. She was startled to find she had considerably more funds at her disposal than she had thought and belatedly grasped that fighting the king's wars had been quite profitable for her. Sharing the news with Raff he too found his accounts were looking healthy. Privately he was relieved as he would need many new study books and equipment when he transferred to the Healer School, and was painfully aware his parents had already funded his warrior training.

The debriefing meeting the day after that, had apparently started early, but Raff and Callie were left to kick their heels in the outer-chambers for quite a while before they were called in. It felt strange to be facing their father as members of his fighting force and Raff wondered what, if anything, they could add to the information they had shared with him the previous night, but there were several other military men present who wanted to pose their own questions to eyewitnesses, which made sense. They were finally dismissed just before lunch, a quick meal in Raff's case as he was scheduled to meet Master Elton, the Senior Healer, for some sort of assessment and discussion.

Callie found herself free and paid a leisurely visit to Jessa before returning to her Academy room. Flinging herself on her bed she was considering which of Master Lauder's books to pick up next when she dozed off. At first her dreams were the usual disjointed nonsense, then she found herself flying – hurtling over snow-covered fields and frozen rivers. A change of direction and she was looking down from the peaks of high mountains. At first the land was mottled green and white; vegetation peeping through snowfall, but in the distance was a darkness, a pooling of black and purple shadows. As she watched the shadows spread forming tainted patches that moved over the land, all linked back to a single point of origin.

There was a feeling of old, old power and once again that roiling malevolent will. This time she felt a sense of searching, seeking directed towards the west. She tried to turn but could not. She tried to look away, but could not. Panic surged through her paralysed body then there was a thunderous noise and her eyes opened wide. She lay still for a moment, disorientated and terrified; her heart thumping.

"Callie, are you there? Halloo." Someone was hammering at her door.

She rolled off the bed and snapped the door open. Chloe and Leon stood outside. "You're…" She flung herself into Leon's arms, shaking, "back." He looked startled but held her tightly.

"Callie, what's happened?"

"Nightmare."

He stroked her hair while Chloe fetched her some water. "Must have been bad. You're as white as a sheet." He led her back to her bed, and Callie finally released her death-grip.

"Goddess," she looked at her friends, "that was perfect timing; I couldn't wake up."

"You, my friend, have obviously been under far too much stress." He held up a finger to block any argument she cared to make. "So it's a good thing we have come to take you to The Broken Arrow. We want to hear all about your adventures."

"If only half of what's being said is true, it must have been amazing. Did you really kill two entire Frystian clans?" Leon looked suitably awed.

"And I want to hear all about the Prince. Did you throw yourself at him? Did he try and seduce you?" Chloe's eyes twinkled and Callie found herself grinning as she grabbed her cloak.

"So, Mighty Mage," Leon continued his questions as they ambled towards the town.

"The Frystians... tell all?"

"I didn't kill two entire clans, but I did help put three clans to sleep."

"You put them to sleep? Why? Were they tired?" Chloe looked entirely confused.

"Who knows? I just couldn't face all that death. It worked."

"That's amazing." Leon pondered for a moment.

"And as for the Prince, sorry Chloe. He didn't try to seduce me and the two times I did fall at his feet, I was unconscious, so of course I can't remember if he did have his wicked way with me."

The light-hearted chattering and banter continued as they walked down the street and by the time they reached The Broken Arrow, Callie felt almost normal again. Raff and others of their friends were already ensconced at their table at the back of the room, and Callie dropped on to the bench beside her brother as Leon went to get their drinks.

Raff seemed to be in genuinely high spirits. Master Elton had greeted him with open arms, making light of his deficiencies and much of his talent. He had then worked out a personal programme for him that would allow Raff a very high level of practical work, appropriate to his age. Callie was happy for her brother. He seemed totally contented in a way she realised she had not seen in a long time; as if he had just come fully alive. She was staring into her beer mulling this over when Chloe nudged her and started waving. "Look Callie, over there, it's Rhys. Rhys, over here." Raff and Callie exchanged glances. So the Prince was back already.

The new arrival shed his cloak and headed in their direction, signalling for one of the barmaids. "Chloe, how nice to see you again. Raff, Callie." He nodded genially towards the rest of the table. "How are things?"

"We're good. Have you been away as well?" Chloe smiled at him. "Raff and Callie have just got back. They were at Nilsport with your cousin."

"Actually, yes, I have been away… on family business."

"Oh right. So what does your family do?" Leon asked.

"Land management and development," Jerran answered shortly, and Raff nearly choked on his drink. "But from what I hear Raff and Callie have had a much more exciting time."

"Oh. Information at last. Do you actually know what they did? It's like getting blood from a stone trying to get them to tell us. I heard that Callie sank some ships. Is that true?"

"Totally true and not just some ships, almost the whole Ice-lander fleet."

"Goddess." Expressions of amazement ran like wildfire up and down the table while Callie reddened.

"What else did you want to know?" The prince was obviously enjoying himself.

Chloe leant closer and lowered her voice. "I wanted to know if Prince Jerran tried to seduce her – you know he has such a reputation with the ladies."

"Chloe." Callie, outraged, tried to silence her friend but to no avail.

"Oh come on, Callie. He's very good looking. Weren't you even tempted? We all want to know."

"Yes we do." Jerran echoed Chloe's words struggling to keep his voice steady, while Callie again flushed scarlet and glared daggers at the Prince.

"I was not tempted. Not at all."

"Callie says the only time she was close to the Prince she was unconscious, so she couldn't remember if he had his wicked way with her or not. What do you make of that?" Chloe giggled.

There was a long silence; surely long enough Callie thought, for the ground to open up and swallow her. She had never been so mortified in her life and Raff nearly shaking with laughter beside her, really didn't help. Finally, the Prince spoke. "Chloe, I think Callie's virtue is probably intact. As I hear it, if the Prince had had his wicked way with her she would most definitely have remembered." The table erupted in peals of laughter.

Jerran finally looked in her direction and offered the tiniest wink, then taking pity on her turned the conversation by asking if they had all heard the news that there was to be a Winter Light Ball, to celebrate both the end of the Nilsport incursion and the formal betrothal of Prince Mikheli. The news was met with universal cheering and took the discussion in a different direction. For that at least, Callie was grateful.

Chapter 33

It was cold and grey the next morning and Callie's turn to wait, perched on the stone window sill, outside the Dean's office. She was due to see Master Lauder and the Dean once they had finished with her brother.

When the door finally opened Master Elton stepped out, closely followed by Raff who nodded at her as they turned away. Master Lauder, with his hand on the door was still finishing his conversation with the Dean, when Raff stopped and called back to his sister.

"Callie, don't forget to ask about that dream and the Heart of Darkness." He pointed a finger at her and turned again only to walk straight into Master Elton's back. The Mage had stopped dead in his tracks and so too had the Dean and Master Lauder. There was an ominous silence, and then Master Lauder walked slowly towards her.

"Did you say The Heart of Darkness?"

Raff reappeared beside his sister. "Yes."

"Callandra. Please tell me this is just something you have come across in your recent reading." It seemed like all three masters were waiting for her answer with varying degrees of alarm.

Callie hesitated. "She's had a nightmare about it," Raff chipped in.

"A nightmare?" the Dean asked quietly.

"Nightmares, actually. I had another one yesterday."

The Mages exchanged glances and walked slowly back into the Dean's office beckoning the twins to follow. "I think you had better tell us all about it, Callie." Master Lauder pushed her gently into a chair.

She shrugged. "It was only a dream."

Dean Skyro looked at her sympathetically. "Let us hope so."

It didn't take that long to tell them what she had seen and what she had felt. Callie didn't realise she was actually shaking until Raff put a hand on her shoulder. When she finally stopped speaking, the Mages looked undeniably serious. Dean Skyros opened a corner cupboard beside his bookshelves and produced a large black bottle and five glasses which he filled to the brim. Callie found it ironic that this gesture of kindness worried her far more than anything else had.

"So. What is it? The Heart of Darkness," Raff finally asked. The Dean paused to gather his thoughts.

"It's part of our history, Raff – a very dark part." He waved to Master Lauder to continue.

"During the time of the Arch Mages there was a lot of contact between the 'benign' races. Many wonderful things were crafted – talismans, crystals, amulets all imbued with magics and created when humans, elves and dwarves blended their talents. Since the sundering there have been no more made, as many of the original techniques were lost, but some of the artefacts themselves survived. Among many lesser creations, three great pieces were fashioned, called the Triquetrae. Have you heard of them?"

Raff shook his head but Callie nodded. "Liss told me a little. He knew about them."

"He would; considering what they cost his people." He continued, "They had various innate qualities but more than anything else, they magnified magical power. They were much treasured. Oddly enough a Mage had to be very powerful already, before he or she was able to activate such a jewel.

"The Arch-Mage Grevis used the first Triquetra to defeat the orc and goblin armies at the battle of Ostland, where he died. That Triquetra was destroyed in his final strike." Raff and Callie nodded;

this was a story they knew.

"The second Triquetra came into the possession of Serpin the Black Sorcerer. He used it to launch a reign of terror, the Dark Ages. He enslaved thousands, turning them into bloodthirsty savages, without will or conscience. They lived to obey his commands and the atrocities they committed in his name were vile beyond belief. To create his mindless hordes, he devised a magical ritual. It was blood magic combined with his own power and the power of the Triquetra. The ritual was called 'The Heart of Darkness'.

"Eventually the Arch-Mages prevailed. They managed to defeat him, although most died in the attempt. They destroyed the second Triquetra. The third disappeared and records note that it was broken up. It was understood that all knowledge of the Rite itself was removed from any record or scroll anywhere."

Callie slowly reached for her pendant and let it drop outside her shirt. "You don't think this could possibly be…?" She passed it to Dean Skyros who studied it thoughtfully, but it was Master Lauder who spoke.

"When you showed it to me, Callie, many possibilities occurred to me – even this one, but only as the faintest of chances. In those times there were many similar objects created, of lesser pedigree and far less power but I'll admit I find your dreaming very disturbing."

"We should test it." Master Elton now held the pendant and looked at his colleagues.

"How?" Raff queried, looking at his anxious sister. Master Elton passed the pendant to Master Lauder and moved a candle in front of him.

"Andre can you use the smallest amount of power to create the tiniest flame, and then pick up the pendant?"

Master Lauder looked at the candle. A second later a minute flame blossomed on the wick. Then he picked up the pendant. There was no change. "Hmm. Dean?"

The Faculty Master repeated the experiment with the same result. "Now you, Callie. Do not draw on your elemental gift. Just light the candle the way you would have before that power emerged." She nodded, observing peripherally that all three Mages had stepped back.

Her tiny flame bobbed on the candlewick, then firmly reining in her elemental power she reached for the pendant. The moment it touched her hand the flame roared upwards in a white-hot column that began to discolour the ceiling. She was so startled she dropped the pendant, which fell to the floor. As it did so the flame shrank and Master Elton extinguished the last spark guttering in a puddle of wax; all that remained of the candle.

No-one spoke for a moment or two, then Master Lauder leaned forward quite calmly for a man who had nearly lost his eyebrows. "Now Callie, are you sure you were not using elemental magic just then?" Callie shook her head. She was rattled but certain.

"No. It's hard to explain but it's like I keep that power in a different place. I have to consciously access it and I didn't." She picked up the pendant. "Look, if there's the slightest chance this may be the third Triquetra you'd better have it." She tried to pass it to the old Mage but he put up a hand to stop her.

"Callie, I couldn't use it. I'm not powerful enough." He waved a hand at his colleagues. "We, none of us are. We are neither powerful enough to use it nor to protect it, if that becomes necessary. I'm afraid, my dear, that it is going to be down to you."

He gazed at the scorched ceiling deep in thought. "I have some very old sources in my personal library that I will consult. In the meantime Callie, take great care of it and avoid using it unless you are in a life or death situation; and I mean that exactly as it sounds. I'll send for you in a couple of days and until then…" Dean Skyros cleared his throat. "Until then, Callandra, keep your fighting skills up and your friends close."

Master Elton opened the study door once more, resting a hand on her shoulder as he went past. "Try not to worry, Callie, until we know there is something to worry about, and if you can't get any untroubled sleep come and see me."

Chapter 34

Callie struggled through the next couple of days. She had attended one of her magecraft classes only to find the other students were all working simple spells using power levels a fraction of her own. Both she and the teacher realised it was no longer appropriate for her, no longer relevant, and she was given permission to withdraw, which was a relief in one way but also left her feeling displaced and isolated.

Another unsettling factor was Raff. He had always been nearby and now that was no longer the case, she found she actually missed him. He had embraced his Healer training whole-heartedly and when they did meet, could talk of little else, except possibly Melina, the healer trainee he had been paired with; a young woman who was, according to Raff, in every way perfect.

A vigorous sparring session under the watchful eyes of Weapons Master Vigo had done little to raise her spirits. He had taught her several new, unarmed combat moves after she had confessed her helplessness during the Frystian ambush on the Nilsport coast road, but practising them had increased her bruises rather than her confidence.

All in all she was in a fairly low mood when she headed back to her Academy room. Picking up the notes and messages from her student pigeonhole she was intrigued to see a thick cream envelope, ornately addressed to her, but less than thrilled when she opened it. She was invited to the Winters Light Ball at court. "Invited," Callie groaned inwardly. A court invitation was a command by any other name, and as her parents would both automatically attend, there was no way she could think of to avoid it.

When the court held a major function, such as the Solstice Ball, a secondary celebration was always arranged for the Academy students, and that was where she had hoped to be. Perhaps she could put in a brief appearance then escape? A slip of paper was attached to the back of the envelope in her father's handwriting. "Callie my dear I'm afraid you really must attend. The King wishes to meet you. All love. F." She sighed – he knew her too well. She decided she might as well head back to the town house. She would need to make sure she had something fit to wear.

The Winters Light Festival really marked the winter solstice; the turn of the year when the hours of daylight began to grow longer than the hours of darkness. It was marked by families coming together to exchange gifts, and many private parties. The one thing they all had in common was the 'Midnight Light'. Shortly before midnight, all the candles, lamps, torches and fires were extinguished and when the hour struck they were relit to much celebration. It was traditional to steal kisses or an embrace in the darkness, and some of the younger girls laid careful plans to make sure they were near someone they liked at that time. Although the 'darkness' was only meant to last a minute or two, it had been known to last considerably longer at the Academy Ball.

Raff, it turned out, had also been commanded to appear at court, and was no better pleased than his sister, having made plans of his own involving Melina. Callie had no doubt that he would disappear at the earliest moment possible. It would be harder for her to do so, as she had had a higher profile at Nilsport, and was much more recognised. Neither did she wish to embarrass her parents. Her mother had insisted on taking her shopping after an examination of the contents of her wardrobe had proved unsatisfactory, and the obvious pleasure Lady D'Arcourt displayed anticipating the event made Callie bite her tongue and try, for once, to act the role of biddable daughter.

The gown Esme had finally bought her was really stunning. It was formal in style, but instead of the insipid pastel shades debutantes and young women were expected to wear, it was a vivid kingfisher blue trimmed in bronze. As she dressed she speculated idly on who would be at court. The King, obviously. Mikheli with Princess Serenna. Jerran would likely be there but probably immersed in royal duties. The Senior Courtiers would be present and the Senior Mages, with high ranking members of the military, so nobody she actually wanted to talk to.

Her mind wondered as Sara, Esme's maid arranged her hair, and flew north.

She thought about Liss for the first time in days. Was he still in the Barrens or already heading back to Derryn? Perhaps he had stayed at Winters Keep with Lord Dexter. Thinking of him and their last encounter brought a smile to her face. She wondered how he and his brother celebrated Winter Light in their fierce northern castle. Perhaps he was in the watch tower, looking up towards Spring River and brooding over the Frystians. And then she knew he wasn't. Staring at the mirror on her dressing table she saw a picture take shape. Riding his grey stallion Chalin, she saw Dexter stop briefly to be identified by the guards at the huge entrance gates of Barnard's Castle. His brother rode behind him, turning to smile at another companion whose hood had slipped back from silver-white hair. Liss.

"Milady, milady are you alright?" Sarah was chafing her hands and looking very anxious.

"Sara, I'm fine. Why shouldn't I be?" She met the maid's alarmed eyes, puzzled.

"You were quite gone there for a minute, milady. I called but you didn't seem to hear me. I nearly went to get your mother. Did you have a dizzy spell?" Callie laughed.

"No I didn't, Sara – it's something to do with my Mage gift."

"Oh, magic!" Sara sniffed. "Well, if you're sure. Perhaps you shouldn't go out tonight after all. I know you don't want to."

"Really, it will be fine. Raff and I have planned our escape but don't tell Mother." Sara smiled and dusted an invisible speck from Callie's white shoulders.

"As if I would. There now, I've finished with you and you are looking really very lovely."

Callie stepped over to the long mirror. Her burnished copper hair was curled and pinned on top of her head, just one ringlet tumbling down beside her delicate heart-shaped face. Her blue eyes were as vivid as her dress and sparkled beneath long dark lashes. The woman in the mirror looked stunning; Callie saw her as a stranger.

*

The Winters Light Ball did not have an early start, as it had to run past the Midnight Light rituals and the D'Arcourt carriage arrived at court about half a mark past nine. They waited in the antechamber with many other guests until they were announced and entered the State Ballroom, which had been beautifully decorated with winter greenery. The air was scented with pine and cedar and bowls of the white ice-lilies glowed here and there.

At the top of the chamber on the semi-circular dais the King sat nodding to his guests, both his sons standing behind him. Prince Mikheli was slightly behind another seat, occupied by an attractive young woman whom Callie assumed must be the Princess Serenna.

The first part of the evening was given to mingling and light social chat. Callie stayed by her mother knowing she would be called to meet the King. When her turn came, she offered him a deep graceful curtsey, eyes demurely on the ground. As she arose at his command she saw he was looking at her in a puzzled, bemused way from twinkling grey-brown eyes.

"My dear Lady Callandra, forgive me for staring but having heard the remarkable things you have achieved for Lithia in the last few weeks, I somehow had pictured you quite differently." Callie wasn't sure what to make of that, tilting her head and raising an errant eyebrow.

Jerran leant forward, eyes dancing. "I think Father was expecting bigger biceps – a broken nose and maybe a hairy chest."

The King backhanded his son across the arm but reluctantly smiled. Callie just burst out laughing. King Theon took her hand in his. "You are a lovely creature, my dear, and simply breath-taking when you smile." Callie blushed and bobbed a further curtsey. The King's face grew serious. "I do truly thank you, Callandra. You have saved lives; Lithian lives, and there's nothing I value more." He released her hand. "Now go and enjoy yourself."

Callie retreated gracefully, returning to her mother's side. The King had obviously limited the number of people to be presented because shortly afterwards he gave a signal for the dancing to begin. It was while she was sitting out, trying to cool down that Jerran approached her with Princess Serenna. Callie rose to her feet and curtseyed. "Serenna, may I introduce the Lady Callandra D'Arcourt."

The Princess had a smile plastered across her pretty face but looked tense and a little nervous. "Prince Jerran has told me some of your adventures, Callandra. You must be so brave."

Callie shook her head. "Mostly, Highness, I wasn't in any real danger. Prince Jerran and the rest of my bodyguards kept me safe. You are far braver than me. I can't imagine being a stranger in a strange land as you are." She waved her arm at their surroundings. Serenna gave the tiniest sigh, then shrugged.

"I've always known that this was going to happen and it could be very much worse. One of my brothers was married off to a Princess from the Summer Isles, who is considerably older than he is, and if I say she is plain, that would be putting it kindly." Callie giggled and after a moment Serenna joined in.

"Where's Prince Mikheli now?" Callie asked, looking around.

"He has gone to the card rooms." The young woman's face closed up, and her voice became expressionless. "He did not wish me to accompany him."

"That's good," Callie declared airily. "I'm sure you would prefer to dance anyway and there are some delightful officers here who are really talented."

The Princess hesitated. "I'm not sure if I should?" She looked towards Jerran questioningly but he grinned.

"If my idiot brother prefers cards to the company of such a lovely lady he'll have to face the consequences. May I have the pleasure, Serenna?" The Princess nodded, blushing slightly as he took her hand and led her on to the dance floor.

A moment later Callie was led out by one of her father's younger staff officers and it was several dances later before she managed to take a rest. She had completely lost track of time and was startled when Raff appeared beside her with an air of urgency. "Callie, it's not long till midnight. We really need to go."

Callie looked about her. Perfect. Neither of their parents was in sight. "Come on then, now."

They made a beeline for the nearest exit. Once through the huge doors the twins exchanged relieved glances, then Raff grabbed one of her hands. With the other she girded up her skirts and they started running along the corridor.

The Ball in the Mess Hall had a very different feel to it. The music was faster and louder than at the royal assembly and the tables, generously covered with food held as many beer tankards as wine glasses; many of which were empty.

Leon immediately whirled Callie onto the floor. She made no objection, having a mild fondness for her brother's friend. They had only completed one full circuit of the room when the great Palace clock began to boom out the Midnight Light. One by one all the candles and lamps were extinguished. In moments it was pitch black. There were shrieks and giggling throughout the hall. Callie felt people moving around her and jostled, dropped Leon's hands for a moment before he reached for her again. She felt his hand slide up her back to her neck and then his lips were pressed gently to her cheek, before he turned her head and kissed her lips lightly.

It was not the first kiss Callie had had from Leon but strangely it felt like it. She was aware of her stomach performing somersaults. Leon drew back a moment, and she sensed, it was far too dark to see, that he was also startled. Then he reached for her again, framing her face with his hands as he lowered his mouth to hers this time hard and demanding. Recklessly she pulled him closer as an aching pleasure awoke deep within her. Against hers, his body felt leaner and harder than she had remembered. She felt the wicked flicker of his tongue across her parting lips and was lost in the moment, wondering how a kiss could last forever and still not be long enough.

A first candle blossomed into life at the far side of the room, then another and another as couples disengaged themselves, turning to share hugs with other friends to a loudly shouted chorus of Winters Light wishes.

As the light grew Callie stared at the man in front of her in absolute shock. His hands dropped to her shoulders but no further, as if he simply didn't want to let her go. She found herself staring into hazel eyes, darkened by some strong emotion.

"I'm so glad we made it." Raff materialised beside her, with an arm around Melina.

"I can't say I was expecting to see you here… Rhys." He looked from Callie to Prince Jerran, who finally let his hands drop from her shoulders, his expression unreadable. Then before Callie could do anything, say anything, even think anything, he spun on his heels and walked out.

"What was that about?" Raff looked back at his sister. Callie touched her fingers to her swollen lips. Lips that still tingled. She took a deep breath then shook her head.

"I have absolutely no idea."

Chapter 35

Nobody was in a hurry to get up the next morning and when Callie read the note from Master Lauder requesting her presence she only made it by skipping breakfast. She must have looked exactly how she felt because the old Mage threw her an amused glance then poured her some coffee from the tray on his table. "Callie. Good morning. I see I have forgotten how hard you young people celebrate Winters Light. I should have asked you to come later." Callie grinned.

"I'm just glad you've called me at all, sir, if that means you have found something out."

"I have indeed – although it's not been easy." He shuffled the papers at one side of his desk until a piece of ancient vellum was on top. It had a diagram on it, hedged about with what must once have been notes – now sadly illegible.

"Is that a Triquetra?" she asked, turning the diagram towards her.

"It is." Master Lauder nodded.

"Well, it doesn't look like mine. Thank the Goddess for that." The Mage shook his head.

"Not so fast, Callie. May I?" He held out a hand and she passed him her pendant. He placed it on the drawing where it sat neatly in the central section.

"I don't understand."

"No, it took me a while." He picked her pendant up and turning it sideways held a small scrap of metal near it, which instantly attached itself. "It's magnetic?"

"Well it's iridium so it's only magnetic because it is bespelled. Under a magnifying lens, it is possible to see that two lobes were attached to it, but not now. And see here." He indicated the plain circle on the lower part of the pendant. "I believe there was once a stone there."

"What sort of stone?"

"Almost certainly an opal."

"An opal?"

"Yes – upala – precious stone, or Opallios to see a change of colour." He shook himself out of his academic reverie. "And now for a history lesson, Callandra. The Third Triquetra was ordered to be broken up by King Tavare IV. It has always been assumed that 'broken up' meant destroyed, but I now suspect we have misunderstood. During the King's reign there was constant warfare with Ostland. "The Marshall responsible for defending that border was Lord Geralt."

"That was my mother's family," Callie interrupted.

"That's right. His line held both the Border Keep and the Landermark title until about sixty years ago, when it passed elsewhere as there was no son to inherit. There are several references to Shalmis the citadel having 'inviolable power'."

"You think my part of the Triquetra was there?"

"This is all supposition, but it does make sense. Didn't you say it was your grandmother who gifted you the pendant?" Callie nodded. "And she was of that house. If I'm right, the Triquetra fell into disuse once Ostland had become a territory of city states presenting no real military threat and so over time the provenance of the pendant was lost." Callie struggled to take in the story that was unfolding before her.

"In that case, have you found out anything about the missing parts?"

"Nothing definite."

For a moment it looked as though he would say nothing more. "But there's something in your mind." Callie prodded gently. The old Mage studied her.

"Callie…"

"Sir. I need to know." She looked down at her hands. "Those nightmares were beyond terrifying. I felt as though something immensely powerful and purely evil was gathering and about to spill over our land. I know that sounds melodramatic, but Master Lauder, I have been in battle now. I have been, and I have seen. This was so very much worse." Her voice tailed off.

The old Mage studied her thoughtfully, for a long moment, then reached for a map. "Callandra, what are the vulnerable points of our Kingdom?"

"Shalmis, Nilsport, Arco's Gap and Winters Keep." She pointed them out.

"And their defences?"

"Nilsport is a walled city with a permanent garrison. Shalmis is a border fortress like Winters Keep, and Arco's Gap has natural defences plus an outpost and patrols from Barnard's Keep."

"Very good, but does the name Eastwold mean anything to you?" She shook her head. "It was a defensive fortress about five marks north of Arco's Gap. About fifteen years ago, a massive Kerrian Force descended on it. They captured it, then destroyed it completely and then withdrew."

"Why? This doesn't make sense."

"No it doesn't, does it? There was so little of the fortress left that King Theon decided he would not rebuild it, and the outpost that you know, was constructed instead, at a less vulnerable position." Callie sat quietly, not quite understanding where Master Lauder's thread was leading. "Then ten years ago there was another massive attack that didn't make sense." He waited.

"Winters Keep, the Massacre?"

Master Lauder nodded. "We didn't connect those two events at first because we believed Winters Keep was a Frystian assault and in a way that was true, but we now think it was all orchestrated by Kerrians."

"What?" Callie frowned.

"Callie, there is a pattern. The Kerrians made no attempt to hold those fortresses. They expended many men to win them, then abandoned them shortly afterwards, so they were not seeking military advantage or a territorial foothold. No. They were after something else and I desperately hope I am wrong about this. I think they were seeking the missing parts of your Triquetra."

Callie looked at the Mage. His kind eyes looked bleak, and her expression must have been as grim as he opened his mouth to speak. "No sir." She held up her hand. "I know what you are going to say. This is all theory, just speculation. We don't really know, and so on. But you don't actually believe that, do you?" Master Lauder slowly shook his head. She was very perceptive.

"So we have to assume that there is someone, a very powerful Mage in Kerria who has rediscovered The Heart of Darkness. Someone who has been plotting for many years and who may now, possibly, hold two parts of the Triquetra?"

Master Lauder nodded. "Possibly."

"Or, possibly not." Callie looked up thoughtfully.

"Possibly not?"

"When I was at Winters Keep my pendant was trying to lead me to something. I didn't have time to carry on looking. I must go back." Her tutor looked startled.

"Indeed you must. I am to discuss all of this with the King later today, as it may affect the safety of the realm. Please join us, Callie, and it might be wise to make sure your affairs here are all in order."

Her feet felt leaden as she made her way back to her room. Once there she sorted out winter travel clothing and checked her weapons. She wrote two simple notes, one for her parents and one for Raff explaining she was possibly being sent north on the King's service and left them on her desk, ready if they should be needed. When Raff knocked on her door shortly before noon she was sitting on her bed staring blankly into space. He plonked himself down beside her. "What's up, little sister? Is it Jerran? If he's causing you problems, I am happy to poison him for you. I've learnt lots of really useful stuff in my toxicology lectures."

"Jerran?" Callie shook her head. "No. I've no idea what he was thinking last night but it's nothing to do with him. I've just been to see Master Lauder."

Her brother's face became instantly serious. "Tell me." She did.

Raff was a good listener, he always had been and yet again Callie wondered how they had all missed the way his talents shouted 'healer' rather than 'warrior'. When she had finished her brother was as silent as she had been trying to absorb and digest so much information.

"So you are likely to be heading back to Winters Keep sometime soon?"

She nodded. "I think that's likely. I expect it will be decided at the meeting with the King later." The distant lunch bell rang and they set off together for the Mess Hall.

"I expect they will want me here for communications, won't they?"

"I really don't know but that does seem likely. I've no idea how this will play out. I need to go to Winters Keep. Jerran wants to go into Frystian lands to try and find out what is really going on in the North. He hopes that Snow Fox Clan might help him, if their resettlement has gone well. He did ask me to go along too, if he was given permission, but maybe he'll just go with Liss."

"Oh yes. I forgot Liss is at Winters Keep."

"Actually now I think of it, he isn't. He and Dexter are at Barnard's Castle at the moment to celebrate Winters Light."

"And you know that how?" her brother asked sceptically.

"When I linked to Dexter yesterday I saw them arriving at the Keep."

"Oh, right." Raff said nothing more until they were both sitting in front of loaded trays. Then he turned to her curiously. "Callie, you didn't identify the link rings that work with your pendant until you got back here after Arco's Gap before you went to Nilsport. So when did you give one to Dexter?"

"Oh, I didn't." He raised an eyebrow, waiting for an explanation. "I discovered at Winters Keep that I can easily link with him."

"Like you do with me and Father?"

"Yes, I suppose so."

"That's odd," he frowned. "But he's alright with that?"

"Of course, I mean. Oh Goddess, Raff, I never told him."

"Callie." Raff's voice was very disapproving. "Callie, that's really unethical. How would you like it if someone was snooping on you and you were unaware of it?" Callie found herself blushing.

"I you put it like that it sounds horrible, but it's only happened twice. The second time was yesterday. I've no actual idea how it happened; so stop looking at me as if I've grown horns." Raff relented slightly.

"I suppose you are only just learning how all your talents work. Still Callie, intrusion and privacy may be things to consider in future." He sounded so pompous that Callie hit him with her spoon.

"Enough, Raff. Did you have medical ethics as well as toxicology this morning? I really don't need anything else to worry about right now."

"That's true. Sorry for the lecture. If there's anything I can do?"

"There is."

"What?"

"Give me the rest of your roast potatoes, I missed breakfast."

Her brother sighed but pushed his entire plate in her direction. "Go ahead and feast, Mighty Mage."

Chapter 36

When Callie presented herself at the Secretariat after lunch she was directed to one of the smaller meeting rooms. Master Lauder was already there sitting at the table in quiet conversation with Mage Terran. Her father was seated beside them and he smiled up at her as she dropped onto the next chair. Just a few minutes later the door opened and the King entered followed by both his sons.

When once they were settled, Master Lauder explained all he had discovered about Callie's pendant and his thoughts thereon. The King listened attentively, and when the tale was told, sat silently for a few minutes drumming his fingers on the table. Finally, he spoke.

"As I see it, this situation could turn out to be a storm in a teacup," he held a hand up as Master Lauder made to remonstrate, "or, it could be the start of very serious trouble for the Kingdom. The first thing we need is more information."

"Father, the first thing we need, is to put this immensely powerful weapon in appropriate hands."

Mikheli offered Callie a patronising smile. "I'm sure the Lady Callandra does her best, but the fact remains that she is still only an Academy student. Is that really appropriate in a matter potentially concerning the defence of the realm?"

Callie couldn't believe what she was hearing, and would have leapt to her feet to protest if her father's iron grip had not pinned her down. Then she heard Jerran's voice – "Which bit of, she annihilated the Kerrian army at Arco's Gap and destroyed the entire Ice-lander fleet, ending the Nilsport War did you miss, brother?"

Mikheli looked taken aback. "She has certainly been fortunate so far, Jerran, but next time…"

"Fortune played no part in it. I should know. I was there."

"Jerran, I mean no disrespect to Lady Callandra but surely even you can see that such a weapon should be in the hands of a Mage with experience that so far the lady lacks."

"Prince Mikheli." Terran's voice chipped in. "As Master Lauder said, it takes an immensely powerful Mage to use a Triquetra or any part of it. Callandra is the only one of us who can."

"Are you saying that with her pendant Callandra is more powerful than any of you are?" His voice was entirely disbelieving.

"No, I'm saying that without the pendant, Callie is more powerful than any of us. With the pendant as well; only time will show us the limits of her capabilities." The Crown Prince paled, his jaw dropping as he looked at Callandra almost nervously.

The King cleared his throat. "As I was saying, we need information. This means a covert expedition to Frystland or Kerria, but do you think it wise for the Triquetra to go north into danger, assuming the Lady Callandra is willing?" Master Lauder and Mage Terran exchanged glances.

"Sire, we have considered this. It may not be entirely wise, certainly there are risks, but, if a Mage has obtained the other parts of the Triquetra intending to use it for conquest and subjugation, Callandra is the only hope of stopping it and for that she will need her pendant."

[No pressure then.] Callie jumped, giving an involuntary grin at the sound of Jerran's voice in her head. He was pointedly looking away from her but must have seen her getting tense at the heavy responsibility she might be fielding.

The King pondered a moment or two longer then nodded. "Lady Callandra, would you be willing to involve yourself in this venture?"

"Of course, Majesty." She nodded her head, pleased that he still acknowledged the choice was hers to make. Her father fidgeted and King Theon looked his way.

"Sire, we need to avoid provocation of either the Frystlanders or the Kerrians. Our forces have been run ragged over the last couple of years, so I strongly recommend a small party that cannot be mistaken in any way for an armed incursion."

"You are right of course, Ivar. So we start with you, Callandra, and while I do not doubt your abilities, you might, as Mikheli suggested benefit from the help of another Mage. Terran, you already know. He is between postings and is willing to go with you if you want him?"

"Yes indeed." Callie smiled, pleased.

"You will have bodyguards of course and Liss is very good at that sort of thing and already in the Marches. I wouldn't be surprised if Lord Dexter joined you too, for at least some of the time. He won't want to leave Winters Keep for too long with events moving so fast." He paused in thought.

[Callie.] Jerran's voice was very quiet in her head. [If I apologise whole heartedly for last night and absolutely swear to be on my best behaviour will you please ask if I can come?] His eyes were fixed on her, his jaw tense, as she hesitated.

[You're apologising? So you are sorry you kissed me last night?]

[Yes. I mean no; that is…]

[So you didn't enjoy it?]

[Well obviously I did.]

[So you aren't sorry?]

[No I… yes. Callie!!]

[I'll think about it.] She broke the contact.

A jumble of images crashed through her mind. Jerran holding her steady as she used her magic, his hands pulling her to safety on the battlefield. His lips kissing her hard and demanding in the darkness of the Ball, and gently brushing her hair in the darkness of their tent as she shook from a nightmare; they worked well together. "Sire, is there any chance you can spare Prince Jerran to come with us?" The

King paused and looked at his younger son, consideringly.

"I suppose it might be useful. Jerran can act for the Crown, but in that case perhaps it should be Mikheli?"

[Goddess, no.] Callie wasn't aware that she had mentally sent out her response until she saw Jerran trying not to laugh. She assumed a diplomatic tone. "Unfortunately Sire, although I can link to Prince Jerran, I don't seem to be able to do so to Prince Mikheli and that might be crucial." The white lie tripped convincingly off her tongue.

"I see. Well we need to give this foray every advantage, and Mikheli really needs to be here with Princess Serenna, so Jerran it shall be." He rose and they all stood as the King moved away. "Find me later, Jerran. I want to go over the fine details of the settlement with the Snow Fox Clan." He nodded at them all and left with Prince Mikheli at his heels, his voice already beginning a litany of complaints.

They all slumped in their chairs as the meeting relaxed. Jerran rounded the table to Callie's side.

"Thank you, Callie. When do you want to leave?"

"As soon as possible, Callandra." Master Lauder's voice answered Jerran's question.

"First thing in the morning?" she asked aloud, looking at Terran and the Prince.

"Fine. If I arrange our bodyguard and horses Terran, can you see to supplies? You'll know what we need." The older Mage nodded. "And Callie, can you make sure Raff knows what we are doing as he may have to field messages."

"Right away. Anything else?"

Terran frowned. "I do hope we find Liss at Winters Keep. You can't link with him, can you Callie?"

"Sorry, no." He looked disappointed so she added, "But I can contact Lord Dexter. They were both at Barnard's Castle."

"Useful to know. Please tell Lord Dexter we are heading his way and ask him to get Liss back to the fortress."

"I will." The old Mage smiled and left the room.

"So Lord Dexter has one of your rings, Callie?" Jerran's voice had a slight edge to it. Callie found she was reluctant to mention the natural link she had with the northern Lord; a link independent of any ring.

"I thought it might be useful," she half lied, "and it seems I was right. I'll go and find Raff." She edged towards the door.

"And when you do find him, bring him home for dinner with your mother and me," Callie's father called after her. She waved her agreement and trotted off.

Callie had found that linking with other people was easier for her, if she was able to imagine where they might be and what they might be doing, so she decided to wait until evening to try and contact Lord Dexter. Dinner at home had been pleasant and useful as her father had shared with her the meagre, but most recent information he had on Kerria.

Back at the Academy she settled on her bed, wrapping a comforter around her in case it took a long time, then cleared her mind and dropped into a trance. She let her thoughts fill with pictures of the harsh northern lands, the snow-covered pines and the purple-grey rocks. She recreated her first view of Winters Keep and tried to feel the spark that was Dexter, but although the 'scent' of him was everywhere, it grew no stronger. She relaxed for a little while, sipping some tea, then decided to try again but shifted her focus to Barnard's Castle.

Here the sense of him lit up almost immediately like a beacon and she breathed a sigh of relief. With Raff's words still in her ears she tried to concentrate on speech and avoid any visual element to the contact. She planned to call his name quietly, but as she settled the link she heard him shouting at her. First there was a string of gibberish then, [You are an unholy turd and your mother obviously lay with a bear.]

[I, what?]

[Who said that?]

Callie, not knowing what was happening fell silent. After another minute she heard some more gibberish then, [And your arse is so huge it could be mistaken for a walrus.]

[Dexter,] she protested. [I'm sorry if you object to this sort of contact, but it is really important and there is no need to be so rude.] She waited.

[Callie?] Dexter sounded amazed but far more normal than he had a moment previously. [Is that really you I can hear or have I finally gone mad?]

[It is me, Dex. You aren't going mad. I'm using my Magery to mind-link with you.]

She waited while he digested that. [So where are you calling from?]

[I'm home in Derryn.]

[So far.] He marvelled. [I'm in… Barnard's Keep.]

[Yes, I know. I honestly wouldn't have forced myself into your mind if it wasn't urgent, so please don't be angry.]

[Angry? I'm not angry.]

[Then why all the insults?]

Dexter burst out laughing. [Sorry, Callie. I'm trying to learn Frystian as Snow Fox Clan looks like a permanent fixture and I'm told that to be held in respect, I must practise my insults; they weren't actually intended for you.]

[Oh, I see. Well thank haven for that. Is Liss still with you?]

[Yes, he's here. But how did you know that?]

[I just… Look, I promise I'll explain it all to you when I see you.]

[You're coming north?] He sounded pleased.

[Yes, I need to visit Winters Keep, then Prince Jerran needs to contact Snow Fox Clan and possibly slip over the border into Frystland. The King wants information. Are you able to meet us there?]

[Certainly. We are heading back tomorrow anyway so we'll be there well before you are.]

[Thank the Goddess, then we'll see you in a few days.]

[Wind at your back, Callie. See you soon. Goodnight.]

Chapter 37

The journey north was uneventful, with the road fairly clear of snow although it seemed busier than previously. They were a small group. Jerran had only brought Will and Gilligan for scouting and bodyguard duties, reasoning that the presence of Terran, an experienced Battle Mage, made up for numbers.

Their coming was looked for and when they rode through the gateway of Winters Keep at dusk on their fourth day of travel, Lord Dexter and his brother were both on the steps to greet them. Callie dismounted slowly, stiff from the long ride, and had hardly handed her reins to a stable boy before she was enveloped in a bear hug. "Callie, my favourite awe-inspiring Mage. It's good to see you." Blaine's exuberance swept her off her feet, quite literally, but she had to smile.

"It's good to see you too Blaine."

She saw Lord Dexter greet the Prince civilly if not with great enthusiasm and recalled their previous conflict over the Snow Fox Clan. It would be interesting to find out how things were developing there when they met before dinner.

Jerran too, had wondered if Lord Dexter might still be angry at the Crown allowing the settlement of a Frystian clan so near to Winters Keep. He was relieved that neither Dexter's words nor body language were overtly hostile to him, while he greeted Callie with surprising warmth. Surprising, because it was an open secret at court that after the butchery of his family, Dexter had become socially withdrawn. Unfailingly civil and always courteous, he discouraged close male friendships and women he simply avoided altogether. All but the most persistent matchmaking dowagers had given him up as a hopeless cause and yet he seemed to have made an exception for Callie. Actually, Jerran mused, as he followed a servant to his chamber, quite a few people made exceptions for Callie, himself included.

She was unlike anyone else he knew and he was delighted to be working with her again, and not just because it took him away from court life. The small group he had assembled meshed well. Liss might join them, and he was a man the Prince trusted implicitly. Dexter he knew less well, but judging him on their time at Arco's Gap he was sound, dependable, an able warrior and blessed with a steady and reasonable nature. He felt the next few weeks promised to be interesting.

After directing the scouts to their quarters and seeing his guests to their chambers, Lord Dexter took himself back to his study. There were matters to be dealt with that had arisen when he had been away, even so briefly, at Barnard's Castle, but his mind was no longer on estate business and he didn't want to admit even to himself where it had strayed.

Dexter told himself that he would see Callie at dinner, as agreed. He told himself she needed time to bathe and change, having been travelling for several days, so he couldn't explain how his feet led him to her door. He stood outside for a moment trying to think of any good reason to knock, other than the simple fact of wanting to see her. He had just about convinced himself to walk away, when she opened the door and smiled at him. "I..." He got no further, the power of speech deserting him when she grabbed the front of his tunic and pulled him inside.

"Thank Haven you've come, Dex, I was just going to look for you."

"You were?"

She nodded. "It's about the mind-link Magery I seem to have."

Dexter dropped into a chair and leaned forward. "Tell me everything." She had his total attention. Callie explained as best she could and even admitted her unintentional snooping as it didn't feel right to conceal it. She was relieved when he brushed it off as the experiment it actually was and reminded her that the outcome had been his rescue from a fire, which made her feel a lot better.

When she had finished talking he sat quietly for a moment while Callie rooted through her pack looking for her link rings. "So Dexter, will you please wear one of these?" She offered the small bag.

"But I don't actually need one, do I Callie? If I've understood what you've been telling me. So shouldn't you save them for people you struggle to link with?"

Callie hesitated. "I have been trying to make contact with all sorts of people," she confessed. "With Liss, for example, I cannot link at all. With others I can make a link but without the boost from the ring it can be hard work and there are a very few people I see to have a natural link with, so it's as easy as chatting."

"Your family?"

"Yes."

"And me?"

"Yes." He considered this for a few minutes then cocked an eyebrow at her. "You still didn't answer my question. Why do you want me to wear one, Callie?"

She huffed. He wasn't going to be put off. "Jerran!"

"The Prince? What about him. Is he causing you problems?"

"No, Dex. Absolutely not. When we were together at Nilsport he was amazing really. I don't know how many times he actually saved my life. He's a superb swordsman, and he's a lot more than that. He has an… I don't know, instinctive overview of what's going on and all the implications. He reads situations really well. In fact, if we can keep him away from that pit of self-interest known as the court, I think we could turn him into a reasonable human being given time."

"You sound like an admirer."

"Well in a way I am."

"But?"

"But he is a bit possessive." Dexter raised an eyebrow. She shook her head. "No, not like that and not stupidly so," she firmly repressed her memory of that Winters Light kiss, "just sometimes he acts like I'm his personal Mage. I think it's partly because we both started new ventures together, when we went to Barnard's Castle. He has a lot of good qualities, but in some ways he's still a true royal and he won't like it if you can do something he can't, even if it's only talking to me." Dexter grinned.

"Yes, I see." He untied the bag and shook out the rings. Then grew absolutely still.

"Dexter?"

After a moment he looked up, his expression unreadable. "I think I know why you were able to contact me, Callie." He held up his hand. On the smallest finger a silver ring caught the light.

She looked at it, confused. "You already have one." He nodded and pulling it off handed it to her. It was just like the rest.

"But how? Where did you get it, Dex?"

He swallowed hard as he slid the ring back onto his hand and looked away. "I took it from what was left of my mother's body after the massacre. She always wore it." For a moment his ever present genial mask fell. He looked so bleak that Callie sprang to her feet and impulsively hugged him, wrapping her arms about him where he sat, holding him tightly.

"Goddess, Dex. I'm so sorry to spring that upon you; bring that back to your mind." The faint tremor she had felt run through his body steadied and she pulled away.

"It's always in my mind, Callie. Don't blame yourself." He looked at the ring, turning it on his finger. "Well at least that's one mystery solved. Let's go meet the others. I want to hear all your news and we have quite a story to tell from the Snow Fox Clan."

They chatted amiably as Dexter led the way back to a small salon where Terran and Liss were talking in front of a blazing fire, unaware that Prince Jerran had emerged from his own room further along the corridor in time to see the two of them come out of Callie's chamber. When the Prince reached the Salon a moment or two after them, his expression was thoughtful.

Conversation at dinner was a give and take catch-up of north and south news. Dexter was delighted to hear the Nilsport conflict was over, as his estate's logging shipments had been delayed by problems at the port. Lord Barnard had not been so much affected, as the metals and gems from his mines were mostly used within Lithia itself. By tacit agreement no mention was made of the real reason for Jerran and Callie's visit until the party regrouped after a satisfying meal and it was Dexter who set the ball rolling.

"Highness – friends – I am always happy to welcome guests to Winters Keep, but I am well aware that you have your own reasons for being here and I think it's time these matters saw the light of day, but where to start?"

"It starts with Callie." Terran gave her a reassuring smile.

Aware that she was the centre of attention she took a moment to gather her thoughts then tugged her pendant into view. "This," she fingered it gently, "is an heirloom that has been in my family for generations, passed on every time to a descendant with Mage gift. Master Lauder believes it is the central section of one of the three great Triquetrae." All but Terran looked blank. "It is a magical artefact that, among other things, increases a Mage's power exponentially, and given that a Mage must be powerful to use it at all, it could be a formidable tool for good or ill."

They nodded. "Master Lauder thinks two 'lobes' are missing, here and here," she pointed. "His research has led him to believe that in times past, the parts were held in the great fortresses to defend Lithia's borders."

"Which fortresses?" Dexter queried.

"Salamis, where this part came from as a dowry. Eastwold."

"Wasn't Eastwold the old fortress beyond Arco's Gap?" Blaine's voice. Callie nodded.

"And Winters Keep." Liss spoke softly and she looked up to see him exchange a long look with Lord Dexter. "Go on."

Callie shrugged. "There's not much more for me to tell… Jerran?" The Prince took over.

"When I was held by the Frystians, they did not know that I spoke their language so I overheard several strange things. When the time came to bring me back here, no-one wanted to be my escort. They didn't want to come anywhere near Winters Keep. They said it was cursed and called it the 'Shame of the Frystian Nation' and this seemed to be linked to one particular clan."

"Was it by any change the White Wolves?" Dexter hazarded.

Jerran looked surprised but nodded. "Yes, the White Wolves. How did you know?"

"I'll say my piece in a moment, what more do you have?"

"Einar told us the clans were facing starvation and the herds failing. He admitted there had been conflict among the different tribes, but wouldn't tell us why. We have lost touch with all our agents in Kerria, and just before we came away my father had a report that refugees have started to appear in the border towns of Ostland." This was news to all of them. Callie picked up the tale again.

"Master Lauder fears that a Mage or Sorcerer of great power may have located the missing parts of the Triquetra and learnt how to perform 'The Heart of Darkness', a ritual that would enable him to create an army directed by his mind and will alone. An army of fighters without humanity or conscience." There was a horrified silence as they digested this and Blaine went round refilling wine goblets. Jerran turned to Liss and Lord Dexter.

"So what can you add to all this?"

"Highness."

"Jerran please, when we're in the field."

"Jerran. As you know I was opposed to the settlement of the Snow Fox Clan in the Barrens. After our family and the other inmates of Winters Keep were slaughtered, and the fortress was recovered, some of the enemy dead were Kerrians but many were clansmen. I could not, would not, make any accord with those butchers." His voice shook slightly and Blaine pressed a goblet into his hand. "Nevertheless as King Theon commanded I went with Liss to the Snow Fox Camp. There were discussions with the clan elders and the initial agreement was made, on the terms laid down by your father, Jerran. The people of the Snow Fox Clan were immensely grateful and Einar ordered a celebration feast.

"While this was being prepared the Shaman sent for me. He said that my heart was black with rage and hate because of the Winters Keep Massacre and although he understood this, he felt to leave such a wound untreated would make good relations with his clan much harder, so he had decided to tell me something I should know, although the telling brought him grief and shame.

"He told me that as the herds failed and hunting became harder, the clans had scattered more widely than usual, moving into areas they did not normally travel. The White Wolves Clan had gone east and crossed the Kerrian border. Then they seemed to go missing entirely. Nothing was heard of them for several months, until two injured warriors staggered into a Raven Clan campsite. They were nearly dead and had had their tongues ripped out, but before they succumbed to their wounds they managed to show the Raven Clan Shaman where they had come from; Winters Keep.

"Raven Clan sent scouts to the fortress where they found our countrymen, every man, woman and child slaughtered. There were a few Kerrians on the point of leaving so it must have been before the royal forces arrived and there were three members of the White Wolves Clan still alive. The clansmen seemed possessed and attacked them. It took considerable force to restrain and bind them, which they did before taking them back to the Raven Clan Shaman.

"Apparently they raved and fought for about three days then seemed to 'wake up', becoming aware of themselves once more and also remembering and understanding what they had done at Winters Keep. They all killed themselves. The Shaman said they had been controlled by blood magic." Dexter took a long drink of wine.

"The Shaman wanted me to understand that Snow Fox Clan had no part in the atrocity at Winters Keep, nor did any clan but the White Wolves, who are now outlawed if any still live, from the Frystian nation."

Liss put a hand on the young Lord's shoulder and moved forward in turn. "It never made sense that nomads would overrun a fortress and then abandon it so soon afterwards; two fortresses if Eastwold is counted. But if they were looking for the Triquetra a pattern emerges – a truly alarming pattern."

"I think it likely that the Sorcerer who bespelled the White Wolves

Clan (if that is what happened) has at least one piece of the pendant, but Dexter tells me that you think the other part might still be here, Callie?"

"Possibly. My pendant reacted to something the last time I was at Winters Keep but I didn't have time to seek it out, so that's the next thing I must do." She yawned. "But I think it will have to wait until morning. If you'll excuse me, I'll see you after breakfast, gentlemen."

Chapter 38

The infirmary in the tower consisted of three main rooms, with a sluice to one side. One of the rooms, with a large window, Miri had used as an examination room, the second held several cots. The third room lit by the weak winter sun was really a still room and it was here Miri had prepared her remedies and here she had stored her herbs and other ingredients.

The walls were shelved and housed row upon row of jars. There were gaps here and there and Dexter explained that precious or rare items had been transferred to the new infirmary, but for the most part the current healer had chosen to use her own medicines.

It was fairly dark in the stillroom and the glow from Callie's pendant was easily visible. She moved about slowly until the glow remained steady facing perhaps a dozen containers. She and Terran took them to the work bench and one by one tipped out their contents, smoothing them with metal spatulas. Nothing. "I just don't understand it." Callie sat back on a bench, perplexed. "If there's nothing here what is my pendant reacting to?"

"We must be missing something but what?" Terran scratched his head.

"Callie, can you turn round between the shelves and the work bench?" Dexter was studying the pendant closely. She obliged. "Is it me or is the glow now brighter facing the work bench?"

"It is," Terran agreed, "but we've been through all these containers and found nothing."

"Callie, try that one again." The old Mage pointed. "It's salt, isn't it?" She nodded and upended the jar once more. Terran spread the salt crystals widely across the table. "Well there's no sign of our missing pieces there."

"But what's this?" Dexter running his fingers through the salt plucked a larger piece from the mess on the table and brushed away debris. This isn't salt crystal; it looks like a gem –possibly an opal?"

"An opal... Master Lauder thought... Here, let me."

Callie took the jewel from his hand and brought it close to her pendant. Before they actually touched it, it leapt from her fingers and settled into the circular depression near the base, with an audible click. They all exchanged glances. "Well it's disappointing that we haven't found another lobe of the Triquetra but joining those two together must be a good thing." Terran observed. "There's nothing else here. The glow from your pendant has gone. Perhaps they found a part of the Triquetra here and either missed or discounted the gem."

"You mentioned Master Lauder," Dexter queried.

"Yes, he predicted the gem would be an opal."

"Why?"

"Opals are brittle and hard to work; only the elves still have the skill but they can store immense power. Their magic can be used in many ways but is strongest in healing."

"That seems a bit odd for a weapon."

"The Triquetra wasn't made to be a weapon, Lord Dexter," Terran shook his head, "it was meant to be a force for good. It is as ever the greed and ambition of men that have changed its purpose."

"So now what?" Dexter looked at the two of them.

"I think we have to assume that the Sorcerer who sent the White Wolves down on Winters Keep has the rest of the talisman. We have to find out what he is planning and, if it bodes ill for Lithia how we can stop him."

"Jerran and Liss won't be back for hours yet. Whether or not Snow Fox Clan will give us a guide, we need to plan a trip to the far north of Frystland or more likely Kerria so let's get to the maps." Dexter led them back inside.

Liss and Jerran did not return to the castle until the afternoon and brought no good news with them.

Einar was apologetic, but unwilling to lend them a guide for several weeks. With Snow Fox Clan barely settled in new territory he needed all his scouts and hunters to rebuild their almost non-existent food reserves, and could not be persuaded otherwise.

Jerran, mulling it over, found he was unwilling to wait. Like Callie, he had an uneasy sense of trouble brewing and was happy to fall in with Dexter's alternative suggestion that instead of heading directly north they should go east and travel up into Kerria from the Ostland borders. "That is quite a trip you're planning, Highness." Terran eyed the Prince thoughtfully. "Likely to take many weeks. Are you certain your father won't object?" Jerran reddened slightly.

"About that. I was going to ask Callie to let him know what we have decided; preferably via her father." He gave Callie a pleading look and she giggled.

"We're back to the 'better to seek forgiveness than ask permission' scenario aren't we?" He grinned and nodded.

"Well I was going to report back anyway. I want to update Master Lauder on the Triquetra. Let's find somewhere quiet." Callie and Jerran slipped away into the empty library leaving Liss alone as Dexter had been called to see unexpected company.

The Isseni looked again at the maps, shuffling them until he found the one he was looking for. It was on a much smaller scale than those they had studied earlier and encompassed the skeletal borders of far more distant countries. His long fingers ran down the long jagged land that was his home, a land he had not seen for decades and his heart turned over within him. If Callie's quest for the Triquetra succeeded, he just might be able to return.

Although it took no time now for Callie to slip into her trance, her father was busy with other people and it was a little while before she could gain his attention. He was amused that he was to 'inform' the King of his son's plans but not at all surprised and promised to deal with the matter as diplomatically as possible. He also agreed to pass on the latest developments regarding the Triquetra to Master Lauder, before breaking contact. Callie was about to return to her room when the library door was flung open. "There you are." Blaine rushed in. "I've been looking everywhere, Callie, I need you urgently."

"Why? What's wrong?"

"You need to save my brother."

"Dexter? Is he in danger?" The cheerful expression fell from Callie's face.

"Of the greatest sort." He looked her over. "You need to change."

"I what? Why?" She looked at Jerran in confusion. He cocked an eyebrow at the younger man.

"Blaine, settle down. I think we'd have noticed if the castle was under attack, so what exactly is the nature of the danger facing your brother?"

"Miss Lucille Merner."

"And she is… one of your local gentry?" The Prince hazarded.

"That's not how I'd describe her. She's appalling and her mother is a predator. They won't be put off and they've got Dexter cornered in the solar."

Callie chuckled and Blaine offered a reluctant smile himself, but it faded quickly. "Yes, I know it seems amusing but it's really wearing Dex down. He's too kind to give her the only kind of snub she would understand and I'm frankly terrified he'll give in and I'll end up with that deluded snobby little bitch as my sister-in-law!"

"I'm sorry Blaine, but…"

"Callie," he pleaded, "you like Dex."

"Yes I do. I would help if I could but I have only working clothes with me." Blaine scratched his head.

"I know, follow me." He trotted back down the corridor and Callie sprinted after him, leaving the Prince standing at the library door grinning, an expression that vanished when he heard her voice in his head.

[Jerran, you can stop laughing. You are our plan B.]

[Our what?]

[Plan B. If I can't repel the vultures, you need to swan in and do the condescending royal thing and put your crown on.]

[I do not condescend. I'm not sure I even know how.]

[No you don't. That's true. Just pretend to be your brother.]

[Callie! Insulting the royal family like that might just be treason and I don't actually travel with a crown.]

[You'll think of something.] She broke the contact. The Prince sighed but headed back to his chambers.

When Callie approached the double doors to the solar, she paused for a moment to tuck a wayward curl behind the jewelled headband that now circled her chestnut hair. She could hear a high-pitched, artificial giggle that instantly rubbed her nerves, and the clear tenor that was Blaine. Dexter must be inside too, but he always spoke softly. She smoothed a crease from the green silk dress that Blaine had provided and pushed the doors open.

Four pairs of eyes looked her up and down, one startled, one appreciative and two instantly hostile. Callie tripped across the room to Dexter's side and slipped her arm through his in an affectionate and possessive manner. "Dexter. You didn't tell me we had company." She gazed adoringly into his eyes and spoke in his mind.

[Dexter, try and look pleased to see me.]

[I am pleased to see you, I don't have to try.]

Callie's smile became genuinely warm as she gave him an infinitesimal wink.

"My dear, my apologies. This is Lady Merner and her daughter Miss Lucille Merner, who are near neighbours. They were passing and called in to surprise us."

"How kind of them." She dropped into a perfect court curtsey.

"This is Lady Callandra D'Arcourt, at least for the moment." Dexter gave her a doting smile, which set Blaine spluttering into his tea. Mother and daughter exchanged furious glances.

"You are staying here, Lady D'Arcourt?"

There was a wealth of innuendo in the brief comment. Callie raised a withering eyebrow, every bit the court lady. "Indeed I am, Lady Merner, although briefly. His Highness Prince Jerran and my fi— and Lord Dexter are escorting me to Salmis to family. It's so kind of them."

"It's absolutely our pleasure." Jerran's voice was formal as he strolled into the room, taking Callie's hand and kissing it before eyeing the visitors as if they were insects. He was gloriously dressed in a velvet jacket with a wealth of lace at his throat and a thin metal fillet around his head.

Lady Merner sank into a low curtsey slightly ahead of her plump daughter. Jerran waited an unconscionable time before waving a languid hand at them. "Oh, do rise. No need for formality here. Did you come to congratulate Lord Dexter on his betrothal?" He eyed Callie appreciatively. "We all think he's a very lucky man."

"His betrothal?" Lady Merner looked shocked. "We hadn't heard. Lord Dexter, is this recent?"

"Very recent indeed." Dexter patted Callie's hand. "The matter isn't public knowledge so I know we can rely on your discretion. Not all Callandra's family have been informed as yet."

"Of course we won't breathe a word." Lady Merner choked the words out. Her daughter overwhelmed by the company merely nodded vigorously.

"Lord Dexter." The dowager rose and managed to wrap her dignity around her. "Please accept our very best wishes and many congratulations. We must take our leave of you and your guests. Prince Jerran." They curtseyed again and Blaine saw them out. The others held their positions like a tableau until Blaine re-entered the room with a whoop of laughter and demanded a kiss from his brother's betrothed.

Callie flopped into a chair laughing. "Jerran what are you wearing?" The Prince's eyes were alight with fun as he pulled the lace from his neck and shook it out to reveal a servant's mob cap. "And where did you get the crown?" He remembered the circlet and dropped it on a low table. "I don't know what it is but the cook wants it back."

Liss arriving at that moment was met by a scene of hysterical laughter. He could not recall the last time he had seen Prince Jerran or Lord Dexter in such high spirits and his gaze rested thoughtfully on the lovely young women who sat between them.

Chapter 39

They set off early the next day heading for Barnard's Castle, where Dexter hoped to borrow Reece from the marcher Lord. As King Theon had predicted, Dexter fully intended to be part of the expedition, despite his brother's loudly voiced objections. He would undoubtedly be an asset, familiar as he was with the northern lands, and speaking Kerrian, so Callie was mildly surprised at Jerran's tepid enthusiasm at his inclusion.

Overnighting at the way stations, three days of steady riding brought them back to Lord Barnard's Castle. The Earl listened to all their news with great interest and was happy for them to borrow his woodsman Reece, having his own concerns about what might be happening just beyond his borders. Once that was settled Dexter and Jerran went to speak to the latest patrol about snow conditions, while Terran arranged a resupply for their onward journey.

Callie, at a loose end for a little while, was curled up in a corner of the library with a book on Kerrian customs when Lord Barnard appeared. "Found you at last."

His craggy face smiled. "I was beginning to think I'd mislaid another guest!"

"Is there something I can do for you, milord?" Callie closed her book curiously.

"Just spare me a few minutes of your time, my dear." He beckoned and she followed him until they reached his study. "I have a little gift for you, Callandra." He opened a drawer in the long desk that dominated the room and withdrew a small carved box, which he passed to her.

"Thank you milord, but, why?"

He smiled again. "Two reasons. Firstly, I wished to mark my appreciation for what you did when last you were here." He held up a hand to forestall her objections. "You are going to say that many people fought bravely and contributed and so on, and you are absolutely right. But the fact remains that without you the outcome could have been very different, and many more lives would have been lost. Secondly, this piece reminded me very much of your pendant. It's not a huge gift but it has long been treasured by my family and I really feel it should go to you." He gestured and she opened the box.

Inside lay a small brooch. The design was a snowflake picked out in tiny chips of opal and diamond and trailing a comet-like tail of minute runes. The design, the craftsmanship and the style were identical to the pendant she pulled out from her tunic. "I thought so." The Earl looked pleased.

"It's absolutely lovely. Are you certain you can bear to part with it? Shouldn't it stay in your family?" Lord Barnard smiled at her pleasure but shook his head.

"It's odd but I just know that it belongs with the pendant and I follow my feelings. I've never been sure if it's a snowflake, or a comet? Either would make it appropriate for you as a weather witch or Elemental Mage or whatever you are now." Callie's face fell and her mouth straightened. "Are you worried?" The Earl's voice was even, uncritical.

"Yes," she admitted. "I am. I'm very new to my power and we really don't know what we may be walking into."

"That's true but you are seeking information, not confrontation, and you have good companions. I'm glad Dexter is going with you; he's a good man to have when things get difficult. Terran has all the field experience you lack, and the Prince, well he is a bonny fighter. I do have a question though?"

"What's that?"

"Which of them is in charge?"

Callie's smile returned as she headed to the door. "I think that would be me!" She left the room to the Earl's bellowed laughter.

*

After taking advice, the next day they loaded their supplies on shaggy mountain ponies that seemed as wide as they were high. It was an early start, the sun still low in the sky when they reached Arco's Gap, where Callie was puzzled to find their guide leading them into the Iron Valley rather than to the north road she had expected.

It seemed there was another path through the Skyfall mountains into Kerria. Known to few and often sealed by snow, it was hidden in the folds of the peaks beyond Silver Stream Mine. As they trotted past Blackstone and Deep Delve, Callie wondered if the avalanche she had triggered would be a problem, but the miners had cleared a road up to the back trail that was to be their starting point.

Turning aside they rode in single file, the path getting steeper as it zig-zagged up the side of the mountain between the trees. The light was dim under the pines as the sun had not yet risen above the peaks. After an hour or two Callie had begun to shiver despite her many layers of clothing. A third hour brought them clear of the treeline to a small plateau with no visible exit.

Reece dismounted and took Will and Gilly towards a rocky outcrop framed by two massive fir trees and after a brief conversation all three men began to shovel snow. Jerran approached Callie, stamping his feet to bring back feeling to them. He held out a hip flask, which she reached for eagerly. "Medr?" He nodded and went to check on the digging, which now revealed the entrance to a tunnel.

Callie thought it looked distinctly unappealing. Not very wide, it was dark and smelt of cold stone and mustiness but the ponies at least seemed unbothered by it. Once inside, with torches to light their way she was soon simply grateful to be out of the wind so constant, high in the mountains. They moved slowly but steadily stopping once for trail food and hours later in a natural cave to spend the night.

Some small adaptations had been made to the area. A hearth had been constructed with a flue leading off somewhere they couldn't see.

A pen for livestock was sturdily built and a trickle of water running down one wall had been fed into a catch basin where they refilled their water skins before letting their mounts drink.

Straw was piled in heaps at once side, with untouched bales stacked nearby.

Terran was fascinated and made a Mage light to explore when his torch was confiscated, but he had found no clues to explain its construction when he returned to the fireside. "It's called the Snakeskin," Dexter informed him. "Legend has it that a hunter after eagle eggs took shelter in it during a snowstorm. It was abandoned even then and there was nothing inside except an enormous empty snakeskin, or dragon skin depending on the version you hear.

"There are, or were, only about four or five people who knew of it before today so we must ask you never to speak of it." He held everyone's gaze until he was satisfied. "We will be through by afternoon tomorrow if we start early so we should all get some sleep."

Callie flung her bedroll onto the straw in a corner, made a pillow of her cloak and curled up under her blanket. Terran seemed to be heading in her direction, only to be intercepted by the Prince. She couldn't hear their quietly spoken exchange, but a moment later Jerran settled down beside her. She raised an eyebrow and he smiled and mind spoke to her.

[I could say that I prefer sleeping next to a beautiful woman rather than any of the men, but that would just annoy you. The fact is, I am, your bodyguard and I'd like to keep our magic sources apart just in case.]

[That makes sense,] she agreed.

[I'm glad you think so. I'm not sure Dexter does.]

He lay down and she was able to see the northern Lord glaring in the Prince's direction.

[Jerran. What did you do? He looks really put out.]

[Nothing much. I just pointed out that I'm already used to sleeping with you.]

[You did what??] Callie's jaw dropped and she blushed scarlet. The

Prince, eyes closed rolled deeper into his blanket, but she couldn't miss the mischievous smile that curved his lips. She groaned.

Callie was tired but sleep eluded her. As she listened to the steady breathing of her companions her mind turned to the one who was missing… Liss. She was sure he had intended to come with them and his sudden decision not to, had been a shock. She knew it had something to do with the Triquetra, or more accurately its companion piece, the cloak pin Lord Barnard had given her. She had worn it to their last dinner and when the Isseni's eyes had fallen on it he had frozen in what looked like shock. He had taken it to study with shaking hands, studying her with an extraordinary mix of hope and fear and even reverence. She had had the feeling that at any moment he would bow before her. He had been silent during the rest of the meal, apparently deep in thought, and when he finally spoke it was to announce gently but firmly that he would not be able to go on with them after all, as unexpectedly urgent business called him elsewhere.

When they had risen in the morning, early as it was, Liss had gone. It was deeply puzzling.

Chapter 40

The Snakeskin Pass took a downward direction the next day, finally ending at a gateway covered by a sheet of rippling green light. Faintly through it they could see snow-clad trees and shrubs and a rough hillside. Reece approached the light curtain and spoke softly.

The curtain vanished and he beckoned them through, resetting the ward when they were all clear. Looking back, the tunnel entrance had vanished. The mountainside looked solid; a uniform jumble of snow covered rocks and scrub. Callie doubted that any of them would be able to find the place again without the help of Dexter or Reece.

They headed slightly south towards Montis, the nearest Kerrian town, arriving just as heavy bells rang out. Dexter and Reece exchanged glances.

"It looks like they have a curfew. Let's find a place to stay." Dexter chivvied them along. The first two inns they tried were full, which they all found odd, as winter was not the season for travel, but from the second they were directed to a roadhouse on the edge of the town. When the found it, they realised it was attached to a caravanserai, so possibly the innkeeper had mistaken them for caravan guards or sell-swords looking for hire.

Once they had secured rooms they settled in the taproom to enjoy a glowing fire and a hot meal. While they waited for their food Dexter chatted quietly to their host before returning to the table as their meal arrived.

"What news?"

"Where to start? The inns are full because people are fleeing from the north. Our host is a canny fellow and says at first he disregarded the wild stories he was being told but no longer. The refugees are telling tales of slaughter and capture. Apparently, whole villages have been found deserted, every single person vanished without trace, or only the old folk left behind. In others there have been scenes of carnage and bloody fighting. He says people are terrified. The reason he has room for us is that several families moved on this morning saying they wouldn't feel safe until they crossed the border."

"They are leaving Kerria?"

"Yes, heading for Ostland."

"I take it this mayhem is not the work of Lord Axtra and his supporters?" Jerran leaned forward looking grim.

"No, for once that bloody Warlord is fighting for the people, and his barons are with him under his banner."

"But who exactly, are they fighting?" Callie queried.

"The story goes that a few years back a little known northern Lord came to power. In Kerria this happens all the time, so it didn't draw much attention, until he had conquered many of his neighbours. Finally, Lord Axtra recognised a threat. There has been fighting for several years now. Axtra is holding the south but hasn't managed to defeat the northerner."

"So there is civil war?"

"Indeed!"

"Lithia's treaty, such as it is, is with Axtra, so the attacks at Arco's Gap might not have been down to him, if someone else is wielding a lot of power."

The Prince looked pensive. "Did he say anything else?"

"Not about the fighting but he warned that an illness is spreading through the land. The local healers and apothecaries are at a loss and claim it is unnatural and stems from the blackest Sorcery."

"They do tend to say that whenever they can't cure someone," Terran remarked wryly.

"True," Dexter nodded, "but in this case it might be the truth. There is a family in the barn with a son infected by the 'shadow sickness' as they are calling it and our host says it is terrifying. It's greatly to his credit that he hasn't thrown them out."

"We'd better take a look." Terran signalled to Callie.

"Isn't that a rather unnecessary risk?" Dexter looked anxious.

"There's always a risk, but if only one child is sick, it can't be very infectious. It might be Sorcery and there's only one way to find out." Terran swallowed the last of his ale. "Can you speak to the innkeeper?" Dexter snagged the man's attention and after a brief conversation the man's shout into the kitchens, was answered by the arrival of a sturdy red-cheeked woman with an apron tied around her ample waist.

She listened for a minute or two then when they had finished eating, beckoned them to the side door. Jerran rose to his feet to follow Callie but she stayed him with a gesture. "We may need a translator but it had better be Dexter until we know more of the nature of the illness. It shouldn't be you, Jerran." He winced but the fact of his royal blood could not be discounted.

The barn was large and airy, scented with clean straw. Families had set up camp in every corner. They offered the Innkeeper's wife brief troubled smiles and shot wary glances towards the Mages and Lord Dexter. "Who are these, Marsha?" A man rose to his feet from a crate he had been perching on.

"They are travellers, Simon; no more, but they claim to have some healing skill and offer their help."

"Is this true?" The man's eyes held little hope. "Can you save my son?"

Callie stepped forward. "May we see him? We can't make any promises except that we will do no harm." The man stepped aside and they saw a young child of maybe five or six years lying under a patchwork coverlet on a bed of straw. A woman was mopping his face with cold water. The boy was very thin and except where a fever had caused a hectic flush, he was very pale.

Terran knelt down and took the boy's limp hand. He sent his awareness through the young body and searched. He could find no infection. The muscles, the heart and lungs were all sound. Puzzled, he moved on until finally he brushed against the lad's unconscious mind and flinched.

Callie shook his arm, bringing him back to the now. "What did you find?"

The old Mage shook his head. "This is no natural disease. There is what looks like a Sorcerer's compulsion seeded in his brain, the sort of thing that would allow someone else to control his mind, once triggered. He is still fighting it at the moment but it is growing and if it overwhelms him, then I cannot imagine what he might become, or how he might be used." He sat back on his haunches.

"Can you cure it?"

"I think not; but you might be able to, or we might be able to together."

Callie looked doubtful. "Terran, I'm not really a healer, beyond what I was taught for the battlefield." The old Mage ran his fingers through his unruly grey hair.

"I know a fair amount and I've picked up tricks over the years but I lack the power. You have that, plus the ability to mind-link, as well as the healing bias of your pendant's opal.

"This lad, if I'm hearing it right, was caught at the edge of the Sorcery. If he had been closer his whole mind would be shadowed and he would already be lost, a mindless puppet." He met her gaze levelly. "He still has a chance if we act now and I mean right now."

Callie took a deep breath. "Dexter we are going to try to heal the child. It may look like we are hurting him, but no-one must interfere once we start. Can you explain?"

Dexter nodded and spoke quietly to the boy's parents for a few minutes, then turned back to the Mages. "Go ahead, these are practical people; they know they have nothing to lose."

Terran took one of Callie's hands and one of the boy's. With her other hand Callie reached for her pendant, sliding her fingers over the opal, then nodded at the older Mage, and opened her mind-link. It was different this time. Instead of being simply a power source,

Callie's awareness showed her what Terran saw. A patch of darkness had settled into the boy's brain like some parasitic plant and dark tendrils were already twisting and winding outwards, the way infection spread from a wound.

"We need to contain it then move in," Terran whispered and formed a sphere around the growth. Sweat began to bead his forehead and beneath her fingers Callie felt the opal warming and tingling.

"Terran, let me." She felt the older Mage struggling and realised she knew what to do, although she did not know how she knew. She let a pulse of multi-coloured light feed through her body from her pendant, guided it into the child and at a nod from Terran she pushed it into his sphere.

The child convulsed, his body arching in pain. His limbs thrashed wildly until they were pinned down by Dexter and his father. Dimly she heard gasps and sobbing but she had no attention to spare. Her light and the seed of darkness boiled and churned wildly in her mind's eye. The child's skin reddened and he howled for what seemed like an age, then thick black tears oozed from his eyes and his body fell limply back on the straw. The shadow was gone leaving healthy tissue, a little raw and sore but sound. Terran muttered a simple cantrip to dull the pain before slowly withdrawing his mind and breaking his connection to Callie.

They dropped their hands and sat back.

Callie became aware that all the people in the barn had gathered round watching. Marsha released her grip on the boy's mother, who dropped down beside her child, wiping his face, just as he gave an enormous yawn and opened startled eyes. "Mam?" He saw his mother. "Mam what happened? Are you alright?"

He propped himself up on his elbows looking about him in bewilderment.

The woman brushed away her tears as she hugged her son tightly.

Callie and Terran stood up and stepped away. The boy's father reached for Terran's hand. "Sir, I have no way to thank you. Everything I have is yours." Terran clapped the man on the back and shook his hand.

"No thanks needed but perhaps tomorrow you could spare the

time to tell us your story? We are trying to understand what is happening here." The boy's father nodded vigorously then turned back to his family.

They walked beside Marsha as they returned to the inn. "That's the first one I've seen healed." She studied Terran warily. "That was Sorcery, wasn't it?"

"Most definitely not." Terran's voice was stern. "That was Magery. Do not confuse the two. Sorcery is fundamentally evil. Magery is not. Have there been many with this sickness?" She nodded.

"Once it's really taken them, they head north. You can't stop them, we've tried. We had one," she shuddered, "he turned into a mindless animal. When his family tried to restrain him, the young man attacked his father and mother. In the end the people they were travelling with killed him to save themselves."

"They headed north? Where to?"

"We're not rightly sure, but always the area controlled by Tol Gath."

"Tol Gath?"

"The Black Lord. The Sorcerer of the Ice-lands."

In the tap room Callie slumped back into her chair. She had lost track of time but figured it must be late as most of the patrons who had been drinking earlier had gone. Dexter put a small glass by her hand and she took a gulp, not even bothering to ask what it was, and ignored the laughter as the raw spirit scorched her throat and set her spluttering. Terran sipped from a similar glass and eyed her with sympathy.

"You should get some sleep, Callie." She nodded.

"I feel like I've just been into battle."

"In a way, you have. That was a nasty piece of work but you handled it really well. I'm exhausted too and I had your strength to draw on. Go on, lass. Up the stairs with you." She yawned and waved a weary goodnight to Dexter and Terran. Jerran she noticed was talking to two men at another table but he gave her a brief smile as she made for the stairs, and a mimed round of applause.

Chapter 41

"…And, here she is." Dexter's voice penetrated the early morning fog that still clouded Callie's brain. She had slept badly, her half-remembered dreams dark and foreboding, but she tried to conjure up half a smile for her companions. Dexter drew out a chair for her and Jerran poured Kaffi.

"Callie, I was talking to two merchants last night, while you were in the barn. They have been stuck here for ten days now, unable to hire enough guards for their caravan. Those traders still going north are taking double the amount of men because of the unrest. We could sign up with them if we wanted to be less conspicuous. Caravans are a normal sight on the Kerrian roads and we would attract less attention. On the other hand, it would give us less freedom and responsibilities we can well do without. What do you think?"

"I'm not keen." Terran shook his head. "I know we are an unusual group and likely to attract more attention than we want, but as yet Lithia is not officially at war with Kerria so theoretically we are free to travel where we choose."

"I think I agree with Terran." Callie gave it some thought. "If we encountered trouble and had to really use our Magery it would also expose us to the Sorcerer."

"But didn't you use Magery in your healing?" Dexter queried. She smiled.

"It's really not the same."

"Very well." Jerran didn't seem particularly disappointed with the decision. "I'll ask Marsha to let them know."

He rose to his feet but Dexter called him back. "We still need to talk to the refugees. We need more information on what we might have to deal with and you should probably hear what they have to say."

The Prince nodded. "True, I'll be right back." He headed for the kitchen while Callie ate her breakfast and Dexter slipped out to talk to Will and Gilly.

They had barely reassembled when the side door of the inn swung open and the man they now knew as Sim, stepped nervously through followed by two others. Terran rose to meet him with a friendly smile. "Sim, Good morning and how is your lad today?"

The man's eyes lit up. "As fine as five pence, sir. Already up to mischief." Terran laughed.

"Let's take that as a good sign. Now, will you sit with us a while and tell us your story? Are your companions in the same fix as you?" Sim nodded, and the Tawney man beside him offered a hand, while the third, whom Callie now realised was a middle-aged woman, bobbed a curtsey despite her breeches.

The Kerrians were a little wary as they sat down; hesitant to speak, but Terran's kindliness soon melted their reserve and slowly at first their stories spilled out. Sim and Bran were brothers who lived in a small village, west and slightly north of Skava. Sim, with his wife and two sons had had a smallholding with a few animals to farm and Bran had made his living as a forester and huntsman.

When trouble began, Falun being quite isolated, had not really noticed what was happening. Travellers and pedlars had never been common and their timing always erratic so their absence went unremarked. If the village had enough need, a wagon would make the trip into Skava and buy whatever they lacked. Gilb, their headman, had made the last trip and came back disturbed, saying Skava was full of people fleeing from the north. Hearing talk of villages being overrun by northern warriors, led by some sort of priests, he had sought out some of those heading south and asked question after question until he felt he had a true picture of events.

The refugees told him that when a troop of the dark-clad warriors reached a village or settlement the 'priests' would demand that all the young men be handed over to them to fight 'for the return of Kerria's glory', and young women be handed over to serve their master, Tol Gath. If their demands were refused, and to begin with they were, the darklings, as people were now calling the black-clad soldiers, would withdraw, only to return later in much greater force, slaughtering the old and frail and rounding up those they wanted anyway.

"Did anyone fight back?" Jerran asked quietly.

"Some did," Lauren, the old woman growled. "My man was one of them. They gutted him like a fish. He was always a bonnie fighter but stood no chance when they used Sorcery. She turned and spat on the sawdust floor. "You say they used Sorcery? Are you certain?" Terran pressed.

"Tell them what you saw, Bran." Sim elbowed his brother and Callie noticed the huntsman's hands were fists as he cleared his throat.

"It was back along. I was out after game; had been since daybreak so I'd covered a lot of ground. I was about five miles north of our village, almost at the edge of the forest. Well, I'd had no luck and with the sun high, I knew there'd be slim chance of anything until evening, so I was thinking to drop down into Drev in the next valley. We have cousins there.

"So, one moment all is quiet and the next all hell breaks loose. These men all in black gear with a fancy sign on their chests just appeared out of nowhere. They had the whole village surrounded then they moved in and went from house to house forcing people from their homes. They just chopped down and butchered any of the older ones who resisted and stunned and knocked out the younger men and women. Before long they had everyone penned on the village green. Then this man dressed like a priest does something. He chants at them and they all stop struggling and just stand there like they were asleep.

"Well, a few oldsters working outside the village arrived back. They had hardly a weapon between them but they upped and attacked those darklings. The priest man laughed then said something more to the prisoners and they just went mad. They turned on their own kin, their own fathers and brothers like wild beasts. They ripped them apart while the soldiers just stood looking on. I wouldn't have believed it if I hadn't seen it myself." He fell silent, the horrors he had witnessed playing across his face.

"Then what happened?"

"When the fighting was over, the ones still alive just stood there again like puppets until the Sorcerer gave them another command and they all marched away. I saw some of them were badly injured but they still tried to march away." He shook his head in disbelief.

"Did they head north?" Dexter's voice was gentle but firm.

"North-west."

"You're sure?"

The man nodded. "I followed them a way."

"You are a brave man."

"A brave man?" The hunter flushed. "Was it brave to hide in the trees and watch my neighbours, my cousins slaughtered?"

"Well you could have stepped in and got yourself killed as well." Callie's crisp voice and unsympathetic comment startled her companions. "Or you could have done what I expect you did do – race back to Falun to give warning."

"That he did." Sim dropped a hand on his brother's shoulder. "We are country folk; tied to the land. I did not want to leave our place but he made me. He warned our neighbours and friends. Some of them left like we did. Others would not and I pray the Goddess's mercy for them. We loaded our wagon heading for Skava by the back roads. That's where we met up with Lauren." He nodded at the old woman.

"We stopped a night just outside Anzi where we lost Lucus, our eldest boy."

"You already lost a son?" Callie was aghast. "How did that happen?"

"Bran had put out a few traps before we slept, not far from our camp. We aimed to leave early in the morning so Lucas went to check them. He took Nile, our youngest, with him. There was a hamlet, only a few houses, just beyond the woods. As the boys were checking the last snares they saw a group of the northmen arriving with one of those priests. Lucas wanted to get closer to watch them. Nile was frightened and started heading back to our camp. We think they got caught in the Priest's dark magic.

"When Lucas didn't return, we went looking for him and found him unconscious. His eyes had turned entirely black and he felt very cold. We put him in the wagon, hoping to find a healer when we reached Skava. After a couple of days..." The man gulped, his voice ragged. "After a couple of days he sort of woke up but didn't really seem to be all there. Then a few miles outside Skava he comes to and leaps out of the wagon and starts walking off. When Nile and his mother tried to stop him, he attacked them. I had to tie him up. The next night he got loose and when I got in his way he came at me with a knife. My own son took a knife to me! He was savage, mindless. He laid open my arm and Verna hit him over the head with the hatchet. In the end he died." Tears ran down the man's wrinkled face and Terran proffered his ever present flask.

"And when you got to Skava?" Jerran addressed the question to Bran.

"The town was full of people like us, with the same story or worse – so we just kept heading south."

"Will you be staying here?" Dexter queried. The Kerrians shook their heads.

"Not on your life."

"Montis then?"

"Sirs, we are heading to Ostland and I'm no way sure even that will be far enough." Terran grimaced.

"I'm sorry we asked you to live through those terrible events again, but please believe we did not do so lightly. We are trying to understand what is happening here in Kerria and how to stop whatever, or whoever has unleashed this great evil." The men nodded.

Sim held out a scrap of parchment. "This is the sign the darklings were wearing. Don't mean nothing to me, but perhaps you know it." Callie reached for it as the Kerrians left. At the door Sim turned back briefly.

"Thanks to you I still have one son left. May your God or Goddess protect you."

There was silence around the table as the travel companions looked at one another. Jerran reached for Terran's flask. "Terran – I don't know how much of this stuff you brought," he took a gulp, "but I'm beginning to think it won't be nearly enough."

Chapter 42

Two more days found them camped halfway between Rist and Secker at a site just off the highway. The towns had been full of anxious travellers, and the little accommodation available was squalid and unpleasant. The road was busy, although they seemed to be the only party heading north. At noon the previous day they had sat at the side of the road watching a seemingly endless stream of people crawl past. Some had carts or mules, but many walked with all their worldly possessions on their backs.

When circumstances allowed, Jerran and Dexter talked to the other travellers, gleaning what information they could. To begin with the Kerrians were invariably wary and hostile, but if Callie and Terran offered healing help, the barriers fell swiftly. As they tended the injured and ill they pieced together a picture of a land plunging into chaos. Skava and Skelfborg it seemed, remained in the hands of Axtra and his allies, but no word came from further north. Beyond Koepce and Is-festning all the towns were known to be under the control of the Ice Lord, Tol Gath.

Sitting round their campfire they studied their maps, marking in villages and settlements they knew to be compromised, trying to see a pattern. "Tol Gath has been moving down the west, while Axtra and the southern Warlords are holding position north of Skava but not much more." Jerran was thoughtful.

"It looks to me pretty much like a stand-off." Dexter agreed.

"Not surprising." Terran joined them. "Kerria has never paid much attention to Magery – it is very rare in their general population. This 'Ice Lord' seems to be very powerful so although Axtra has far more trained men, he won't want to commit them in case they can be turned against him."

"There's something I've been wondering." Dexter threw more wood on the fire. "If we find ourselves in close contact with the Sorcerer or his priests, I imagine you and Callie can defend yourselves from magical assault, but the rest of us are vulnerable. Is there any way you can give us some sort of anti-magic protection?"

The Battle Mage looked thoughtful. "That's a very good point – we'll have to come up with something or you won't be able to help when you are really needed. I'll think on it. Now, are we going to leave the highway and test the water in the countryside, or not?"

"I think we should." Jerran eyed his companions in turn. "If we head west beyond Secker we can go through Falun and Anzi and circle back to the north road between Skelfborg and Skava. You all know what we've heard and what we might find but we really need to see for ourselves."

Nobody was keen but nobody argued. What the Prince had said was true, and in the morning they set a brisk pace for Secker where they bought what supplies they could find. They also managed a night in a halfway decent inn, which had rooms because the outrageous prices it was charging were much too high for the local travellers.

Callie had a single room, not large but clean, and almost perfect when they had a bath brought up for her. Stripping off her travel-stained clothes, she was soon neck deep in hot soapy water and even managed to wash her hair. Afterwards, wrapped in a towel, she decided to wash some of her clothing and emptied the pockets, finding the folded scrap of parchment the farmer Sim had given her back in Montis. It looked like an abstract design and she tossed it on the clothes chest while she finished her laundry.

She was just dressed and brushing her hair when there was a tap on her door and at her shout Jerran's head appeared. "A quick word, Callie?" She beckoned him in. "When you send your next update back to Raff I was going to ask if you can check on Liss – I want to know if he returned to Derryn." The Prince watched her smile fade.

"Of course I will. I do hope he is alright. He changed his mind so suddenly and I was certain he meant to come with us. It was strange." She saw something curious in Jerran's face. "What are you not telling me?"

"It's nothing."

"Jerran!"

"Well, nothing I can put my finger on. He said unexpected business had come up." Jerran's voice was expressionless, as if he was trying not to colour his words.

"You didn't believe him?"

The Prince hesitated. "I felt he was hiding something. These days I am following my instincts far more than I used to and they are shouting that Liss has his own agenda. I also think this 'unexpected business' concerns you in some way."

He looked at the young woman before him awaiting her reaction. Her face was thoughtful as she wound her fingers through her damp and glorious hair. He trusted her to take him seriously and she did. "I'll certainly ask after him. In fact, I could ask Raff to do some quiet investigating – find out what Liss really is up to, if he's back in Derryn. My brother is perfectly placed for that."

"So he is. Thank you."

She smiled, her generous mouth quirking. "I'm concerned about him too, Jerran – he is just so…"

"Unique." They spoke the word together and laughed.

The Prince turned to go then stopped staring at the wooden chest. "You figured it out!"

"What?" Callie stepped closer. The square of vellum lay where she had tossed it and her pendant, removed while she washed her hair, lay on top of it. By chance or design it rested across the sigil and in so doing, completed the shape of a Triquetra. They stared at it and at each other. "Oh damn," Callie swore softly and scooped her pendant up to drop it back over her head.

*

The going was slower once they had left the high road and headed along the western spur towards Falun. Making camp for the second time, they were finishing a late supper when Terran called for their attention.

"I have been considering Dexter's request for some 'anti-magic' and I think we can do it. As Mages we are taught to shield ourselves. Some people without any Mage gift still have strong natural shields and many people who work in 'public life' develop them." Jerran nodded. "Everyone is different so we need to test each one of you to establish what additional help you might need. That would require you to let Callie or myself enter your mind, so it has to be your decision."

"You can do me, Terran." Dexter looked at the older Mage.

"And me," Jerran agreed.

"I could—" Callie started only to be interrupted by the Prince.

"Why don't you do Will and Gilly if they are agreeable?"

"Oh, alright." Callie felt oddly rebuffed. It seemed both men were avoiding her gaze and she wondered whether she was being paranoid or oversensitive.

"Me first, then." Gilly came over to her. "I take it this is not going to hurt?" He winked at her and she felt a little better.

"Hold my hand, Gilly."

"Finally!" He clutched her arm and she grinned then steadied herself to go exploring in the strange landscape of another man's mind. Gilly had some shields; not complete but definitely there. Will was pretty much the same. When Callie withdrew Terran was waiting for her. "These two are partial." She looked at him.

"Jerran is perhaps three-quarters shielded. Lord Dexter has some interesting internal barriers, but nothing that would repel magic."

"So can you construct or complete shields for us?" Dexter asked.

"We can," Terran agreed.

"Will we still be able to mind speak – or will that be blocked too?" Jerran queried.

"That won't be affected. The shields will only repel magical attack or assault. They should only block any communications that are forced on you. Do you still want us to go ahead?" He waited.

"Would these shields be permanent?" Gilly asked.

"They certainly don't have to be."

"Fire away then. Do I get to hold your hand again, Callie?"

"Actually, you get to hold mine." Terran moved to sit by the scout. "Callie will power me if I need it."

The Mages linked and Callie, sitting and staring into the dancing flames of the fire felt the slightest pull on her source. Will was followed by Jerran. Dexter was last and Callie realised the draw on her power was markedly stronger. When all were finished they turned in for the night, setting a sentry for the first time. Callie lay awake, weary as she was, wishing she was home or at least in a comfortable bed. She tried to distract herself by re-running the way Terran had created shields for their companions – a new use of her Mage-gift she found fascinating, until it brought her back to the strong feeling she had got that neither Dexter nor Jerran wanted her in their minds. She was still puzzling over that when she finally dropped off.

Chapter 43

"Is my father free right now?" Raff directed a charming smile at the General's aide.

"If it's another report from Callandra, I can take it, Raff." The man smiled obligingly and put out a hand.

"It is, but there are a couple of things I wanted to ask him. Please?"

His father's aide smiled and knocked on the door behind him, speaking a few words into the room beyond. "Go on in but be quick. He is due in Council shortly."

"Thanks." Raff dived into General D'Arcourt's office. His father smiled at him and reached for the report he was holding out. "Raff. Thank you. These are proving really useful, but what do you need to see me about?"

"There is something Callie has asked me to do that I haven't included in the report for obvious reasons, and I'm not sure I feel comfortable about it?"

"Go on." General D'Arcourt looked at his son with calm interest.

"She and Prince Jerran want me to check up on Liss."

"Liss?" Raff could see that his father was startled. "Is there some suggestion of misdoings on his part?"

"Not at all." Raff shook his head vigorously. "Callie likes and trusts him and Jerran has known him forever. The thing is, you know he was meant to be part of their party?"

"Yes. But didn't I hear he became unwell and felt he couldn't go on?"

Raff grimaced.

"Is that not the case?"

"I'm not sure. Callie said he withdrew saying unexpected business had come up. When he got back here the story was that he was unwell. I managed to look at his medical notes – he is staying in a room in the healers' wing and basically they are a load of vague nonsense. Also I've made excuses to see him three times now."

"And?"

"The first time he was having a very serious discussion with Master Lauder so I withdrew."

"And the other times?"

"He wasn't actually there." His father raised an eyebrow.

"Perhaps he…"

"Sir, I checked all the treatment rooms and all the facilities. He really wasn't there."

"How curious. You are implying that he isn't actually ill – so using that as a cover for other activities?" Raff loved how quick his father was on the uptake.

"I really don't know – but it is odd. Liss is well-liked and highly regarded – I realise all this – but he's still not a Lithian. I wondered whether you knew anything – I mean anything you are allowed to share with me?"

General D'Arcourt shook his hand. "No I don't." He paused thoughtfully. "Liss has been a friend to Lithia for many years and I see no reason why that should have changed – also if he is involved in something, he is colluding with Master Lauder and presumably, Master Elton, both of whom I regard as above suspicion."

"So, what do I do? Callie wants me to keep watch on him."

"Well…" the General spoke slowly. "If you can be unobtrusive it can't do any harm, Raff. Stay observant and be on the lookout for anything odd. Trust your instinct. You have a wide network of friends and contacts. Ask the ones you truly trust to be alert – to keep watch for strangers – anything out of the ordinary around the campus and academy. You can imply that I fear some infiltrations and have asked you, to do this to raise the level of security. You, specifically, can continue watching Liss or ask your healer girlfriend to." Raff didn't bother asking how his father knew he had a girlfriend, who was also studying healing. It surprised him not at all.

"Now, dear boy, I have to go to the Privy Council." They walked together to the door. "I'm glad you came to see me, Raff. It was the right thing to do. If anything happens, you know where to find me if you need help." Raff nodded and trotted away as his father stopped to collect papers for his meeting. He couldn't decide whether he would mention seeing the General when next he spoke to his sister.

*

A wooden fingerpost, faded and half smothered by brambles, indicated a further divide of the western spur road towards Falun and Drev. The weather had stayed dry but an increasing wind from the north had sent the temperatures diving although it was nearly mid-day. As well as the promise of sleet or snow it carried another smell. One that had them exchanging worried glances and wrapping scarves across their faces.

As the first few village buildings came into view, the sense of wrongness grew. The only sounds were a few chickens scratching in the muddy street, and somewhere a cow lowing in apparent distress. Dexter held up a hand. "Arm yourselves – move in pairs." Callie he beckoned up beside him as he dismounted, and waved the scouts forward. "Jerran, Terran, start checking these houses." He pointed to a short row of houses on the left as he led Callie to the right.

Dexter walked up to the nearest cot and stepped up onto the raised veranda. Callie wondered if he would knock or shout, but his hand had barely grazed the door before it swung open. It was a simple dwelling. One large room with a table and hearth occupied most of the ground floor. An area at the lowest level had been partitioned off, obviously for livestock, and a sleeping platform was visible at the top of a simple ladder.

Dexter froze in the doorway. His sudden intake of breath was ill-advised as the stench set him coughing. The owners of the property lay on the floor, their bodies swarming with flies and he heard the scurry of a rat moving away from where it had evidently been feasting. He stepped back outside, pushing Callie before him.

Looking at his expression, she said not a word.

They moved slowly from house to house; there was obviously no need to hurry.

Terran was swearing violently by the time they met at the end of the street and Jerran wore the bleakest expression Callie had ever seen.

"Over here!" Gilly shouted to them from the doorway of a large barn, that lay a little further on. It was dim inside, but when their eyes had adjusted to the semi-darkness they saw Will crouched beside a bundle of rags in the straw. A very, very old man lay half under an empty manger. Will trickled a little water between his parched lips as Terran and Callie dropped down beside him. "He's alive?"

The scout nodded. "Only just. He groaned a moment or two ago. Goddess knows how long he's been here like this."

The man's eyes opened slowly as he licked his lips. He didn't reach for the water skin and Terran saw his hands were pressed against his stomach, holding together the tops of a wide and ghastly-looking wound. Looking at it, he shook his head. After another small sip of water some awareness seemed to come into the man's eyes. He tried to speak and failed then tried and failed again. "Callie, he's trying to tell us something. Can you link with him? You have more mind skills than I do."

She leaned forward and gently stroked the old man's blood-soaked hair. "Translate for me, Dex?"

He nodded. "Sir, we are Mages." The man flinched, his eyes widening in fear. She grasped his hand. "No! Not Sorcerers. Mages from Lithia. If there is something you need to tell us, something we need to know, I may be able to make a link with you and take it from your mind. It wouldn't hurt at all – all you would need to do is think about what happened here. I shall not force you." She waited, unsure if he had understood or was willing, but after a moment or two he gave the smallest nod. With a quick glance at Terran, Callie let her awareness slide gently into the old man's mind. She didn't know what to expect – words, pictures, feelings. Only Terran's confidence gave her the courage to try.

For a moment there was nothing and she began to sit back when a kaleidoscope of pictures flashed past and she realised, stunned, that she was actually seeing the man's memories.

She saw the start of a normal day; the village coming awake, people going about their business. She heard an alarm raised, shouting, running feet, screams. She saw the dark-clad invaders, so many of them, moving inwards as they tightened a noose around the village. She watched those who tried to resist cut down without thought or mercy. She saw the younger people driven into the barn – among them a comely woman of early middle age with a young lass beside her – people who meant the world to the old man. She experienced his valiant but hopeless attempt to save them, armed only with a pitchfork – an attack that earned him the wound that had all but disembowelled him. She felt she peered semi-conscious through the straw as the youth of the village were lightly bound and led away, unresisting under the watchful eyes and control of a 'priest' and then she saw nothing, but immense terrifying darkness.

"Callie." Dexter steadied her. "He's gone." Callie shuddered in revulsion to be so closely linked to a dying mind. They waited, giving her time to collect herself. When she thought she could speak, without her voice shaking, she related what she had seen.

They found no-one else alive in the village. The dead lay everywhere, where they had fallen – all the old or very young – those the invaders had deemed useless. They retrieved their mounts and rode silently onwards towards Drev, in dread of what they would find there. It was smaller than Falun, a hamlet nestled below a forested hillside. There were no sounds or signs of life, so Will and Gilly rode in with Terran leaving the others waiting at the roadside.

Callie dropped down from her saddle and made her way to the half-frozen steam that had followed the road for the last mile or two. It was a pretty scene. Most of the trees were trimmed with snow and clumps of snowbells pushed up through the thin covering still on the ground. The water was icy but Callie splashed it on her face anyway; anything to draw her out of the old man's memories. Dexter came and squatted beside her. He didn't say anything. There was nothing to say.

After a while Jerran, minding the horses, shouted down to them that the others were returning.

Dexter drew Callie up beside him. "Are you alright?" She met his quiet, concerned gaze.

"No, but I will be." He nodded, hugging her briefly before reclaiming his mount.

They decided to skirt round Anzi, having no desire to experience another destroyed village and after two simple camps they turned back onto the great north road, perhaps four or five miles beyond Skelfborg. The road was empty; a reminder if they needed it, that they were approaching a war zone. After checking with Terran that it would not call attention to them, Callie scanned the area for people but the countryside was deserted.

Jerran was loath to get too close to Skava until they knew who held the town, so Will and Gilly offered to scout ahead the following day unless they encountered any other travellers. There was an undeniably raised level of tension as they made camp. As Jerran passed Callie walking the first watch he noticed the rest of the camp was still awake. Will and Terran hadn't even retired to their bedrolls when it was time for them to take over.

Chapter 44

When Jerran opened his eyes, jarred awake by some external noise that was out of place, he found himself looking up the length of a sturdy longsword. His groping hand registered that his own weapons had already been removed.

"Get up." The owner of the sword stepped back a short distance, blue eyes watchful. The Prince rose slowly and once on his feet was pushed by his captor out of the tent towards the fire. The others were all standing there under guard. Gilly was bleeding and Terran, his partner on watch, was clutching his head.

"Is that all of them?" Jerran's captor nodded even as he bound the Prince's hands together. In the moonlight it was obvious that the men were not dressed in the dark clothing of the Ice Lord. They wore typical Kerrian dress, brightly coloured and trimmed with fur. The man asking the questions, obviously their leader, looked them over appraisingly. "Who are you and what are you doing here?" He directed the question somewhere between Jerran and Dexter. "Do not lie; it would not be in your best interests."

"We are Lithians on a mission from King Theon." The warrior raised an eyebrow.

"And what is this mission?"

"It is something we can only discuss with Lord Axtra. We are making our way to Skava, which we understand is his present base."

"And how do I know you are not spies or agents of the usurper? You have documents?" The Prince shook his head.

"In a land at war, carrying such things is as likely to get you slaughtered, as to save you – but I do have this." He held up his bound hands, indicating a ring he wore. The warrior studied it, seeming to understand what he was seeing. He barked a few commands to his men who swiftly struck the camp and loaded everything onto their horses.

"Mount up, you are coming with us."

"Where to?" Dexter queried. The warrior smiled.

"You say you wish to meet Lord Axtra – now you will and you'll even have an escort on the way!"

[Callie, are you okay?] Dexter's voice was quietly anxious in her mind.

[I'm fine, Dex. Jerran told me to just go along with things for the moment until we see how this plays out. We were probably going to have to make contact with Axtra at some point anyway. I just hope we can convince them we are on the same side.]

[Well, if we don't, you do pack a lot of power – enough to free us for sure, but I'm with Jerran on this one. We'll save that as a last resort.] He broke the contact and they fell silent, concentrating on riding, hands bound, in the half-light before dawn surrounded on all sides by Kerrian warriors.

Skava was what passed for a city in Kerria. The buildings were a strange mix of wood and stone, steeply roofed against the heavy snows. The streets were narrow and the whole was enclosed by a substantial wall. They had made good time on the great north road and it was barely mid-morning before they were riding through the southern gate. Solders watched the road and eyed them curiously, but their escort was obviously recognised as they were allowed to enter unchallenged.

Callie had had butterflies in her stomach from the moment she had been hauled to her feet from the warmth of her bedroll. She had almost panicked and lashed out when one of the Kerrians had run an appreciative hand over her backside. She had recognised the look on the man's face and had spent most of the journey thinking of imaginative ways of dealing with any attempted rape but now she was simply hungry. Even fear it seemed lost its edge after several hours.

Shouted commands drew her attention back to her surroundings. Their horses' hooves clattered as they moved from the dirt streets to a stone-paved courtyard in front of what looked like a barracks and stables. "We are here." The commander dismounted and threw his reins to one of his men, gesturing for them to do the same, which was not easy. Callie bit her lip as their mounts were led away; she had become fond of her shaggy pony.

She was startled by a light touch on her shoulder and turned to see one of the Kerrians watching her. He spoke briefly and she looked to Jerran for a translation. "He says the horses will be well cared for. Horses are valued here." Callie nodded and offered a slight smile to the man as she watched all but four of their escort depart. The remaining guards, swords drawn, surrounded them and they were led into the fortified building on the fourth side of the square and nudged onwards until they came to a simple but windowless chamber.

It had a fire, a table and chairs and torches on the walls for light but nothing else. "Wait here." Their captor stood in the doorway. "Do not try to leave. It will not be allowed." He stepped away, closing the door behind him.

Just before it slammed shut Dexter heard another voice. "Did you get them?"

"Yes, we did." Then the bolt was thrown. Now that was interesting. Their capture hadn't been by chance or accident – it sounded like the Kerrians had been looking for them. He shared the news with the others.

"Have either of you ever met Axtra?" Terran had dropped into a chair where he was worrying at his bond with strong white teeth. He aimed the question at Dexter and the Prince.

"Not me." Dexter shook his head.

Jerran frowned. "I think I was at court when he signed the last accord, but as I had no part in it, I only saw him from a distance."

"What do we know of him?" Callie held up her freed hands before starting to untie the others.

Jerran took a moment to think. "He is very astute, ruthless, a talented war leader."

"He is a callous, calculating untrustworthy warmonger." Dexter's voice was cold.

Jerran eyed the northern Lord warily then continued. "My father and yours, Callie, say he reads people well. Everyone thinks of the Kerrians as barbarians, but Axtra has been in power for many years and that's not just by force of arms."

"No, that's right." Callie looked thoughtful. "I remember now, my father suspected he had a very extensive spy network. That's probably how they found us." She dragged Gilly beneath one of the wall torches to re-check his head wound and was relieved to see it was not too deep despite the copious blood. "So what now? Do we have to fight our way out?"

"I think not yet." Dexter frowned. "Yes, we are being detained, but this is hardly a dungeon. I think…" He stopped speaking as the door opened. The guards ignored the fact that they were now untied but waved them to the back of the room as several servants entered with food and washing water, which they placed haphazardly on the table before silently withdrawing. As they considered this their captor reappeared and looked over the provisions carefully. He frowned, shook his head and walked out.

"What was that about?" Jerran queried as they approached the table.

Dexter cast a measuring eye then he too frowned. "No salt."

Callie looked at him, confused. "If you want salt perhaps we could just ask for some?"

Dexter shook his head. "Not in Kerria. Here, if someone offers you food and their intentions towards you are benign they give you salt. It confers guest rights and ensures your safety."

"Perhaps they just forg—"

"Callie, it wouldn't have been a mistake. It's much too important for that. We'd best be on our guard until we find out what the Warlord has planned for us."

Chapter 45

Once they had eaten time passed slowly. There was little they could plan for, when their movements were under someone else's control, so it was almost a relief when the door opened again and they were beckoned out and led down draughty corridors into a large chamber, bright with wall hangings and scented by the sputtering pine logs in the huge fireplace.

There were several men in the room and no women. All hard men – all warriors dressed in fur and leather but there was no question which one had to be Warlord Axtra. He rose to his considerable height as they entered, pushing what looked to be a bearskin clear of the enormous sword his hand rested on so casually.

He studied them in silence for a few minutes, his eyes glacial blue and piercing. Finally, he seemed satisfied and resumed his ornate seat. "Sit." He spoke heavily accented Common, as he waved them to chairs set in a semi-circle. As they took their seats, armed warriors stepped up to stand behind each one of them. "When I heard there were visitors in my land I was surprised. The season and the war have discouraged most travellers." He held up a hand as Dexter made to speak. "When I heard who our visitors were – I was fascinated." He paused as they absorbed the comment.

"Yes, I do know who some of you are so we need not waste time on inventive stories as to why you are here. You, Prince Jerran, have been watched since your arrival at Montis – and Lord Dexter is known to very many Kerrians." There was an edge to his voice as he glared on the border Lord. "But we do not know the rest of your company, so perhaps you could introduce them?"

Dexter and Jerran exchanged glances. "These," Dexter began, "are scouts or bodyguards."

Axtra dismissed Will and Gilly with a casual wave of his hand. "But who is this?" He eyed Terran with great interest.

"Terran Lenster." The Mage spoke for himself.

"And you are?"

Terran hesitated briefly. "A warrior."

"A warrior?" The Warlord quirked an eyebrow. "And is that all you are, Terran Lenster?"

"He is also a Mage." Jerran's voice answered the question.

[Jerran!!] Callie scolded him mentally, even as she noticed a swift exchange of glances between Axtra and his captains.

[Callie.] Jerran spoke in her mind. [He already knows. I'll take money on his spies watching you two healing the refugees on our way here. Trust me. There's something he wants or needs from us – so please follow my lead.] He hesitated. [Don't take offence if you are ignored. Women are very much second-class citizens in Kerria.]

The Warlord's eyes moved from Terran and settled on Callie, looking her over coolly. "The woman is attractive. Which one of you does she belong to? Or do you share her?"

Jerran suppressed any reaction to the jolt of outrage he felt from Callie at this question. "She's mine," he made the announcement a trivial matter, "but she is also apprenticed to Mage Terran as she has some slight healing skill."

"Another Mage then. Good." Axtra leant forward, his attention focused on the Prince. "My agents tell me that your actions in Kerria have caused no trouble. On the contrary, on several occasions you have helped people fleeing the fighting. They believe you are gathering facts – collecting information – and I ask myself, what do you plan to do with the knowledge that Kerria is in turmoil?"

"Lithia is absolutely not seeking any military advantage from your situation, Lord Axtra." The Prince spoke firmly. "We are here because of incursions into our own land. A large force of Kerrians and Frystlanders forced their way through Arco's Gap trying to capture our eastern mines. I suppose you know nothing of that?"

The Warlord shrugged and assumed a blatantly false expression of innocence. "You surely cannot think I would sanction such an act of aggression when we have a treaty?"

Dexter observed some of the Kerrian captains smirking and looking away. Jerran simply raised a cynical eyebrow. "Renegades then or, perhaps, outlaws. Almost an entire army, of renegades and outlaws. How remarkable. As it happens we were able to defeat these intruders, but in view of that 'incursion' and the wild stories reaching us from the traders we felt a visit to Kerria might be timely." He paused.

"We have been trying to find out what happens here and now we think we know."

The Warlord's face was expressionless. "And what exactly do you think you know?"

The Prince took a deep breath. "Kerrians are fierce warriors, but to send them against your current enemy, would be to paint the snow with blood, to no purpose. They cannot defeat a Sorcerer and his mind-controlled troops by strength of arms alone."

Axtra sat back and ran a hand through his greying blond hair, finally raising his eyes to Jerran and nodding. "There you have it. Kerrians have no magic. Sometimes the Frystland shamans drift across our borders, but their gifts are of hoof and horn – not the great magics that we now find unleashed against us by Tol Gath. Tol Gath is the Sorcerer in the north."

"We have heard the name," Dexter confirmed.

"He is also claiming to be one of our folk heroes come again – 'The Ice-Lord'. It is not the way of Kerrians to seek help beyond our borders – and certainly not from Lithians." He spoke as if the words left a bad taste in his mouth. "But here you are, arrived like a gift from Krig himself, when the fighting has all but reached a stalemate. And as you said yourself we are allies by treaty Prince Jerran – are we not?"

The Prince nodded.

"As Tol Goth's actions have already affected Lithia – and may do so again – are you willing to aid us?"

"Lithia will always assist her allies, Lord Axtra. I think my father would allow a contingent of Mages to come here to deal with your rogue Sorcerer."

The Warlord shook his head. "No, you will not bring a force of magicians into my lands."

"Lord Axtra, I doubt Mage Terran for all his skill is powerful enough to defeat Tol Gath by himself."

"Still, my answer is no. Your intentions may be as you say, but civil war always offers tempting opportunities. Your Mage can at least try."

They both looked towards Terran who gave a half-smile and shrugged.

"That's why I'm here."

The Warlord grinned with a self-satisfied expression. "Come." He led them into a smaller room where a round table was covered with maps. Lines drawn across the northern reaches and markings seemed to show the disposition of troops.

Dexter and Jerran moved closer. "What is this?" Dexter put his finger to a large dot.

"That is Jaan Linna." It was their captor who spoke up. "It means The Ice Fortress."

"I thought that was just a legend." Dexter looked startled.

"No, it's real enough. No-one knows how it was built or even who built it, but it has always been there. Preserved we believe by some Sorcery. Tol Gath has made it his base. And here," the man they now knew as Arild pointed to clusters of dots surrounding the fortress, "he has troops. They are in," he searched for words, "villages with barracks. There are no fences, a few guards. The people he has conscripted are controlled by his priests."

Dexter heard Callie's mind-speech. [Can you ask if Jaan Linna is fortified? Is there a town?] He met her eyes briefly before she looked meekly down at the ground. He realised she was trying to make herself invisible, insignificant. Dexter relayed her question.

"There is a small walled settlement around the actual fortress, but our scouts have not been able to penetrate it. Those who have gone in haven't come back out."

"Do you still hold Koepce?" Jerran ran his fingers along the road to the northern town. The Warlord shrugged.

"We did yesterday. We may not tomorrow. Most of my men are here now." He pointed to a cross west, and slightly south of Jaan Linna.

"This is Is-festning."

"Ice-castle?" Jerran tried a translation. Arild nodded.

"It is really little more than a fortified farmhouse; a place that is only used in summer, but as close to the fortress as we can get. We shall ride there tomorrow? Yes?" The Warlord waited for their consent.

[Is everyone alright with this or should I try and stall him?] Jerran mind spoke and Callie relayed his question.

[It's really what we came for.] said Dexter.

[No point in delaying if Callie is willing?] Terran added.

Callie nodded without looking up.

"Agreed." Jerran nodded at Lord Axtra.

"That is well. We will leave in the morning." He sketched a brief bow and without another word turned and departed through a side door followed by several of his advisers.

"Come." Arild led them out once more and they followed him through a warren of passages until passing through a pair of heavy iron-bound doors, they reached a short corridor that had an air of dust and disuse. There were several chambers. He opened the first and pointed at Will and Gilly. The room held two beds, a table and chairs and a stand for armour. It was simple but clean. The second room was the same and the Kerrian directed Dexter and Terran towards it. The third room had an ornate doorway, which had to be unlocked and opened on to a suite. The living room was thickly carpeted. A fire burned in the grate and flickered off some beautifully carved wooden furniture. Other doors led out of it. Jerran and Callie walked in.

"Your things will be brought to you soon. Your weapons will be returned to you tomorrow and tonight there will be a feast." Jerran simply nodded while Callie made her way to the window, which actually had real glass in it; a rare sight this far north. To her surprise the view was of dark pine forest. The Warlord's compound was obviously at the edge of Skava, and not centrally in the town as she had thought.

Arild made to leave, then stopped in the doorway looking at her hesitantly. She offered him a smile and he stepped back into the room. "Milady, they say you are a healer?" He spoke in Common, understandably if not fluently.

"I have some skill. Why? Do you need my help?"

"Some of my men were badly wounded in the fighting at Koepce. Our healers have done what they can but…"

She hesitated and the hopeful expression on his face faded. "You are right. If it is the will of Krigsgud that their time is come, I should not deny them. They will be honoured in the afterlife for earning their wounds in battle." He turned on his heels and reached for the door.

"No, no, wait." Callie raised her hand. "I will help your men, no question, but I am only as Prince Jerran said – an apprentice. Terran has far more knowledge and healing skill than I do." Arid shook his head.

"That would not be allowed. He is a warrior. You are only a woman. Perhaps I should not interfere."

Callie swallowed the casual insult, only raising an eyebrow. "Let me help. If Krig wishes the company of your warriors, rest assured he will take them anyway, and it might be by Krig's hand that I come to be here just when I am needed."

"That's true." The Kerrian's face brightened. "Now?"

"Certainly. I need to wash my hands." He pointed towards one of the internal doors and Callie opened it. It was a splendid wood panelled bed-chamber, dominated by a huge bed covered in furs. Callie swallowed hard and opened the next one, where she found a bathing chamber and quickly cleaned herself up.

"Arild, if I have to use healing power, I will need one of my companions to serve as an anchor. The captain looked puzzled, obviously unfamiliar with the word. "To assist me." She tried again.

"The Prince may come."

"Jerran but not Terran? Doesn't he count as a warrior too?"

"The Prince is of the blood that signed the treaty with my uncle."

"Axtra is your uncle?" Jerran queried.

"He is." The Kerrian's assent was brusque. "Shall we go?"

Chapter 46

They left the 'guest wing', which was, Jerran noticed, now guarded, and Arild led them out across the courtyard to the barracks. Entering through a door at one end they found themselves in a large room with simple cots in rows. It was alarmingly full.

Their escort left them for a moment returning with two women, whom he introduced as Gerda and Helga. Both were in their middle years and their expressions, as they looked at Callie, if not outrightly hostile, were wary. "How do you want to do this?" Jerran asked her in a low voice.

"They will know who are the most seriously injured – ask where they most need help."

The Prince turned a charming smile on the glaring women. He was obviously laying it on thickly and Callie thought she saw Arild hide a grin. As an observer Callie was impressed. In minutes the women melted and started pointing about the room. "Over here." He steered Callie to one of the cots and one of the women, Helga, began to unwrap a bandage from the shoulder of a young warrior whose face was grey with pain. "They think part of the arrow is still inside and infection has set in." Callie nodded, aware of a putrid smell and looking at the insidious red tendrils spreading from the wound site, she grabbed a stool and settled herself, while Jerran perched on the edge of the bed.

[Jerran.]

[I know. If you look like you're in too deep, I'll call you back.]

Callie steadied her breathing and using the techniques she had been learning from Terran, she scanned the wound. It was jagged and deep. She closed her eyes and sent her awareness into the man's body. Buried beneath layers of muscle a lump of metal and filthy fabric had created a puddle of infection. It had to come out. "Jerran, tell Arild and Helga to hold him down, this is going to hurt." She heard him speak softly then she gathered her will, reached for and grasped the debris, pulling it back along its entry route, past raw suppurating flesh. The man thrashed and writhed. Callie was vaguely aware of Gerda putting a leather strap between his teeth before leaning her not inconsiderable weight across his legs.

With an unpleasant pop the arrowhead surfaced and fell away from the wound, followed by a flood of stinking pus. Helga cheered – her face alight as she started mopping up. "Tell her to wait." Callie felt her way back into the warrior's shoulder. "I'm going to cauterize the wound – hold him." She summoned the minutest flame her mind could form and let it flame white hot for barely a second. The man screamed and fainted. She chased the strands of infection, burning them out one by one, before she was satisfied.

"Callie." Jerran's hand tightened on her shoulder. After a minute or two she was able to meet his watchful gaze.

"Ask if they have yarrow or comfrey they can pack in the wound." The Prince obliged.

"They ask if he'll survive?"

"I think now, he may well." The youth's eyes opened wide, as if to confirm this. No longer hazy with disease, but alert and watching her with interest. Arild leant forward. "Thank you, healer," then he led the way to the next patient.

After a couple of hours Helga dragged Callie into a side room and sat her down, ignoring her protests, until she had had a hot drink and some squares of a local biscuit, so sweet it made her teeth ache. It seemed she had gone from enemy of the people to favoured niece in short order.

By the time they stopped Callie had had the satisfaction of putting several of Arild's company back on their feet and had undoubtedly saved the lives and limbs of at least three men, whose injuries were too severe for the local Kerrian healers to handle. Arild had been immensely grateful. To Jerran it was clear the Kerrian captain cared about his men and his men knew it. He had seemed very nervous as Callie attended to the last of the seriously injured young warriors – a youth who Gerda informed them, was actually Arild's younger brother. If she had not spoken, they would not have known. The captain showed no favouritism, although they both saw tension fall away from the Kerrian once he realised his sibling would live.

A while later, as they walked slowly out of the room many, many eyes were upon them. Then one of the men reached down beside his bed and grabbed his sword. Jerran, unarmed, looked wildly about him for anything he could use as a weapon but Arild laid a firm hand on the Prince's sword arm and offered a smile. The soldier started tapping the frame of his bed in a heavy rhythm. In seconds all those able to handle their weapons had joined in. The noise was tremendous and brought smiles to the faces of the Lithians.

Arild closed the door behind him. "They honour you."

He laughed, white teeth flashing. "Very noisily." He turned to Callandra. "I was going to take you to see your horse, milady, but you look like you may need to rest?" He was right, Jerran realised. She looked pale, as though she needed to lie down before she fell down. He snagged her arm. "Go on back, Callie, and I'll see to the horses." She was too tired to object instead followed one of Arild's men back to their quarters while Jerran and the Captain made their way onwards to the stables.

Back in their chamber Callie flung herself across the huge bed and her eyes closed. She was asleep in seconds.

When Jerran returned to the guest quarters with Arild's promise to retrieve them before the evening feast, he found the rest of the company had also drifted to their various beds, their pre-dawn start having caught up with them. He opened the door to the bedchamber in the suite. Callie was curled up fast asleep, her auburn hair spilling from her simple leather tie making a vivid splash of colour against the dark furs on which she lay.

He stood quietly looking down at her for a minute or two. Her long dark eyelashes flickered as she dreamt. Asleep she looked very lovely and very young. Jerran slipped silently past and tried the final door in the chamber, which as he suspected led into a 'dressing room' with a simple single bed. He dropped onto it, trying to identify the strange feeling that had surged through him as he had looked at Callie. Not desire, although he was honest enough to admit that existed. Not camaraderie – although in so many ways she treated him as a true friend. No, what he felt was a strong desire to protect her and he wished it was his right to do so.

Rather ironic, he thought wryly, as no woman he knew had ever needed his protection less. He was still puzzling it over when he, too, fell asleep.

*

As they had been told, Is-festning, for all its grand name was little more than a fortified farmhouse surrounded by many extra wooden buildings and a sea of Kerrian hide tents, thickly lined with felt. They were left to their own devices while Axtra met with his captains but were soon called to join them.

The Kerrian warriors greeted Terran with enthusiasm, Jerran and Dexter with cautious respect and Callie with amusement and ribald comments that Dexter was unwilling to translate for her. She wasn't actually excluded from the meeting room but found herself very much discounted. From the back of the room she watched and listened, observing that in the current situation Dexter was taking the lead. His years of border warfare and instinctive understanding of the northern lands very evident.

Although the Kerrians had still failed to get scouts in and out of Jaan Linna, the fortress, they had finally managed to scale the town walls and prepare rough maps of the settlement. They had identified the barracks and a building that saw the constant coming and going of 'priests' and the delivery of prisoners who did not re-emerge. Terran and Callie exchanged worried glances at this last information.

The key to defeating the Ice Lord had to be in breaking the spell that held the pressed Kerrians in thrall. If that could be done Axtra was confident his trained warriors would have no problem fighting off Tol Gath's forces – if fighting would even be necessary. It was not unlikely that released from coercion, the Kerrians would either turn on their captors or simply flee.

[I need to study the magic at close quarters.] Callie spoke in Terran's mind. [How far is Tol Gath's nearest camp and can we go there?]

The old Mage asked the questions as his own and Axtra cautiously agreed that they should be taken to observe the ensorcelled Kerrians for themselves. They snatched the briefest of meals, then found themselves back in their saddles, heading slightly north.

Their guides were unsmiling fighting men and they were all relieved that Arild too, had chosen to accompany them. After a cold ride they reached Axtra's observation post and were led silently through the dense woodland until they reached a position with a view down onto one of Tol Gath's bases. When they were finally in a position to look down Callie's heart sank. From the shelter of the trees the hamlet appeared unguarded. There were no visible patrols, no high fences, nothing in fact to stop the captured Kerrians from walking away except magic. Magic that must be very powerful.

The Warlord's men tasked with watching the encampment reported that there were probably only half a dozen guards but they appeared to have free will. These men managed the prisoners and the settlement in daily, mundane matters. A single priest was also quartered there, who emerged to perform some strange ritual every night or two. A ritual that seemed to reinforce the prisoners' obedience. As it hadn't happened the night before, they were almost certain the priest would appear with the last of the daylight. They waited crouched low in the undergrowth, their breath clouding in the freezing air.

Just when Callie was certain one of her legs had gone to sleep a horn sounded, the noise building up to a long sustained note. "They will come now." Arild relayed the whispered comment from one of their guides.

As they watched, the doors of several large barn-like buildings opened and a stream of men and women spilled out. They made their way slowly, steadily and almost silently to a large area of muddy open ground central to the buildings. Then they stood still apparently waiting.

[Terran, we need to get down there.] Callie's eyes marked the few guardsmen. [We can join in with the stragglers – see if we can break their thrall.]

The older Mage's eyebrows shot up but he simply nodded and turned to the others. "Wait here, we'll do a recce."

Jerran's eyes flashed. "If you're taking Callie, I'm coming."

"No."

"I'm her bodyguard."

"True. But your presence with us would make her more vulnerable. Hold here." Terran held the Prince's gaze until he saw Jerran's reluctant acceptance, then turned and crept after Callie down through the thinning trees. The two of them fell in behind the last few stragglers and followed until they reached the gathering ground. Callie was relieved no-one spoke so their speech would not give them away and dressed in clothing provided by the Warlord they really looked little different from the captive Kerrians.

They had only a short time to wait before the door of one of the smaller buildings was opened by a dark-clad soldier. He ran his eyes over the gathered crowd, and apparently satisfied blew the bugle-like horn he was holding. All the shuffling and fidgeting stopped abruptly, as the captured Kerrians faced towards the raised dais outside the small building, now occupied by a priest.

The man wasn't tall but certainly had an air of command about him. His long black robe was emblazoned with the Ice Lord's sigil. Callie felt butterflies in her stomach, and it occurred to her that her experience of hostile Mages and Sorcerers was very, very limited. She was just deciding whether she was going to have a full-blown panic attack when Terran mind spoke to her.

[Callie, use your Mage sight on the prisoners.]

[What am I looking for?]

[Look at their heads.] She looked out over the crowd then drew her focus to one or two Kerrians standing close to her. [What is that?] Her close inspection showed an almost invisible purple-black mesh resting like a skull cap on each and every one of them. The faintest of threads led away back to Tol Goth's priest, who had started chanting. She turned her attention back to the cowled figure, copying the motions of the people around her. They had begun to shuffle and twitch as if in discomfort.

"Ugh." Terran hissed. [Callie, reinforce your shields.]

The rest of what he said was mumbled, but came across as a selection of inventive swear words. [Ware!] She nudged the older Mage as the priest's voice rose. The ritual was obviously reaching a climax, and he drew an ornate dagger and slashed it down his arm. His blood ran freely and after a moment or two he shook the residue off where it dappled those standing closest to hm. Then he barked a long clear command, before simply turning his back and walking away.

The soldier sounded his horn again and the Kerrians walked slowly back the way they had come.

[Are you coming back now?] Jerran's voice in her head sounded distinctly unhappy.

[Not yet. These are so casually watched we should be able to slip into one of their barracks.]

[But—] She broke the link and walked slowly forward beside Terran.

The barn-like building in which they shortly found themselves was really little more than it appeared. Wooden bunks filled most of the room and a long table and benches ran down the centre. People pitched themselves back on their simple beds, or settled at the table, eyes blank and unfocused.

Callie sat on the end of a bed occupied by a healthy-looking young woman, who paid her no attention at all. Terran dropped down beside a man at the table. [Let's try]. She nodded and reached out to the young woman. She studied the net with her Mage sight and brought her powers to bear on it. It would not freeze and shatter. It would not burn. She tried dispel with no luck. Anything more powerful would likely kill the woman and certainly attract the kind of attention they were trying to avoid.

[Terran – I'm getting nowhere. You?] She turned towards him and saw sweat beaded his face as he shook his head. [We should probably think of getting out.] He rose to his feet. Callie's shoulders dropped, discouraged. If she could heal diseases why couldn't she fix this?

Perhaps that was the answer. [Let me just try one more thing.] She located the faint thread that led away from the woman. [I'm going to use a healing magic, taking this as the point of infection.] She shaped her will and let it build then brought it to bear. There was a moment of resistance then the 'strand' unravelled and vanished.

The young woman gave a gasp, looking about her with the startled eyes of someone who has just woken up. "Qai?" She froze as Callie put a hand across her mouth.

[Ask her if she can be silent if I remove my hand.] Callie turned to Terran, whose Kerrian was basic but just about up to the task. He smiled at the woman whose eyes darted between the two of them in fear.

"We mean you no harm." Terran spoke his stumbling Kerrian. The girl flinched.

"There is danger – no noise. Right?" The girl nodded and Callie removed her hand.

"What is danger? Who are you? Where am I?" The girl's eyes had moved beyond her bed trying to make sense of what she saw in the rest of the room.

"We must escape. Come." Terran beckoned and the girl barely hesitated before wrapping an old blanket around her and climbing to her feet.

Terran opened the door a fraction and peered out into the gathering gloom.

[Can you check for life forms, Callie?]

[Sorry, no – too many people – we'll just have to risk it.] They slipped into the darkness skirting the building and scuttled at speed into the tree-line. Terran took the girl's arm. Without Mage sight she tripped and stumbled over tree roots and brambles and hung on to him gratefully. Callie followed behind, checking on their back trail, but there was no sign of pursuit.

Finding their way out of the camp and up through the trees seemed to take longer than it should have to Callie and she was just wondering if they had missed their companions and gone astray when Dexter mind spoke to her. [We're just to your right, Callie. Who is that you've brought with you?]

[One of the captives. We managed to release her but we haven't been able to explain much because of the language barrier – could you or Jerran talk to her when we reach you?]

[I'll get Jerran to. He can always get around women.]

[Right.] She broke the contact feeling strangely irritated.

"There you are!" Terran spoke quietly but aloud as they found themselves once more back in the shallow dell that had been their observation point. The young woman seemed to relax slightly as she saw the uniform Arild wore, so Jerran stepped away and let the Kerrian commander field the girl's questions while he simply listened in.

By the time they mounted up to ride back to Is-festning Callie felt like an icicle. She was tired, she was dirty and she was hungry, and more anxious than she was prepared to admit. The Sorcery used on the Kerrians, was powerful and tainted, and it had battered at her mind although only delivered by one of Tol Gath's underlings.

If she stopped to consider how strong that made the Ice Lord himself, she thought she might turn tail and run.

There was little conversation on the ride back. Jerran reported that 'Mira' could remember nothing of her time in the camp. Her last memory was walking to the stables at an inn just beyond Anzi to retrieve her horse and that, she struggled to accept, had been nearly five weeks ago. Jerran held his position beside her where she rode double with one of Arild's men but shared no more information, so Callie was left with her thoughts.

Out of habit she scanned her companions. Will and Gilly were looking forward to food and warmth and Terran was half asleep. Dexter felt strangely preoccupied. Finally, she mind-spoke to him. [Dex? What's up? I can tell something's bothering you.]

He half smiled in her direction but didn't reply for a moment or two. [Just thinking. You know I don't and never will trust most Kerrians.] It was a statement – no answer required. [I was wondering why Axtra didn't want Jerran to come out with us on this trip; because he really didn't.] Callie stopped to think.

[He said he wanted to go over strategies for our attempt on the Ice Fortress, with him.]

[True – but in all humility, I am the strategist – not Jerran. He seemed very keen to keep the Prince away from danger.]

[But Jerran came anyway.]

[After he insisted. Oh, forget it, Callie – suspicion is my middle name where Kerrians are concerned. I'm probably seeing shadows where there are none. Anyway, when we get back we'll have more plans to settle. How do you want to play things? Do we continue to make them think Terran is the force to be reckoned with and you his menial assistant?]

[Absolutely. Let's not put all our cards on the table just yet. I'll let the others know.]

*

The Warlord and his advisers listened intently to Terran's report. Mira had not been able to add much to their knowledge having been present in body but absent in mind for the weeks she had spent at the camp. She had had a roof over her head and simple but regular meals. She thought she remembered some basic training with staffs and scars and cuts indicated some contact with edged weapons, but that was all.

It was finally agreed that Terran would lead their group into Jaan Linna town the next night while, on signal, Axtra's men launched simultaneous attacks on all Tol Gath's training camps with the sole purpose of killing the priests, at whatever cost. An action he had refused to consider before, because unless Tol Gath himself could be neutralised there was nothing to prevent the Ice Lord from simply creating more of his underlings. Timing would be crucial and relied on Terran signalling to watchers as they attempted to engage the Sorcerer. It sounded straight forward as they sat and discussed it in Is-festning's large hall but Callie, looking at her companions realised that not one of them believed it would be so.

The Warlord issued his orders and messenger horses headed out to the forces scattered around Jaan Linna in a loose circle. The Lithians sought some rest, Jerran commandeering a couple of basic rooms with simple cots. The beds were already occupied by a few rather drunk Kerrians but he ejected them by simply tipping them onto the floor. When the men objected Jerran assumed a lofty expression and pointed out that he was a royal Prince and was damned if he was going into mortal danger to try and save their country the next day without a decent night's sleep. It made Callie giggle but as the men crawled away she was quick to grab herself a bed. She felt tired from using her magic and she knew she would need to be at her full strength when they finally faced Tol Gath.

She felt like she had only been sleep for about ten minutes, mainly because she had, only been asleep for ten minutes, when the sound of raised voices forced her back to consciousness. "You can ask her yourself since you've obviously woken her up." Dexter did not sound pleased. Callie heaved herself up on her elbows and reluctantly opened her eyes to see Will and Gilly standing beside her bed looking very sheepish.

"What?" Her voice was a growl. Will, her long-time friend was distinctly avoiding her gaze. He stepped to one side and drew Mira into the light.

"Can Mira stay here with us, Callie?"

"Why?" Callie's gaze snagged on Gilly who was now obviously trying not to laugh. "Is there a problem? Wouldn't she rather be with her own people? I know there are women here and we are a bit crowded."

"The thing is," the scout shuffled his feet, "it's a bit of a sticky situation."

"How so?"

"Well, I'm not sure I really understand it but she is being counted as spoils of war."

"She what?" Callie spluttered, outraged. "That's dreadful. She was captured, abducted and placed under a mind control spell! How does that make her 'spoils of war'?" Will shrugged.

"And..." Jerran who had been watching carefully, chipped in.

"And, I sort of won her in a dice game." He was staring so determinedly at the floor he didn't see Callie's jaw drop, although he certainly heard the laughter from the other men.

"You. What?"

"I thought we were playing for a horse!" More laughter. "I guess my Kerrian's not too good."

"Gods above. Dex, can you tell her she is free to stay for the time being? After Jaan Linna we'll see how the land lies. Now I'm going to sleep!" She turned her back to the room and refused to pay any attention to the whispering and furniture moving that took place on the other side of the room.

*

Raff was on late duty at the Healing Centre. In the still room of one of the wards, he was carefully measuring out doses of medicines that would be dispensed during the night, when he heard a noise. The noise wasn't loud, but it was out of place. A door or window had clicked open or shut. All was quiet in the main room so he moved to the side corridor which led to several single rooms. Patients with possibly contagious diseases were treated here as well as those in their final days.

Liss's room was the third along.

A wave of frustration surged through the young healer. On two recent occasions he had found Liss missing. Leon, watchful at Raff's request, had brought him odd snippets of information. Liss, on his return from Barnard's Castle had sent couriers racing to his distant homeland, some overland and some by sea. Hal had added to the mystery by coming across the Isseni in a very out of the way hostelry in the seedier part of the city where he had been in discussions with three dubious-looking characters.

Raff walked slowly until he stood outside Liss's door. He reviewed everything he knew or had heard about the outlander. Without exception it was all to the Isseni's credit. What the hell! Without giving himself time to reconsider he tapped on the door. "Come." Liss was slowly removing outerwear. He glanced at Raff calmly as he tossed a pair of daggers and what looked like throwing stars on to his bed. "I wondered how long you would stand out there, Raff – have a seat." He indicated the single chair in the small room.

"You look remarkably fit for an ill man, Liss." Raff smiled faintly, as the Isseni walked round the end of his bed and settled on one corner.

"I told the Masters they were making a mistake not including you in our little charade. Your talents may differ from your sister's but you are both intelligent and far too observant."

"Liss – please just tell me what's going on. If it's above board and okay with the Masters, I'm obviously not going to cause problems."

"I know you won't, Raff, and you may be able to help us." He paused for thought. "Where to start? Did Callie ever tell you that the Isseni don't have magic – at least not anymore?" Raff nodded.

"She said you couldn't 'do' magic, although you can sense it and identify it."

"Actually, only some of us can do that. The one strand of magic that remains to our people is foretelling."

"Foretelling?" Raff wondered where this conversation was leading.

"More or less – yes. It's a chancy and vague gift and often more trouble than help, but there are several Seers in our Kingdom. Some 'foresee' years ahead, others months, some only days. When they see something it is recorded and matched."

"Matched?"

"As a rule of thumb, if one Seer sees something it's a 'maybe'. If two Seers see the same thing, it's a 'probably'. If three or more see the same it's almost a certainty." He looked to see if Raff was following. The young man nodded. "Foretellings are not common so when they happen we really do pay attention, but a few months back two came almost together – and in a way they may be linked. One of our Seers had a foretelling that was clear in general intent. Danger and threat to the Lithian Crown." Raff gasped. "But it was vague in detail. Which? What? When? It was also at the time the fighting was fierce in Nilsport, so we wondered if that was it – a warning of the invasion – the possibility that it might succeed."

"But it didn't."

"No. So we relaxed a little."

"I can hear a 'but' coming." Liss nodded.

"Two more of our Seers have reported that same foretelling." Raff explored the idea.

"Yet you still do not know what shape or form the threat will take?"

"No."

"Is that why you did not wish to go on to Kerria?" Even as Raff framed the question, he paused and shook his head. "No, that can't be right. You knew all this before you even set out."

"That's true, I was concerned about leaving the royal court with such a threat looming but nothing indicated immediacy so I thought I would go anyway. Then something happened on the way."

"What? I can understand Prince Jerran as a royal Prince might be vulnerable in Kerria, but you left before that."

"That's true. Jerran might be at risk, but he's with Callie. I cannot imagine a single situation he could possibly find himself in that she couldn't deal with." He held up a hand, anticipating Raff's disbelief. "Really Raff – you, none of you have grasped the immensity of the power she can now command." Raff took a moment to digest that thought.

"So. What happened that brought you back?" Liss was silent for so long Raff began to think he would not answer.

"There was a second foretelling. Brief and cryptic but it relates to a prophecy." Raff groaned.

"A prophecy, not really?"

"Yes. It was seen and recorded centuries ago and generation after generation of Isseni have prayed for its fulfilment. The prophecy is so old it barely makes sense anymore, but the first line reads…" He paused, translating under his breath. "When the Ice jewels are once more united…" Our seer simply said, "The ice jewels stir they begin to gather."

"That's it?"

Liss nodded.

"The ice jewels, do you know what they are?"

"Some of them. The reason I have been here in Lithia for decades is because it was foretold that the first and greatest of the jewels would appear in this land."

"What? So you've been put here to watch out in case they turn up?"

"More or less." He waited eyeing the young healer speculatively. Raff snapped his fingers.

"Callie's pendant!? You think that might be the first and greatest?"

"Indeed I do and as it is incomplete, I thought I should join the trip to find the missing parts but it is not that simple and much remains unclear. The prophecy links the jewels to the "Red Queen", so we have watched and guarded the Lithian royal line for generations!"

"Then?"

"At Barnard's Castle we gathered to eat dinner the night before we departed. Callie sat down opposite me. She was wearing a brooch that shone with power. Lord Barnard had just given it to her in thanks for what she did at Arco's Gap. I questioned him afterwards and he was slightly bemused. He had forgotten the piece completely but when he saw Callie it came to the front of his mind so strongly that he went looking for it. He was absolutely certain she had to have it. It was another of the Ice jewels."

"So your Seer was right; the jewels are stirring. What else did the prophecy say?"

"Raff, I am sorry but I do not think I am free to tell you that. It is not a matter of trust. I dare not say more. If I take a single wrong action, or speak a word out of place that prevents the fulfilment of the prophecy, it would be the end of hope for my people. What I can tell you is, if I am reading it correctly and these matters truly are in motion, the ones at risk are the King and Prince Mikheli."

"So what now?"

"I have an extensive network of contacts in Derryn listening for anything untoward. Extra patrols have been set up. The ports are being watched and the guards at the city gates are checking everyone entering or leaving."

"Why is my father not part of this?"

"He is now. I expect he'll send for you quite soon. He said he had asked you to use the access you have as a healer to listen and question the sort of people who don't come to the attention of the city guards."

Raff nodded. "So has Master Elton declared you ill so you are free of all your court duties?"

"Exactly."

"How is Master Lauder involved?"

"We do not know if an attack would be physical, magical or something else entirely. That is one reason your father was not involved to begin with. He is a soldier. To do what he does so well, he needs to have a tangible enemy to defeat or outwit. Master Lauder and the other Mages are on the look-out for any use of unknown magics."

"I see. Well, what can I do?"

"Carry on as you are, Raff. I was very impressed by one of your friends, Hal?" Raff nodded. "I was surprised to see him in such a little-known inn and I really couldn't tell from his behaviour if he had seen and recognised me?"

"He did!"

"Impressive!"

"So all we can do is stay alert, watch and wait?"

Liss sighed. "I'm afraid so." He brushed his silver hair out of his eyes. "There may be a further foreseeing – and that's a double-edged blade." Raff looked a question. "Another foreseeing might provide useful detail but it would make an event, a possible royal death, imminent and extremely likely."

When Raff returned to the still room, he sat down to consider all that he had learnt. It was a lot to take in and his mind drifted to Callie. He wished, not for the first time that she was nearby – near enough to talk to face to face instead of mind to mind. So much seemed to be happening so fast. It was quite a while before he turned back to the medicines.

Chapter 47

At Is-festning the day dragged. The men checked and re-checked their weapons. All the horses were groomed. It seemed to Jerran that the waiting and anticipating were far worse than the cut and thrust of battle itself. He kept an eye on Callie who was huddled in a corner with Terran discussing magical responses to possible scenarios. She was biting her lip as she always did when she was nervous.

He was glad he wasn't the only one.

Mid-way through the afternoon, snowbirds began arriving, confirming Axtra's men had received their orders and would be in position to attack at moonrise. Terran had not been happy to have the time so predetermined, but without mind-links there was no other way to co-ordinate the attacks. He prayed they were able to penetrate Tol Gath's fortress and tackle the Sorcerer successfully. He knew it would not be easy.

Finished with Terran, Callie took herself off to an empty room and set her mind free to seek her brother. Raff linked so quickly, she felt he must have been waiting for her. It was good to talk to her other half; to talk freely, not minding her words. When she had brought him up to date she found she was reluctant to break the contact and let him chatter for a while. He wanted reassurance that they were all okay, particularly Jerran, which seemed a bit odd but before she could follow that thought a knock at the door brought an end to their interlude as Dexter shouted it was time to leave.

Callie slipped blades into her leathers and she was ready. She could not afford to be late. Axtra had had to be persuaded that an insignificant woman should be included in the coming action at all. Terran had finally convinced him that Callie had a small amount of natural power that he could add to his own, if need be. The Warlord apparently had no trouble accepting her as a mere tool to be used by someone else.

They rode out with perhaps two troops of Axtra's men. The rest were positioned encircling the fortress and town of Jaan Linna. Following a southerly road from Skava to Is-festning, none of them had actually seen the Ice Fortress. When it first appeared it was outlined against the sunset, but even at a distance it was huge. Tall, angular towers clawed at the sky and the lofty walls, made from some pale stone, glimmered with the snow light. They halted their horses for a moment or two, simply staring. The warriors looked grim. To Callie it looked like a castle from her childhood fairy tales and she would have thought it remarkably beautiful if only she didn't have to enter it. That thought made her feel slightly sick.

Axtra was watching them she realised, or at least, Terran. "Do you still think you can get in?"

The older Mage didn't let any doubts colour his voice. "I'm sure we can get in. Getting out again in one piece might be more of a challenge." Axtra laughed and Callie found herself thinking that if they did get in and defeat Tol Gath, the Warlord was not going to be remotely worried whether or not they escaped afterwards.

At the last fortified position, they grabbed a hot drink and left their horses with some of Arild's men. The light was fading and a few clouds muddied the skies, but not enough to block the moon when it rose. They made their silent way through the thinning trees until they were opposite the smallest of the entrance gates into the town of Jaan Linna. There were two visible guards and Callie couldn't detect any others nearby.

"Ready?" Terran pressed her arm. She nodded. "I'll take the left." They focused their magic and simultaneously sent 'sleep' towards the men at the gatehouse, who obligingly slumped to the ground. They darted across the open space, crouching in the shadows of the walls; Dexter and Jerran removed the overtunics from the fallen men, donning them swiftly over their own mail. They edged through the gate while Will and Gilly pulled the dormant sentries to their feet, propping them semi-visibly where Terran froze them in place.

Within the town wall a maze of alleyways spread left and right weaving around buildings of the same grey moonstone. They slipped along the narrow streets moving from shadow to shadow, diving into doorways as soldiers walked past evidently heading to or from the nearby tavern that hummed with activity and even a few notes of music.

None of them had known what to expect, but Dexter summed up the general surprise. [It's just like a normal barracks town.] He used mind speech as Callie was holding an open link so everyone could hear.

Terran cast an assessing eye along the lanes. [These men are not under any compulsion so I imagine Tol Gath is making sure their wants are met. I think there's another ale-house that way,] he jerked his head, [and that looks like a brothel.] He pointed to another anonymous building, which Callie stared at, wondering how he could tell, even as her companions agreed with him.

They continued on, working their way inwards as they did so, noting the ground was gradually rising. [Hold,] Jerran hissed as they rounded a corner and nearly wandered out into an open area that was buzzing with activity. Near a long building fronted by shallow stone steps and ornate pillars, a crocodile of men and women were waiting. They were bound and even in the half-light it was evident that many had been beaten or injured. One frail woman was only on her feet because a young man beside her was holding her up. A contingent of armed guards surrounded them, some with swords drawn, others with staffs at the ready.

As they watched two 'priests' descended the steps and looked the prisoners over – for all the world as if they were assessing cattle at the sale ring. Finally, they nodded and the captives were pushed and prodded inside the building. [That must be the Temple.] Jerran stared into the darkness. [We need to deal with these priests before we go to Tol Gath or he may be able to call for reinforcements.]

[If as we suspect, the priests are mind-linked to him, he'll know as soon as we take them down.] Terran looked concerned.

[Can't be helped.] Dexter shook his head. [We daren't leave any more enemies behind us than we have to. Let's do it.] A murmur of agreement swept across the link and Dexter waved for Will, Gilly and the Mages to move clear of concealment, as he and Jerran walked boldly across the square where the last two of the guards remained.

One looked up and grinned at Jerran. "Finally, are you are reliefs?"

Jerran smiled, reversing the grip on his sword. "In a way." He clubbed the man with his sword hilt and Dexter took out his partner. "Will! Gilly!" The scouts stripped the men's tabards as quickly as they could before dragging their bodies behind the pillars and tying them up.

[Now we free those people. I counted eight guards so still at least six inside and the priests. Form up!] Dexter and Jerran stepped in front of Terran and Callie who clasped their hands behind their backs as if they were tied. Will and Gilly fell in behind and they marched through the temple door as if they had every right to do so.

If the temple had seemed silvery and light from the outside, within it was all darkness. On a raised dais straight ahead of them was an altar; a stone table on which one of the prisoners, already tied down with leather straps writhed and struggled. The other prisoners were on their knees, still bound and many of them weeping.

The soldiers standing in a semi-circle in front of them, weapons drawn, looked bored and disinterested. They had obviously witnessed it all before. There were four priests in front of the altar. Three of them, black clad, hands linked, were chanting softly. The fourth in red held a ritual dagger that he raised aloft even as they approached. The blade was black, and rippled in the reddish light thrown by the candles edging the space. He looked up at Dexter and Jerran and paused as they approached obviously annoyed.

"Why do you interrupt the ritual, you fools?" His voice was thin and rather high.

Dexter shrugged, looking the picture of an ignorant soldier. "Two more." He stepped to one side seeming to push Callie forward but essentially giving her a clear angle of attack as Jerran did the same beside Terran.

The priest looked them over for a moment then nodded. "Oh, very well." He gestured for them to be added to the prisoners on the floor then turned his attention back to the ritual, raising his dagger high once more as he resumed his incantations.

[Now!] Dexter's command brought instant results. Terran sprang forward and grabbed the ritual dagger from the chief priest and used it to stab the man through the heart before slashing the bloody blade across the leather straps that pinned the prisoner to the stone table.

Callie dived past the startled soldiers to where the other priests froze briefly, before their shock turned to fury. She felt a surge of magic and flung up the wide concave shield that Terran had taught her, extending it until it also covered the prisoners. One of the priests slammed a bolt of energy at her and his eyes bulged as it ricocheted back at him, extinguishing his life like a snuffed candle.

Terran stepping calmly over the High Priest's body, grabbed another of the priests unbalanced by the edge of the blast, slitting his throat before he could recover then spun on his heel, bringing his sword down to cleave the final celebrant from shoulder to hip.

Callie swallowed hard then spun round in her turn, looking beyond the prisoners who stood wide eyed, their faces showing a mix of terror and hope. The six soldiers were giving a fairly good account of themselves but were obviously outclassed. One of them looked as though he wanted to drop his weapon and Callie winced as she saw the tip of Dexter's blade emerge through his back but there could be no quarter given. As Jerran had said, these men were not mind controlled. They had chosen to ally themselves with a Sorcerer whose tactics included massacre, rape and the butchery of young children. As she impaled one of the men on her own sword, she finally and fully understood that knowing a man deserved to die did not make delivering that ultimate sentence any easier.

It was all over in a very short time. Will and Gilly moved among the captives untying them. Several, shaking with terror and on the verge of collapse, slumped to the floor. "Who are you?"

The man who minutes before had been lashed to the altar, had pulled himself together enough to approach them. "We are here on a mission for Lord Axtra." Dexter kept it brief.

"He really sent you to get us out?" one of the women asked

disbelievingly.

Dexter grimaced. "Not exactly – we are on our way to a reckoning with the Sorcerer Tol Gath. I'm afraid it was pure chance that our paths crossed."

"We thank the gods for that, but what do we do now? If we leave the temple his soldiers will recapture us."

"True. Will, Gilly, can you check all the anterooms?"

The scouts slipped away and returned in short order. "All clear. There's only one back entrance and we've secure it."

"Good, now listen. When we leave, barricade the temple entrance behind us. If we succeed in our mission, Lord Axtra's men will enter Jaan Linna and deal with the soldiers." He paused as a loud bell tolled from above. "What's that? Have they raised the alarm?"

"No." The prisoner shook his head. "That's the curfew bell. Even the soldiers have to return to their barracks when it sounds. Afterwards, you mustn't be seen out."

"Damn. Well, as I was saying – don't leave the temple until we let you know it is safe." The man nodded. They turned to go.

"What if you don't make it back?" The Kerrian kept his voice low.

Dexter shrugged. "Then, good luck."

They headed back to the entrance, the scouts checking ahead, but all was quiet. They slipped noiselessly along the next street, but the third time they had to take cover Dexter mind-spoke them all. [It's like he said, these soldiers are all heading for their barracks, and though that tells us we are going in the right direction, we are going to be discovered before long. You see that building over there?] He indicated a derelict house with most of its roof and one wall missing. [We'd best hide out there until the traffic dies down.]

They darted across the roadway and settled themselves to wait. It was hard to gauge the passing of time, but fewer and fewer soldiers appeared until at last, the streets were empty. "Time to go!"

Will and Gilly moved up to the next corner, then Will came racing back. "The inner entrance to the Keep is up ahead past three alleyways. There are guards."

"Terran." Dexter looked to the older Mage who nodded and crept forward with Jerran beside him.

"Callie?" Dexter stepped over the broken wall and they trotted swiftly after the others. Automatically Callie scanned for body heat and swore as she grabbed Dexter's arm. "Dex, there are people coming."

"Where from?"

"Some behind us and more from the first alley on the left. Take cover." Jerran and Terran disappeared down the second alley and Will and Gilly simply vanished. "Come on!" Dexter took Callie's hand and they ran to the right, only to be brought up short. Their alley was a dead end with not even a doorway for cover, and unfortunately well lit. The heavy footsteps and jangling armour of the approaching solders was almost upon them. Dexter, looking about him frantically began to draw his sword.

"No, wait!" Callie swung round, putting her back to the wall. "Dexter. Kiss me."

"What?"

"Now!" She grabbed the front of his stolen tunic, pulling him close, then wrapped her arms around his neck, lowering his face to hers.

"Callie are you sure this—"

"Dexter! Just do it!" He let his lips brush hers gently.

"Goddess!" Callie swore. "Can you make a bit more effort? Pretend I'm Penny Plain!"

"Who?"

"I'll tell you later or ask Jerran!" Dexter pulled Callie closer, sliding his thigh between hers, and kissed her firmly. Her lips were soft and warm in the cold night air and her body a delightful combination of toned muscle and womanly curves. She leaned into his embrace, running her hands up his back beneath the tabard. He tried for control, aware that his breathing was becoming uneven. He honestly tried, then her tongue darted into his mouth. His hand slid along her thigh as a surge of entirely inappropriate desire fired his blood.

Callie sensed the tension sweeping through his body and almost faltered; almost drew back, then on the edge of her awareness she heard the soldiers stopping at the end of their alleyway and shouting at them. She recognised the word for 'curfew' and ribald laughter that followed a few comments. Dexter took his hand from her thigh and made a universal gesture that provoked other lewd comments and laughter before the soldiers finally moved on.

After a minute Dexter straightened up, not quite releasing her. He swallowed hard. "Callie."

"I think you can let her go now." Prince Jerran stood at the alley entrance. His voice was cold.

"Do I have to?" Dexter tried for a light tone but he sounded hoarse and he studiously avoided looking at Callie.

Terran stepped forward and patted her on the back. "Quick thinking, lass. Now, from where we were hiding, we could see the inner gateway and what looks to be the main barracks, it's through and just to the right. I think we should go and give them all sweet dreams before we call on our Sorcerer – or do you think that would use up too much energy?"

Callie gathered her scattered wits. "I think that's a good idea but let's set a time limit on it. I don't like to think of even those soldiers being butchered by Axtra's men in their sleep, and I wouldn't put it past them."

They approached the gatehouse keeping to the shadows with Callie concealed in their midst. The guard walked out at Gilly's wave and for a moment Callie thought the scout was whispering to him, before she saw the man keel over. Jerran raised his voice. "There's something wrong out here!" Two other guards ran out and were instantly dispatched. There were no others.

The Mages walked through the gates towards the long barn-like building and Terran placed a hand on the wall. "How many, Callie?"

She felt for the sparks within; more than she had thought. "About thirty, I would say." Terran nodded and closed his eyes, while the others kept watch, swords drawn. After a few minutes he blinked and looked about him.

"Done?" Jerran asked. He nodded. "Right then. Let's see if we can cut off the head of this snake."

Chapter 48

Across a courtyard they saw the grand entrance to the Ice Fortress of Jaan Linna. A tall archway, intricately carved, was inset with some stone that flickered as starlight played over it. The stone walls themselves were the same silver grey as the exterior and as they crept forward they could see the ceiling rose, vaulted high above them. There was no-one in the echoing antechambers. Here and there, torches burning in wall sconces threw red-gold light over the path they took threading their way between huge pillars.

There was no sound at all: no people, no activity, but Terran and Callie both felt a presence, an awareness. Darkness pressed at their shields. Immense tainted power rolled over them and Callie thought her knees might buckle. She shuddered and felt warm fingers snag her hand. Their arrival had not gone unnoticed. The long hallway led to a vast staircase that rose one level before dividing. [Which way?] Jerran thought to the Mages. They both pointed to the left without a moment's hesitation. As they moved silently up the stairs, past ancient suits of armour, Will's bow snagged on the chain mail of one ancient warrior and the metal rang and echoed. [Quiet!] Jerran hissed and Will looked suitably chastened but Callie raised a hand.

[I hate to say this, Jerran, but it doesn't matter. He knows we are here. I can feel it.] She looked sideways at Terran who nodded in grim agreement.

At the top of the stairs they walked through two interconnecting rooms. They were full of ornate furniture from a time long gone by, but showed no sign of age or decay. Callie glanced at Terran questioningly. [A stasis spell, and a very good one,] he murmured, looking about him admiringly.

At last, looming out of the darkness they saw a huge pair of doors. They approached warily, nerves so taut that Callie jumped when Dexter tapped her shoulder. [Callie, your pendant.] He pointed and she saw the outline of the gem glowing softly through her outer clothing. It felt warm when she touched it. Warm and almost alive. [I know this sounds crazy, but I think it senses its missing parts; it wants to be made whole again!]

[And hopefully it soon will be. Callie, can you check what lies beyond these doors? The emptiness out here feels so orchestrated; I think we can expect a warm reception.]

Callie extended her awareness cautiously and flinched. [The room is crowded; there are people straight ahead. Men on either side of the doors and others somehow high up.]

[Probably a gallery.] Dexter seemed unsurprised. [I expect they will be archers.]

[There are several more priests!]

[You can tell they are priests?]

[Yes. They sort of taste tainted.] Her face blanched and she took an uncertain step backwards until she was steadied by the Prince.

[Callie, watch your wards!] She nodded at Terran and strengthened her shields.

[Is it the Sorcerer?] Dexter asked.

[I think so. Dear Gods! Whatever it is, it is barely human anymore, and so powerful!] Her voice quavered. [I'm not sure I can do this!]

Terran grabbed her shoulders and he spun her to face him. [Callandra,] he shook her gently, [fear and self-doubt are both his weapons. Remember who you are – an Elemental Mage.]

[But I'm not that powerful!]

[Not that powerful! An Elemental Mage? Goddess! The north wind will do your bidding; the snow will fall at your direction. You can command the very rocks and earth beneath this fortress and play with the fire glimmering from these torches on our sword blades. All these are here for you to use. You may not be sure you can do this – but I am absolutely certain.] She read the total conviction written on his craggy face, took a deep breath and raised her head. Her auburn hair fluttered around her face, twirling on unseen currents of air and flames danced in her eyes.

For a moment she looked like some figure from legend.

A whisper from Dexter stole into her mind. [It's performance anxiety – we all get it!]. The comment was loaded with dubious innuendo. Callie clapped hand over her mouth before she burst out laughing, and became her simple self again.

[What?] Jerran queried. She shook her head and saw the frown on the Prince's face deepen as he looked between her and Dexter.

[Terran, Callie – the archers in the gallery before we go in.] Dexter drew them back to the moment.

[Now?]

[Now!] The Mages cast the sleep spell in the direction Callie indicated. The sound of chanting, humming through the doors did not falter but it was punctuated by thuds and clashes that they prayed were bowmen collapsing.

Then, before they could make another move, the great doors swung silently open, and they were finally face to face with the Sorcerer of Jaan Linna.

The great hall before them was circular or hexagonal; it was difficult to tell in the flickering candle light. On either side of the doors stood squadrons of soldiers, alert, well-armed and absolutely silent, weapons drawn.

Ahead and to one side of the hall, several red-robed priests were chanting over twenty or so Kerrians poorly dressed and unarmed, who shuffled frantically but were surrounded by more solders in a ring of steel. The priests ignored the intruders and continued with their vile ritual.

Tol Gath sat on an ornate throne-like chair of carved obsidian set on a raised dais. He was watching them. [Damn and blast,] Terran swore under his breath as he reeled from the power the Sorcerer exuded. The Ice Lord rose to his feet. He was very tall, dark and skeletally thin and appeared a lot younger than they had unknowingly been expecting. There was an air of mockery about him.

"And finally we meet." He spoke trade tongue with an accent they did not recognise. "Your little group has caused me considerable annoyance, but I am in a forgiving mood as you have brought me the rest of the Triquetra." His dark eyes fixed hungrily on the pendant now glowing brightly at Callie's throat. "At last the pieces will be united."

"To do what?" Callie was proud that her voice remained steady.

"To save time." He laughed coldly. "I intend to control all of Kerria, then Lithia. This will happen – but it will happen faster when I hold the full power of the Triquetra. Now – please." He held out his hand as if he expected her simply to hand it over.

Callie shook her head. "I'm sorry but I really can't agree to that."

The Sorcerer sighed. "If you still believe you can stop me you are deluded. If you resist, your friends and these innocents," he waved his hand at the captive Kerrians, "will all die – are you prepared for that?"

[Now!] Terran shouted as he launched an energy bolt at the Sorcerer. Callie matched and surpassed it with the power she flung towards Tol Goth only to see it dissipate as it hit a smoky grey shield. Behind her she could hear the sound of sword fighting, as the soldiers attacked. She sent blast after blast towards Tol Gath knowing her companions needed her to succeed before they were overwhelmed by sheer numbers. [I have to get closer!] she mind-spoke Terran and ran forward with him on her heels. They launched lightning together, compounding the power. For a moment, her eyes still dazzled by the after image of fire, it seemed to Callie that Tol Gath wavered. Wavered? Not staggered – wavered – her mind raced. "Terran, that's not him – it's a construct. So where is he?"

"Right here," a voice hissed behind her. She whirled round as a mesh of blue light dropped over her, freezing her in place. She could see, but she could not move and she could not feel her magic. What she did see nearly broke her heart. Before her eyes the shielding she and Terran had put on their companions faded to nothing. The men were all bleeding but fighting on until with a snap of his fingers Tol

Gath disarmed them and sent them to their knees. Jerran fell where he stood but to her horror she saw Dexter stagger backwards and stumble into the group of Kerrian captives, where he collapsed and lay still.

Tol Gath looked about him smiling. "That's better. Now, I won't kill you immediately – not until you've shared all you know of my wonderful pendant." He turned back to her and calmly lifted the Triquetra from her neck and dropped it over his own head where it lay next to two others, so shaped and glowing they could only be the missing lobes of the amulet. "I will deal with you later, my dear. Your interference has finally given Axtra sufficient backbone to attack my forces. It was a good plan. He has killed most of my priests. Fortunately, with the triquetra complete they are now redundant anyway. Let me show you to your chamber – it's been specially prepared!" He signalled one of his men. Callie could not turn to see what he did but the next moment the floor slid away beneath her feet and she fell helpless to save herself down a long filth-encrusted chute that finally spat her onto the floor of some sort of cell. A thud and groan told her Terran had fallen nearby.

It was pitch black. The straw she felt beneath her was damp and rustling. The place was probably riddled with vermin. Half-stunned, she hadn't moved before rough hands grabbed her and turned her over, tying her wrists and feet. She assumed the same was happening to Terran, although worryingly he had made no further sound. She opened her mouth to shout, scream, bite – she had no idea what, only to find strong fingers pinching her nostrils while some sort of flask was tilted at her lips. She tried to turn away and was slapped across the face so hard her teeth rattled. She swallowed, choked and swallowed again. Whatever her captives were pouring down her throat tasted bitter and oily.

A minute or two later they let go of her and she fell back onto the straw. She could not see how many guards were in the cell but a low mumbled conversation was taking place nearby, where she thought Terran lay. The voices became more distant. There was a heavy clang as the cell door shut. Then a grid of bright blue light sprang up, dazzling her. The front wall of the cell holding her was entirely barred and each metal strut flickered with coruscating blue flames.

Callie moved gingerly, almost feeling her bruises develop. She tested her bonds, without much hope, only to find she could slip her hands free with little difficulty and thereby untie her ankles. So the bonds had only been meant to hold her while she was drugged: at least that's what she reasoned. She rose unsteadily and made her way to Terran. When she shook his shoulder he groaned faintly but did not stir. She ran her hands over his body. He winced as she touched one of his wrists, but it didn't actually feel broken. When she reached his head a damp stickiness coated her fingers and the smell of blood caught the back of her throat.

Her landing had been hard but she had obviously been luckier than Terran.

Callie sat back on her haunches and tried to settle herself; to calm her racing heart. It took longer than usual but finally as her breathing steadied she reached inside herself for the spark that was her magic. She reached and reached again, uncomprehending. There was only emptiness. She reeled with the shock of it. Her magic, the huge swirling chaos of it that coloured every strand of her heart and soul, was gone.

She crouched on the damp straw for long minutes, shaking, unaware that hot tears were trickling down her face. Terran groaned again. With trembling fingers Callie ripped her scarf and bound it round his head. She could barely see his wound and had no means to clean it. She could do nothing more. She crawled to the wall and leant back against the chill stone, thinking.

She knew somewhere above her, her companions were taken capture. They had no shielding and even if they still lived, they had no chance of breaking free. They had all thought she would be able to deal with the Sorcerer. Honestly she had thought so too and cursed herself for her hubris, for letting them all down. Tol Gath had been well prepared for her and now she was a prisoner in a magically warded dungeon – her life hanging by the merest thread, and worst of all, the Sorcerer of Jaan Linna now wore the great Triquetra.

Chapter 49

In another part of the fortress someone lifted Jerran's head and he profoundly wished they hadn't as the world spun wildly. When he finally managed to open his eyes he saw Gilly was holding him up. His mouth was dry, his head ached and the wounds he knew he had taken, although superficial, stung, every one. He winced.

Will came and knelt by his other side and helped him edge back against a wall. Many pairs of eyes watched the three of them. "What can you tell me?" he asked quietly. "Are we all here?" His gaze searched for Callie, for Dexter, for Terran. Will shook his head.

"Just the three of us. Callie and Terran were trapped when Tol Gath dropped some kind of magic web over them, then they disappeared through a trap door. We three were brought down here and thrown in with this lot." He tilted his head towards the people around them. Kerrians all by their looks. "They tell me it's a sort of holding pen. Every day the solders come and take some of them away; they aren't seen again." He fell silent. It was obvious that the prisoners would be taken to Tol Gath's priests to be bound to him with the mindless loyalty imposed by his dark magic.

"So Callie and Terran are trapped by magic. We three are here. Where's Dexter?" Neither scout would meet his eyes.

Finally, Will swore under his breath. "When he fell he ended up right where the priests were performing their ritual. He may have been caught by it."

Jerran shuddered. His eyes snagged on his ring and he rubbed it absently. [Callie? Callie? Terran?] No response. Nothing. He hadn't thought there would be.

A disturbance at the front of the room brought him from his thoughts. Several of the Kerrians around them rose and moved forwards. Gilly joined them then returned. "Soldiers and drudges bringing the food and water. Makes sense. Tol Gath will need them to be healthy if he intends to use them to fight."

"How many soldiers?"

"Four armed men, two with swords, two with crossbows, staying well clear of the door and drudges with the actual food." Once a scout always a scout, Jerran reflected wryly. "We need to get out of here and soon. I wonder how often they come."

"Twice a day," a new voice addressed them. A powerfully built man stood looking down at them. "They come in the morning, bring bread and water and empty the slop buckets. The same at night. It's the only time we see them unless they need another batch of 'volunteers' for the priests." His mouth twisted in distaste.

Jerran rose slowly, to his not inconsiderable height, and found he still had to look up to the man. "Who are you?"

The man looked at him challengingly. "I am a Kerrian, so more to the point, who are you?" Jerran grinned.

"Fair enough. I am – we all are Lithians as I'm sure you've realised, but we came here with Lord Axtra's forces. Two of our companions are Mages. We hoped to put an end to the Ice Lord and his Sorcery." The Kerrian cocked an eyebrow.

"It doesn't look like things have gone to plan?"

"Unfortunately not."

"Kedan." The man held out a massive hand and gripped the Prince's forearm.

"Rhys," he offered without hesitation. "I was a bodyguard to the Mages with Will and Gilly here. Are you a soldier?" The Kerrian grimaced.

"Not exactly. I've seen some service but I was a blacksmith not far from Anzl. Did I hear you say you intend to get out of here?"

"Yes," Jerran answered bluntly. "As soon as we can."

"How?" The Kerrian looked sceptical. "We can hardly jump the guards with our bare hands, and there is not a thing in here you could turn into a weapon. I've looked."

"As to that…" Will began to feel along the seams of his clothing, seeing which Gilly began doing the same. A few minutes later Jerran found himself staring open-mouthed at a fascinating collection of objects. He fingered them warily – a fine wire garrotte, two double ended needle-like stilettos and tubes that rattled. He reached for one curiously, but Will stayed his hand. "Darts and blow pipe. They are poisoned."

"Now that's more like it." Kedan grinned. "I suggest we keep it simple. If these two take out the bowmen, you and I will need to tackle the guards. They won't be expecting it – none of these folk here are fighters but I'll get some of them to drag the drudges out of the way when the door's unlocked."

"Sounds good." The Lithians nodded. "But friend, after that we need to locate the dungeons where our Mages are being held. Do you know where they are?"

"No," the Blacksmith shook his head, "but I expect the drudges will – I'm sure they can be 'persuaded' to show you the way. I'll warn our cellmates what to expect. Once the doors are open we'll keep quiet until the alarm is given then we'll see how much confusion we can create." He saw the look of surprise on Jerran's face and read it accurately. "They aren't fighters, but they are Kerrians. Just about everyone here has lost someone to that bastard Sorcerer. They all know what is at stake!" He wandered away, leaving Jerran and the scouts sharing out the weapons. They could see him pause and talk quietly to one person after another. Those he left all turned their eyes towards the Lithians. Jerran nearly flinched at the burgeoning hope he saw on their faces.

Knowing there was no more to be done until morning the men sat quietly, lost in their own thoughts. The Prince finally allowed himself to think about their missing companions. He prayed Dexter had escaped the vile mind control of the Sorcerer's ritual, and that Terran was not too badly injured. As for Callie, when he thought about her he felt strangely hollow inside. He simply didn't know if she was alive or dead. If she was alive and powerless she must be terrified. Now Tol Gath had all the Triquetra was there any reason at all that he would keep her alive? He was still trying to think of one when the last of the torches spluttered and died.

*

There was no way to gauge the passing of time, Callie realised in the blue-shot darkness of the warded dungeon. It could have been hours or days for all she knew as she sat and shivered. Terran was still unconscious and when she noticed he too was shaking, she curled up against him to share her body's meagre warmth. She must have finally dozed off, because a gentle hand on her hair startled her to instant wakefulness. "Terran?"

"Aye lass, I think I'm back with you. Are you alright?"

Callie gave a mirthless laugh. "That's a difficult one to answer. We are imprisoned in a shielded cell – we have both been drugged. I cannot feel a single spark of magic inside me and the Ice Lord has the Triquetra, so, I've been better." Terran chuckled.

"Well lass – as long as it hasn't got you down. Where are the others?"

"I really don't know."

Terran heaved himself to his feet, shuffled to one side and spat. He approached the cell door and studied the light flickering up and down thoughtfully. "Hmm!"

"What?" Callie really wasn't in the mood for cryptic.

"The cell is warded."

"I think I'd spotted that." Callie winced at the sarcasm in her voice. "Sorry Terran, I guess I'm a little – tense? No, that's not the word. Terrified?"

"That's alright, lass. What I was going to say was the cell is warded but we've been drugged so Tol Gath isn't taking any chances. He is guessing that our magic may be internal. That means that if we can get it back, the cell door probably won't be enough to hold us."

Briefly that seemed like good news to Callie, then she shook her head. "But how can we get our magic back?"

She watched Terran drop back to his knees, his eyes darting around their prison. After a moment or two he began to sift the fouled straw carefully through his fingers.

She was just about to ask what he was doing when he rose on his haunches, smiling. "Yes! We're in luck! Callie, see this." He waved a small sprig of something in front of her face. "We need to find as much of it as we can. It's a field herb and often found in poorer quality bedding. Start looking." There was a distinct teacher-student tone in Terran's voice and Callie obediently began to sift the mat of sorted stems she sat on. It wasn't a pleasant task but, after a while they had a fairly large pile.

"What now?"

Terran looked at her, measuringly. "Now we eat it." Callie frowned. The tiny herbs were crushed, dirty and covered in Goddess knew what. Before she could speak Terran went on, "This herb is called pulk flower. Locals call it puke flower. It is a very strong emetic. When you've eaten enough you will be sick. Really sick – so please choose a corner! I hope it will be enough to counteract the magic suppressant Tol Gath gave us. I recognised the taste – mage bane. It is sometimes used in interrogation when a magic user is involved." He met her eyes steadily but Callie didn't flinch from his regard. She was not naïve. Her father had explained bluntly some of the methods that were used to extricate information from those who rose against the Crown.

She nodded and she and Terran shared their unsavoury crop. Waiting wouldn't make it any better. She pushed the dried herbs into her mouth and swallowed as quickly as she could. The first wave of nausea hit her scant minutes after she had chewed her portion and she vomited violently, continuously, gasping for breath. By the sound of it Terran was similarly occupied. It was really one of the most unpleasant half hours Callie thought she had ever experienced. When it was over she crawled away from the mess, wishing desperately for water to cleanse her mouth.

Terran settled beside her and looped an arm about her shoulders. "Well done. This is the sort of experience you only get in the field."

"I'll try to be grateful." Callie's dry tone made him chuckle.

His hand tightened on her shoulder. "Looks like we may have company." She raised her eyes. Lights, normal torchlights were flickering beyond the cell doors and approaching. "Try and looked dazed – uncoordinated."

"At the moment that really won't be too difficult!" she responded quietly as she looked through the bars.

Tol Gath himself stood outside the cell with a small troop of soldiers. He glared at the Mages as they rose to their feet then waved his arms at the cell warding which blinked out. "Bring them." He pivoted on his heels and walked away – no, stormed away. The Ice Lord looked distinctly angry.

As the soldiers unlocked their cell, Terran leaned towards Callie. "We have to play for time. He thinks we have no power but I hope we soon will have." He followed the gesturing soldiers and they began to climb a very long flight of stairs which ended, eventually, when they reached a massive locked door that opened onto a corridor. There were no windows but somehow the darkness was less intense, making Callie believe that they were now above ground level. Their guards finally shepherded them into a moderately sized chambers with a fire burning. The furnishings were sparse, but apart from one jarring anomaly, it could have been some dowager's entrance hall. Callie was dropped on to a well-padded seat, her wrists locked into cuffs. Terran was pushed and prodded forward and chained to a curious blackened pillar. It could have been stone or some sort of petrified wood, she could not tell.

[This doesn't look too promising.]

[Terran! I can hear you. Can you hear me?]

[I can!] Callie was overcome with relief. If their magic was returning they could contact the others and might at least stand a chance.

One of Tol Gath's soldiers approached them. "You will wait. The Ice Lord comes," he managed in strangled trade tongue. Neither answered as the guards retreated to the doorway. It was not as if they had a choice.

More time passed. The room in which they were confined did have a window and although it was shuttered the first light of day began to seep in. As it did Callie made several attempts to contact the rest of their party with no success. At first it felt strange like swimming through treacle, but each time she tried, it felt a bit easier, until, [Callie! Is that you?] Jerran's unmistakable mind-voice elicited an excited squeak from her. [You're alive – we feared the worst. Are Terran and Dexter with you? Are they okay?]

[Terran's here. Head injury but otherwise in one piece. Dexter isn't with us. Have you got Will and Gilly?]

[Yes. We are being held in a large prison cell with lots of Kerrians. We plan to break out when the guards and drudges make their morning visit!]

[Goddess, I hope that won't be long. We've been taken from the dungeon and are shortly to be 'questioned' by the Ice Lord himself. Terran is chained up and I don't think it's going to be tea and conversation.]

[Can you describe the room you are in? We intend to use the drudges as guides to find you.]

Callie gave him as much detail as she could and he relayed several questions to her from the scouts. She was just telling him how many steps they had climbed when the soldiers at the door straightened to attention. Callie felt her heart sink. Some shade of her feeling must have crossed the link because Jerran paused. [What?]

[He's here.] Callie braced herself as Tol Gath strode into the room.

[Goddess speed, Callie]. The link broke and the Mages found themselves facing a furious Sorcerer once again.

Tol Gath came to a halt in front of Callie and her eyes were instantly drawn to the Triquetra now reassembled that glowed upon his chest. He saw where her gaze lingered and fingered the jewel provocatively. "A thing of beauty, is it not? Beauty and power. Now you will tell me all you know of it." Callie hesitated. What was he expecting from her? "Speak." His voice became harsher. "What uses have you put it to?"

"I, I'm not sure what you mean. It's the Triquetra, it enhances the power you already have but you already know that."

"Have you used it to communicate? What method did you use?"

"The same as you, I imagine."

"Don't imagine! Tell me. I know what I do – I wish to know what you do!"

"I'm not sure." Callie hesitated, uncertain how to answer. Tol Gath hissed and immediately turned towards Terran, sending a whip of fire lashing across his face – just missing his eyes and laying open his cheek to the bone. There was a smell of cooked meat.

"Answer me," he said.

Callie gasped, tearing her eyes away from her companion. "I just reach for the minds I know and the boost to my own power helps me form a link." This was obviously not the answer Tol Goth had wanted to hear.

"How do you kill with it?" He leaned towards her his black eyes narrowed.

"I don't." She shook her head.

"How?" The Mage sent another stream of flame towards Terran and Callie saw one of his arms begin to smoulder and the skin on his hand begin to shrivel. He winced before he managed to snuff the flames.

"Don't, please stop it," she begged.

"I will when you answer me properly." He struck again, sending a bolt of energy and Terran reeled back against the pillar, shuddering.

"How can I answer you? I've only used it for a power boost and healing."

"Healing! What use have I for healing? If you do not tell me all you have learnt of the Triquetra's power your companion will die – slowly." He walked over to Terran and Callie watched in horror as he ran a nail down the man's face which split open and oozed blood.

"No, please – what do you want to know?" Tol Gath turned back to her.

[Callie.] Terran's mind voice was weak and strained. [The Triquetra – it's not working for him – or not fully. That's what this is all about. The Triquetra was a creation of the light – it may be that once again intact it will not allow its power to be corrupted by his dark magic. Try and give him something to think about. Tell him some of its history!]

[But you...]

[The next thing he does to me I'll pretend to collapse. There's no point in him torturing me if I'm unconscious.]

Callie cleared her throat. "The Triquetra has been in Lithia for centuries. It is a treasured heirloom that has been passed down in the Guardian Families from generation to generation." He stared at her silently. "It has been said that its full power will only respond to one of those bloodlines." She fell silent and swallowed hard. Something she had said seemed to strike a chord with the Sorcerer, he frowned seemingly deep in thought.

"You'd best hope that is not the case, little weather witch, because if it is, I will make you one of my slaves and you will carry out all my commands through the power of the talisman." He whirled about and stalked out of the room.

"Terran? Terran can you hear me?" The old Mage lifted his head. His face was sheeted with blood and he looked dazed.

"I'm still here, lass. Could you tell our Prince that if he's planning a rescue – now would be a good time!" He stopped speaking and slid down the pole until he rested on the floor, his head drooping. Callie broadcast a call. There was still that deafening silence from Dexter but after a moment Jerran was back with her.

[Callie – keep trying with Dexter. If you regain your elemental power will you be able to break free of your manacles?]

[Possibly – but even if I can, I may hold off until you're free. I know I'll need help and Terran is struggling.]

[Right. Any idea what Tol Gath is up to?]

[Not really. I can't read him, but something I said rattled him. It almost felt like he'd gone to check something out but I'm only guessing.]

[That's all we can do for the moment. Now we just have to wait.] The Prince fell silent and Callie was left to her thoughts.

Perhaps an hour later Gilly nudged the Prince. The torchlight beyond the holding cell doors slowly grew stronger. It was accompanied by jangling and rattling, which proved to be a trolley affair laden with provisions, pushed by two drudges. Four armed guards strolled along behind. Although the first two men had their swords drawn, they only looked half awake, unlike the two bowmen who trailed behind. Jerran followed Will and Gilly towards the door then glanced around, puzzled when he couldn't see Kedan. "I'm right behind you," the blacksmith kept his deep voice low, "but I tend to make them nervous." He was crouching down behind two larger Kerrians, farmers by the looks of them, who were also edging forward with purpose.

The guards placed themselves on either side of the doorway, and motioned to one of the drudges, who unlocked the cell doors pushing them inwards.

"Now," Jerran murmured and everything happened at once. With an almost silent hiss the blow darts found their marks on the necks of the archers who staggered, dropping their crossbows. Kedan rose to his full height as his compatriots grabbed the drudges, dragging them clear of the doorway.

At the same moment Jerran flung his blade at the nearest swordsman, piercing him in the eye. His partner who had half-turned to see what ailed the archers fell forward on to his knees as the blacksmith pulled the other blade from his back. It was all over in minutes.

Jerran and the Kerrian walked back to the drudges while Will and Gilly armed themselves and moved to keep watch on the passageway. The servants, both oldish men, looked shocked, so Jerran left it to Kedan to try and extract information from them. It didn't take long. They were both familiar with the room Callie and Terran had been taken to when he described it and moments later they were out and running. [Callie – we're on our way. Hold fast.]

[Thank the Goddess – see if the drudges have any idea where Dexter might be!]

As they climbed the stairs Jerran and Kedan milked the helpers for information. The men were more than happy to talk given the chance of freedom but shook their heads grimly when Jerran told them where they had last seen Dexter. Other servants had told them of the scene in the great hall.

They knew that two Mages had been imprisoned in the shielded dungeon and had themselves helped bring Jerran's party down to the holding pen along with a new batch of Kerrian prisoners, but Dexter had not been among them. The priests had continued with their ritual. Once it was completed the newly bespelled slaves would have been commanded to remain where they were until they were sent to a camp or fighting arena. If Dexter hadn't been moved, he might still be in the Great Hall, and if he was in the Great Hall and had endured the ritual unshielded he might have been enslaved along with the Kerrians. Jerran felt sick at the thought.

They moved swiftly and silently. For once Lady Fortune was on their side and they didn't run into any more guards. Jerran was beginning to wonder if they would reach their destination before the alarm was raised when one more corridor brought them to a corner with an archway ahead. Here the drudges halted and edged forward cautiously, muttering at Kedan. "They say we must pass the entrance to the Great Hall to get to your friends and there are sometimes soldiers here."

One of the men drew his head back. "It's clear." They moved forward then Jerran hesitated.

"Dexter might still be in there, I'm going in." Will and Gilly took guard as he slid one of the huge doors silently ajar. It was dark inside but he could hear the slight sounds of people breathing, a cough here, and a throat cleared there.

As his eyes adjusted to the gloom he could see the only people in the room were the Kerrians who had cowered before Tol Gath's priests the previous day. They stood in a pack, silently, eyes closed, unmoving. He approached them cautiously but no-one stirred. They seemed completely unaware of his presence as he walked among them.

It was unnerving but he pressed on, his eyes scouring every face. He could not see Dexter. "We need to go." Kedan's whisper from the doorway. "Perhaps your friend has been moved after all?" Reluctantly the Prince nodded and turned to leave, stumbling as he did so. A man lay on the floor. Face pale and eyes closed, Dexter curled at his feet. There were ominous stains on his clothing. Jerran fell to his knees and shook the northern Lord's shoulder. He did not respond.

"I've found him – we need to get him out of here." Kedan moved fully into the room and joined Jerran. He dropped to the floor beside the unconscious man and with gentle fingers prised open one of

Dexter's eyes. A black pit stared up at them. "Dear God." Jerran flinched. The Kerrian dropped a hand to his shoulder.

"I'm sorry but unless your Mages defeat the Sorcerer I think it's too late for your companion."

[Jerran.] Callie's voice sounded anxiously in his head. [Where are you? We are being moved.]

Jerran swore under his breath. [We are back in the Great Hall. The drudges thought Dexter might be there and I've just found him.]

[How is he?]

Jerran hesitated.

[He's injured. We need to get him out of here.]

[You're in the Great Hall? I think that's where we are heading. Tol Gath stormed in just now. He has two red priests with him and a couple of soldiers. You need to get out of there.]

Jerran's mind raced. [Callie, no. We are staying. We'll hide amongst the Kerrians. Tol Gath won't know we are here until we attack. Be ready.]

Callie was pushed into the Great Hall by one of the Ice Lord's soldiers. Terran staggered beside her. With a wave of his hand the Sorcerer sent fire to the torches around the walls and made his way to his throne.

"Prepare her." His voice was cold, like the hands of the red priests who pinned her between them and began to lead her towards the stone altar.

Concealed amongst the mass of Kerrian prisoners Will and Gilly waited for Callie to move a step or two to the side, then sent their lethal darts shooting towards the Ice Lord. One struck in his throat and one his hand. He crumpled and lurched to one side and for a moment Callie was certain he was dead. Then his lips drew back in a snarl as he pushed himself upright once more. "Now, Callie!" Jerran leapt on one of the priests while Kedan stabbed the other.

Callie raised her head and sent her mind questing for her favourite element – air. She willed it to move and it obeyed, spinning her captors away. She turned her gaze to the Dark Lord. His eyes shone with rage and one hand flickered a spell casting, even as he clutched the Triquetra with the other, muttering as he rubbed the opal healing stone. The poisoned darts slid gently from his body. Another incantation and red and purple flames roared up around him, wreathing his body. He extended one arm and launched fire straight at Callie. She flung up a shield, staggering from the sheer magical force he commanded and watched, horrified as her defences burnt away. The Sorcerer smiled as he raised his arm again. Callie thought her final moment had come. Unconsciously she took a step backwards and stumbled over a fallen warrior, tumbling to one side. Tol Gath's fire bolt missed her by inches, setting two of the paralysed Kerrian prisoners ablaze, burning them alive and filling the Great Hall with the scent of human flesh. Callie retched and felt a hand slip into hers. Terran had dragged himself back to her side, and injured as he was he offered her his strength. [Callie. He may have the Triquetra, but you have more, you are an Elemental Mage!] His faith in her, even now, drove the doubt and fear from her heart as the Ice Lord loomed over her, using his remaining strength to wrap himself in shield upon shield.

"Not this time, Tol Gath!" She reached for and stole the air above the Sorcerer below the Sorcerer, around him, then from his very lungs. Gasping and gurgling, he fell to his knees clutching his throat, then desperately pointed at the Kerrians and hissed, "Kill them," before he collapsed.

The crowd of commoners stirred. They opened eyes like black pits from the deepest of hells and began to move towards the Lithians. Caught by surprise the scouts were dragged down by the frenzied mob who clawed and bit to obey their Master. Behind them Callie saw Jerran and a huge Kerrian trying to subdue another of the prisoners who was fighting like a demon. As they reeled into the torchlight Callie saw the man's face. It was Dexter, but not Dexter as she had ever seen him.

His lips were drawn back in a snarl and froth edged his mouth. She froze in horror.

"Callie – Callie – if they are still controlled then Tol Gath isn't dead. We must…" Terran's voice failed and she saw with shock that he had fallen unconscious. She found her feet, plucked a ritual dagger from the dead hand of the red priest, then crept to where the Ice-Lord lay. He raised a shaking hand and looked at her from cold eyes.

She flinched. He should be dead without air to breathe. His magic had counteracted the poison on the darts. Had the power of the Triquetra saved him?

The next moment the Sorcerer dragged a small dagger across his palms.

He clutched the Triquetra where it hung on a heavy chain around his neck, smearing the petals with blood, and Callie was sure she felt his power surge, and sensed the healing power of the opal stir into life once more. A huge feeling of anger and revulsion swept through her. The mosaic pieces that had brought her to this time and place spilled across her mind in a fraction of a second. Kaleidoscopic pictures. Refugees crawling up the road with all their worldly goods on their backs. Dexter's butchered family. The black destruction wreaked by Tol Gath's mind control spell. The clan lives of simple people warped and twisted.

She gasped for breath as the Sorcerer pressed his foul darkness down on her. His power stank of ancient evil, of bitterness and the pain of thousands of innocents. For a moment she cowered then out of the corner of her eye she saw the man who had been Dexter, grab a sword and fix his gaze on Terran. Terran who, barely aware, stood no chance of rolling clear of the descending blade. Even controlled by the Sorcerer's dark magic, Dexter had lost none of his skill. It had to be stopped and she was the only one who could do it.

She reached down and she reached up. Below the deepest foundations of the fortress she felt for the bedrock and it came to her hands as she called it. She drew a spire of stone ever upwards striking through the fortress itself until she thrust it like a spear into the belly of the Blood Mage. Injured, drugged, he still fought with immense strength, abandoning his attack to spin web upon web of defence and wards around himself. For a moment he kept her out. Callie's fury drove out her fear as she screamed her frustration, and sent the air smashing against the huge windows of the great hall, shattering them into a thousand rainbow fragments. The final constraints of doubt fell away and her awareness was free. She reached up to the edge of the sky where the north wind howled. It was full of ice and snow and she drew it back down, twisting and spinning it until she was satisfied. She met the stunned gaze of the Sorcerer, his face white and disbelieving.

"No." His voice was a whisper. "You can't be. There are no more left." She smiled and released the tornado. It destroyed his defences, peeling them away layer by layer faster than he could rebuild them. She walked closer. The vortex having destroyed his shields began to shred his clothes, then scour his body with a thousand needle points of ice. His screams echoed around the hall, but Callie was only distantly aware of them. She felt herself fraying as the immense forces she handled diminished her humanity. Someone tugged the blade from her hand. Then the screaming stopped. The man she had known as Jerran had drawn the priest's blade across the Sorcerer's throat. Dropping the blade, he stepped to her side. "Sorry, Callie." He spoke out loud. People used to do that, she half remembered.

Then he slapped her across the face. Hard.

*

The hurricane vanished and Callie crumpled to the floor. Terran rousing, settled her briefly then staggered across to the others. Jerran's massive friend had started pulling Kerrians off the scouts. Kerrians who looked around them with bewilderment and shock. Will and Gilly finally emerged from beneath the pile-up of bodies. Mauled and bitten, they were far less damaged then they might have been — so many slaves had attacked at once that they had virtually ended up fighting each other.

Terran dropped heavily beside Dexter who still sat on the floor. "How are you feeling, lad?"

"Strange?" Dexter ran a troubled and shaking hand over his face as if to clear his mind. "What happened? We were all in the hall fighting; it was going badly then nothing."

"You got caught in the ritual, lad. You should be alright now. Tol Gath is dead."

"Truly? Well thank the Goddess, where's Callie?" Terran pointed across the hall where Jerran knelt beside the young woman. Dexter rose slowly and walked across towards them. He paused looking down at the Sorcerer's body and retrieved the Triquetra, wiping away the blood and dropping it in his pocket.

Jerran glanced round as he approached, a warm smile lighting up his face. "Dex, Thank God. We thought we'd lost you for a while there."

"You did lose me for a while there, but I think I'm back. Is Callie okay?"

"More or less. Terran says she drew so much power to fight the Ice Lord she nearly lost herself to it. It's one of the dangers the Elemental Mages always faced and she is very new to her power."

"So what now?"

"We need to let Axtra know that Tol Gath is dead and he can move his men in. Then they can deal with all these displaced Kerrians."

"I'll see if our stuff is where we stashed it. If it is I'll send up the flares, otherwise I'll improvise." He walked away and Terran took his place, watching as the Prince gently brushed the hair back from Callie's white face.

"Jerran lad, she'll be fine and your Kerrian friend looks like he could do with your help." He pointed to where Kedan and several of his countrymen were already arguing. "I don't have much of the language like you – and we do owe him for his help. I'll sit by our lass, so no need to fret, but we're not finished yet."

Chapter 50

By the time Dexter returned from firing a flare to confirm their success to Warlord Axtra, his companions had withdrawn to the great gallery where Callie, pale and shaky, was sitting on a stone bench. She sipped from Terran's flask from time to time, and looked back through the open doors where she could see Jerran calming bemused Kerrians, explaining how they came to be in a fortress in a war zone and identifying those who would be useful in arranging an orderly evacuation. There was some discussion, a little arguing but really they accepted and adjusted to the situation remarkably well. Jerran proposed to lead them back to the Temple where they could wait with the other erstwhile prisoners until it was safe for them to leave. Although Tol Gath was dead, his men had raised arms against Warlord Axtra. They could expect no mercy; no quarter given, so they would fight fiercely to escape, or die in the attempt. The streets would not be safe until Axtra had complete control of Jaan Linna, and most of the Kerrians were happy to seek sanctuary until that happened.

Axtra had not wanted, or needed the Lithians to take part in any mopping up operation and they were all heartily relieved. Every one of them had sustained minor injuries. They were bruised and battered and covered in blood, but to all intents and purposes their mission was accomplished. It had been agreed that they would regroup at Is-festning and then withdraw at leisure back to Skava, as Axtra had indicated there were further matters he wished to discuss with Prince Jerran.

They moved slowly and quietly back through the great fortress, their numbers increasing as others joined them; escaped prisoners slipping out of hiding places; servants freed from servitude by the death of the Ice Lord. Retracing her steps down the great staircase past the tapestries and statues, with a growing band of wide-eyed Kerrians trailing behind, Callie felt dazed and weak. The release of tension that followed the terror of the past few hours made it a real effort for her to simply put one foot in front of another. She was vaguely aware that Will had taken one of her arms. Jerran, sword drawn walked ahead with Gilly and Kedan. Dexter supported Terran and chivvied the Kerrians from the back.

As they approached the fortress entrance once more, the distinct, if distant sounds of fighting reached their ears and Will stepped ahead to see what was happening, while they waited in the shadows. He returned a few minutes later, his face pale. "There are pockets of resistance but they won't last long. Axtra's men are already spreading through the citadel. We should be okay to get back to the Temple. After that we'll just have to avoid the hotspots."

The others nodded as Terran moved forward. "Do we leave the troops asleep in the barracks? They aren't going to wake any time soon."

He stepped towards the building, only to be halted by Will's hand on his arm. "Terran, they aren't going to wake at all." Will's voice was curt. Dexter and Jerran exchanged glances and silently slipped into the shadowy entrance, reappearing moments later. Callie looked at their faces and her questions died unasked.

They set off again retracing the path they had taken the day before. By good fortune the only soldiers they met were a squad of Arild's men, who chose to accompany them. The Kerrians in the Temple were nervously pleased to see them and some were overjoyed to be reunited with friends and family they had thought lost. There was universal relief that Tol Gath was no more, and if not all the danger was past, Arild's men were willing to watch over the Kerrians until it was safe for them to leave. Dexter breathed a sigh of relief at that. He hadn't been looking forward to shepherding a large group of unarmed civilians past pockets of fighting while keeping their own group safe. Callie was noticeably unsteady on her feet and Terran's staff seemed to be all that was keeping him upright.

He was about to signal for them to move on when the most senior of Arild's officers appeared at his side beckoning the others close. "Milords, before you leave may I ask a question?" Dexter nodded wondering what was coming. "Our people." He waved at the large group of Kerrians settling about the chamber. "You have rescued them and for that you have our thanks. They seem well but are they truly free of the Sorcerer's influence?" He hesitated.

"We need to know so we can at least be prepared." So much left unsaid in that statement.

In the silence that followed Terran and Callie exchanged glances then she squared her shoulders. "I'll check. Please ask one of them to come over."

"Kedan," Jerran called across the room and the great blacksmith strode towards them. When they had explained he scratched his head for a moment, then nodded and dropped down in front of Callie. Even on his knees he was nearly as tall as she was.

"Jerran," the Prince stood right beside her, "please explain what I will be doing – it is intrusive but not harmful." The Prince spoke a little Kerrian and as the blacksmith was still consenting, she reached forward and placed her hands on either side of his head.

It was hard to describe the sensation of exploring another's mind. The surface layers were clear and bright and when she moved through memories, beyond noticing the emotions that coloured them, she did not linger, feeling very much a voyeur. She delved deeper and was just about to withdraw when she saw it.

Tiny; contained. A seed of darkness lay inert, deep in the Kerrian's mind.

She flinched and felt Jerran's hand on her arm, steading her. She gathered the shreds of her power and directed a blade of pure energy at the spore. It didn't take long but she was shaking as she withdrew.

Arild's man winced. "So they are still infected?"

Callie stopped to think. "There was a tiny seed of darkness. It was inert; contained. I do not think it would affect them in any way unless they once again came under the influence of a very powerful Sorcerer, with knowledge of the Heart of Darkness Rite, and that is the remotest of possibilities. I really believe they can return to their normal lives, and I certainly don't have the strength to cauterize every one of them."

"Very well." The man offered her a brief bow, and smile. "Again, my thanks. I'll detain you no longer."

Dexter led their party out of the Temple. They could still hear the shouting of men and the clash of weapons echoing through the narrow lanes but they were close to the gate before they actually saw anything and what they did see brought a smile to one or two faces. A spirited action was taking place outside a solid building, with much larger windows than they had noticed so far.

In the street, and trying to gain entry to the building were a number of men from Axtra's forces. They were being bombarded by random items thrown by several very angry and very scantily clad women. As Callie watched, one of Axtra's warriors was almost stunned by what looked like a chamber-pot hitting him on the head. Terran came and stood beside her, trying hard not to laugh. "One of the brothels I presume?" He nodded.

"Apparently not all the soldiers did return to barracks at curfew."

"And?"

"Axtra's men want to capture them, but the ladies are afraid they won't get paid unless they, er, fulfil their duties, so they won't give them up."

Dexter's face briefly lost its grim expression. "Definitely giving a new meaning to *coitus interruptus*," he murmured under his breath to Terran who groaned.

He turned to Callie. "That reminds me – who is Penny Plain? You never did say outside the fortress."

"Oh – according to barracks gossip, in his younger days, our Prince's favourite whore." Dexter burst out laughing. Jerran froze in shock and outrage, which only made the laughter louder.

"Callandra – I can't believe what you just said – no lady would even know of such matters let alone refer to them in that offhand way."

"Sorry Jerran," Callie shrugged, "but it's hardly a secret is it? You must be aware that most of what you do feeds the gossip mills." She offered a semi-apologetic smile as she walked on, leaving the Prince reeling.

They edged round the whorehouse and saw the great gateway ahead; their horses tethered and guarded just a small distance further on. "Wonderful! The perfect way to end the day – an hour of riding through snow." Callie winced as she climbed into her saddle. She was cold and so tired she could hardly hold herself upright. She knew in theory, that any Mage could bring him or herself to exhaustion by overusing magical energy but it hadn't really worked like that for her. An Elemental Mage, she had resources immensely greater than other magic users at her fingertips, but the control and the guidance for what she did, came from within and that particular well had run dry.

They rode slowly, in near silence back along the road to Isfestning. The day was cold and overcast. Dexter looking troubled led the party with Terran. Jerran rode behind Callie and studied her with hooded, watchful eyes.

As they moved through the quiet of winter, the events of the previous twenty-four hours flickered through his mind; the vile red priests, the terrified Kerrians, Dexter bespelled, Terran tortured and Tol Gath dying but it lingered stubbornly, on Callie. Callie blazing with power; Callie lying unconscious, and Callie locked in a heated embrace with Dexter as they tried to avoid the soldiers near the entrance to the fortress of Jaan Linna. That last memory bothered him deeply. It had looked so real. Her behaviour was outrageous, wanton. The way she had spoken of his affairs, even her awareness of his dalliances angered him and he couldn't or wouldn't acknowledge why. He told himself he was disgusted, dismissing his state of mind as exhaustion and tension.

Watching her so closely, he was the first to notice her swaying in the saddle. "Callie!" His call alerted the others and as he nudged Warrior forward, Dexter dropped back. The young Mage lurched to one side and would have fallen if Dexter had not caught her up. The border Lord, wild-eyed and anxious, scooped her from her mount, pulling her in front of him. She hardly stirred. Terran had turned his mount and looked at the two young men. Jerran had snagged her horse's reigns; his icy gaze was fixed on Dexter as he settled Callie on his mount. He looked angry and anxious in equal parts.

"Terran that's the third or fourth time this has happened; is she alright?" Dexter queried quietly.

"She is. Don't worry." Terran's voice was calm. "She is still adjusting to the massive power she is using. A couple of months ago she was a student weather-witch and now – well, now she controls the very elements. This," he gestured, "is likely to happen for a fair few weeks yet – but she will recover quickly and it should hit her less every time. She has to learn to pace herself – not always possible in life and death situations."

Nodding, Dexter urged his horse forward and they resumed their journey. An hour or so later they passed Axtra's outer sentries and saw the fortress a little further on – bustling with activity. Dexter felt Callie stir in his arms and gripped her more firmly. She opened vivid blue eyes and he could see she was trying to make sense of her situation. "Where are we?" She peered up at him, tugging down the edge of his enveloping cloak.

"We're nearly back at Is-festning."

"Did I fall asleep?" she queried, astonished.

"Something like that!" There was a distinct smile in his voice. "Terran said not to worry – that it's some sort of magic-using exhaustion." He felt Callie nod against his chest where her head tucked neatly under his chin.

Chapter 51

The hooves of their horses sounded the change from snow-covered road to cleared cobbles as they drew to a weary halt. Jerran handed off Callie's reins to one of Axtra's men and Terran helped her down, steadying her until she found her feet. They walked slowly into the main hall of the fortress. The fire crackled and the air was scented with the hot spiced wine the servants brought them. A couple of the garrison warriors hurried up to ask for news only to be bowled aside by a female whirlwind, Mira. She flung herself at Will, clutched him for a moment or two then to Callie's open-mouthed amazement began to run her hands all over the scout's body checking for injuries. When she had assured herself that he was undamaged, she grasped his face between her hands and kissed him heatedly.

Although Will's face reddened, he obviously had no difficulty in responding until he saw Callie's expression. Then, finally aware of the rest of the company observing him, he grabbed Mira's roving hands in some embarrassment.

"Callandra, milady. I'm sorry." His sheepish apology was interrupted by Jerran.

"In the light of her own behaviour I hardly think Callandra warrants an apology from you, Will." He gave them all a cool dismissive look and walked away, heading for the stairs. Silence fell as

Callie tried to digest the remark.

"What? What did he mean by that?" No-one met her eyes. "What is the matter with him?"

Dexter sighed. "You really don't know, do you, Callie?" She regarded him blankly.

"If I did I wouldn't ask but I'm certainly going to find out." She turned.

"That's probably not a good idea right now." Dexter's voice, carrying a note of warning tailed off as he realised he was talking to empty space.

Callie walked firmly up the stairs to the men's room and tapped on the door. There was no answer but she was not in the mood to be deterred and walked in. It wasn't Jerran who stood facing her, it was 'Prince Jerran.'

"I did not give you permission to enter." His voice was chilly and distant.

"That's true." Callie looked at the man in front of her in bewilderment.

He shrugged. "I suppose I shouldn't be surprised that you think it's acceptable to enter a man's bed chamber uninvited. You apparently have no idea how to behave with any proper decorum."

"I – what?" The Prince turned his back on her and began to remove his weapons. "Prince Jerran," Callie's voice sounded unnaturally formal, "in exactly what way has my behaviour offended you? How have I shown a lack of decorum?"

"How can you ask?" There was anger in his tone and he turned round rapidly his eyes flashing.

"In Jaan Linna you acted like a slut. It was appalling. You are a member of the nobility, Lady Callandra, and a Mage. At a certain level your informality can be refreshing but acting the way you did with Lord Dexter will soon sully your reputation."

"Lord Dexter?" Callie's mind raced backwards until she reached the alleyway in Jaan Linna. "That?" Her bewilderment turned to fury. "Highness – I am sorry that I have not comported myself as you feel a lady should. The next time I'm about to be attacked by enemy soldiers on a mission for the good of the Kingdom I'll try to ensure my actions do not contravene court etiquette."

"Good," he snapped at her. "And perhaps bear in mind that it is not usual to entertain single gentlemen in your bedchamber either."

Callie turned on her heels and stormed out of the room slamming the door behind her. The sound echoed down the stairs to Terran and Dexter who exchanged wry glances.

No-one rose early the following morning. Dexter, after breakfasting alone made his way to the stables to check on the horses. He was surprised to find Arild in the yard. The Kerrian looked unwontedly serious and seemed reluctant to talk.

"Looks like you are heading off?"

"Yes." The monosyllabic answer struck Dexter as odd.

"So, we won't be riding back to Skava together?" Arild didn't meet his eyes.

"I will not be going to Skava just yet. I am ordered to Koepce."

He didn't seem at all happy about it, and Dexter had a feeling he was missing something. "Then my friend may good fortune ride with you. After Skava we will be heading home."

Arild's hands stilled on the horse's tack. He turned slowly. "Lord Dexter, I wish you well." He hesitated, glancing at his men who were preparing their mounts nearby and lowered his voice. "There may be danger on your road home. Be on your guard." He shook his head and turned away leaving Dexter feeling distinctly uneasy.

Jerran also found himself alone at the table until Terran arrived, yawning as widely as the stitches across his cheek allowed, but looking much better than the day before.

"Are you recovered?" the Prince asked cordially.

"Pretty much." The Mage loaded his plate with bread and ham. "I'm just getting too old. I think this will probably be my last field trip. When we get back to Derryn I might just stay at the academy or the hospital. They can always use Mages with field experience." He settled himself on a large chair, concentrating on his food for a while.

Jerran soon finished eating but made no move to leave, instead staring out of the window at the comings and goings in the yard.

Terran looked at the young man thoughtfully. "Have you seen Dexter or Callie this morning?"

He noticed the Prince stiffen slightly. "I believe Dexter has gone to check the horses. I haven't seen Callandra." He didn't turn.

"About Callandra."

"I do not wish to talk about her, Terran."

"Fine, Prince Jerran. Don't talk: just listen. Your behaviour yesterday did you no credit. You really owe the lass an apology." Jerran finally turned toward the Mage, his expression icy.

"That's not going to happen. As for my behaviour – what about hers?" Even to himself the Prince sounded childish.

"You know quite well that Callie was acting a part with Lord Dexter."

"She…"

"No!" The Mage stopped the angry young man. "Listen, Jerran. As far as I know Callie regards Dexter as a friend and nothing more – at least not yet." He noted the Prince's swiftly raised eyebrow. "But, has it occurred to you that there is no reason at all why there shouldn't be something more for those two if their friendship were to develop that way? They are of an age and rank and Lord Dexter, unlike you, Jerran, is free to choose his own wife." The Prince scowled.

"Actually, within reason I too am free to choose my own wife." He saw Terran's surprise. "Unlike Mikheli I am not Crown Prince, and he is betrothed to Serenna, the only foreign Princess of suitable age currently available."

Terran digested this information along with a third piece of toast. "No doubt then, when the time comes you will bestow your name and rank on one of the court beauties who can be guaranteed to behave impeccably at all times, otherwise you would do well to consider the real reason you are so angry about Callie and Lord Dexter." The Prince said nothing. Terran finished his Kaffi and rose to his feet. "I'll go and pack. Do you have any idea how long we'll need to stay at Skava?"

The Prince shook his head. "I've no idea what Axtra wants from me – maybe a day or two."

Terran nodded and left the room passing Dexter on his way. "Jerran." Dexter addressed the Prince with his usual amiability. "What is your opinion of Arild?"

Jerran looked quizzical. "I think he's a good man – a bit more thoughtful and far less aggressive than some of his countrymen. Why do you ask?" Dexter relayed his encounter in the stables. "So a veiled warning. That is a bit odd and he was meant to be riding with us to Skava. I've noticed he doesn't always agree with Axtra's orders, so perhaps he's spoken out of turn once too often."

"Well there's not much we can do right now except stay alert."

"True. So if we are travelling by ourselves, when Callie gets up, we can be on our way." He headed for the stairs.

"Oh, she is up. She had a tray in her room."

Jerran paused, a frown darkening his face. "And how exactly do you know that?" he muttered under his breath.

It was about mid-morning when they finally left Is-festning behind. They rode steadily, familiar with the road which was fairly clear after the passage of many troops and wagons. Approaching the turn-off for Jaan Linna they saw a crowd of people ahead and Will and Gilly rode forward to investigate, returning shortly afterwards accompanied by Sven, Arild's second in command. "So, what's going on?" Terran moved up to the Kerrian speakers curiously.

"Refugees," Will explained. "Apparently Arild thought there might be some on the road and brought extra food supplies with him, but there are many who have been brought great distances and are in no way fit enough to make their own way back to their villages. He's commandeered all these," he pointed to wagons, carts and sleds, "from Jaan Linna and means to see them on their way so they'll at least stand a chance. The local people have dispersed but many of these are weak and injured, and far from home."

"That's a very humane way to treat the people," Dexter mused out loud. "Not exactly what I would have expected from a Warlord." He met the Kerrian's assessing gaze.

"That's because the orders came from Commander Arild, not Warlord Axtra. He would never countenance such actions. He believes only the strong have a right to survive. Commander Arild is this way." He turned his mount and rode off, leaving Dexter to wonder as he followed, whether he was of the same mind as the Warlord or not.

Arild greeted him with a slight but genuine smile. "It seems we may travel together after all; unless you ride in haste?"

"Not really – we will no doubt be killing time until Lord Axtra himself returns to Skava."

"In that case we would appreciate your company. Many of our people are in a poor state and with the failure of Tol Gath's revolt there will certainly be danger from those of his troops who evaded capture."

Dexter nodded "True – I'll speak to the others." He made his way back to where the Lithians were gathered watching as the sleds and carts filled rapidly. No-one objected to the escort duty, so they fell in alongside and the convoy moved on surprisingly quickly.

Callie watched as Arild rode up and down the line exchanging a word here and there and offering what encouragement he could. It was a long, cold day for everyone, and when the camp was finally set for the night all she really wanted to do was toast herself, unmoving by the campfire but Terran almost immediately began to move among the refugees offering healing and pain relief and ashamed of her laziness she squared her shoulders and joined him.

Their fire had burnt low by the time they got back to it, but the thick stew Will had made for them was tasty and helped ease the exhaustion they both felt.

Callie was content to sit silently beside the old Mage. For some reason she always found his company restful. She stared into the flames but Terran studied her. He began quietly. "Callie, are you alright; really alright?" She looked up at him questioningly. "It's just you seemed very angry with our Prince last night." Callie huffed but made no comment. "He had no right to say what he did. I hope you didn't take it to heart?"

"Of course not. We are all tense, worn out and wound up. Jerran can be such an idiot sometimes. A complete royal idiot with a right royal temper but when he calms down he'll know he was in the wrong. Forget it. I intend to."

Terran winked at her and patted her shoulder, glad to know she wasn't still upset and thinking Jerran had got off lightly.

As they finished speaking Arild dropped down on to a log beside them. "My thanks." He offered them a half-bow. "It is no duty of yours to give help to our people, that was kindly done."

Terran shook his head. "It was the right thing to do. Your people have been through a lot and still have far to go." Arild stared into the fire.

"Tol Gath certainly inflicted much suffering. Whole communities have been destroyed. He took the young and the strong. Recovery will not be swift. I wish with all my heart that our leaders would spend their strength and energy in helping the people instead of waging endless wars that benefit so few." He sighed and offered a rueful smile. "I must be truly weary to say such a thing to our enemies."

"Are we your enemies?" Terran raised an eyebrow at the Kerrian commander who rose slowly to his feet.

"On a personal level, no. Indeed, in other circumstances, I would be honoured to call you friends." He vanished into the night.

Chapter 52

The following day they reached the great north road and the convoy was reordered with some of the wagons turning off to Koepce with Arild and his men. Jerran who had been riding with Arild and Sven for most of the morning now made his way back to his companions, calling them all together.

"Do you have any objections to continuing as escort to the refugees heading for Skava?" He eyed them hopefully. "Arild doesn't actually think there will be any trouble now we are on the high road but while Tol Gath held sway this whole area was overrun with bandits and thugs. Just a small armed presence should be enough to deter any chancers. He feels these people have suffered enough."

"No problem." Terran spoke for the rest of them. "It may slow us but not much." They moved into position around the refugees who would continue south with them and were greeted with effusive thanks by the haggard men and women, grateful for any support even if it came from Lithians.

Sven led away the party heading for Koepce. As the last sled slid reluctantly on the increasingly soft snow, Arild drew his horse close to Dexter and Jerran. He grasped each man in turn elbow to elbow then shook his head, gazing after the departing wagons.

"Is there something you need to tell us, Arild?" Jerran was

watching the Kerrian closely.

"There is nothing I actually know, but again I say to you, be wary. I do not know all my uncle's plans and I am no traitor but he is beginning to feel his age; he and most of his closest advisers. To my mind his determination to show he is still strong has made him harsher and more ruthless than he used to be. You have done him, and Kerria a great service in ridding us of Tol Gath, but I wish I was more certain that gratitude is all you will find in Skava." He gave them a semi-bow and raced off after the disappearing convoy.

Dexter and Jerran exchanged worried glances. "We could of course make our way straight home and avoid Skava altogether," Dexter suggested mildly.

The Prince considered for a moment then shook his head. "We have a treaty with Axtra we must not jeopardise. Lithia still needs time to recover from the war in the west. We will have to go and see what our Warlord intends – and as Arild said – be wary." Dexter nodded reluctantly then cantered off to the front of the wagons while Jerran brought up the rear.

Late evening brought them finally and wearily into the courtyard at Skava. Callie was so stiff and cold her knees nearly buckled as she dismounted and she made no argument when the stable hands approached to claim her reins and led her horse off for a thorough grooming and a well-deserved feed. The steward welcomed them back in cordial, if not enthusiastic tones and they were soon reinstalled in the 'guest' rooms they had previously occupied. The dinner hour was long past but they were barely settled before servants arrived to build up the fires and lay out a spread of cold meats and ale, for which they were all suitably grateful.

Callie was exhausted and after a brief meal and a skimpy wash departed to her bed. The others soon followed suit and Dexter presently found himself alone in the main room. He felt unsettled and restless even though he too was tired.

Giving up his attempt to sleep, he flung his cloak back around his shoulders and left the suite of rooms thinking he would check on the horses after all. It was late and very quiet so the jangling sound that signified armour and weaponry was clearly audible to him as he approached the outer doors. Dexter drew a dagger and silently turned the door handle. It wouldn't budge; it was obviously locked.

After a moment he rapped firmly on the frame and it was opened slowly by a guard, who blocked the entrance. He was an older man with a look of experience about him. "Yes?" he asked as though nothing about the situation was odd.

"Why is this door locked?"

"Sir, Lord Axtra left orders. Until he is certain that none of the Sorcerer's forces are still at large he wants to ensure you are in no danger."

"I see." Dexter frowned, wondering how much danger there could be in the Warlord's own fortress. "I wish to go and check on my horse, I think he was favouring his left leg."

A second guard moved into view. "I'm sure your horses have been well tended, milord."

"I expect you're right but I would like to see for myself."

The older guard hesitated for a moment then nodded to his companion. "Vorst will accompany you." The second guard was once again an older man. He nodded and led Dexter back towards the courtyard which was fuller than previously.

"Are those Lord Axtra's personal guards?" He eyed a number of soldiers demounting and leading horses away.

"Some of them." The guard's response was curt and Dexter was hurried past the activity to the peripheral stabling where the Lithian mounts were located. The horses were all in sturdy stalls with fresh hay and water. Their tack had been roughly cleaned and hung on pegs that ran along the wall opposite the stalls. Dexter gently patted Argus and ran gentle hands down his foreleg, feeling for any damage, but the horse seemed comfortable enough. Satisfied, he rewarded the shaggy creature with an apple from the stable barrel and stepped away.

"Are you satisfied?" There was a hostile edge to the guard's voice but Dexter ignored it and refused to be hurried. Back in the courtyard the guard followed at his shoulder making sure that he did not stray and as he stepped back through the doors of the guest wing he heard the key again turn in the lock behind him. He took himself to his bed wondering if they were indeed guests or prisoners.

The next morning was halfway gone before Terran, the heaviest sleeper, joined the rest of the company where they lounged at the table after a very late breakfast. He listened thoughtfully as they discussed Dexter's experience the previous night, but there was really nothing to be done until Axtra showed his hand. The steward, arriving with servants to clear the meal, informed them that Lord Axtra expected to reach Skava by early afternoon. In the evening they were to be guests at a feast to celebrate the defeat of Tol Gath. He was perfectly civil and made arrangements for them all to visit the bathhouses before bowing himself out.

"So, maybe we are honoured guests after all, Dex." Callie looked more cheerful.

"Let us hope so." He was sorry to see the way her face fell. "You're probably right, Callie. Perhaps I am being paranoid."

"No you're not." Jerran shook his head. "There's definitely something up – all my instincts are telling me so." Callie looked from one to the other in dismay.

Recently it had begun to seem as if Jerran and Dexter disagreed on everything, so the fact that they were of one mind was a little alarming.

"Is there anything we can do to prepare?" Terran grimaced.

"Get some rest. Stay alert!"

"Right, I'm heading for the baths." She went to her room to gather clean clothes and stepping back into the corridor found Dexter waiting for her.

"This could do with a wash, or whatever you do to such things." He held out the Triquetra, petals still smeared with blood dangling on the chain that he had removed from the Sorcerer's neck. Callie reached for it slowly.

"Thank you." She expected him to leave but he did not. He looked troubled. "Dex?"

"Callie, I need a favour."

"You've only to ask!"

He hesitated. "As I understand it, somewhere in my mind is the seed of darkness left by Tol Gath's priests?"

"Yes, I believe so."

"I know you said it won't cause me problems unless I fall under the influence of another megalomaniac Black Sorcerer – and I realise that is extremely unlikely but…"

"You want me to destroy it." He nodded.

"I can't bear the thought of it – not after what he cost my family."

Callie looked at him with sympathy. "Dexter – I am perfectly willing to do this but are you sure? When it came to creating wards you weren't keen for me to be inside your head."

"Callie, that wasn't because I don't trust you. I do implicitly, but you would have seen memories that still give me nightmares." She was not surprised to find that he had been trying to protect her. She punched his shoulder.

"Come to my room once I'm clean and we'll take care of it straightaway." He gave her a grateful smile and moved off.

Lord Axtra's bathhouses were well appointed and efficiently run. After weeks on winter campaign it was little short of bliss to linger in the hot water and steam rooms. Jerran was surprised and delighted to be offered a massage, which soothed many of his aches and pains, so he was the last to return to their living quarters. Terran was dozing by the fire. Will and Gilly were playing dice but there was no sign of Callie or Dexter. "Where's Dexter?" Jerran wasn't going to ask about Callie if his life depended upon it. Will looked up briefly.

"He's with Callie. She said they weren't to be disturbed." He winked and turned back to his game.

Jerran took a deep breath and dropped into a chair the other side of the fire trying very hard not to imagine what the Mage and the border Lord were doing that demanded privacy in her room.

Callie had settled Dexter on the floor near the hearth in her bedchamber and drawn up a chair behind him. When she gently tugged his hair away from his forehead she could feel the muscles of his face smiling. "That is so much better than I was expecting!"

"Idiot! You know I haven't started yet." She giggled.

"Damn. Okay, do your worst!" His words were light but she could feel the underlying tension.

"Close your eyes and just think of something – neutral. I'll try not to pry. As this is all so recent I really won't have to go through much." She felt Dexter grow calm beneath her hands and she created a gentle link, which his mind accepted, then slipped into the landscape of his thoughts and memories. He was thinking about horses: the splendid horses he bred at Winters Keep, and longing to be riding in the fields below the woodland far from blood and death.

She moved as if she was turning pages of his memories. She found the final confrontation with Tol Gath seen through his bespelled eyes and then beyond it, shadow. She moved slowly through the darkness until she found the source, the nucleus, the perilous seed and concentrating her focus annihilated it with a burst of white energy. Dexter didn't react and she remembered Terran telling her the mind had few nerves to transmit pain. She was almost done. She decided to check back a little further to be absolutely certain and found she was looking at herself as Dexter must once have, in the alley below Jaan Linna. She read the hesitation as she had pressed herself upon him – the quick comprehension of what she intended. Then the way he had felt as they kissed – desire and physical pleasure, well, not so surprising but behind it a warm tenderness. He cared for her. He admired her and he wondered if he dared to allow himself to feel more, but was terrified to do so, since all but one of those he loved had been torn from him.

Callie pulled herself together and slowly withdrew from his thoughts. "All done?" Dexter turned his head to look up at her.

"Absolutely. You're once again as pure as the driven snow – and I didn't need to go far to find it."

"Thanks Callie." He climbed to his feet. "I'll leave you to rest before the feast. I'd better return to the main room before your over-possessive royal bodyguard has a fit. No need to provide him with more ammunition about your wanton behaviour!" He winked and departed, leaving Callie to her thoughts. She really did like Dexter. She liked his good temper, his humour and calm intelligence, but was not at all sure the warmth she felt for him would ever turn to fire.

Chapter 53

The 'Feast' was not in the Great Hall, as they had expected, but in another chamber, smaller but still richly appointed. A round table dominated the space and each of the Lithians found themselves seated between two Kerrians, with Axtra as the centre point. The food was well cooked, the wine and beers good quality but Dexter noticed that their hosts drank very little. There was palpable tension in the room.

Once the final course had been served, the Warlord snapped his fingers and the servers withdrew. Jerran thought he heard a locking bar slide across the outside of the door and loosened the dagger at his belt with a concerned look at Dexter. Axtra raised a hand for silence and leaned forward across the table, his eyes fixed on the Prince. "Highness. First let me thank you for all you and your companions have done for Kerria." His smile was cold and did not reach his eyes.

Jerran nodded courteously. "We are always happy to assist our allies." His voice was carefully neutral.

"It's good to hear you say that," Axtra steepled his fingers, "as there is another matter in which your help is going to be – crucial." He paused as Jerran offered him a questioning look. "Yes, the matter of the Iron Mines."

The Prince's face remained blank, but his lips tightened. "The Iron Mines?"

"Yes, Prince Jerran. Kerria, as you know needs iron ore."

Jerran frowned slightly. "Lord Axtra, we are happy to trade iron ore with any neighbouring country. There is no reason why Kerria should not be one of them."

Axtra offered his half-smile again. "Perhaps I am not making myself clear. I am not looking for a trading arrangement; I want you to cede Deep Delve Mine to us."

"What?" Jerran's astonishment was plain to see. "What on earth makes you think my father would consider that suggestion for a moment?"

"Oh." Axtra made a pretence of scratching his head in thought. "I think he might accept it as a fair price to ransom the Crown Prince of Lithia!" Jerran made a move to rise as the enormity of Axtra's words sank in, only to feel the point of a sword prick his back. The guardsmen placed around the walls were now directly behind him and all of his companions. He dropped back into his seat, composing himself.

"Your treachery will not succeed, Axtra. I am not the Crown Prince. My father will always put our country's needs before his personal feelings: even if that means sacrificing the spare heir." He heard Callie's tiny gasp.

"To some extent that is true, boy." The Warlord made no further effort to hide his contempt. "But he would do almost anything to avoid the chaos that fell on your country the last time there was no direct heir!"

Dexter shook his head. "But Prince Mikheli?"

The Warlord offered an affected sigh. "I'm so sorry to be the bearer of dark tidings, Highness, guests, but Prince Mikheli has suffered a fatal accident."

"What? How?" Jerran's eyes met those of the two Mages, who both minutely shook their heads. They knew nothing. "When?" His voice sounded harsh, disbelieving.

This time Axtra's smile was genuine. "Tomorrow."

"You bastard!" Jerran sprang towards the Warlord only to be pinned on either side by Axtra's guards. "Now, now, Jerran, as a Prince you need to take a more pragmatic view; think of it as a promotion. There is nothing you can do to stop it from here anyway."

[Callie.] He mind-called her in desperation. She was staring with total concentration into her wine goblet – for all the world as if she could not bear to watch the scene playing out, but he sensed rather than saw the minute nod that meant she was even now trying to contact her brother.

Raff had been lying on his bed reading and relaxing after a day that had included a particularly challenging orienteering exercise when Callie's mind call blazed through his sleepiness.

[Raff!] Every shade of fear coloured her call.

He shot upright. [Callie. What's wrong?]

[Everything. Just listen. There's going to be an attempt on Prince Mikheli's life in the next twenty-four hours.]

[What? How? Why?]

[We don't know how, and I'll tell you why later. Just go. Make sure the Prince is safe. Tell the King and father. Now go!]

Axtra sipped his wine. "Let me tell you what is going to happen next." The Warlord rocked his chair back and looked at his Council, who one and all were smirking or offering admiring glances. "Lord Dexter will take your seal ring to your father with my terms for your safe release. That release will not happen until Kerrians are occupying Deep Delve Mine. Mind you, Highness – I am not ungrateful for what you have all done so I'll let you keep your whore while you wait." He half-turned in Callie's direction.

"Tol Gath was proving to be quite a problem – powerful Mages are so unpredictable. So unpredictable I prefer not to have them around when they have completed their tasks. They tend to interfere and so…" He gave a small wave of his hand and Dexter followed the direction of his gaze to see Terran suddenly slump forward across the table – a sword through his back.

"No!" Callie wailed in horror and sprang to her feet, pushing past her laughing guard to get to Terran's side. "What can I do?" She felt for her magic, then so very faintly she heard Terran whisper in her mind. [Callie, don't. The wound is mortal. They must not know what you are if the rest of you are to survive.]

[But…] she wept.

[Sweetling. I bless all the gods that I got to meet one such as you – with the power and will to do so much good. Bless you.] And in that moment he was gone. Callie raised her tear-stained face and fixed her startling blue eyes on the Warlord. He would pay. Oh yes, he would pay. Lord Axtra smiled. "Take them away." He turned as they were marched out of the room.

Raff raced across the compounds, taking the side entrance to the palace and sprinting past the state offices until he skidded to a halt outside his father's chambers. To his relief a light still showed beneath the oak door and he flung it open.

"Raff?" The General looked up, startled. "What's happened?"

"Callie just called." He relayed the information and before he had even finished found himself being dragged along the corridors that led from the King's working area to the royal family's private quarters. The guards looked at Raff doubtfully but in the company of the King's senior General, waved them through.

Raff's father knocked briskly at an undistinguished white door and waited impatiently until the King's voice growled permission to enter. Theon was settled in an old chair by the fire flicking through reams of papers. His expression, far from welcoming at this late interruption, softened as he recognised his visitor. "Ivor?"

"Majesty."

"At this time of night, this can hardly be a social call, so what brings you to my door – and with Raff?"

"You need to call Vris." The King gave him a long look and reached for a bell pull, hanging nearby. "Tell me." General D'Arcourt gestured Raff forward.

"Callie, my sister just called me with a message from Prince Jerran."

"Is Jerran alright?"

"So far, but there's going to be an attempt on Prince Mikheli's life."

"Mikheli? When? How?"

"They don't know how, but within the next twenty-four hours. As to why, she said we can speak again soon but wanted me to make sure the Prince was safe first." Abruptly he staggered, his face paling.

"Raff?" His father steadied him; his face tight with concern.

"Terran! The Kerrians just executed Terran."

"Are you sure? Are you in contact with Callie right now?"

Raff shook his head. "No, not exactly. I think because we're twins I sometimes pick up echoes. They stabbed him in the back."

The King flinched then nodded as the door opened to admit two pages. "Fetch Commander Vris and the Isseni ambassador Liss, if he is still in the medical wing. Go quickly and get them to meet me at Prince Mikheli's suite." He strode to the door and beckoned for them to follow him.

The Crown Prince had a large suite of rooms occupying nearly all one side corridor of the royal apartments. The sounds of voices and laughter were clearly audible as they approached. Evidently Mikheli had company. The King swore under his breath and signalled for Raff and his father to wait, tapping lightly on the door. It was pulled open by a bright-eyed and obviously inebriated young Lord who looked taken aback to be facing his sovereign but still managed a fairly creditable bow. "Majesty."

"Lord Simons – I hate to intrude but I'm afraid I must have urgent words with my son."

"Oh, oh of course." The young man seemed to become aware that he was blocking the doorway and hastily stepped to one side.

"Raff, come with me. Ivor, bring Vris and Liss in when they arrive." Raff followed the King into a large reception room, which held quite a crowd of young nobles and several young women who did not appear to be of the same class at all.

"Father." Mikheli lurched toward the King grinning broadly. "Have you come to wish me a Happy Name Day?" Theon conjured a half smile and put a hand on his son's shoulder.

"I do indeed wish you a Happy Name Day, my son, and I'm sorry to intrude into your celebrations, but we need to speak on a rather serious matter – and no." He obviously anticipated his son's objection. "No, it won't wait." Whatever words Mikheli was about to utter died on his lips as he saw General D'Arcourt appear behind his father with the head of Lithian special services and the Isseni ambassador in tow.

The Prince led the way into a small study and stood looking uncertainly at each man in turn. Theon nodded and Raff's father stepped forward. "As most of you will know my daughter Callandra is in Kerria with Prince Jerran and Lord Dexter. They went to try and deal with a northern Sorcerer, Tol Gath, whose depredations had begun to affect Lithia. With regard to Tol Gath, they have been successful and the Sorcerer is dead. Through Callie's mind link with her brother," he waved at Raff, "we have been kept informed of events. Prince Jerran notified us that Warlord Axtra had asked him to return to Skava, his fortress, before heading home, as there were matters he wished to discuss. We do not know all that has happened but Callandra contacted Raff about half a mark ago with an urgent warning that an attempt is going to be made on your life, Prince Mikheli. Very soon."

"What?" The Prince looked stunned. "But why? Are you sure this is serious?"

"Very serious, Highness. Callie said they had murdered Terran, in case he was able to interfere."

"Terran's dead?" Liss looked, appalled.

Vris plucked a notebook from some invisible pocket and rapidly scribbled a longish note, which he despatched with one of the loitering pages. "My men will guard you, Highness, until we can be certain you are safe. For now, we need more information. Raff. Can you?" Liss settled the young man in a chair where he took a deep breath and rubbed the satellite ring he wore, looking for the bright thread he recognised as his twin sister.

[Callie?] He spoke out loud for the benefit of his audience. The pause before he made contact felt longer than it really was, under the many concerned eyes turned on him. He winced at the grief that coloured her mental tone. [Callie, I'm with King Theon, Prince Mikheli, Father, Liss and Commander Vris. What more can you tell us?]

Callie was concise, explaining that Prince Jerran was being held hostage and would not be released unless Lithia ceded Deep Delve Mine to the Kerrians. Vaguely Raff heard the gasps of outrage around him. [You yourself are still free and yet they murdered Terran. How is that?]

He heard the equivalent of Callie's mental laugh. [The Kerrians wouldn't believe for a moment that I have any real power. They think I am Prince Jerran's – companion.] She tested the word for suitability. [They plan to send Lord Dexter back to Derryn with the Prince's signet ring and Axtra's terms. They have no idea that we are able to contact you all. Is Prince Mikheli safe?]

[Prince Mikheli will be under the protection of Commander Vris's men.]

[Well thank the Gods for that. What does His Majesty wish me to do? I could probably blast us out of here but we would still be a long way from home.]

Raff waited while a low-voiced discussion took place around him. Finally, the King himself dropped a hand on Raff's shoulder.

"Tell her to do nothing as yet. We will send our forces to Barnard's Keep. Ivor." His look was all the command General D'Arcourt required. Raff's father spun on his heels and left the room at speed. "Tell Lord Dexter to head for Barnard's Keep. We may need his guidance in Kerria or through the Snakeshead Pass. We will give warning before we make any move and we need updates of what is happening." Raff relayed the King's words.

[She asks, is that all for now?]

King Theon looked suddenly weary but managed a fleeting smile. "Please thank her for the warning and tell her to take care of herself and my other son." Raff passed the message and finally broke the contact.

"Mikheli." The King turned to the Crown Prince who still seemed to be struggling to take in what had just happened. "You need to bid goodnight to your guests." The Prince nodded reluctantly. "And I need you to stay in your quarters until we have checked the palace and surrounds."

"But Father – surely I'm safe here – and it's my Name Day." He sounded so like a petulant five-year-old Raff didn't quite know where to look. The King seemed similarly unimpressed.

"Yes, it is your Name Day, Mikheli, and if you want to live to see another one you will respect my wishes." He eyed the young man appraisingly and added, "I think I shall make that a royal command. Understood?"

"Yes, Sire." The Prince released a disgruntled sigh and flounced through the study door to where his guests were chatting in much more subdued tones. Raff heard him muttering about a security problem as they were ushered out.

Theon stood and watched until only the five of them remained. Mikheli flung himself moodily onto one of the sofas. "Son, you have everything you actually need here. Vris's elites will be guarding your doors and Master Lauder will renew the wards on the building outside against the unlikely chance that the Kerrian attack turns out to be a magical one. We will keep you informed of developments. Raff," he raised his hand, "constant contact with your sister, please." Raff nodded, having already formed the intention of contacting her again, when he could do so without an audience.

The King placed a hand on his son's shoulder. "Perhaps you should get an early night, Mikheli?"

The Prince shook his head. "I doubt if I would sleep after all this. I think I'll drown my sorrows in one of the bottles Jerran left me for a Name Day gift."

King Theon sighed. "Don't overdo it." He waved them all out and closed the door behind him. There were four men outside and two immediately stepped across the entrance, the torches tracing the silver piping on their black uniforms that marked them as elite arms men.

At the door to the King's study Theon turned again to Raff. "Thank you, Raff. Come and see me in the morning." He stepped into his room followed by Liss and Vris. Raff made his way slowly back to his quarters, his mind racing.

Chapter 54

When Raff broke their connection Callie slumped back into her cushions and stared blankly at Jerran who sat facing her. He let out a long breath. "Thank the Goddess. That was a swift response." She half nodded, her expression bewildered.

"Jerran – how did it all go so wrong so quickly? When I think of Terran…" Her voice choked and her eyes filled with tears.

Jerran moved to sit beside her on the couch, slipping his arm around her shoulders. "Terran was a good man." Her voice was barely a whisper. "He helped me so much. He helped the Kerrians so much and they murdered him. It was an execution!" She raised a tear-stained face to him as if he could help her make sense of something intrinsically senseless. Jerran had no words to offer, but sat silently holding her until her sobs subsided, then rose and fetched her a glass of wine, his footsteps loud in the room that now seemed so empty. Dexter, Will and Gilly had already been sent on their way.

"Jerran, what will they do when they realise their scheme has failed?"

The Prince poured wine for himself and stared into his goblet. "Nothing good – that's for certain, but as long as they think I might be useful I will be safe, and you thanks to the Goddess, they have already discounted. We now know, to our cost, exactly how ruthless they can be, but they don't hold all the cards, Callie." He counted points off on his fingers. "One: Lithia is aware of their treachery and already taking steps. Two: we have a covert way to communicate with all our contacts, and three: we have you – the first Elemental Mage for several lifetimes with more power than anyone else – and that was before you had the entire Triquetra in your hands."

"Have you done anything with it yet?"

Callie bit her lip. "Actually – I forgot all about it." She blushed slightly.

"What?" Jerran stared at her in disbelief, then chuckled when he realised she was serious.

"Only you, Callie – only you. You have your hands on one of the greatest magical relics of the ages and you manage to forget about it!"

"Hey!" she objected. "I did wash it."

"You washed it. Well I suppose that's a start." Jerran was pleased he had managed to distract her. "Perhaps you could try drying it next or – I don't know, maybe polishing it?" Her lips twitched.

"Okay, okay. I take your point – I am curious about it."

"Well, go and play with it but only after you go and talk to Raff like you promised. He should be free of all those terrible old men by now."

Callie headed for her own room where she could be private. Jerran watched her go then topped up his wine. In truth the casual brutality of Terran's death had shaken him badly too. In their time in Kerria, he had begun to find Dexter's constant mistrust and wariness of the people irritating, even knowing his past history but it seemed the northern Lord's attitude had been sadly justified. Dexter, he forced himself to acknowledge was a perceptive and decent man as well as a fine warrior; the sort of man he should have been pleased to call friend. He reluctantly acknowledged the reason such friendship had not developed was entirely due to him. He had hated seeing Callie so comfortable in Dexter's company. Jealousy, and it could be called nothing else, was never attractive and he was only glad that Callie hadn't taken permanent offence at his petty behaviour. Her friendship mattered to him. She mattered to him: a lot. Terran had been right, he really did owe her an apology.

Callie curled up on her bed. Raff responded so quickly he must have been waiting for her contact. It was a great relief to talk to him with no-one else listening in. She told him again in detail all that had happened and his care and concern for her were very soothing. With her twin so little needed to actually be said. He restored her perspective, reminded her that there was a world beyond the nightmare she was currently enduring.

It was maybe half a mark later that she wandered back into the main chamber. "Better? The Prince smiled at her. She grinned back and nodded.

"Everyone is worried about us, but trusting that we can take care of ourselves. The army call up is in full swing and several of the Mages, who were almost burnt out after Nilsport feel ready to take the field again. Terran was well liked."

"And my Princely brother is safe."

Callie laughed. "Raff said he was most put out that he had to cancel his Name Day party. When they left him confined to his quarters he had decided to drink himself to oblivion on the wine you sent for his Name Day present." Callie had expected a smile as she told her tale and was startled by Jerran's suddenly grim expression.

"Callie – I didn't send wine for Mikheli's Name Day – I got him a new dagger." She froze as the implication of his words sank in.

[Raff!] she screamed across the mind-link to her brother.

[Goddess. What now?]

[Jerran didn't send any wine to his brother for his Name Day. It may be...]

[I'm on it.] For the second time Raff raced towards the palace, not even pausing to answer the sentry's challenge, which meant that when he arrived in front of the Crown Prince's rooms, there were four guards chasing him. He bent double, breathless, chest heaving and gasped out his news to Vris's elites, who flung open the Prince's door without a moment's hesitation.

Prince Mikheli was sitting in an armchair near the fire, with his head back and his eyes closed. He looked as if he was sleeping, but his right hand hung down limply. A wine goblet lay on the floor where it had fallen, ruby liquor puddled around it like blood.

Raff raced across the room and gently shook the Prince's shoulder. Mikheli's head slipped to one side and with shaking hands Raff felt for the pulse at his throat. There was nothing. "Fetch a healer – tell them poison, get Vris and call the King." The arms men raced away as Raff stared at the Crown Prince, his mind blank. Then he turned and ran into the Prince's bathing chamber returning with a small mirror, but not the faintest mist shadowed the glass. He was still holding Mikheli's wrist when Vris and the King burst through the door.

"Dear Goddess. No!" The King reached for his son and shook him urgently, willing him to somehow wake up. He was firmly pushed to one side as Master Elton arrived, his bag jangling. He flicked a glance at Raff, who minutely shook his head, then began the same series of checks Raff had performed minutes earlier; each one slower than the last. Finally, he stepped away and turned to the King.

"Majesty – I'm so sorry." Theon shook his head in denial.

"No. There must be something you can do." The healer shook his head sadly.

"I'm afraid we are too late."

"Perhaps Master Lauder…"

"Theon." Elton's voice was calm but firm. "He's gone." The King reached for his son with shaking hands, drawing him into a last embrace. He kissed the young man's hair as tears made slow tracks down his face, rocking back and forth, a strong man overthrown by grief.

Raff had retired to the back of the room, wishing desperately to be anywhere else, but not daring to leave. Questions would certainly be coming his way. Master Elton opened his bag and withdrew a phial. "Raff – water." When he returned with a tumbler the healer offered both to the King who hesitated then accepted the potion, swallowing hard, his eyes still on his son.

The King spoke softly. "Raff, wait in my office. All of you please leave me." They emptied the room.

Sitting in the firelight it seemed to Callie that each minute stretched longer than the one before. It would take a little time for Raff to reach the palace and get to the Prince's chambers. Or perhaps he was already there and the wine was fine, or Mikheli had decided to start on his favourite brandy instead. Endless permutations seethed through her mind. Jerran sat silently, his head on one hand. He knew Raff would contact Callie as soon as there was news.

At last she stirred, brushing her fingers across her pendant to include him in the contact. Raff's voice sounded thin and harsh and very subdued. [Callie, are you there?]

[Yes, we are both here.] Jerran realised she was gently warning her brother that he would be able to hear anything that was said.

There was a noticeable pause, then Raff spoke quietly. [I'm very sorry, but we were too late. He's… Prince Mikheli is dead.] Callie heard Jerran's sudden intake of breath.

[Master Elton recognised the poison. He said it was something that acts very swiftly. The Prince would not have suffered. The King's orders remain as before. He reminds you that you must pretend ignorance of Mikheli's death or you might compromise your own safety.

[His Majesty has retired to the royal chapel to light candles for Mikheli's death and Prince Jerran's life. He will keep vigil this night. Tell Jerran I'm so sorry, Callie.] His voice faltered. [We'll speak again tomorrow. Goodnight, Cal. Goddess Bless.]

Callie turned her eyes away from the fire. Jerran's hands covered his face. He made no sound but his body was taut with tension. She uncurled and rose to her feet. "Jerran. I'm so sorry too." She brushed a hand across his shoulders. "I'm right next door if you need me." She made her way quietly from the room, shutting the door behind her to give him some privacy.

Alone, Jerran slid onto the floor. Tears fell slowly at first then he gave way to his grief. He wept and raged. He cried for his brother who, for all his faults had been there for him in the dark times, following the death of their mother. He raged for the loss of the future he had hoped for, then wept again at the injustice of a life so vilely taken.

Callie drifted in and out of sleep. She heard the first outpouring of Jerran's grief and hoped that exhaustion would finally dull his pain and let him sleep, although her Mage senses told her that he had not gone to bed. As the grey light of false dawn crept through her window she pulled a shawl over her night robe and slipped back into the main room. Jerran, sprawled on the floor, was gazing blankly at the last embers of the fire. His face looked ravaged and he was visibly shivering.

Callie darted into his bedchamber, grabbing a thick woven blanket, which she dropped over his unresisting frame. She coaxed some life back into the fire, adding logs as the flames grew then pulled the trivet forward and filled the copper with ale. Jerran watched her actions in a detached way, although he did pull the blanket closer about himself. They did not speak. Then the tang of warm ale began to scent the air. Callie put the poker into the flames. She poured ale into a tankard and plunged the poker into the frothy liquid before forcing Jerran to take it. He growled a thank you from a swollen throat, finally turning to look at her.

Her hair was wild. Her feet were bare and the shawl did not cover much of the almost sheer night robe she wore – and she really didn't care. She wasn't trying to make an impression. She wasn't thinking of herself at all. She was there because she cared about him. It was clear in her eyes; written on her face. That and the mulled ale slowly brought some life back to his chilled body.

"Did you get any sleep?" she asked gently. He shook his head.

"I just keep thinking it can't be true. Mikheli could be an idiot, but he didn't deserve to die like that."

"Tell me about him."

Jerran studied her face.

"Why? I know you didn't really like him." She didn't try to deny it, instead she looked thoughtful.

"There were certainly things about him I found aggravating, but I barely knew him and there must have been more to him than I could see or you wouldn't care so much." He nodded, accepting her words.

After a pause he started speaking slowly. "Mikheli was six years older than me. After him it was thought my mother would not bear again, so my arrival was a bit of a shock for everyone."

"Did he resent you?"

"No. There was no need. When we were young we were like two

single children – at very different stages of our lives. Then my mother died and everything changed."

"How old were you then?"

"Eight. My father – he was devastated. He withdrew from us and spent all his time working."

"So you almost lost both parents?" Jerran nodded.

"Exactly. Mikheli was nearly fifteen but he saw what effect it was having on me and sort of took my life in hand. Making sure I made friends, making sure my tutors were decent and kind and badgering my father until he paid me some attention." He chuckled. "On my twelfth birthday I was going to get my first full-sized horse and Father had promised that he would take me out riding. I had really been looking forward to it, then it looked like Father was going to cry off for some meeting or other. Mikheli set a small fire in the Council Chamber and when everyone evacuated the building, he locked all the doors and hid the keys so Father couldn't actually get to his work. I think he got into a lot of trouble, but it was the best day ever." He grinned at the memory, then his smile dropped.

"I thought and hoped we would become closer when I become an adult but that didn't happen. I really don't, didn't, care for most of my brother's friends. Mikheli was always arrogant but it seemed to me they encouraged his worst characteristics. He didn't spend much time thinking – he was all action – so he really didn't see how people tried to use him and gain his friendship for the sake of his influence. Even so, I knew with absolute certainty that if my back was to the wall, he would always have been there for me." Jerran emptied the dregs of his ale onto the greying ashes at the end of the hearth and yawned.

"Go to bed." Callie relieved him of his tankard. "When we do get up we will need to put on a convincing performance and we need to make some plans."

Chapter 55

It wasn't early when Callie finally dressed and dragged herself to the breakfast table and she ate alone. She had opened Jerran's door to find his room in darkness and hear the faintest sound of snoring.

When she had eaten she settled herself on her bed and unwrapped the Triquetra. It was impossible to tell that it had existed in three separate parts for centuries; no seam or join was even vaguely visible. It felt cool and heavy in her hands yet somehow more alive. She slipped it back over her head and brushed it lightly for an energy boost as she sent her mind outwards looking for Dexter and the scouts. She needed to tell him the news of Mikheli's death and check that he, at least was alright. She had hardly settled her focus and breathing when she found him.

[Callie!] She heard his mental voice but for a moment she was too startled to speak. Linking with Dexter had always been easy for her but now, with the full power of the Triquetra, she could actually see him. A scene unfolded before her in miniature; an eagle's-eye view. He was riding steadily with Will and Gilly, followed by two of Axtra's men, and it looked like they were nearing Secker.

She willed herself closer, tightening the contact until she could see every detail of his face. He looked stern, a slight breeze whipped his hair into his eyes but there was warmth in his tone.

[Is that you, Callie? – What news?]

She pulled herself together. [The worst. Despite our warning they managed to kill Prince Mikheli.] She saw him swear under his breath, trying to conceal his reaction from the watchful Kerrians. [The King has issued a call to arms and the army will be heading to the Snakeshead Pass. Then wants you to be there to lead them through – so you'll have to shed your guards before too long.]

[So it will be war?]

[I fear so.]

He sighed. [I will obviously do what you say. It's a good thing our guards chose to take the southern route – at least we are heading in the right direction. Please take care of yourself, Callie – I know you'll look out for Jerran. As well as losing a brother he is now facing a future he has never wanted or expected. I know he can be difficult – particularly where you are concerned – but actually he's a really decent man!]

[Yes Dex. I do know that. I'd better break off now in case Raff needs to contact me. God speed.] As she broke the link she heard the sound of movement from the other room and reflected silently how odd it was to feel sorry for a Prince.

Jerran had, in the end, slept deeply and when he was fully awake, realised that the first awful shock of his brother's death felt less raw. After some breakfast and three cups of Kaffi he went through his pack until he found his maps of Kerria.

He was still studying them when Callie joined him.

"What are you up to?" She peered over his shoulder.

"Just trying to work out timings and what might face the army if and when it gets here."

Callie frowned. "Isn't there any way we can avoid more bloodshed?" The Prince's mouth flattened. "Yes, Jerran, I know you want justice for your brother's death, but that atrocity was down to a few power-hungry old men. This country is in dire straits. Just think what we've seen – the poverty, the famine, the lawlessness. It's the ordinary people who are suffering and there's damned all they can do about it."

"Callie, you may be right but…"

"And our people," she went on. "We've just finished fighting in the west. Most of the families I know have lost someone – a brother, a son, a cousin, whatever. It needs to stop."

The Prince heard the sincerity in her voice and ran a hand through his increasingly shaggy hair. "Callie, look, everything you say is true but how can we stop it? If you can think of a way, as long as you give me Axtra I'm right with you." She knew he meant it. She poured herself another cup of Kaffi and looked down at the Triquetra.

"I need to think and perhaps explore a little."

"Then I'll see if they will let me visit the horses. Don't take any wild risks."

Callie, settled in a deep window embrasure, was on the whole relieved, when half a mark later Raff's mind voice interrupted her less than successful experiments.

[Callie?]

[I'm here – has something happened?]

[No. Yes. Maybe.] She smiled in spite of herself.

[Which one of the three answers shall I go with?] Her brother chuckled.

[Sorry. No other disasters, but Master Lauder wants to speak to you urgently about your pendant. He wants a direct link, so please can you make contact with him?]

[Certainly, now?]

[If you could.] His mental voice withdrew.

Callie resettled herself and visualised the old master. Sure enough, he appeared in front of her sitting at his chaotic desk making notes, from what looked like a scroll.

[Sir?] He looked up alertly, obviously hearing her even if he couldn't see her.

[Callandra my dear, thank you for getting in touch – I have news.]

[About the Triquetra?]

[Indeed, indeed. As you know my students and I scoured the

library looking for information with little success. Well, I mentioned it to Elias, that's Master Elton to you, and it stirred his memory. It hadn't occurred to me to search the medical library but that's where we struck gold. Liss and Raff found this.] He held up the scroll. [This is all about 'a' Triquetra.]

['A' Triquetra?"]

[Yes exactly, I told you there were several made. We need to identify yours. First things first – you have the pendant with you right now?"

[Yes sir.]

[Can you look at the back of the mounting ring and tell me what you see?]

Callie tipped the talisman towards the window light until a tiny row of dots and dashes became visible. [Well there are marks, I suppose they could be runes but they really look like tiny bird footprints.] She heard Master Lauder laugh.

[That's a good description. Now; one by one.]

She told him what she saw and heard him muttering in a low voice, [Isa, mannuz, perth, ehwaz, raido, isa, vruz, mannuz. That's remarkable – truly remarkable!] Silence fell. If it wasn't for the fact that Callie could actually see her old master leaning back in his chair, nodding to himself, she might have thought he had broken off contact.

[Sir, what is remarkable?] she prompted gently.

[Oh, Callie, sorry. These runes mean we can definitely identify your pendant as the Imperum Triquetra – and this entire scroll is about it. It was certainly one of the most, if not **the**, most powerful talismans ever made. You've already found how it magnifies your power, but what makes this particular piece priceless, as well as terrifying, is the same reason the information was held in the restricted section of the medical library. It could be a tool for mind control.]

[What? Did I hear you right?]

[You did. It's ironic, isn't it? You set out to prevent a Sorcerer using a mind-control ritual when you were actually wearing something capable of the same thing yourself. Once you have mastered it – and it does require immense personal power to achieve that – it would allow you entry into anyone's mind.]

[To do what exactly?]

[To do whatever you wished.]

[That's frightening.]

[I'm glad to hear you say so. Callie, you need to think through the implication. The scroll indicates that a Mage with just enough power to trigger it could plant 'suggestions' in someone else's mind and encourage them to perform a deed or action to which they were not fundamentally opposed. Someone truly powerful could force another to do absolutely anything, whether they wanted to or not; no ritual needed. You could erase someone's entire memories, change their perceptions and personality, plant a geas in their mind to be the compass for their whole life. It's probably part of the reason it lent itself so well to the Heart of Darkness rite.

[We believe Tol Gath used one single part of the Triquetra to perform that ritual on the White Wolf Clan and force them to Winters Keep; and you know the result.]

[The massacre.]

[Exactly.]

[Good Goddess, what were they thinking to create such a dangerous weapon – because that's what it is.]

[Those were dangerous times, Callandra. People were desperate. As soon as peace was achieved the Triquetra was 'dismantled'. It was designed for that to be possible. The holders or guardians were men and women of impeccable integrity and principle. To be chosen as such was a supreme honour. And there's more, so much more. I wish I could get this scroll to you.] There was a long silence.

[Callie?]

[I'm still here, Master, just trying to take in what you have told me. If the Triquetra is so powerful there must be some way to use it to stop Lord Axtra.]

[Indeed there must. I'm beginning to believe that the only limiting factors are your willpower, and we both know you have plenty of that, and the ideas you can come up with. Why not try some mild suggestions on the servants or Prince Jerran until you get a feel for it?] He chuckled. [Oh, one thing more. It was occasionally used in matters of Supreme Justice. A Mage wearing it would always be able to know if someone spoke the truth or lied.] Callie groaned.

[Now King Theon wants to hold a Council of War in about two marks. If you are agreeable, he will use Raff's ring – so be ready – and if you are able to link in Prince Jerran and Lord Dexter that would be excellent.] Master Lauder's thoughtful gaze stared back at her then his expression changed to one of near panic.

[Heavens, Callie, I'm late for my class – I must go.] She saw him leap to his feet and grab an apparently random handful of papers before he shot out of the study. She sat still, her throbbing head pressed against the cold glass of the windowpane.

When Jerran returned he found Callie pacing the room in frustration. He listened attentively while she relayed her conversation with Master Lauder – and whistled aloud as she concluded. She looked very worried and resumed her pacing. "I wish I had that scroll. Knowledge is power and I don't know enough, but it's in Derryn with all my other books, and I'm in Skava." She threw her hands up in disgust.

Jerran gave her a sympathetic smile. "Callie, all your books are back in Derryn but didn't you spend a week just reading before we went to Nilsport?" She nodded. "So what can you remember?" She shrugged.

"It was random stuff apart from historical battles. The Elemental and Arch-Mages were rather an eccentric bunch."

"In what way?"

"Well, for example, Tardon the traveller used his earth power to create new roads whenever he went on a journey. Alessor the archer used to go hunting and barbeque her kills with lightning bolts and Wisher the Arch-Mage built himself a mansion with little in the way of plumbing. If he wanted a shower he summoned a rain cloud."

"Are you making that up?"

"Unfortunately, no. Havens, Jerran! Do you think I'll ever get a notable nickname like them?"

"Actually, I do but I think that's likely to be 'Callandra the Bloody Annoying' unless you try a bit harder." She glowered.

"Callie, I know there were some Mages who did good things – now think."

"Well, Isden turned back the great wave that would have swamped the lowlands."

"True, but not useful – no water. Wasn't there someone called Battry? I'm sure I remember him from my own studies."

"Battris."

"That's it! Didn't he save half the population during the great famine, when the seas froze over?"

"He did – but once again, we don't have a food shortage."

"No. But how did he do it? Load cattle on a passing cloud and blow it over?"

She laughed. "No he…" Her voice died away and her expression changed completely.

"He what?"

"He opened a portal."

"A portal?"

"Absolutely, I did read that. Jerran, you are brilliant." She danced across the room and hugged him.

"Do you think you might be able to do something similar?"

"I don't see why not. I have the power and my Magery lends itself to matters of movement and distance. I certainly have the will as Master Lauder said." She glanced at the ornate timepiece over the mantle.

"We'll be speaking to your father and the others in about a mark and a half. What will your father want to do, or want us to do about Kerria?"

The Prince hesitated. "I can't speak for the King."

"No, but you probably have a good idea how he would choose to deal with the present situation?"

Jerran gathered his thoughts. "When I said to Axtra that Lithia had no thoughts of conquest towards Kerria, I was telling the truth. My father has often said that he has his hands more than full with our own Kingdom. What he would ideally like, would be for Kerria to be led by a leader or Council who would actually abide by a treaty so we could spend less on defence and build up trade between the two nations."

"The Kerrians don't have a Council, do they?"

"Not really – or not like ours. About forty years ago the country was a patchwork of territories held by different leaders. The fighting was constant. Over time Axtra overran or defeated most of the other Warlords. That man is a ruthless bastard, but a masterly tactician.

"Eventually, bowing to the inevitable the remaining opposition conceded defeat. As a sop to their pride they were given places on a 'Council of Advisers'. I believe those were the men at dinner last night. They were the right age and certainly looked the part."

"So they all need to be removed?" Jerran nodded.

"There's really no chance of permanent change while they hold power."

"But if we did manage to get rid of them – someone would have to take over?"

"Yes. Or things would only get worse." Callie was silent for a while. "Callie." She looked up to see Jerran had perched himself beside her. "We'll find another way."

"What?"

"That's why you always lose at Sarties – your face shows exactly what you are thinking."

"You don't know what I'm thinking!"

"No? Well let me see. You want to get rid of Axtra and his cronies and feel they should pay for what they have done to us and to their own people. Although you have the power to do it, the idea of killing them all fills you with horror." She made to speak but he raised his hand to stop her. "You could possibly do it in the heat of battle, but not in cold blood. This time you know that just putting them to sleep will not be enough. Unless they die, Lithia will be at war again and more lives will be lost. But if you kill them you are not sure you would be able to live with yourself."

Callie stared at the man beside her, speechless for once.

"How did I do?"

She shook her head. "I'm that easy to read?"

"Not always. Not when you guard yourself and not by everyone, but Callie," he paused, "we've been through quite a lot together these last few months, and I have been working as a diplomat for the last five years."

"True." She looked at him, considering. If they managed to walk free from their present captivity, some day he would make a magnificent King.

Chapter 56

Callie spent the next hour working with the Triquetra, tracing the subtleties of its communication link and then decided to test the 'veracity' strand – a function she was relieved to discover she had to actually invoke.

"Jerran – I need to practise – can you tell me a lie?" The Prince still pondering the Kerrian maps looked briefly puzzled but seeing her fiddling with the pendant quickly grasped what she was doing. "Okay, er – I'm not really a Prince and my name is Jeremy."

"Ouch." Callie dropped the Triquetra, rubbing her fingertips.

"What did it do?"

"It went really ice cold. So cold is false. Now say something true."

"Derryn is the capital of Lithia."

"Warm – so true."

"My favourite food is reedfish."

"Icy cold."

"Yes, I really hate it."

"Can you do one more?" The Prince broke eye contact and turned to stare at the wintry view beyond the window. He spoke quietly. "I really don't want to be King." Burning hot. Callie suppressed the gasp that came to her lips. A silence grew as Jerran walked away and leaned his head against the window frame.

[Callie.] Raff's mind call was a blessed interruption.

[We're here, Raff.]

[If you can make contact with Dexter I'll pass my ring to His Majesty. Master Lauder is here with his and Liss and father are here too.]

[Just give me a minute.] Callie reached for Dexter, whose rapid response showed he had been waiting. The next voice she heard only slightly distorted by magic and distance had the same timbre as Jerran's although the pitch was deeper.

[Lady Callandra this is King Theon speaking, can you hear me?]

[I can, Sire, and in a moment I'll be able to see you too and perhaps you… there.] Jerran turned away from the window to see her clutch her pendant. What looked like a dark mirror appeared in front of her and grew until it reached the size of quite a large cheval glass. Through it he could clearly see his father and the others gathered round the large desk in the King's study.

Master Lauder bobbed with excitement. [That's my girl, Callie… how did you?] She smiled.

[I tried combining the Triquetra's communication thread with the scrying technique Terran taught me, and it works.]

The old Mage was patently delighted. [Excellent, excellent, when you get back Callie, I think…]

[Andre,] the King interrupted mildly. [We have to actually get them back first.] The master looked mildly embarrassed.

[Of course, Sire – apologies.]

[Are you well, son?] Theon's eyes were directed slightly to one side of Callie and she realised Jerran had moved to stand behind her.

[I'm fine, sir.] His voice was neutral but calm. [What would you have us do here?]

[We must resolve the situation in Kerria, and if at all possible, I would like a long-term solution.] They nodded. [Apart from the fact that I have no territorial ambitions – if we tried to conquer or annexe

Kerria, in its current state it would simply be a huge drain on our resources. That being said, we cannot achieve the change we need unless we remove those currently in power.]

[We had come to the same conclusion,] the Prince agreed.

[Correct me if I'm wrong, Jerran, but does Axtra still soothe his supporters by that pretence of a Council of Advisers?]

[He does. They were all there when he announced his plans for me and executed Terran.] He saw his father and General D'Arcourt wince and share a look.

[Very well. Now tell me, have any of you encountered any Kerrians that you feel we might be able to trust, or we might at least be able to work with?]

After a brief pause Callie and Jerran spoke together and an echo indicated Dexter too had spoken. [Arild.]

[The man who originally took you prisoner? Isn't he Axtra's nephew?] General D'Arcourt sounded sceptical.

[He is,] Dexter confirmed, [but in all our dealings he has shown himself to be humane and honourable. Jerran?]

[I agree. He has the respect of his own fighting men but still cares for those innocents caught up in Tol Gath's plot.] The King looked thoughtful.

[A scion of Axtra's family might be the best answer if he proves trustworthy. He would have some sort of claim to the leadership.]

[If he proves trustworthy.] General D'Arcourt still sounded unconvinced.

[He would be more acceptable to the Kerrians than any Lithian and I trust Jerran's judgement.]

There were several more minutes of low-voiced discussion in the King's study while Callie and Jerran waited quietly. [Very well. This may not work out but we can't leave a power vacuum in Kerria. If it does succeed, well we might avoid any military conflict at all – and even partial success would give Lithia some respite. This is what we want you to do. Callie, can you put a compulsion on Lord Dexter's guards? Would you be able to manage that over the distance?] Her eyes widened but she saw no problem.

[Yes, Sire.]

[Good. Send them to Arild with the message that he and all his forces are to return to Skava immediately. Dexter you, Will and Gilly head back to Skava as fast as you can. Go to Axtra and tell him you have a response from me to Jerran, about his ransom demands. If he questions how you could have this answer so soon, emphasise our mage abilities.

[As Arild's men approach, let Jerran and Callie know. Jerran, you will demand to take this matter to the whole Council – act as if you are going to agree to his terms. Callie,] the King's expression softened as he eyed the young woman, [it will then be down to you.]

Jerran saw her clench her hands in her lap, but before he could speak his father went on. [I am not a butcher. Axtra will be executed for the murder of Mage Terran, which he ordered and the death of my son, which he sanctioned. I have no intention of asking you to kill these men, no matter how much they may deserve that fate.] Jerran dropped a hand to Callie's shoulder and felt the tension go out of her.

[Callie.] Master Lauder smiled gently at her. [We have been studying the Triquetra scroll. Although we have barely scratched the surface, based on Isseni lore, Liss sent us looking for very specific information on…]

[Portals?] Callie chipped in.

[Why yes – I see you got there before us. I always said you were my brightest student.]

[Actually that's not at all what I remember you saying.] General D'Arcourt's lips quirked and Callie blushed faintly.

[It's all here. The how, is clearly spelt out and the creation seems simple as I read it but I suspect you are the only living Mage with enough power to actually do it.] He fell silent and the King resumed.

[Our hope is that if you can create one, we can send the Kerrian Councillors into distant exile with a geas so that they can live out their remaining days unable to return and doing some actual good.]

[Do you have somewhere in mind?] Dexter queried.

[Oh yes indeed.] General D'Arcourt's mirthless laugh boded ill. [If Arild proves cooperative we will support him as leader of the

Kerrians. If not, our fall-back plan would be to create other portals and use them to feed our own military to the hot spots in Kerria we have identified. Is that all clear?]

There was a chorus of assent. Master Lauder moved forward. [Callie, I'll read out what you need to know when you are ready, and then you need to deal with Lord Dexter's guards. After that...] He looked to one side and Callie turned her attention back to the King.

[Callandra, is it possible for you to hold this link in a way that allows me a few minutes' private conversation with my son?]

[Yes, Sire. I'll withdraw.] She rose, holding her pendant, and walked out of the room, trying not to wish for time to speak to her own father privately too.

Back in her own room Callie settled at a small table and scribbled notes as Master Lauder read out the information on portals, contained in the Triquetra scroll. It didn't seem complicated; in fact, not dissimilar to the visual contact she had already managed. When she had finished, a faint buzz at the back of her mind told her the King and his son were still talking, so she turned her mind to Dexter.

As soon as he appeared she saw he had acted swiftly. Their unwary guards had already been immobilised, bound and gagged. [What do I do now, Callie?] Dexter's mind voice was warm and clear.

[Put your hands on each man's head and I will work through you. I'm going to make it a very simple command. Are you ready?]

[Yes, go ahead.] Callie planted the compulsion in both men's minds, as if they had received new orders from their commander. They were to ride with all speed to Koepka and order Arild back to Skava, which they must avoid on route.

Callie knew the directive would cause them no harm but still didn't like the necessity. She soothed her conscience by telling herself that she was truly obeying a royal command. When she broke the link she returned to her notes, studying them until she was sure she knew what to do.

Unconsciously, Callie had expected Jerran to let her know when he and the King had concluded their conversation but as time passed and that didn't happen she finally wandered out. Jerran was sitting in front of the fire, looking serious and subdued. "Jerran?" He tried for a smile with no great success. "Has something happened?" He looked at her almost sadly. "Nothing unexpected."

"If there's anything I…" He brushed her concern away almost curtly. "Callie, please. It's confidential. I can't talk about it." He left the room swiftly, only reappearing later to share an almost silent evening meal.

*

Dexter patted his horse as he watched their erstwhile guards turn their mounts. The men would retrace their route for a few miles before heading north-east to Koepka. When Callie had put the compulsion on them, he hadn't known what to expect, but surely some sort of fireworks. In fact, they simply acted as though they had been given new orders that needed to be executed promptly and they even gave brief farewell waves as they settled their horses into the ground-eating stride that would take them swiftly to their destination.

He signalled to Will and Gilly and they in turn headed east on a road that would take them to the outskirts of Skava. The three of them had taken turns to slow the progress of their outwards journey to the Eastwold Pass as much as possible as a return to Axtra's headquarters had always seemed likely.

As they rode Dexter found himself reviewing the plan. What it amounted to was a coup; the conquest of another country by a grand total of five people. When he thought of it like that it did seem utterly ridiculous and impossible, but it wasn't, because one of those five people was so remarkable. Callandra, extraordinary, kind, powerful, funny, feisty and vulnerable, she had become a close friend to him in next to no time and he recognised how strange that was.

Losing his entire family in the worst possible way had hurt him so badly that he had re-drawn his defences, setting everyone apart from Blaine at a distance. Then Callie had come along. He knew from experience that a close bond often formed between these who had endured and survived extreme danger together, so perhaps he had connected with her because events over the past few weeks had been so intense. He mused on it as the hours and the miles passed by, finally concluding that no matter how things might eventually turn out he was glad to have her in his life.

When Callie next woke, she felt distinct butterflies in her stomach.

If all went well Arild and his men might reach Skava that very night and the power play would begin. Jerran seemed to have recovered his balance after a night's sleep and was perfectly ready to go with her to the healer hall after they had breakfasted; permission having easily been obtained as long as they took guards.

Gerda and Helga greeted them warmly and they moved through the rooms, helping where they could. Jerran translated and Callie healed, or eased pain. They worked well together, but at mid-day Jerran pulled her firmly away. There was no way to predict when she might need all the Mage strength she could muster.

After lunch a game of Sartis whiled away an hour or two then Callie dozed off over one of the few books the fortress could provide. She woke fully when a servant brought more wood for the fire, to realise the daylight was fading. Jerran lounged on the sofa nearby simply staring at the flames, yesterday's bleak expression again visible in the firelight. When she stirred he produced a quick unconvincing smile and set about lighting candles. Their evening meal had not yet arrived when a clatter of hooves on the cobbles drew the Prince to the window.

"I think – yes, it's them." Dexter and one of the scouts were briefly illuminated by the stable lamps. Callie's stomach flipped over. She and Jerran stood in near darkness watching as Dexter walked to the main entrance where he spoke briefly to the steward before they disappeared inside.

Callie hissed, "Jerran tell me again that I can do this. Tell me that I am really powerful and…" He moved closer and unexpectedly wrapped his arms around her. She started, but stilled as he hugged her. She could feel his warmth, his strength. The rise and fall of his chest. It felt really good.

"Callie, you can do this. You have great power, great intelligence, great perception, great courage, a really great backside and a pair of very— ouch!" Jerran released her as she giggled and thumped him.

"That's *lèse majesté* I'll have you know; violation of the dignity of a royal prince."

"What dignity?"

"Touché." She grinned warmly at his ploy to prevent her having a full-blown panic attack and her smile almost took his breath away.

He stepped back, turning as the door opened to admit servants with their dinner.

They had barely eaten a mouthful of it when they heard the voices they had been anticipating. "Leave some for us." Lord Dexter stood in the doorway with Gilly who moved at speed to the fire.

"Ye Gods, it's bitter out there." Gilly flung a wet cloak over the nearest chair and tried to roast himself. Dexter moved at a more leisurely pace, looking them over.

"It's good to see you both safe and well. We've set things in motion and Will has headed north to watch out for Arild. Axtra's steward has gone to inform his master of our return so I imagine we will have company shortly. Best to be prepared." They nodded.

The travellers quickly changed out of their damp travel gear and settled at the dinner table where they addressed themselves to the food with a single-mindedness that spoke of camp rations.

"That's better." Dexter finally sat back. "Any more news from home?"

Callie shook her head but Jerran grimaced. "When the situation is resolved my father wants…" The sentence went unfinished as the door was slammed open. Axtra himself stood there glowering. He stalked towards the table, planting himself opposite Dexter.

"My steward told me you had returned. Did I not make myself clear? You were to return with King Theon's answer to my demands – on which the life of your noble Prince here depends." Dexter rose calmly to his feet.

"And so indeed I have."

"Don't take me for a fool." Axtra's scowl deepened. "You have not had time to reach Lithia – let alone go there and return."

"Lord Axtra, forgive me." Dexter's extreme courtesy was insulting in itself. "It is true that we did not journey all the way to Lithia, but we approached close enough that we could use Magery to deliver your demands to our King. He gave due consideration to your words – and your actions, and has returned his answer. I have already shared his decision with Prince Jerran." He smiled blandly while Callie looked away. Was Axtra so ignorant of Magery that he would believe this?

It took the Warlord a moment to understand what Dexter was saying, then his expression changed to one of confident self-satisfaction.

"And? What did he say?" Prince Jerran rose in turn.

"Lord Axtra. My father commands that I give you his response – in front of your whole Council."

"You'll give it to me now, you insolent cub, or—"

"Or what, milord? You'll have me killed? Even if that is to be my fate, it would not further your plans if you were to execute me right now."

A muscle twitched below the Warlord's eye. "I don't trust you." He eyed the men thoughtfully as Dexter gave a mirthless laugh.

"You – don't trust us? How ironic."

"Dexter." Jerran quelled him with a gesture.

"Lord Axtra my father said an alliance was sworn with you, with the consent of your Council. You have chosen by your actions to dissolve it, and he wishes to be certain that this is also by the will of your Council. Is that a problem for you?" His voice held a challenge.

"Why should it be?" The Warlord eyed him consideringly. "Very well, I will agree to this but it will do you no good, Princeling. I control my Council. They do my bidding. Always. We will meet in the morning." He spun on his heels and stormed away, his footsteps heavy in the passage until the outer door slammed shut.

Callie let out a breath she didn't even know she had been holding. Jerran held up two fingers. "Step two. Now we wait for tomorrow – and Arild."

Gilly, warm and fed soon headed for his bed. Dexter was about to follow their example when Callie turned to Jerran once again sprawled in front of the fire. "Jerran, just before Axtra arrived you started to say something about your father?"

Jerran's face clouded. He glanced at her and sighed. "When this is all over he wants me home as soon as possible."

"Meaning?" Dexter moved to join them.

"Meaning he wants Callie to send me to Derryn though a portal."

"Oh." Callie felt strangely put out.

"Could you do that, Callie?" Dexter sounded dubious. She shrugged.

"There's no reason why not. If it's urgent?" She looked a question at the Prince.

"I need to be there when they hold Mikheli's state funeral. He's held in a stasis spell."

"Goddess Jerran, that's grim," Callie muttered sympathetically.

"Obviously you would want to say your farewells to your brother, Jerran, but couldn't they have held the funeral and let you do something privately later?" Dexter looked concerned.

Jerran shook his head. "It's not that simple, because Mikheli was Crown Prince. All the nobles will gather to see him interred and they won't be able to leave afterwards until I am there to receive their oaths of acceptance as the new heir to the Crown. Then I will have to take on my brother's role, and many of my brother's... duties." There was a distinct pause before that last word. Callie's heart fell as the import of his words sank in. For Jerran, no more roving the country with a handful of companions; no more revelry at the Broken Arrow, no chance to use his formidable fighting skills on real battlefields. He would lose so much, and so, a selfish corner of her mind, acknowledged so would she. No more royal bodyguard to save her from blades and nightmares, and offer intuitive support in her healing; no affectionate mockery to rescue her from panic and no more well-informed, unpatronising conversation.

Jerran, as Crown Prince, would once again be surrounded by the courtiers, councils and meetings she thought she had rescued him from. She knew just how much he would hate it. Looking up she saw Dexter watching her and tried to gather her thoughts. "Of course I will send you to Derryn as the King commands. I suppose that could even be tomorrow."

"Actually," the Prince offered a genuine smile, "not tomorrow."

"Not tomorrow?"

"Well you will have to send the Council into exile and Axtra to prison. I told my father that after that you would be too exhausted to do anything more."

"Oh, I don't think…" She saw Jerran's eyebrow quirk and understood. He was trying to grasp a last few days of freedom. "Jerran, that is so thoughtful of you – I'll be absolutely exhausted. It might take me several days to recover."

"Exactly what I thought. If we make our way slowly home, I imagine you might be sufficiently recovered to attempt it by the time we reach Barnard's Castle? And of course as your bodyguard, it would be unthinkable to abandon you in a hostile land, even with Lord Dexter's strong sword arm to support you."

An inexplicable wave of relief washed over Callie and she chuckled. "Well I'd better go and build up by strength. Goodnight, gentlemen."

Chapter 57

Truth be told none of them slept well. A cold sleeting rain had set in about midnight and done nothing to raise their spirits even though Will had returned, confirming Arild was on his way. Their discussions were low voiced and tense and it was almost a relief when one of Axtra's officers arrived with a squad of men to escort them to the meeting chamber.

The Council of Advisers, all the lesser Warlords who governed land under Axtra, were present. They mostly wore their studded leather armour but their weapons, apart from the daggers on their belts were piled outside the doors. They eyed the Lithians with expressions ranging from amusement and curiosity to annoyance, but none of them offered greetings. Axtra was not present and after a quarter mark a certain restlessness spread over the company.

Finally, the rear door opened to admit the Warlord, his second-in-command, and following behind a warrior in travel gear, who calmly settled himself at the end of the table. "Arild!" Callie heard a sigh of relief from Dexter and a low muttered 'perfect' from Jerran.

Axtra glanced at the Lithians then ignoring them, turned to his Council.

"Before we hear from our royal 'guest', there is a small matter I would like to clarify. I ordered my nephew to Koepka," he pointed at

Arild, "so I am puzzled how he comes to be here. He tells me he received orders to return to Skava with all speed and I have never found him to lie, so I am wondering who took it upon himself to issue such an order?"

There was no answer, as the Kerrians looked at each other suspiciously. Axtra hammered a huge fist on the table. "Who dares to usurp my authority? Who did this?"

Jerran gave Callie a wink, his fingers tangling briefly with hers as she took a breath and stepped forward. "That would be me, Lord Axtra. I gave the order." Her voice was firm and calm. The old Warlord turned to look at her.

"You!" He laughed and turned away as Jerran stepped beside her.

"Lady Callandra did give that order, although I commanded her to do so."

Axtra looked at the young woman again. "Indeed? Well, by command or not, your whore will pay the price for her impudence. Guards! Take her to the dungeons." The guards by the doorway stepped forward, or tried to, as the stone floor softened across the room and washed up their legs and those of Axtra's entire Council, like a wave of muddy water, setting hard and holding them all in place as if they were half-men, half statues. Only Axtra remained free. "What in the seven hells?" Axtra drew the only sword in the room and raised it high as he rushed at Callie, to be brought up short as she drew the air from his lungs, bringing him crashing to his knees, eyes bulging.

Dexter and Will stepped forward swiftly, disarming him and dragging him back to his seat, where Callie bound him in place.

The Kerrians failing to break free from their stone bonds were now shouting as loudly as they could. Jerran moved to stand in front of the semi-circular table and bellowed, "Enough! Cease this noise. The Lady Callandra has sealed this chamber so your calls for help will not be heard. You were brought here to listen and so you shall. I and my companions came into Kerria peacefully. By our skills and at great personal risk, Tol Gath, the dark Sorcerer, who inflicted great suffering on the people of Kerria was brought down. When we returned to Skava, at your behest Lord Axtra, you imprisoned us, butchered Mage Terran then held me hostage, even while you arranged the assassination of my brother the Crown Prince of Lithia

– a country with whom you had a treaty."

"Krig's blud." Arild looked stunned and stared at his uncle in disbelief. "No Kerrian would behave so. Uncle – tell him."

Axtra sneered. "You are soft, sister-son. Sometimes hard decisions have to be made. We need metal. A mine would not be a high price to pay for a Crown Prince!"

"We could trade for metal!"

"That is not the Kerrian way!"

"Then perhaps it should be! I didn't know it was the Kerrian way to send assassins." He turned to Jerran. "Your brother is dead?" The Prince nodded curtly. "He died defending himself?"

"He was poisoned." A murmur of disgust rippled round Axra's advisers. Obviously this fact had been concealed and did not meet with the approval of warriors, who counted themselves blessed if they died with weapon in hand.

"My father, King Theon of Lithia, utterly rejects your demands, Axtra."

"Then he is a fool. When your whore's little magic tricks fail, do you really think you'll have any chance of reaching Lithia before my men capture and kill you?"

"The thing is – they will no longer be your men. You see – I'm not leaving. You are." Axtra for the first time looked uncertain.

"You are unfit to rule. Your people suffer while you play war games, and speaking for Lithia, you are a bad neighbour. My father's patience is at an end. He feels it is time for a change. You, Axtra, will be executed for the death of my brother, but your 'loyal' men, this collection of short-sighted warmongers will be exiled."

The Council men began shouting again. "Wherever you send us, you Lithian dog, we will return and free Kerria."

"I think not. You see Tol Gath was not the only one with mind magic. My 'whore' as you so charmingly titled her is a very powerful Mage; far more so than Terran whom you executed. She will put a compulsion on all of you that you will never leave your new home and your only desire will be to help and defend the local people in any way that you can."

Axtra spat. "Kerrians will never accept the rule of Lithian scum."

"Then it's as well they won't have to." A stunned silence greeted that statement.

"Days ago, I said Lithia had no territorial ambition regarding Kerria and that is the simple truth. Your nephew Arild will have the daunting task of bringing Kerria back from the brink of disaster where you have dragged it."

"What?" Arild, finding he was free from restraint rose to his feet, stunned. "Prince Jerran, Lord Dexter, Lady Callandra. I cannot argue with the justice you intend to deliver here, and I would see Kerria change but if you want a puppet under the control of your King I am not that man. My loyalty and my sword belong to Kerria."

"Arild, we want no more than I have said," Jerran began but Arild interrupted him in blatant disbelief.

"You control magical forces that make our warriors look like children. You hold Kerria in the palm of your hand and you expect me to believe that you will simply walk away?" Jerran faltered, unsure how to prove his good faith but Dexter stepped forward.

"Arild, do you remember when Callandra was helping the healers and the axeman who kept lying about what had happened?"

The Commander nodded, puzzled. "Callandra used a truth spell on him."

"She did," he acknowledged slowly.

"If she puts one on Prince Jerran would that satisfy you? After a brief hesitation the Kerrian nodded and Callie touched her pendant. "Jerran?"

"Do it." She closed her eyes and seconds later a light settled about the Prince.

"I Jerran Prince of Lithia do give oath that if Arild Stormson becomes Lord of Kerria, Lithia will not make any claim on the territory, nor seek to interfere, encroach or seek any influence in this land."

The Pendant almost glowed with heat. True! Arild looked at it for a long moment, then nodded. "He speaks Truth." His eyes ran across the faces of his uncle's cronies. Callie wondered whether he saw what she did, corruption, greed. arrogance and cruelty.

He took a deep breath and drew himself taller. "For the sake of Kerria, it shall be as you say.

"Traitor," Axtra snarled. "Plotting to overthrow your own blood with these Kerrian dogs."

"Uncle, if the Mage placed her truth spell on me it would prove that I knew nothing of this plan. I have served you loyally but no more. It is you who have betrayed our peoplc. They deserve better. Your time is over." He walked across to stand by Dexter.

Callie moved into the centre of the room and with a flicker of her hand cast a light sleep on all the soldiers and Warlords. Then she closed her eyes and reached out until the power of the Triquetra filled her and her vision of the world deepened and shifted, revealing ever more levels for her to know. She sought and found the sparks that represented the minds of the sleeping men and settled to her work. The compulsions she placed deeply and strongly. These men must never leave their new home; their only purpose would be to serve and save the people there. That work would drive them for the rest of their lives.

When she was satisfied, she released the molten stone holding them and let it puddle back into stone flags. Then she turned and faced the hearth where a fire was eating its way through giant logs. She reached for this element and used it to fashion a circle of darkness that grew at her command until it was as tall as she was – a portal.

"Their weapons will be outside, may they…?" Arild asked and Dexter went with him to fetch them. Jerran stayed beside Callie, one hand steady on her shoulder. The portal, which had been pitch black began to lighten and as if someone was drawing back veils, a scene began to emerge. Callie bit her lip in concentration, carefully replicating the image that had been given to her by Master Lauder. When it exactly matched, she signalled and all the Kerrian war leaders rose obediently to their feet like sleepwalkers. They collected their arms from Arild and Dexter and without a word, without hesitation, without a backward glance they walked through the portal out onto a scrubby hillside.

"Where is it?" Arild asked quietly, as the last men walked away.

"Leprossa." Dexter's voice was carefully neutral.

"The lepers' isle?" Arild blanched. "Then truly they will never return."

"No, but while they live they will be able to help the unfortunates. It's almost unbelievable but raiders have been landing there and stealing their few cattle. Most of the lepers cannot even hold a weapon let alone defend themselves."

"Callie." Dexter turned to the young Mage. "Do you want to send Axtra now or rest first?" She turned towards him. Her concentration wavered for only a split second but Axtra was on his feet, belt knife in hand and lunging for the Prince. Callie flung herself in front of Jerran, colliding with Dexter as she did so, but fast as they were, Arild was faster. The sword he had retrieved and had not even had time to sheathe, skewered the Warlord from the groin to chest.

Axtra fell backwards, a groan taking his last breath as he slithered down a yard of bloody steel to the floor. Arild looked down at the man who had been the supreme ruler of Kerria since before he was born and nudged his uncle's body clear with his foot.

For a moment no-one spoke. Then Jerran pulled himself together. "Arild, I thank you." He bowed shakily, then spun on his heels, grabbed Callie and shook her hard. "Don't you ever – and I mean ever, do anything like that again. If anything happened to you I don't know what I'd…" His voice trailed off as he realised he was the focus of everyone's attention.

"And I expect you feel like that about me too?" Dexter chipped in.

"Certainly." The Prince laughed, reluctantly released Callie and took a deep breath.

"Arild? Is there more we need to do?"

The Kerrian shook his head. "My own men are here with me. I can secure the capital. There are some holdings where I will have to fight to establish my authority, but our soldiers are weary, their numbers depleted and there are many, many Kerrians who would accept the djvelen himself as ruler if it meant the end to war. In many ways times are changing, and we must change with them." He squared his shoulders. "Spring approaches. By the end of this year I give you my word our land will be at peace." He held out his arm and

Jerran clasped it.

"Then with your leave, Lord Arild, may we make ready to depart?"

"Lord Arild – I think I like the sound of that – and it would be wise for you to leave now. When time allows, Kerria will thank you properly for dealing with Tol Gath, but for now ride safe and may your Gods go with you." He offered them a formal bow and they filed slowly out of the great chamber.

Chapter 58

They headed south along the great road carrying with them news of Axtra's passing and in some towns they delivered sealed messages from Arild to the local commanders and militia. These local leaders, understanding what was happening seemed for the most part relieved, a sign of how great Axtra's oppression had become.

Finally, they reached Montis and the last inn before they turned west to seek the Snakeshead Pass. Marsha, as stout as ever, welcomed them with open arms and bustled off immediately to arrange wine and hot meals, but when they had blunted their appetites and melted the cold from their bones she and her husband came to sit with them, eager to catch up on happenings in the wider world. Learning that Axtra was gone had them exchanging worried glances. His hand had been heavy but he had controlled some of the more lawless elements in their land, but hearing the news that Arild Stormson had taken power was met with honest delight. Dexter had been uncertain how widely the young man would be known, but his reputation had grown quietly but steadily as his attempts to alleviate the suffering of the common people had been noticed and whispered about.

After a long day in the saddle Callie was exhausted by the time she felt she could politely withdraw to her room. Weary as she was she still dragged herself to the bathhouse, shedding the dirt of several days on the road and washing out her hair. The following night they would camp in the Snakeshead tunnel and the day beyond would bring them to Barnard's Castle.

Finishing her bath, Callie cursed herself, realising she hadn't brought clean clothes with her, and unwilling to dress again in her travel-stained gear, she peeped cautiously out of the bathing rooms. The corridor was empty so she wrapped herself up in a huge towel and sprinted swiftly up the stairs, regaining her own room without being seen and shutting the door firmly behind her. She was just about to towel her wet hair, when a sound made her spin round. Jerran was perched on the edge of her bed, rather deliberately clearing his throat.

"Jerran? Why are you in my room?" He rose and walked slowly towards her. "I wanted to," he shrugged, looking anxious and uncomfortable, "I don't know – talk to you. Tomorrow we'll he in the pass. The day after at Barnard's Keep and then I must return to Derryn."

Standing in front of her he looked down and she saw deep sadness in his bright hazel eyes. Her fingers tightened on the towel. "I wanted to thank you, Callie – and to say goodbye."

"Why do you need to thank me?" He offered her a lopsided grin.

"I've lived more in the months since you came into my life than in all the previous twenty-four years. I will always be grateful for that."

Callie found it difficult to meet his gaze but understood his words and shook her head, brushing off his gratitude. "But Jerran – why goodbye? You will be at court. I'll be there sometimes. Will we no longer be friends?"

"Friends? Well maybe, but many things will change when I return to Derryn. Perhaps our 'friendship' can continue, but not..." his voice tailed off. His eyes held hers and she read in them longing and distress. Slowly, almost against his will, he reached for her and put his hands on her naked shoulders, brushing away her damp tangled hair. He leaned forward, his intention obviously to plant a kiss on her forehead and everything inside her rebelled. She reached for his head and pulled it down to hers, her mouth seeking his. He froze for the shortest of moments, then his body was pressed to hers so tightly that her towel, the only thing she wore, ceased its perilous descent.

One of his hands caressed her neck and plunged into her wet hair as he tilted her head and planted a line of hot kisses up her throat. Then his lips brushed across her cheeks before his tongue invaded her mouth. A flame as hot as her elemental magic ignited deep within her body. Her hands stroked down his broad shoulders and back and she felt his breathing grow ragged. Their tongues danced and the Prince's eyes grew darker, heavy lidded, as his thigh pressed between her legs and she felt his body harden through the thin sheeting. Then he groaned.

With a huge effort Jerran drew back, even as Callie protested, and her towel slipped to reveal rosebud pink nipples. She did not move to cover herself and after a moment his gaze shifted to see her dark blue eyes soft with desire, and he swallowed hard.

"Goddess – Callie – forgive me." He released her as if her touch burnt him, then he was gone. Callandra stood alone in her room, aching. Her shoulders were marked where the Prince's hands had gripped her so tightly and she wondered, in curious detachment, whether her heart was marked in the same way.

Callie rode in near silence the next day. When she reached the breakfast room, Jerran had already gone to check the horses and as hours passed he kept as far from her as civility allowed. They made good time, reaching the tunnel camp earlier than on their outward journey. Callie wished they needn't stop at all but the horses were weary. After simple trail food she retired to her bedroll, the Prince settling himself on the opposite side of the area. Lying wide awake with eyes closed Callie recalled bitterly Jerran's determination to be by her side on their way into Kerria, insisting it was his place as her bodyguard. Apparently that no longer mattered.

A hand pulled her blanket higher and startled her. She opened her eyes to see Dexter's concerned face. "Sorry Callie, did I wake you? I thought I saw you shivering."

"No." She shook her head as he resettled her blanket. He hesitated as if he might speak, but she closed her eyes again and turned away. Gradually the noises of the camp faded and eventually only the occasional whicker of the horses and the steady breathing of sleepers disturbed the night.

Callie, in the privacy of the darkness, allowed her eyes to fill with tears. She made no noise. She didn't sob, but she was simply unable to stop them trickling down her face. In her head those last moments she had shared with Jerran played and replayed like a Winter-light play. Callie was not very experienced with men, but neither was she completely innocent. She had had her share of kisses and caresses, but never before had she felt the deep ache and fire that Jerran's embrace had stirred in her. She blushed with shame and humiliation, remembering how he had gazed at her naked breasts, then turned away.

How could she have so misread the man? She wished desperately to be elsewhere, to be with her ordinary companions, not Lords and Princes, not Warlords and Mages. She wished her magic could change time so that she could go back and undo that last encounter, or go forward and be back home. It was nearly dawn before she slept.

Dexter left Callie for as long as he could in the morning, only gently shaking her awake when the Kaffi was brewed and most of their equipment already loaded on the horses. To his eyes, she looked wan and pale, although a brisk wash in chilly water hadn't entirely removed a suspicious red puffiness around her eyes. Still, she took her drink with polite thanks and quickly prepared to ride.

When they emerged with relief on to the Lithian plateau on the western side of the Skyfall Mountains, the view was strikingly different. Most of the snow had melted leaving only rags of slush tucked into corners and occasional ice pockets. The mountain streams were running fast as they picked their way down to the River Road. It was challenging terrain and no-one had attention for anything other than the trail until the road flattened out. Will and Gilly were in high spirits, obviously happy to be back on home territory and their occasional laughter punctuated the quiet.

Jerran rode at the front, apparently lost in thought. With only a few miles of their journey left Dexter let his horse fall back to ride alongside Callandra. "We'll be back at Barnard's Keep within a mark and once you've sent the Prince on his way you'll be a lady of leisure once more, Callie." She smiled but said nothing. "Do you return to the Academy? After all you've done I imagine that might be strange."

It would too. For the first time Callie gave a moment's thought to the future and wondered what she might choose to do. "I think," she answered slowly, glancing at him, "that I won't make any decision for a while." She shook her head as if trying to clear cobwebs. "I am tired in a way I've never known."

Dexter nodded. "That's the delayed reaction to what you've been doing. In life and death situations, when each moment could be your last, your body is on high alert. Afterwards, well, lassitude and a week or two of almost sleep walking."

"That's exactly it! You mean you get it too?"

"Indeed I do, and," his gaze rested pointedly on the Prince riding ahead, "I haven't had as much to deal with as you."

Callie refused to be drawn, turning the conversation back on him. "Do you go to Derryn or home?" Dexter frowned.

"I must go to Derryn, as I have to give oath before the King like everyone else, but I really need to go to Winters Keep first. Blaine will be going mad by now, and when I do turn up and have to leave again almost immediately, he'll be furious."

"Dexter, I can send you to Winters Keep in no time, so why not give yourself a day or two there then bring Blaine on with you to Derryn? He'd be much more forgiving of your long absence if you did."

"Callie, that's brilliant. I keep forgetting what you can do. Why not come with me?"

She sighed. "I only wish I could. I can create portals for other people to use but I'm not yet certain how to hold it and cross myself. I'll probably arrive in Derryn at the same time you do."

"You'll only have Will and Gilly with you – is that okay?" His voice was uncertain. He was obviously anxious for her safety while well aware of the immense power she commanded.

"It will be just fine. I used to train with Will and Gilly when they were finishing at battle school. Speaking of which…" Her roving gaze had noticed them waving and pointing. The tallest turrets of Bernard's Keep had come into view and it looked like they had been spotted as a mirror signal flashed towards them. Their journey was all but over.

*

Warmth, clean clothes and a comfortable room – small things helped

Callie put herself back together while Jerran and Dexter updated Gideon on the happenings in Kerria. With nothing more to do, Callie decided to contact her brother.

[Raff?]

[Callie! At last! Please tell me you are on your way home!]

[I can certainly do that. We've just reached Barnard's Keep.]

[That's brilliant – so only a few more days.]

[You missed me then?]

[Certainly not. Well, you know.] There was a short pause. She did know. The bond she shared with her twin was fathoms deeper than even her closest friendships.

[So what's wrong?] Raff asked gently.

[Who said anything's wrong? We've completed our mission, more or less successfully.] The memory of Terran ruffled the edge of her mind.

[Callie – oh, never mind. You'll tell me when you get here. We'll have the whole family together for a while! Megan's back.]

[Really? Oh, fantastic. I can't wait to see her. Has she changed at all? Is she all grown up and superior?]

He laughed. [She always was all grown up and it's not in her to be superior.] That was true. Their sister, older by five years had been away since the previous spring living and working with the horses of the hill people. When she had been at the academy, Megan's Mage gift had led her into Healer training, where she had become perfectly competent but not outstanding. A fortuitous accident had turned her attention to animals instead. Here her skills had proved little short of miraculous and she had persuaded her parents to let her do her elective study with the horse breeders of West Lithia. Callie had not expected to see her so soon.

[So, how is she?]

[So full of all she has learnt, you won't get a word in edgeways.]

[I thought she wasn't coming back until mid-summer?]

[That still holds. The tribal leaders were bringing horses to Derryn and she managed to tag along. They weren't going to stay long, but the tribesman in charge is of high enough status to offer the loyal oath to Jerran. You are sending him back, aren't you?]

[Yes.] Her response was curt.

[About time. The word is that the King was furious at his refusal to hurry.]

[Well he'll be back at court tomorrow – or even later tonight.] She wasn't aware that her tone of voice had changed, but her twin knew her very, very well.

[Oh, I see.]

[You see what?]

[Well you didn't say 'and good riddance' but I'll swear it was there.]

[I was just…] She was interrupted by a tap on the door and a page appeared to tell her dinner would be served in half a mark.

[Raff, I have to go and dress, then possibly create a portal or two. Giver my love to the ancients.] She automatically used their private name for their parents.

[I'll do that, mighty Mage. See you soon.] And he broke the contact, leaving Callie to dress speedily while swallowing down a massive bout of homesickness.

The meal was served in one of the smaller chambers, and apart from Dexter and Jerran, with Lord Barnard away in Derryn, Gideon had only included Healer Terrill, and Cestris, the arms master at Barnard Keep. Although Terrill had questions in abundance about the mind sickness Tol Gath had created and spread, most of the conversation revolved around the military situation in Kerria and Callie's concentration drifted away. She was called back to the present when she heard her name mentioned.

"So Lady Callandra will be sending you home shortly, Your Highness."

"After dinner if she will be so kind." It was almost a request but he still did not look at her. "I'm sorry I cannot stay, Gideon, but you know the circumstances." Lord Barnard's heir nodded. "And you are going to Winters Keep before you set out for Derryn, Dexter?"

"Yes, I need to check things are well, then Blaine and I will both head to the capital."

"Callandra." Gideon turned to his third visitor. "Are there any particular needs to be met before you can create these portals?" She shook her head.

"I do find an archway or a fireplace gives me a useful anchor but it's not essential."

"Then let's be about it. As you'll need your horses and gear, shall we say in half a mark at the Castle gateway?" He directed his remarks to Jerran and Dexter. "I'll fetch those letters for my father."

The company dispersed; Jerran and Dexter to ready themselves for their onward journeys and Gideon to the Castle's office. Callie drifted back to her room and curled up with a book knowing she would be called when needed.

In the stable Jerran found Warrior already saddled so it took no time to put his few personal possessions into his saddle bags. He was doing up the last buckle, when he felt a tap on his shoulder and turned to see Lord Dexter looking at him very measuringly. "Prince Jerran." The northern Lord pronounced his words slowly as if they left a bad taste in his mouth. "Prince Jerran, a private word if I may?" The Prince raised an eyebrow.

"A private word before Callie arrives." Jerran turned back to his task.

Dexter's voice was low. "It would be obvious to a blind man that you have upset Lady Callandra very badly. I don't know how, or why, but I just wanted to tell you, if you cause her any more grief, Prince or not, I'm probably going to break every bone in your body." His tone was calm, almost conversational, but held a ring of total conviction. The Prince's hands stilled at his task. "The thing is, I really care about Callie." Jerran spun round.

"And you think I don't." He spat out the words, rage and despair written over his face. Then he shook his head and reached to mount his horse. In the saddle he threw a glance back at the northern Lord. "You'll understand soon enough." Then he rode Warrior out towards the gate as Callie and Gideon walked down the steps from the great hall.

Chapter 59

Home! Callie's aching heart lifted as she trotted Jessa into Derryn City. Although they'd had no deadline to keep, by unspoken agreement, the three remaining travellers had ridden long hard days to get back, cutting their journey time almost in half. Callie didn't stop at the Academy or barracks. She wasn't ready for the curiosity and questions that would inevitably come her way. She rode slowly to the D'Arcourt town house and dismounting wearily from her beloved mare, she stood unsteadily in the courtyard until Winston and his stable lads engulfed her, petting her as much as they did Jessa.

She entered the house quietly, not sure if anyone would even be there. The demands on her parents were many, Raff had duties, and she had no idea of Megan's movements. A hum of conversation drew her to the family salon and she warily opened the door to find for once the Gods were smiling at her. Her family, all her family and only her family were sitting chatting. Four pairs of eyes glanced her way then she was wrapped in hug after healing hug. It felt wonderful. The pain and anger that had coloured her last few days were lost in the warmth and comfort of her family. When her eyes filled with tears, which then fell freely, no questions were asked, no eyebrows raised. Perhaps Esma and Raff exchanged a quick glance before he put a goblet of wine in her hand but nothing more.

When she had emptied it, her mother announced that Callie was worn out and shooed her up the stairs to her room, where Sarah undressed her, brushing out her wind tangled hair. After extracting a promise that Callie would try to sleep, her mother's maid finally left her with a single candle and departed, closing the door firmly behind her.

Callie lay back on her fine pillows. The candlelight flickered across the opal firestone of the Triquetra that lay on her night table. The pendant looked like a simple piece of jewellery, a decoration casually dropped by a lady as she undressed after a dance, all sparkling prettiness, but it was not. All that it meant and all that it could mean to her and others danced across her thoughts as she fell asleep.

*

It was as rare for General D'Arcourt to lunch at home as it was for Callie to sleep almost the entire morning away, but both things happened the next day. Callie had slept long and deeply in secure and familiar surroundings. When she got up in a very leisurely manner she felt much recovered. As lunch was nearly ready and breakfast long gone, she grabbed some Kaffi and wandered through the family rooms. The door to her father's study was ajar and she recognised his gruff tones, in conversation with Raff.

"Callie!" Her father caught sight of her and beckoned. "I've been watching for you. You look a lot less like a wraith than you did last night so I assume you slept well?"

"Absolutely." She circled behind her father, wrapping her arms around his neck and planting a kiss on his thick grey hair. "Oh, it's so good to be home – but I am surprised to see you here and at this time of day?" Her voice lifted in a question.

"I pulled rank." Her father gave her a wink. "You know the routine. All your party need to be individually debriefed on your Kerrian trip. Prince Jerran has already submitted very comprehensive reports, so we know the main events, but each one of you will have a different perspective, something to add and that can be useful. I decided there was no reason why you and I couldn't do yours at home." A gong sounded from the hallway. "After we have some lunch if that's alright?"

"Or breakfast in your case, Callie," her brother butted in.

"That's fine, sir." She turned and punched Raff on the arm and walked after her father towards the dining room, only to feel her brother's fingers dart into her hair, pulling out her clasp so that it came tumbling down. She elbowed him in the ribs hard enough to make him grunt. General D'Arcourt didn't turn. He just stood perfectly still.

"Callandra, Raff – refresh my memory. How old are the two of you?"

"Sorry sir," they echoed. Callie bit her lip to quell a giggle and knew her brother was doing the same. She realised with relief that she still knew how to laugh.

It took the best part of the afternoon for Callie to give her account of Kerria and answer all her father's questions, while he took copious notes. She didn't mind that Raff sat quietly at the back of the room listening. She would have told him everything anyway.

Finally finished, General D'Arcourt looked his daughter over carefully. She seemed older and somehow less innocent; inevitable consequences of doing what she had done and seeing what she had seen. He didn't believe for a minute that she had told him every last thing. There were matters she had skirted around and others she had hurried past, that suggested to him that there had been tensions within the group, although not enough to prevent their success. He thought he might learn more of that when he spoke to Lord Dexter, who was due to reach Derryn within the next day or two.

"Thank you, Callie. I hope I won't have to revisit any of this – I'll put the report together myself. Now, I know you plan on some time off and that will do you good but I'm afraid there is one formal event you cannot avoid. The King wishes to honour you, Lord Dexter and Prince Jerran for all you have done and thank you for procuring what we hope will be a more lasting peace with Kerria."

The look of horror on his daughter's face made him chuckle. "Callie, I said 'honour' not torture."

"Same thing." Callie glared at him. "Do I have to?"

"Yes." His voice was firm then after a pause he went on, "Things have been very difficult here, Callie, with Mikheli's death. King Theon is trying to raise the peoples' spirits and restore their confidence. Prince Jerran's return has helped. His brother's death was vile, but to be blunt Jerran will make the far better King when the time comes – and celebrating what your intrepid little band has achieved will continue the good work."

Callie sighed but realised her father was right. "When will it be?"

"As soon as Lord Dexter gets here." She smiled at that.

"Father – can I ask you something?" He didn't look up from his notes.

"The answer is no."

"But I haven't even asked yet?"

"Still no. I know that voice."

Raff burst out laughing. "What were you after, Mighty Mage?"

"I was only going to ask if we could invite Lord Dexter and his brother to dinner?" This certainly did make the General look up. He ostentatiously extended his arm.

"Raff, please pinch me." Raff obliged.

"Father!!"

"Well it seems I'm not actually dreaming. Callandra, did you just ask me to invite an eligible young man to dinner on your behalf?"

"Aaahgh – it's not like that! Dexter is a good friend and a really decent man and Blaine is – well Blaine is an idiot but great fun. Dexter was very good to me. There's an awfully large hole in his life where his family used to be. I just thought…" She tailed off and shrugged.

"An excellent and kind idea. I'll speak to your mother. Do you want us to invite Prince Jerran as well?"

"Certainly not. If I ever see His Highness again it will be far too soon." The sharpness in her voice silenced her father for a moment. He glanced sideways at Raff who gave him an infinitesimal shrug, then returned his attention to his daughter.

"Very well. Now off with you – and don't forget to visit Master Lauder and Master Elton."

"Anyone else?"

"Well Liss has been very worried about you too." She groaned.

*

It was only four days later that Callie found herself walking through the palace corridors between her parents. Outside the throne room they parted as she was drawn aside into an antechamber, where she was pleased to see Will and Gilly also present. Lord Dexter was talking to an older man who looked slightly familiar although she didn't remember ever having met him. They looked up as she entered. Dexter gave her a warm smile and stepped towards her, obviously intending an introduction when Worrall, King Theon's master of ceremonies, bustled into the room.

He offered a brief bow, looking them over for any sartorial mistakes. Callie was wearing something quite unusual. Instead of a demure gown or the dull formal dress of academy students, she wore cobalt blue, close-fitting leggings beneath an asymmetric three-quarter length tunic of the same colour, richly embroidered in red-gold thread. Copper-dusted boots completed the outfit. She looked absolutely stunning; fierce and slightly wild. Callie had been amazed when her mother had brought the clothes to her, but Esma with foreknowledge of the ceremony, had announced that she wanted people to look at her daughter and see her for what she truly was. Callie had been delighted, and in a tiny little corner of her mind was pleased that Prince Jerran would see what he had rejected.

Worrall's voice drew her from her thoughts. "So are you clear on the order? Arms men William and Gilligan will enter together – walk to the dais, bow, separate and stand on either side, followed by Master Lenster. Then Lord Dexter if you will escort Lady Callandra?" Dexter nodded. "After your bow and curtsey, remain in the centre slightly to the left. Prince Jerran will be on the dais with his father and his betrothed, but he will come down to stand on your other side, Lady Callandra, before His Majesty makes the speeches and presentations. Lady Callandra?" The fussy little man hesitated. The lady Mage was suddenly looking faint, all the colour leaching from her face. "Lady Callandra are you alright?" He tutted anxiously as the young woman seemed to sway slightly. Dexter put an arm round her shoulders to steady her as his mind also processed the information Worrall had so casually dropped. He could see the question in Callie's eyes.

"Prince Jerran's betrothed?" he asked quietly for her.

"Havens, I suppose I shouldn't have said that as nothing has been officially confirmed yet, but the whole court is awaiting the announcement." He smacked himself lightly on the forehead. "But then of course you have only just returned."

"What announcement?" Dexter pressed, tightening his hold on Callie as he felt a tremor run through her body.

"Oh, that the Princess Serenna is willing to marry Prince Jerran in place of poor Prince Mikheli, to strengthen ties between Lithia and Westerland. From what I hear." His voice became horribly gossipy. "Although she is of course sorry about Prince Mikheli's death, she has always had a soft spot for Prince Jerran and would much prefer him as a consort. Anyway, that's for another day. Lady Callandra – are you sure you're alright? There's no need to be nervous."

Dexter felt Callie draw in a deep breath and swallow hard. She gave him a tiny smile and a grateful look then walked to the window, collecting a glass of water on the way. A heavy silence fell over the room and perhaps in contrast from beyond the doors the volume of noise increased. Callie stared blankly down at the palace gardens. It all made sense now. It was after his private conversation with his father that Jerran had been distressed and distant. He had known his duty had to override his personal feelings. In a strange way that almost made her feel better; almost, but not very much.

A knock sounded on the outer door. Dexter took her hand and squeezed it.

"It's time, Callie." She squared her shoulders as they lined up to make their entrance.

The courtiers, the advisers, the nobility and all those who had come to Derryn to swear oaths to Prince Jerran as the new Crown Prince, thronged the court, but as a fanfare sounded they drew to the sides of the great throne room, like curtains parting. Revealed at the far end King Theon sat his throne on a raised dais. There were men of power to one side of him; advisors, Mages and the General of his armies. On the other side holding himself stiffly the Crown Prince stood beside Princess Serenna of Westerland, his blank expression a vivid contrast to the quiet smile that she wore.

As Will and Gilly reached the front of the hall the King rose to his feet and raised his hands in applause that was taken up enthusiastically across the room. King Theon was a good speaker. He briefly outlined the mission that had taken their group into Kerria and stressed that none of the actions could have taken place without the groundwork of these skilled foot soldiers. The scouts didn't get stars or ribbons, instead they each got a hefty purse and two weeks' paid leave to their evident delight.

When the man Callie had not recognised walked forward the King stepped down from his dais and offered a short but genuine embrace before introducing him to the court as Liam Lenster, the brother of Battlemage Terran, whose valour had had much to do with the success of the mission. The King spoke for a few minutes about Terran, in a way that showed he had personally known and liked the man.

Then Liam accepted a posthumous honour on his brother's behalf before retiring to stand beside Gilly.

Callie had kept her attention on the central action, but as she approached the throne and dropped into a graceful curtsey she let her gaze slip sideways. Jerran stepped forward, untangling himself firmly from Serenna who had slipped her arm through his. He looked pale but composed and as he walked down the steps and took his place at Callie's right hand, she noticed the briefest exchange of glances between him and Dexter before he turned back to face his father.

Theon was quiet for a moment then the King raised his head, looking out across the hall. "I am not often lost for words," he began, and Callie thought she heard a whispered, [That's true,] ghost through her mind although both of her companions stared straight ahead, "but this time the events in Kerria almost leave me speechless. This small group before you went into a supposedly allied but ultimately hostile land, and by combining their battle skills and Magecraft, defeated the Black Sorcerer Tol Gath. They redeemed one of the ancient guardian amulets of Lithia and against almost impossible odds, when betrayed and captured, managed to overthrow the Warlord Axtra, so long a thorn in our kingdom's side.

"I couldn't be more grateful or prouder of these three Lithians." He stopped as the cheers and clapping drowned his voice. After a few minutes he was able to go on. "There really is no honour that matches their courage and achievement. They are made Freemen of our country with all due ranks and privileges."

A ripple of wonder spread through the hall. Such laurels were so very rare. The King reached for the elaborate sashes that marked their honour and dropped one over Lord Dexter's head, offering a hearty handshake. In the background Callie thought she heard a whoop of delight as Blaine cheered his brother. The King moved in front of her and when the ribbon was in place she started to curtsey, but the King scooped her up in a warm embrace that lifted her feet clear off the ground, murmuring, "Well done, lass." She could not control the smile that lit up her face and it was still there when her gaze followed the King to Jerran's side; their eyes met and she heard his sudden intake of breath before he turned back to his father. A brief hug, a hearty slap on the back and she thought she heard the quietly spoken words. "No father has ever been prouder," before they both walked back to the dais and resumed their places.

Callie, Dexter and the others bowed and walked back out of the hall, the walls ringing with the cheering and clapping of people who understood what future horrors they had spared Lithia.

Chapter 60

Once the King had withdrawn, the court was concluded for the day and Callie was soon introducing Lord Dexter and Blaine to her family before they all piled into coaches to return to the D'Arcourt town house. Dexter had been keeping an anxious eye on Callie. The shock and loss that he had seen in her face at Worrell's words in the antechamber had confirmed what he already suspected. The affection he knew Callie felt for him, was that of a friend or sister and unlikely ever to be more. Pragmatically he decided he needed and would enjoy both of those and be grateful that she had taught him to risk caring once more. In a strange way that left him feeling calmer. He was genuinely fond of Callie but she was not a restful person.

Callandra's family, he was not surprised to find, were rather unusual. There was an all pervasive air of equity amongst them. Everyone was different. Everyone was valued. Blaine instantly found a kindred spirit in Raff and they chatted like the oldest of friends. The General was astute but good humoured. Donna Esma was charming and kind. It was a very long time, he realised, since he had been in any assembly where he had felt so entirely comfortable and relaxed.

Conversation had not moved much past comments on the ceremony and a first drink when Callie arrived at his elbow dragging a very attractive young woman.

"Dex, this is Megan, my sister. You need to talk to her."

"Always a pleasure but…"

"She wants to hear about your plan to develop the Winters Keep horse breeds."

"Surely that would be very boring for…"

"Dex! Megan is a sort of life Mage. She deals in animal breeding and healing. Especially horses. Right now she's based in West Lithia."

"Not with the Hill Tribes!" Dexter's face lit up with boyish enthusiasm. Megan nodded. "That's amazing! My horses are…" And they were off. Callie smiled inwardly and hoped they might discover how much more they had in common than the desire to breed perfect horses. Lunch a little later was a great success and so was tea and eventually even supper.

When Blaine and Dexter finally took their leave, Megan had promised to take Dexter to meet the 'Ekweri' tribal leaders the next day and Blaine was scheduled to do some arms training with Raff. It had all been very pleasant and Callie kept her mind firmly on that thought as she made her way to her bed.

Jerran hoped he had played his part well during the honour ceremony. He had listened attentively as his father spoke to Will and Gilly. He had watched with admiration the way the King had made Liam Lenster feel that Terran's sacrifice had been truly valued. Then he had had to face Callie. She had looked superb. Her vivid blue eyes alert and dangerous; the glory of her auburn hair, hair that he had once run his fingers through, framed her heart-shaped face. She had avoided his gaze until the end and what he read in her face told him she knew about Serenna. He had felt like a traitor when he had stepped down on to the floor at her right hand, untangling Serenna's claws from his arm.

He caught himself up at that thought. He was being unfair. He had always known that Serenna had feelings for him that he simply didn't return. He had always known that she had not cared much for his brother but had been willing to marry him anyway to bring their nations closer together. Serenna had accepted her duty. Surely he must be willing to do the same and yet when he had stepped to

Callie's side, everything in him cried out that this was his proper place. The place he was meant to be.

The royal party had gathered for a light luncheon after the Reception and Jerran had tried to make an effort for his father's sake. The day after his return to Derryn he had stood by the King's side as his brother was committed to the care of the Goddess and taken to the royal crypt. Mikheli had lain in an open coffin. The stasis spell, which would only be cancelled when his coffin was sealed, had made him seem as if he only slept. He had looked so young and Jerran had felt a huge anger at the waste of such a life, taken at the Warlord's command. He remembered the last few moments of Lord Axtra's own life as he slid gutted like a wild boar from Arild's longsword, aware of his approaching death, in agony and powerless to prevent it. It felt like justice.

"Jerran?" He shrugged off his dark thoughts as he heard his name.

"Sorry sir?"

"I was just saying that Master Lauder wants Callandra to be declared an Arch-Mage. What do you make of that?"

He shrugged. "It's simply what she is."

"Really?" Serenna asked doubtfully. "She's really that powerful?"

"She really is." He smiled ruefully. "If she wasn't on our side and so principled, her power would keep me awake at night."

"That sounds worrying. Is there perhaps some way she could be restrained?"

"What?"

"Well suppose she decided to move against our countries for whatever reason."

"She wouldn't."

"She might."

"She wouldn't."

"I'll grant you it's unlikely but you can't know that."

"I think I can."

"You think you know her that well?" There was a long silence. It seemed to Jerran that everyone at the table was listening. "Yes. I do."

He turned away to find his father watching him thoughtfully and tried for a different topic of conversation. "Father, I thought I'd go and see the horses the Ekweri have brought. Have you had any chance to look them over?"

"No, I haven't been down to the pens yet. Lord Barnard was telling me that he and Lord Dexter have begun a breeding programme to develop stronger, sturdier work horses for use in the ore trade and the mountains, so don't be surprised if you see him down there too. Now I must be about my business. What are you young people doing for the rest of the day?"

"As it is fine we are taking a short ride to the Sea Tower. I've never been there." Serenna smiled at the King. "Well enjoy yourselves." They stood as the monarch left the room.

Jerran looked down at his rich clothing and honour sash. "I obviously need to change, Serenna, so shall we meet in the courtyard in half a mark?"

The Princess frowned. "Jerran, I need to change too so it will have to be more than half a mark."

"A mark then? We cannot set out too late, Serenna, the days are still short."

"I'll do my best then. Why not order the horses before we go to change? That will make things quicker."

"True, but it won't take long to ready Warrior and Daystar."

Serenna looked on the Prince with a bemused expression. "What about the horses for my attendants and the guards?"

"Sorry?" The Prince looked blank.

"It's nice that you want to be alone with me, Jerran, but it would be totally inappropriate. We aren't even officially betrothed yet. It would do such damage to my reputation." Jerran blinked and took a deep breath.

"How thoughtless of me. How many horses do you think we'll need?"

She counted on her fingers. "Seven?"

"I'll see to it at once." He bowed and headed for the palace exit nearest the stables as the Princess strolled back to her apartments.

Although Jerran had not anticipated riding out with an entourage, the trip to the Sea Tower didn't take as long as he'd feared. Serenna was a passable horsewoman, although she made no effort to mount or dismount without assistance. The Tower itself stood alone on a high outcropping of stone just off the road from Derryn to the sea. Once used as a lookout for raiders, it had become a popular leisure ride commanding a magnificent view of Windwhistle Bay. As they approached the coast and the road gained height they finally dismounted and climbed up the footpath, the sea-scented breeze beginning to tug at their cloaks.

Gazing out, Jerran found himself remembering another stretch of coast on the road outside Nilsport when they had been attacked. Callie had been knocked from her horse and pinned under a huge Frystland Warrior before he had been able to intervene. Bruised and covered in blood she had scrambled to her feet to continue fighting at his back. He smiled inwardly, remembering how very impressed she had been by the cool way he had quickly checked her over and resumed battle. Only it hadn't been *sang froid* that had made him act like that. It was the fact that his heart had seemed to stop when he thought she was about to die and as far as he could tell it hadn't been working properly since.

"Jerran! Jerran!" The note of irritation in Serenna's voice told him she had been trying to get his attention for some time.

"Pardon me. I was miles away."

Serenna looked at him thoughtfully. "So I see. It's chillier than I thought it would be."

He nodded and didn't try to tease her about the very stylish but not entirely practical riding habit she had chosen to wear for a winter's ride. "I'll fetch you a rug." He turned to move back towards the horses but she caught his hand.

"I don't imagine we will stay much longer – so perhaps I can share your cloak?" She offered him a warm smile.

Jerran found himself flinching. "I'm not sure that would be entirely proper, Highness – we must remember your reputation."

Serenna pouted and sighed. "I suppose you are right."

When he reached the horses to ask the servants to unpack a thick rug he found the Princess had followed him down – "Jerran, don't worry. I think I would like to go back now anyway."

They chatted on the way back in a perfectly friendly way. Serenna was pleasant and once or twice they managed the gentle laughter that had marked their earlier friendship, so Jerran was slightly surprised, if relieved, when the Princess excused herself from their later supper engagement. Since his return from Kerria it seemed to the Prince that he never got a moment to himself anymore. As heir apparent, he had acquired many new duties and he was also expected to court and escort the Westerland Princess. When she claimed she had let herself get chilled through and intended an early night, his sympathy was as real as his relief.

In fact, once warm and comfortable with a glass of mulled cider in her hand Serenna dismissed her ladies and sat for a long time staring into her fire deep in thought. Finally, she came to a decision. At her desk she penned a brief note then rang for a page and arranged for its delivery to Lord Dexter the following day. It was a long time before she retired.

*

Callie had not for one moment taken her father's mention of visiting Masters Lauder and Elton as only suggestions. When she left her home at mid-morning to seek them out, the house was quiet. Raff would be out most of the day, having duty at the Healer's Hall and then plans to annihilate Blaine in the combat arenas. Megan would be at the horse pens, where Dexter was due to join her and her father would be in his office at the palace, so she had only herself to please as to time-keeping.

She was walking slowly along the corridor towards Master Lauder's office when he hailed her from behind.

"Callandra. I was wondering when I would be seeing you. Was it me you were looking for?"

"Yes sir, and then I'm to go and speak to Master Elton."

"Well my dear you can kill two birds with one stone as he will be coming here shortly." The old Mage unlocked the door to his study with a wave of his hand. "Come in, come in and take a seat." Callie settled close to Master Lauder's desk and was just unclasping the Triquetra from her neck when Master Elton walked in.

"Oh, Callie, excellent. I have so many questions." The healer looked her over sharply. "How are you bearing up? For a first field trip you have certainly been through the mincer."

"I guess I'm still in one piece," she winced, "but some of it was grim." They nodded in complete understanding.

"And this is it." Master Lauder picked up the pendant. "The Imperium Triquetra in its entirely. I never thought I'd see such a thing in my lifetime. Here," he reached to a shelf behind him, "is the scroll we found." He hung on to it for a moment. "Now Callie, the Dean called a meeting to discuss how you should complete your education here at the Academy, and how best we might help you in the light of your abilities and recent events." She looked up with interest. "You still have five months left before you graduate?" She nodded. "So, our thinking is this. You will need to continue if not increase your combat training. It's essential for field work." He smiled at her obvious agreement.

"You have had the same basic healer training that all students receive, but with the power of the Triquetra's healing gem, it is quite likely you will be called on to do far more extensive interventions. In fact, that has already happened, hasn't it?" She nodded again.

Master Elton leaned forward. "Your pendant will help you to do quite remarkable things, Callie, but the outcomes will be better if you build on a foundation of greater medical knowledge – so you will be spending some further time in the House of Healing."

"And you and I, Callie, will be studying this." He finally proffered the scroll. "You may take this one to study at your leisure. It's a copy I had made for you, and you may want to add to it."

"Add to it?"

"Yes indeed. It is apparent that each guardian had a different experience using the amulet. It seems to relate to their innate and individual Mage gifts. Your experiences, as an Elemental Mage and weather witch, might one day be a help to someone else."

"That makes sense," Callie agreed as she considered it.

"We have set up your schedule to resume after the next weekend, but for now, we want a blow-by-blow account of how you used your magic and healing, if you can bear it?" Could she bear it? Again? Callie winced but her objections died unspoken as Master Elton leaned forward, his grey eyes twinkling. "I brought a cake."

Chapter 61

The holding pens and paddocks for horses newly arrived in Derryn were on the very western edge of the city. The day was shaping up to be bright but still chilly and Dexter turned his horse towards the stable blocks, looking forward to getting out of the wind for a few minutes. Beyond the fields a small cluster of felt tents added a splash of colour to the still wintry landscape and he realised this must be where the Ekweri had set up their camp.

He had wondered if he might be early, but the tack room was already occupied. Bruno and Skep, King Theon's horse masters, were both there and nodded in greeting. Megan, who had been perched on a bench beside the table rose with a smile for him and promptly fetched him some mulled cider. The two other men in the room had the tanned skins and slightly angular features that marked them as Ekweri tribe. They offered him brief bows as introductions were made, but added very little to the general conversation. Dexter's disappointment must have shown as Megan moved close beside him once they set out for the paddocks. "Wait till we reach the horses." She winked and led the way to one of the larger fields.

Dexter had not appreciated how very many horses the Ekweri supplied. The field was teeming. He studied them with interest. Lithia had quite a substantial standing army and the need for replacement mounts was constant. These horses were sturdy, deep chested and almost all of a medium height. They would in fact suit nine out of ten riders, very well, which was impressive. He was running his hands expertly over one of the geldings when he felt a tap on his shoulder. "You like them?" Tiff, one of the Ekweri was beside him watching. Dexter nodded.

"They are very good and I can see they will be ideal military mounts, but I need something different." He began to explain his own needs to the horse master who listened with interest and called to his partner to join them. Megan, who had been checking the feet of some of the mares strolled up as they beckoned Dexter away. "Where am I going?" he whispered to her, slightly bemused.

"They want to show you their own horses, beyond the camp. Feel honoured!" She grinned.

"I do." And he meant it.

The Ekweri's own mounts were almost more pony than horse. They were shaggier, sturdier and heavily muscled. Dexter stopped in his tracks. "This is what I want and need! Will they trade?" He looked at Megan his eyes alight with enthusiasm. "It depends."

"On?"

"On what you have to offer." Teff and his fellow horse master obviously understood the word 'trade' as they began chattering away in their own dialect, their grasp of Common proving inadequate for the task. Megan was all but laughing. "They want to know if you bred the horse you rode here on?" Dexter nodded.

"Actually, yes I did."

"Then they want to know if you would trade him for one of theirs?" Dexter shook his head.

"No, not him, but I have others like him. Winter's Keep and Barnard Castle are a fair way from Derryn. We often have to travel long distances and this line have good speeds and wonderful stamina. I would like to trade, but Ajax is a friend of mine and I couldn't part with him. I don't mean to offend them."

Megan translated as Dexter watched slightly anxiously, but far from being offended both men slapped him on the back. He raised a questioning eyebrow at Megan. "They understand and they approve. They regard the horses as their children. They would like to discuss the matter further with you in their tents; that never happens. You've made quite an impression. When we reach the yurts just do as I do." He nodded agreeably and they made their way to the hill tribe camp.

It was at least a couple of fascinating and successful hours later before Megan led Dexter back towards the stables. As they skirted the tents he was once again brought up short by a vision of horse flesh. In a small enclosure set entirely apart, a mare raised her head to look at them. Her coat was an extraordinary dappled chestnut and her flowing mane and tail were white gold. He had never seen anything so beautiful. "I think I'm in love." Megan giggled.

"She is wonderful, isn't she?"

"What is she doing here? What is she?"

"I heard they brought her as a gift for Jerran's betrothed, but they haven't made any move to present her yet. The Shaman says the time is not yet 'auspicious'."

Her casual comment drew Dexter's thoughts swiftly from horses to the situation his recent companions were dealing with. He was unaware how serious his expression had become until Megan touched his arm. "Dexter, is something wrong?"

"Sorry," he apologised, "I'm afraid my mind was wandering. How's Callie?"

"Callie?" Megan was bewildered by the unexpected question. "Well, I think she's alright. To be honest I've hardly seen anything of her. She was tired after Kerria of course, but since then she seems to be keeping herself very busy. Why do you ask?"

Dexter hesitated. Obviously Callie had not confided in her sister. He hesitated, sighed, and fudged an answer. "She went through a lot on that Kerrian trip. She might appreciate some sisterly support right now." Megan studied the northern Lord carefully. She could see he was genuinely concerned for her sister and wondered what he knew that she didn't.

"Then thanks for mentioning it. Now let's see if there's any mulled cider left."

It was late afternoon when Megan returned to the D'Arcourt town house. She had really enjoyed her day and had been delighted to confirm her first impression of Dexter as an intelligent and thoughtful man. That being said, his words about her sister had worried her quite a lot and once bathed and free from the smells of horse and stable that Lady Esma would not tolerate, she set off in search of Callie, finding her curled up in the library, reading what looked like a scroll.

Callie yawned as Megan dropped into the opposite armchair and eyed her sister speculatively. "How did your day go?"

Megan couldn't help smiling. "It was really good."

"Did Dex turn up?"

"Indeed he did. He truly does know horses. It was amazing. He was really good with Tiff and Vedd too. We actually got invited into their camp, which never happens, and I think they intend to trade with him. Unbelievable!" She was grinning as she spoke, and Callie smiled at her enthusiasm.

"So Dexter – do you like him?"

Megan hesitated, although the very faintest of blushes coloured her cheeks. "Well I hardly know him yet – but if I did – like him – that is – would that be all right with you?"

Callie rolled her eyes heavenwards. "Of course! Why do you think I introduced you?"

Megan laughed. "Well that's true, you did. As I said I've only just met him but Goddess it is such a relief to find an intelligent man who doesn't want to talk about himself all the time." Callie smirked.

"Your problem, my sister, is that you are way too choosy."

"I am not, but yes, I admit I do like your friend, and Callie," she eyed her sister attentively, "he asked about you. He asked me if you are all right – as if there was a reason you might not be?" Megan was not sure what reaction, if any, her question would illicit but to her shock and dismay all the brightness faded from her sister's face, and she turned away. "Callie, what is it? Tell me. You obviously went through a lot on that trip, what is troubling you so much?"

Silence fell for so long that Megan thought her sister really wouldn't answer.

"Was it the fighting, the disease, being held prisoner, Terran?" She persisted. "Good Goddess!" She shook her head. "It does sound so awful when I say it like that." She waited again. Then very quietly Callie spoke.

"All those things were truly terrible. I have nightmares when I think I'm back in Tol Gath's dungeon. I feel sick when I think of the way Terran was tortured and executed. I saw so much suffering, such vileness, but I know that in time I will get over that and call it experience. Yes, it was a hard trip, Megan. The thing is," she faltered, "as well as losing my innocence, in the broadest sense, it seems I also lost my heart and I'm not quite sure how to carry on without it."

Megan looked at her sister, appalled and stunned. Callie was biting her lip and staring down at the hands in her lap. Megan heard her sister's voice waver and watched a large tear drop silently on to the old scroll. Her mind raced. Will and Gilly were old friends of Callie's and she had made it clear she had no interest in Dexter, so, "Jerran?" she blurted out. "The Prince?" Callie gave the faintest nod.

"And he?"

"I thought." Callie shook her head. "It doesn't matter now what I thought. He will soon be officially betrothed to the Princess Serenna."

"You and the Crown Prince." Megan tried to take it in. "Did he? Did you, I mean…" Her voice tailed off.

"Relax, Megan. Nothing inappropriate happened. We just got very close and it felt so right. Then Mikheli died and after he spoke to his father he became very distant, very circumspect. Of course I didn't understand until the day of the Reception. I can't believe he didn't tell me." She looked up at her sister, her eyes swimming with tears. "Megan, I know this, whatever it was between us, is over now and he's hurt me very badly but for all that I still miss him so much." She crumpled and Megan wrapping her in a tight embrace, was achingly aware of how rarely if ever she had seen her brilliant, indomitable little sister brought so low.

Dexter found he was in a buoyant mood when he returned home. Like most of the nobles, his family had a house in Derryn, as well as their estates, and there he found his brother had returned just ahead of him. Blaine listened with interest to his brother's account of the Ekweri horses and the possibility of future trade. If he noticed how many times Dexter's sentences began with 'Megan said' or 'Megan thinks', for once he had the tact not to mention it. Even if this new friendship never developed it would be entirely good for his brother to spend some time in female company where he did not need to be constantly on his guard.

As a young eligible Lord, Dexter had been targeted by many match-making mothers, and after getting his fingers burnt on a couple of occasions had pretty much avoided involvements with any women at all for quite some time. Megan, Blaine thought, was like Callie in the sense of being intelligent and independent but she had struck him as softer and less fierce than her fiery younger sister. She was certainly very unlike the decorative but wholly impractical ladies of the court and that had to be a good thing.

So they were both in good spirits as they got ready to set out for Colonel Ferran's quarters where they had been promised a few hands of cards in strictly male company. Dexter grabbed the handful of notes and invitations from the hall table as he waited for Blaine, flicking through them quickly. Only one caught his eye and he stuffed it in his pocket. It bore the palace messenger crest and he might save himself a trip, if he could deal with it while he was out.

Ferran, although older by a generation than Dexter and his brother was a man whose company they enjoyed and a good host. Liss made the fourth of their party, although as his unreadable features meant he invariably won every card game, they refused to play for high stakes, if he was at the table. It was a convivial evening and it was late when the party broke up. Dexter was donning his coat when the crackle of expensive paper reminded him of the note he had picked up. He slit the envelope quickly while Blaine wrapped himself up against the cold and read the message. It was brief.

"Her Royal Highness Princess Serenna of Westerland begs Lord Dexter of Winters Keep for the favour of a few minutes' private conversation, as soon as this might be arranged."

He stared at the note, trying to make his not very sober brain, work. Why on earth would the Princess want to talk to him? He knew her only slightly, having been formally introduced when she had visited at court. His baffled expression caught Liss's attention. "Not bad news I trust?"

Dexter shrugged and passed the note across. "What do you make of that?" The Isseni read it and looked thoughtful.

"How interesting."

"What do I do?" Dexter knew he felt thick headed.

"You will give her a few minutes' private conversation, Dexter. She is a Princess, so really this counts as a royal command." Liss looked his friend over. "It might be best if you sobered up first – you may need to have your wits about you."

"True, then I think I'll start with sleep." The two brothers took their leave and set off down the street, weaving a not altogether straight path. Liss smiled as he watched them, even while his mind ran through every possible reason the Princess might have for wishing to see Lord Dexter.

The next day, despite an aching head, Dexter settled to catching up on the estate business that had to be dealt with in Derryn. He sent a brief note to the palace assuring Princess Serenna that he would call at her convenience any time in the next three or four days before his intended return to Winters Keep. He had finished ordering supplies and was on the last of his paperwork when Blaine finally surfaced looking somewhat the worse for wear.

After several cups of Kaffi he coaxed Dexter into a trip to the merchant quarters where rumour had it that Lassen, a renowned swordsmith had come by an elder sword. They were actually on the doorstep when a breathless young lad, dressed in messenger uniform raced up to them. He gave a brief bow and held out another envelope. "Are you Lord Dexter, sir?"

"I am."

"A message for you, milord." Dexter was hard pressed not to laugh. The lad was so out of breath his speech was almost unintelligible. He opened the letter. He was requested to attend the Princess Serenna two hours before the court dined. He nodded at the lad. "Please confirm that I will be there."

"Yes milord." The boy smiled at the coin he was tossed and whirled away as they walked on.

"Problem?" Blaine was trying to interpret the puzzled expression on his brother's face.

"I don't think so – but I will have to be at the Palace later so I may as well dine there. There is a musical soiree afterwards I believe…" The expression on Blaine's face made Dexter burst out laughing. "Not really your thing?"

"I'd rather slash my wrists. Anyway Raff and I have plans, we thought…"

Dexter held up his hand. "No, I really, really don't want to know."

Chapter 62

"That is quite enough." Jerran's voice was not raised, but the force of it was sufficient to rock the two rotund merchants before him, back on their heels. He had been sitting as Arbitrator at the Civil Court (why, he wondered, did they call it that when it was anything but civil?), and his headache was now practically giving him double vision.

"But Highness…" One of the merchants was nothing if not persistent.

"Not another word. You, Master Willis, sold these goods to Master Welland at a price you were willing to accept. The fact that the market rose and he was able to sell them on at a profit is his good fortune. You have no recourse in law to try and claim more from him."

"But lad," the grain merchant puffed himself up, "you must see."

Jerran rose to his feet. "Did you just call me 'lad'?"

"I…" The merchant swallowed hard, finally and belatedly realising that he now faced the Crown Prince and not the often disregarded spare heir.

"My ruling is this. The case is thrown out of court. You," he pointed, "will pay all Master Welland's costs for wasting his time and mine, and as a penalty for your disrespect of my rank in this court, you will make a donation of a hundred crowns to the Sisters of

Mercy Orphanage."

"A hundred Crowns – but that's – Highness, please reconsider." Jerran paused, looking with barely concealed distaste at the man's jowls wobbling in outrage. "Very well, I will reconsider. Make that a hundred and twenty crowns and if I see you here before me again, any time soon, I will not be so lenient. See the treasurer on your way out. Court is adjourned."

He stalked out of the room leaving a shocked silence behind him. In the anteroom he poured himself a glass of wine and rubbed his eyes. A few minutes later he heard a timid knock at the door. "Now what?" he snorted, flinging himself on an ancient sofa. The door opened very, very cautiously to show a visibly nervous court clerk. Jerran drew breath and tried to look less threatening. "Yes?"

The young man gulped. "So sorry to trouble Your Highness but when I write up the notes, what charge should Master Willis's penalty be under?"

"Lèsé Majesté," he answered reflexively.

"Thank you, Highness." The door closed as the court official scuttled away at speed.

Lèsé Majesté. He remembered the last time he had used those words. Callie had punched him as they bantered, her face alight with laughter and warmth. His mouth turned up for a moment. Then, alone, as he so seldom was these days, he allowed a heavy sigh to escape him. He had hoped that keeping busy with his new duties and acting the role that fortune had dealt him would get easier but that wasn't happening.

He had to spend some time each day with the Westerland Princess, which had become a special sort of torment. When she had been just a fellow royal and even as Mikheli's betrothed he had liked Serenna well enough. Now every time he saw her, he found her lacking. She liked to be waited on. She was timid, even afraid of spirited horses. She was not above gossip. It took her two marks to change her dress. Then he got angry with himself. None of these things was unusual in a gently bred noblewoman. Nor was her exaggerated attachment to rank and protocol or her indecisiveness, those were just products of her upbringing. They weren't really her fault, and most of all, it was not her fault that she simply wasn't Callie.

Jerran's circle of personal friends had never been large and as the closest Grae and Dirk, who had shared his training and served as squires with him rarely ever came to Derryn, he had allowed himself to be drawn into his brother's. At first those young Lords had seemed sophisticated and worldly wise but before long he had become increasingly disenchanted, disliking their attitudes of superiority and privilege. Mikheli's companions barely concealed their determination to benefit from their connection to the Crown Prince and by degrees Jerran had become socially withdrawn.

In contrast, Callie's friends, drawn from every social class, worked to achieve their goals. They were, for the most part, intelligent, well-meaning people – a really welcome relief and she herself had filled a void he had scarcely been aware of. Her absence had left him lonelier than ever before. He sighed again, he wouldn't, mustn't, think about her – a resolution he had to make afresh every day, usually as his path took him quite unnecessarily near the combat area where she just might be training.

Another firmer knock at the door brought him out of his thoughts. "Highness. Warrior is ready for you." He composed himself as best he could and made ready to ride back to the palace. At least he had the afternoon free to recover from his black mood as Serenna had indicated she would be busy until Court Dinner and the Musical Soirée afterwards.

Dexter had changed into dress that would carry him through the rest of the evening when he presented himself outside Princess Serenna's chambers. He was admitted into an ornately decorated reception room and assured that the Princess would be with him very shortly, when she had finished speaking to the Westerland Ambassador.

Only minutes later one of the internal doors opened and an elaborately dressed courtier exited, offering him a brief bow on his way out. Princess Serenna remained standing in the doorway. "Thank you for coming, Lord Dexter." She smiled and beckoned him into what must be her private study. He was startled on entering, to find they were alone, and Serenna must have noticed his glance as she offered him a seat.

"My ladies are next door if you are feeling nervous, milord, but when I asked you here for a private conversation I meant exactly that." Her expression became serious.

"Highness." He bowed before sitting. "What did you wish to discuss?"

She hesitated, then as if firming her resolve sought and held his gaze. "Your trip to Kerria." Dexter shrugged, still puzzled but nothing much of the venture was confidential. He settled back in his chair.

"What do you wish to know?"

"You were a very small group, weren't you?" He nodded.

"Prince Jerran and myself, Mages Terran and Callandra and our scouts Will and Gilligan."

"You were all together most of the time if I have heard correctly?"

"We were," he agreed. "It was only at the end when Warlord Axtra took Prince Jerran hostage and sent me off with the scouts that we split up."

"That was after he killed Mage Terran?"

"It was."

She sat pensively for a few minutes twirling a lock of her hair. "You went through a lot together?" He simply nodded. "I have heard that sharing life and death situations can create a close bond between people." She looked a question.

"That's true." Dexter began to suspect where the conversation was leading.

"And would you say these 'experiences' might change a person?" She didn't look at him.

"Almost always. Most experiences do." After a short silence the Princess looked up. "Lord Dexter you may well be reluctant to answer what I am going to ask you next but please believe I do not ask out of idle curiosity; the future happiness of two or indeed three people may be affected by your answers."

Dexter tried to lighten the mood. "Now you are scaring me." She dismissed his comment with a shake of her head. She would not be distracted or diverted.

"As you are probably aware, I have known Prince Jerran for many years now." Dexter groaned inwardly. "Since his return from Kerria I have found him changed. Don't mistake me. He is as courteous, civil and kind as he ever was, but there is something different: he is different. It seems to me it must be one of two things; either his brother's death while he was held hostage or," another long pause, "did his friendship with Lady Callandra turn into something else – a liaison perhaps? I really need to know."

"Highness," Dexter spoke firmly. "Although Lady Callandra and Prince Jerran often appeared to be close friends – I am honestly certain they did not have any closer relationship while the whole group of us were together. To be blunt, even if they had been so inclined, there was neither the time nor the opportunity." He shook his head. "You must understand, Princess Serenna. We slept in roadside camps or tiny inns, often all in one room. We rarely shed our armour and on many occasions we were fighting for our lives." He fell silent and so did she as she considered his words.

"Lord Dexter – please answer me honestly. Do you think Jerran cares for Callie?"

"Yes, of course he does. So do I." She looked away.

"Do you think he's in love with her?"

"Princess Serenna," Dexter protested. "How can I be expected to—"

"Lord Dexter, I remind you… the happiness of three people. Do you think he's in love with her?"

Dexter's mind went blank. After a silence that lasted much too long he shook his head. "Highness, I can't answer that."

Serenna looked at him calmly, if sadly. "I think you already have." She rose. "Thank you for coming, Lord Dexter. I apologise for subjecting you to such an uncomfortable interview. May I count on your discretion, regarding our conversation?" He nodded.

"Of course." She rang a hand bell at the table beside her and her ladies reappeared.

He was dismissed.

Retreating from the royal guest apartments, he mopped his brow, thinking he'd rather face a dozen Warlords than a Princess who suspected her intended's affections lay elsewhere. On impulse he detoured through a small open courtyard and made his way to Liss' quarters. He knocked on the door quite vigorously and brushed past the startled Isseni. "Gods above, Liss. I need a drink." His friend took a good look at him and went to fetch the brandy.

Dexter felt distinctly mellow as he entered the court dining room a while later. So much so, that Liss chose to seat them as far from the high table as their rank allowed. Dexter seemed very happy to have his back to the royal party, which allowed Liss to observe them at his leisure. Theon looked to be discussing military matters with his Generals. Probably the vexed question of how to strengthen and rebuild the army after recent engagements. Prince Jerran sat unsmiling beside Princess Serenna, who seemed to be carrying most of the burden of their conversation. He studied the Prince speculatively. Earlier, when Dexter had arrived at his quarters, distinctly rattled, he had admitted having spent the previous hour in conversation with the Westerland royal, but would only say she had wanted clarification on some parts of the Kerrian venture. The Westerland Ambassador's visit that Dexter had referred to in passing also gave Liss cause for thought, but he put the matters aside as the arrival of Colonel Ferran brightened their company.

Dexter drank only water during the meal and as he and his friends strolled to the Long Gallery he was undecided if he would actually stay for the music until he saw Lady D'Arcourt in the distance. As he approached to pay his respects, her companion turned slightly and he realised it was Megan, who smiled when she caught his eye.

Murmuring brief excuses, he made his way through the throng. Megan threw a brief word to her mother then tilted her head towards one of the window embrasures that punctuated one side of the Long Gallery. "Dexter – how fortunate. I wanted to speak to you – but wasn't at all sure I would find you in a place like this." She gestured around her.

"I could say the same, milady, but actually I love music."

"Really?"

"Yes, really. My mother was quite talented and taught me to play the lute when I was young, not that I've had time for it recently. The northern winters are long and when we get snowed in its good to be able to entertain ourselves."

"I'd love to hear you play."

"Trust me, at the moment you really wouldn't." He looked so disgusted with himself she chuckled.

"That's terrible! I can't abide wasting talent. Promise me you'll practise when you get home then."

"For you, my lady, anything. I'll put it on my 'to do' list for Freyasday."

"You're going home on Freyasday?" He was obscurely pleased that she looked disappointed.

"I must. I've only been back two nights since we set out for Kerria all those weeks ago." She frowned.

"Of course, then you came straight here to swear oath. But never mind that right now, I just really wanted to thank you."

"What for?"

Her face darkened. "I now know why you asked about Callie."

"Aah. How is she?"

"Not great."

Dexter swore. "Damn it. She isn't here tonight?" Megan shook her head.

"She really doesn't think she could bear to encounter Jerran at the moment. Personally I'd like to meet him, if only to wring his neck. He's hurt Callie very badly." She glared but he shook his head.

"Megan, you're being unfair. Remember, when they first became friends he was, as far as he knew, a free agent. After Mikheli's death he was much more formal and reserved. Liss told me that King Theon had expressly forbidden Jerran mentioning his proposed betrothal, so he couldn't even explain."

Megan gave him a measuring look. "Dexter."

"Yes?"

"Are you always this reasonable?"

"No."

"Well thank havens for that. We need to take our seats, they are starting."

Chapter 63

Free of other official duties on Sunsday, Jerran had been out with Graeme, King Theon's hunt master and Collis, keeper of the kennels. They had ridden to one of the home farms that supplied the Palace after the steward had received word of the loss of several sheep and an injured calf. Although it had been a horribly early start the Prince found the peace of the dawn countryside and the quiet of his companions an immense relief. It made him realise just how highly strung he was and how wearing he found being constantly observed; his every action weighed and measured.

Collis had brought several dogs with him. They were part bloodhound but of a lighter build and their tracking abilities were amazing. When the farmer had shown them where the animals had been attacked, the dogs quickly picked up a scent and running silently led them away over several other fields into nearby woodland.

Crossing a stream, there were large animal tracks visible in the mud, easily identifiable as wild boar. Master Graeme, getting excited, tried to persuade Jerran to withdraw at this point so that he might arrange a hunt for the court, but the Prince was in no mood to oblige. Any boar large enough to attack farm animals, and so far from the King's hunting grounds, presented a hazard that needed to be dealt with swiftly.

He and his companions all carried multiple weapons and they

loaded their crossbows as they neared the area of rocky outcrops where their prey seemed to have gone to ground. When they were set, Collis sent his dogs forward and shortly after a huge sow appeared. Jerran gave Graeme the first shot while he sat his horse beside the kennel master in case the boar had a mate, or a single shot failed to stop it. When a second boar did appear it was Jerran's bolt that brought it down.

By the time they had arranged for the farmer to send one of the boars up to the palace, leaving the other with him for compensation, mid-day had come and gone, so the Prince cheerfully settled to a plate of fresh bread and cold meats at the farmhouse table.

It had been a good morning, away from the politics of the court and doing something useful and Jerran was feeling much more cheerful when he returned to his apartments; a feeling that ended abruptly as he picked up the notes on his table. One was in his father's own hand. It was brief. His father wished to see him on his return to the palace to discuss his betrothal.

Although he had been expecting it, the King's summons made Jerran feel as if he had just received a violent body blow. It was quite some time before he felt steady enough to set out in search of his father, who turned out to be remarkably elusive. Having drawn a blank in the offices and the King's own apartment, one of the more observant pages mentioned having seen the King walking near the Queen's Solar – a beautiful chamber, seldom if ever, used since Helèn's death. When he reached it, the door was ajar and Jerran saw his father leaning against one of the wildly expensive full-length glass doors that led into the Queen's private garden: a garden she had tended herself.

Theon had obviously heard his son's arrival because he turned and offered a brief smile. "Good, you're back. What did you find?"

"Wild boar; two of them." Jerran didn't ask how his father knew where he'd been or what he'd been doing. Very little escaped the King's notice.

"The reason I called you, Jerran, is to discuss…"

"My betrothal – yes, I know. Are the negotiations concluded? Have you set a date for the announcement?" Jerran knew his words sounded rushed and his voice tense.

"No and no." The King, in contrast, sounded very calm. "Jerran, the Princess Serenna came to see me this morning. She no longer wishes for the proposed betrothal between the two of you to proceed."

There was a silence while Jerran wondered if he had heard his father correctly.

"What? What did you just say?" He looked at his father in stunned disbelief.

"The betrothal is not going to happen." Jerran shook himself.

"I don't understand. If I've done anything…" His father stopped him with a raised hand. "No. She made it quite clear that your behaviour has been irreproachable. Serenna was refreshingly candid. She told me that when her advisers first suggested that she marry you, after Mikheli's unfortunate death, she felt both enthusiastic and optimistic. She felt the two of you were already friends and it was in her mind that in time that friendship might grow into something more." The King watched his son, but Jerran's expression was unreadable.

"However," Theon went on, "after your return from first Nilsport, and more recently Kerria, Serenna felt that things between you had changed. That you had changed. She told me that she had finally realised, you were already in love with someone else, so her hopes for the future would never be realised. Certainly the proposed marriage was a duty, but when Serenna agreed to it, it was in the hope that it might become something more." The King paused but Jerran remained silent.

"The Princess has discussed the matter with her Ambassador, and although a marriage alliance would have strengthened ties between our two countries, they are already sound. She has made it clear that no offence has been taken in this matter."

Jerran dropped into a chair, mainly because he wasn't certain his legs would continue to hold him up, and swallowed hard. The King, studying him thoughtfully watched relief flood across his son's face. Lines of tension almost visibly fell away and Theon berated himself for not being more aware of his son's true feelings in the matter. He was well aware that Jerran would always do what was required of him, no matter the personal cost.

"Would I be right in assuming the Lady, Princess Serenna is thinking of, is our Mage Lady Callandra?" Jerran nodded. "Well," he considered, "as you know, apart from the Westerland Princess there are no other royal matches suitable for you. Callandra is from an excellent family. She is the most powerful Mage for centuries, which must benefit the Crown." He smiled inwardly, seeing his son bridling at the implication that any of his interest in Callie was based on pedigree or power. "And I find her quite delightful." Jerran's radiant smile was a pleasure to see. "Mind you," the King added, lips twitching, "I wouldn't be surprised if she turned out to be quite a handful."

"Tell me about it." Jerran spoke with such feeling his father finally burst out laughing.

"Princess Serenna and her entourage will be leaving tomorrow morning. After they have gone, and I stress after, I have no objection to you seeking to fix your interest with Callandra."

"If she'll have me after all this." Jerran's smile fell away and his father looked mildly startled.

"You're the Crown Prince!"

"So! That doesn't matter to Callie, one bit. I know I hurt her badly and couldn't even explain why." Theon nodded slowly.

"*Mea culpa*. Still, I have always admired your powers of persuasion, son. I'd really like you to have what I had." He waved his hand to indicate the solar. "Having a partner who cared for me as a person, not for my rank and status, was all that kept me going sometimes. Good luck!" He waved his son away and returned his contemplation of the garden where the very first of the spring blossom was beginning to show.

Leaving his father, his head spinning, Jerran walked very slowly towards Princess Serenna's apartment, trying to take in what his father had told him and what it might mean for his future. Maids and footmen were bustling around Serenna's rooms busily packing, but she greeted him with a slight smile and drew him into her study.

"You've seen your father!" She made it a statement; his face looked subtly younger and less tense.

He nodded. "Serenna, I don't really know what to say except

thank you." She shook her head.

"It's for me too, Jerran. You know I'm very fond of you, and I would have found it so painful if we had married, knowing you longed for someone else. I do wish you all the best for your future." She gave him a sincere, if slightly sad smile. "Although I am not the Westerland heir, I am part of a royal family. One day you will be King, and watching my father I've often thought it the hardest of jobs. Having the right person beside you – well, I can't think of anything more important."

Jerran nodded. "That's pretty much what my own father said." She gave him a brief hug. "

We will undoubtedly meet again – now I must calm my people. All my good wishes, Jerran."

"And to you." Another quick hug, a formal bow and he picked his way back through the organised chaos of the outer room.

Chapter 64

Callie, as agreed with the Faculty, found herself back at the Academy on Moonsday. At the House of Healing she had found out how little she actually knew about anatomy and disease and had to work hard to keep up with the other students, although most of them, as Raff pointed out, were actually healers in training.

Lunch, the twins had with their friends, who sarcastically reintroduced themselves to Callie to draw attention to the way she had neglected them, no matter that most of it hadn't been her fault. It was pleasant to be doing something so ordinary, but after a while she began to feel subdued, conscious that there were now so many things, so many experiences she didn't feel comfortable sharing.

Leon, always the most sensitive of the group, soon put an end to her brooding, informing her that her return to student-hood would be marked by a grand session at the Broken Arrow, although not until Thorsday, so that Raff could be there with them. She was still smiling at their antics as she made her way to Master Lauder's study. Ending the day with a quite literally bruising, unarmed combat session, when Callie fell into bed that night, she slept well for the first time in weeks.

On Tuesday morning, after King Theon and his son had stood together on the Palace steps to see the Westerland party depart, the

King had gone to a Council meeting leaving Jerran free at last to look for Callie.

After failing to track her down in all the likeliest places, he finally penned a short note, asking if he could call upon her. The reply shook him badly. The Lady Callandra D'Arcourt, had no desire for such a meeting, or any further correspondence. Sitting looking at her writing, Jerran found himself wondering if he had made her feel as awful as he himself felt right then.

If he could only speak to her, he felt sure he could sort things out, but he was at a loss, how to achieve it. After a little more thought, he made his way to the Palace Offices and enquired if General D'Arcourt was available. He didn't have to wait long before he was standing in front of Callie's father, who rose and saluted. "Highness. How may I serve you?" The General's voice was calm and bland and Jerran wondered what, if anything, he knew about Callie and himself.

"I'm sorry to disturb you, sir, but I was wondering if you might know how I could contact Callandra?" There was a distinct pause.

"My daughter has resumed her Academy Studies, Highness." He hesitated. "If you have 'official' business that concerns her I will make sure that she is aware." There was a slight but undeniable emphasis on the word 'official'. Jerran gave the smallest shake of his head. "Highness," the General frowned. "I find myself in an awkward position here. Callie will certainly do whatever is asked of her for Lithia or our royal family, but on a personal level, she has made it quite clear to her family, that for whatever reason she does not wish to see you at the moment." The General saw the Prince's mouth tighten but he simply bowed.

"I'm sorry to have taken up your time, sir." He withdrew swiftly and cursed all the way to the stables where he ignored the startled stable master and saddled Warrior himself.

He rode wildly for quite some time, churning with anger and fear. Anger at the politics that had put him in his present position and fear that he might not win Callie back. Surely he couldn't lose her now? Now that he was free. The first raindrops from a very threatening cloud finally made him turn back towards Derryn, but he was so deeply lost in thought that he didn't notice he was no longer alone on the road, until Warrior whinnied. Another rider approached astride a splendid bay stallion and leading a ridiculously short and chunky pony. "Jerran, is that you?" The Prince, startled, recognised Dexter's voice.

"Just about." The northern Lord, taking in the Prince's inadequate clothing and haggard expression, drew his own conclusions, but Jerran's attention had strayed.

"What on earth is that?" He pointed at the pony, his curiosity obviously roused.

"She is my newest acquisition and I hope the first of many from the Ekweri. I'm going to try her out at home. We have some tasks that our own horse breeds don't quite suit, and this little lass might be perfect."

"If you say so." The Prince looked more than dubious.

"You weren't at the stables were you, or did I miss seeing you there?"

The Prince shook his head. "No I, I just went for a ride." Dexter pulled his horse to a halt and reaching behind him for a rolled up cloak, tossing it over to Jerran.

"Here, for Goddess' sake put that on. Callie will kill me if anything happens to you."

"I sincerely doubt that, as she is currently refusing to see me, or even read my letters!" There was a pain and bitterness in the Prince's voice.

"Not so surprising." Dexter's voice was neutral.

"Yes I know, but Dexter there's something I need to tell her. It's really important, but I can't tell her if she keeps avoiding me." Dexter regarded the Prince with some sympathy.

"Look Jerran, I know your betrothal was a very unwelcome shock and the whole situation not of your making, but Callie's doing her best to come to terms with it and…"

"Dexter," Jerran interrupted. "In absolute confidence," he waited until the border Lord nodded, "Princess Serenna has decided she does not want our betrothal to proceed!"

"What? So you are free?"

"I am. For various reasons Serenna did not want it to be made public until she had departed, but I have my father's permission to speak to Callie."

"That's brilliant."

"It certainly would be brilliant, if only I could find the damned woman." He sounded so annoyed that Dexter burst out laughing and reluctantly the Prince joined in. "I'm sorry, I shouldn't have said that but I'm pretty much in pieces; it's been horrendous."

Dexter grinned and without thinking leaned across and slapped Jerran on the back. "Right, my Prince. I do, as it happens have a little inside information. Callie's friends will all be at the inn they frequent, on Thursday night. Now what is it called?"

"The Broken Arrow?"

"Yes, that's it."

"You're sure?"

"Absolutely certain. Raff asked Blaine if he would like to join them, but as we are leaving early on Freyasday he declined. Does that help at all?"

"More than you could possibly know." Jerran's whole face brightened and he suddenly seemed to become aware that he was discussing his most personal affairs in the pouring rain in the middle of the road. "Gods, I'm wet through. Let's get into the dry. Liss is hosting supper tonight – you will join us?"

"Is that a royal command?"

"It is!"

"Well, why not?" They headed for the Palace riding side by side.

After two more days of hard study and combat practice, Callie was looking forward to time off and yet not. She wanted a break because she was tired, but unless she kept busy her thoughts strayed and she felt unutterably bleak. Her friends were brilliant. They did not know why she was so unhappy, and had the grace not to ask her. It was enough that she was, and they rallied round to keep her spirits up.

When Thursday evening came, Hal and Chloe arrived at her Academy room to walk her down to the inn, Leon and Raff having set off earlier to secure their table. Others of their year group were getting drinks in as they strolled through the door, including several she hadn't seen since before the Kerrian trip. Their knowledge of her adventures was therefore second or third hand and the stories had grown so much in the telling she soon found herself laughing hysterically.

They were on their second or third round of drinks, apparently courtesy of Megan, when Callie felt Raff freeze beside her for a moment. She looked up to see Prince Jerran approaching their table. "Rhys!" Chloe's voice. "Brilliant timing. You are just the person we need! Did you hear we were having a 'welcome back to being a student' party for Callie?"

"Something like that." The Prince smiled amiably and edged himself on the bench next to Chloe, not particularly close to Raff and Callie.

"I'm leaving," Callie muttered, twisting in her seat.

"No." Raff held her down firmly. [At least not yet.] He spoke in her mind. [It would make a scene, Callie, and be most unfair on your friends who all came here tonight for you. Just sip your drink and keep it together. He isn't actually bothering you, and you will have to learn to deal with him some time.] Callie looked mutinous but picked up the cider and gave it her total attention. As quiet fell at her end of the table Jerran's conversation with Chloe was clearly audible.

"So apart from my obvious charm, why am I just the person you need?" he queried.

"Well, have you been at court recently?"

Jerran nodded, "I was there today, why?"

"Do you know what's going on with the Princess? There are the most amazing rumours!"

Jerran silently blessed Callie's gossipy friend for such an opportunity.

"I do indeed know exactly what's going on with the Princess."

"But will you tell us?" Leon chipped in.

"What do you want to know?" Callie felt Raff's fingers slide into hers.

"Well we all thought the Princess Serenna was going to marry your cousin after Prince Mikheli died."

"That was the plan," Jerran agreed mildly.

"But then there wasn't any announcement and everyone presumed that was out of respect for Prince Mikheli's death. You know; not rushing things?" Chloe finally took a breath.

"Well, you seem to have it right so far."

"But," Hal leaned forward, resting his elbows on the table to peer round Chloe, "the thing is, my cousin is in the palace guards and he says all the people from Westerland left on Tuesday morning, including the Princess." Callie looked up, startled. This was news to her, and Raff was obviously surprised too.

"So what happened? Did they fall out?"

"Not exactly," Jerran spoke slowly.

"Don't keep us in suspense." The Prince straightened up.

"You all seem to know about the betrothal between Prince Mikheli and the Princess. It was agreed years ago." They nodded. "The Princess agreed to it for reasons of state; she was not actually very fond of the Prince."

"It was always Prince Jerran she wanted, or so I've heard," Hal interrupted.

"So when Prince Mikheli died and they offered her the other Prince, she must have been quite pleased?" Chloe picked up the thread again.

"You're right. She was pleased and relieved. She and Prince Jerran had always got on well and been friends for years, although possibly her feelings for him were a bit warmer than simple friendship."

"So, did Prince Jerran refuse to marry her?"

"No, he couldn't do that. He knew he had to accept the betrothal whether he wanted to or not. Then a few days ago Princess Serenna went to see King Theon and told him that she no longer wished to marry Prince Jerran."

"She, broke it off?"

"Yes, she did." Raff, watching his sister as she listened carefully, removed the glass from her trembling hand.

"Was it because of something Prince Jerran had done?"

There was a pause. "I suppose it was in a way."

"Well then, dish the dirt – what did he do?"

"He fell very much in love with someone else."

"Goddess!"

"Oh, how romantic," Chloe gasped amid other exclamations around the table.

"So, Prince Jerran had to agree to a betrothal to one woman, while he wanted another?" Hal queried.

"Exactly."

"That's awful. How did he tell her?"

"He wasn't allowed to tell her or explain."

"That's just cruel. She wouldn't have known what to think."

"No. I'm sure it hurt her very badly."

"Then what? When Princess Serenna found out did she just call it off?"

"Pretty much. She wasn't happy about it, but apparently she said that this way only one person would be miserable: not three. I think she genuinely does care for Prince Jerran."

"So will Prince Jerran get to marry his Lady love now?"

Sophie, one of the other students, was biting her nails as if she was at a wonder play.

"I heard he has the King's permission." Callie heard Raff's sharp intake of breath. "But he's not sure yet if she'll ever forgive him – even once she knows everything." The end of the story was met with an outburst of excited chatter. The Prince's fierce hazel eyes finally rose to meet Callie's. She was pale and he thought he could see her shaking.

"Callie, are you alright? You look like you need a breath of fresh air." He moved swiftly round the table as she rose unsteadily to her feet and drew her unresisting arm through his. "How many of these has she had?" He waved mockingly at the empty glasses on the table, prompting laughter and comments on people who couldn't hold their drink.

Callie wasn't entirely sure she was breathing. She seemed to have forgotten how, until the wintry air stung her. Jerran drew her round the corner of the building into the shadows. "Callie, I'm sorry for that performance but I was getting desperate. I just couldn't find a way to speak to you. And I'm even more sorry for what I've put you through. I was forbidden to explain and I expect you thought…"

"That you had just been amusing yourself with me?" He nodded, wincing. "Only very briefly. Somehow it didn't feel like that." He slid his arms around her shoulder, studying her face anxiously.

"Jerran, it's true, you really aren't betrothed anymore?"

"No." He shook his head.

"And your father isn't furious? He doesn't mind if you choose someone else?"

"He was surprisingly calm and I don't know about choosing someone else, but he doesn't mind if I choose you. He told me that sometimes it was only my mother that kept him going and that sort of bond is worth a dozen treaties. These last few weeks have been hellish."

"I know." She scowled up at him and he hugged her tightly.

"Are you going to forgive me?"

"I'll consider it."

"Because if you are, I'll need to speak to your father."

She gazed up at him with an expression that made his soul sing. He tipped her face towards his and their lips met. Callie thought that such a perfect kiss should never have to end and as the Prince seemed to be of the same mind, it might not have if a bunch of revellers hadn't reeled past and glanced their way.

In the quiet they distinctly heard one of the men point at them and mutter, "Hey, isn't that the Prince?" Jerran groaned.

"Oh Goddess, there goes your reputation."

"As if my reputation was important." She reached for him again.

"Callie, as the future Queen it is!"

"As what? Havens!" The shock in her voice made him draw back a little way.

"Callie?"

"I forgot about that."

He burst out laughing and kissed her again in pure delight. "Only you would think that was unimportant. You're obviously not interested in my rank and title." She snuggled into him, running her hand up his chest, feeling his heart race. His head dropped again and the kisses that followed bruised her lips and set her body on fire as no-one else's ever had.

Finally drawing back she let out a long sigh. "Jerran, I need to go home and sit very still for a while and think about all of this. It's been so hard."

He stroked her hair gently. "I know."

The sound of someone clearing his throat drew Callie's gaze past Jerran to where Raff stood outside the inn. "Is everything alright?" They walked towards him, hands firmly clasped.

"Yes everything is very alright." The Prince smiled. "And Callie wants to go home now."

"I'll take her, I've got to get back."

The Prince leaned down and kissed the top of her hair. "Until tomorrow." She nodded, as he stepped away and Raff took his place, watching as they walked away.

They had only taken a few steps when Callie heard Jerran's voice in her head.

[Callie?]

[Yes?]

[Um. I love you very much. I think I forgot to mention that!]

They were still near enough for him to hear her peal of laughter ringing through the night. He made his way back inside slumping on the bench, his lips unable to stop smiling. "Is everything okay, Rhys?" Leon eyed him quizzically.

"Oh yes!"

"Callie is fine but she decided to go on, so Raff has taken her back. For myself I don't think I have ever felt better so I would like to buy everyone a drink."

Chapter 65

Blaine regarded his brother with a mixture of bewilderment and exasperation. Dexter was sitting on one of the ornamental benches to one side of the main Palace courtyard. "Dex, what are we doing here? I thought we'd be on the road to Winters Keep by now. We packed yesterday and now you seem to be – I don't know – lurking!"

"I am not 'lurking'," his brother answered mildly, "I'm – waiting."

"What for?" Blaine looked around. "Oh, I see, Megan."

"Megan? No, why would you say that?"

"Because she's headed towards us!" Dexter looked past his brother to see the young woman Blaine had spotted entering the courtyard from the stable side.

She smiled in greeting. "Dexter, Blaine! I didn't expect to see you again, I thought you'd be long gone on your way to Winters Keep!"

"That's what I thought too," Blaine agreed, "but he's waiting."

"Waiting? What for?" She looked puzzled.

"There's something I really want to know before we leave."

"Is it whether Megan will come and run your horse breeding programme at Winters Keep?" Blaine offered, helpfully.

"Blaine!" Dexter's voice warned his brother to shut up. "Please ignore him, Megan, he is very much speaking out of turn." Dexter glared at his sibling.

"You need someone to run your horse breeding?"

Megan's eyes darted between the two of them.

"It's not important, Megan."

"That's not what you said yesterday." Blaine's comment earned him a cuff on the head.

"We're only just starting…"

"And you thought of me?" She sounded startled.

"Yes, he did!" Blaine butted in, managing to dodge another cuff.

"Megan, please don't take offence, it was a stupid idea. You are nobility for Haven's sake – hardly someone I can hire, and you'll have far more important projects, I'm sure. I don't imagine moving to a Keep where it's winter for five months of the year is among them."

"Five months!"

"That bit is unfortunately true," Blaine confirmed. "It's part of the reason we have difficulty getting or keeping people in important jobs. Dex has been trying to find a new Mage Healer for months now, since ours is leaving to marry as soon as we can." Dexter winced.

"I must admit on that score I'm at my wits' end. I've offered good pay, but all the healers worth having, want to be in the big cities, where there are more opportunities and greater chances of promotion."

"I suppose that is how most people think," Megan sounded sympathetic, "but your horse breeding. I can't believe you were seriously considering me. I mean…"

"Megan, I apologise again. No offence was intended. Please don't be insulted."

"Insulted? Dexter, I'm not insulted; far from it, I'm really flattered. I would be thrilled to be given such a chance. Would you really consider letting me try?" There was no denying the sincere enthusiasm in Megan's voice.

"Would I let you try? You mean you actually might be interested?"

"There's absolutely nothing I want more! I'll be finished with the Ekweri in about six weeks and was just wondering where I should go next." She looked suddenly nervous. "I know you really need someone with more experience than me, but they will give me a good reference." She was biting her lip, Dexter noticed, the same way Callie did when she was anxious.

"Megan, I don't need your references! I've seen you work. I already know how capable you are."

"You're serious?"

"Never more so!" Blaine and Dexter exchanged delighted glances. "Then welcome to the team at Winters Keep."

Megan's smile was a thing of wonder. Dexter turned to his brother. "Thank you, Blaine. Now if you can only find me a Mage Healer as well."

"Oh." Megan sounded surprised. "You want someone else?" The brothers both looked blank. "Ah, perhaps you didn't realise. You know me as an animal healer, but that means I had to do extra training after I qualified as a natural Mage healer. Out in the country the two jobs are often combined."

"Yes!" Blaine punched the air. "That will solve so many of our problems. You're exactly what my brother needs. What luck that you arrived while my brother was 'waiting'."

"Well, actually it wasn't luck. The Ekweri Shaman cast the runes and announced that the stars are propitious this morning and we had to prepare Fyr and bring her here straight away. I'm not sure how that's going to work out because some people are saying the Princess has returned home." Dexter grinned and looked up to see two pairs of eyes regarding him suspiciously. "I'm not saying a word." He patted the bench beside him. "Now tell me if I need to speak to your father and what other arrangements we need to put in place before you come north to join us."

*

When Jerran rose in the morning, he hadn't had very much sleep, but despite staying at the inn longer than he had intended, he hadn't drunk much at all. Dressing with care he grabbed some breakfast before making his way to the court offices, only to find General

D'Arcourt was in a meeting. He had to muster what patience he could until the assembly room doors opened and several military officers departed.

The General appeared behind them and offered Jerran a bow, before beckoning him into the adjacent study which he had visited only a few days earlier. "Highness. What may I do for you?" There was a definite twinkle in the General's eyes this time that made Jerran wonder if he had some inkling of what was coming.

"Sir, there is something I need to ask you – it concerns your daughter the Lady Callandra and it is both a state matter and a personal one."

The General nodded.

"With your permission I would like to marry Callie." The General looked unsurprised.

"Is she agreeable to this?

"I believe so, yes."

"I'm sure you wouldn't have approached me unless your own father had given his consent?"

"He has."

"Then I can scarcely refuse, can I?" He rose and offered a hand that the Prince grasped eagerly. Waving Jerran into a chair, the General looked at his prospective son-in-law and future monarch thoughtfully. "I'm glad you have resolved your differences, Highness."

"Jerran, please, sir." The General nodded.

"I can see the two of you are very well matched on a personal level, and as a father I think that bodes well for your future happiness, but can I put my other hat on for a moment as a minister of this realm and ask you a question?" Jerran nodded.

"Do you feel, Jerran, that Callandra will one day make a good queen? I love my daughter very much. In fact, of all my children Callie is probably the one I am closest to, but that doesn't make me blind to her faults. She is wilful, obstinate, and sometimes rash. She has the devil's own temper, and pays scant regard to decorum and etiquette!" Jerran grinned.

"Sir, I don't think Callie will make a 'good' queen. Some day I know she will make a 'great' queen. Yes, she is all those things you mention, but she is so much more. She is caring, kind, principled and courageous beyond belief." He paused. "Sir, you have known her for years and I have only really known her for months, but in those months I have fought at her back and beside her on bloody battlefields and anchored her power as she struggled against foul disease and dark magic. She can and has made hard decisions." His voice dropped. "When the horror of the deaths she caused; deaths she could not avoid, threatened to overcome her, I was there to wake her from the nightmares."

He hesitated. "As for me, when I was at my lowest, taken hostage with my brother assassinated and not knowing if I even had a future, she was there at my side.

"No. She won't be a 'good queen' if you mean an 'ordinary queen'. There's precious little 'ordinary' about Callie." His fierce expression grew soft. "And that's why I love her."

There was a very long silence as General D'Arcourt absorbed the Prince's passionate words. It was stunningly clear that the man in front of him knew his daughter better now, than he did himself. After a few moments he rose and bowed deeply. "Jerran, I'm giving you my greatest treasure, you deserve her. Go with my heartfelt blessings." Jerran went.

He left the Palace through one of the side entrances and made his way across one of the smaller courtyards that led to the fencing Salle. Callie, he knew, was scheduled for a one-to-one session with Trevan, one of King Theon's sword masters, and he was sure if she hadn't finished she wouldn't mind the interruption. Trevan was not one of her favourite people; being a stickler for detail and with an exaggerated idea of his own importance.

The Prince walked swiftly. Glancing sideways as he passed an entrance to the great courtyard, he saw Blaine and Dexter and couldn't resist giving them a victory sign that brought a broad smile to the Earl's face.

"What?" Blaine demanded, seeing his brother's grin. He spun round but could see no reason for it.

"Not long now." Dexter chuckled.

"Will you stop being so damned cryptic?"

"No! Oh, there's Liss and Raff, try and get their attention." Blaine followed his line of sight and hallooed until the two men crossed to join them.

"Hey there! Where are you off to?" Blaine addressed Raff.

The younger man shrugged. "I really don't know. Liss came to find me and said we should come here and wait."

"You too?"

"What are we waiting for?"

"Only he knows." He pointed at Dexter. "He says it's important." Liss smiled.

"He's right and it will be of interest to all of you, so have a little patience." He sat with a look of anticipation on his face, gazing towards the roof of the Salle just visible beyond the nearer buildings.

By the time Jerran reached the entrance to the Salle he was almost trotting. His need to find Callie, to finally and conclusively claim her had knocked every other thought from his head. He barged through the doors into the great practice chamber.

It was full of activity. Many men and several women were paired up or working in small groups under the eagle eyes of the sword masters or their senior students. Callie was engaged in single combat with one of the royal guards. They were each armed with sword and dagger and were exchanging blows at a furious rate.

"Callie." Without thinking Jerran called her name and started to move towards her, oblivious to the blades that missed him by inches.

"Highness. Stop." Sword Master Trevan blocked his path. "What are you doing? You know the rules of the Salle, it is extremely dangerous to interrupt and distract warriors, practising with live steel. You or they might be injured. Please withdraw to the perimeter!"

Jerran tried and failed to edge past him, aware that some of the activity in the hall had died away as attention was drawn to his altercation with the sword master.

"Trevan, I need to speak to the Lady Callandra!"

"Highness, surely it can wait? She is in the middle of her final duel."

It's really important."

"With respect, Highness, so is her training." Jerran was dimly aware that Callie had lowered her blade, a point having been scored.

"Trevan, before the next point may I just ask her one question?"

"One question?"

Jerran nodded and they both looked towards the subject of their discussion. Callie was wearing practise leathers. Her hair was darkened with sweat and escaping from a leather tie. Jerran thought she looked beautiful; her eyes were sparkling with laughter. He heard her voice in his head. [Jerran, you can't.]

[Oh yes I can. I've seen your father and I'm not prepared to wait a minute longer.]

"Very well, Highness." Trevan's voice was clearly irritated. "One question." The Crown Prince of Lithia cleared his throat.

"Lady Callandra, if you have no objection, and since my father and yours have given their consent, I wonder if you would agree to be my wife?"

A stunned silence swept through the huge hall and instead of a pin dropping Jerran clearly heard the fall of a weapon or two. Callie brushed her hair from her eyes. "Yes, Prince Jerran, I will. I think I'd like that." She smiled and turned back to her stunned opponent, tossing, "I won't be long," over her shoulder.

Jerran eyed the sword master nonchalantly. "Do carry on." He walked calmly to one of the benches that lined the edge of the room and sprawled on it, hands clasped behind his head, letting the tumult his words had unleashed, simply wash over him.

"Touché." Callie shook hands with her thoroughly unnerved opponent and strolled across to the Prince. She kissed him casually on the lips, for all the world as if he was a stable boy and she a kitchen maid.

Jerran was hard put not to laugh out loud. "I must clean up. I won't be long." She disappeared into the changing rooms at which point all semblance of order vanished in the Salle.

Trainees were darting off in all directions, obviously determined to spread such momentous news. Jerran thought he saw Gilly slip away but it was hard to tell in the moving crowd. Finally, Trevan and two other instructors made their way over to the Prince. The offered formal bows.

"Highness, may we offer you our congratulations?"

"Thank you." Jerran rose and bowed his head in acknowledgement.

"And here comes your betrothed now."

Jerran turned even as he relished the turn of phrase. Callie, damp from a quick shower, hair down to dry, walked straight into his open arms and raised her glowing face for a kiss. "Shall we?" He led her out of the Salle and opened the outer door to be met by a sea of faces. The smaller courtyard was bursting with the soldiers that Callie and Jerran had fought alongside.

As the couple appeared an almighty roar rose from the crowd cheering their Warrior Prince, as he claimed the woman who had saved so many of them. A storm of whooping and cheering followed before the men drew aside to allow the couple to proceed.

"What in the seven hells was that?" Blaine and Raff exchanged glances as the huge explosion of noise reached them.

"That," Dexter grinned, "is what we have been waiting for." Even as he spoke Jerran and Callie walked into the Great Courtyard, hand in hand and simply glowing with happiness. As they drew near Dexter bowed. "I take it congratulations are in order."

"Yes they are! My betrothed and I (Gods above, I love saying that) are shortly going to have lunch with my father. You will have to postpone your departure, Dex, as you are all invited. Raff, your parents already know to come but we want you to go and find Leon, Hal and Chloe and bring them along too. They all played a part in getting us this far, even if they didn't know it!"

Raff laughed. "Chloe will probably have hysterics when she realises you really are the Prince."

Jerran smiled. "I'm counting on it." He slipped his arm back round Callie's waist and walked her up the main steps of the Palace.

Megan dropped back on the bench looking slightly pale. "Megan? Are you okay?" Dexter looked concerned.

"Yes. Yes, I'm fine. I've just realised that one day my wild little sister will be Queen."

"Yes, she will. Weather witch, Mage, Queen-in-waiting. I wonder what else she will do?"

Liss turned his inscrutable silver gaze upon them and spoke very softly. "What indeed?"

ABOUT THE AUTHOR

Jo Cox now lives in Somerset in a tiny village with her husband, although she has also lived in New Zealand and Canada. She has two adult sons who live in Dubai and Australia. When she is not writing, she plays the saxophone, learns Italian and drinks a lot of good wine.

Printed in Great Britain
by Amazon